KENNETH BROMBERG

AMERICAN DREAMS

This is a **FLAME TREE PRESS** book

FLAME TREE PRESS
6 Melbray Mews, London, SW6 3NS, UK
flametreepress.com

Distribution and warehouse:
Marston Book Services Ltd
160 Eastern Avenue, Milton Park, Abingdon, Oxon, OX14 4SB
www.marston.co.uk

Publisher's Note: This is a work of fiction. Names, characters, places, and
incidents are a product of the author's imagination. Locales and public names
are sometimes used for atmospheric purposes. Any resemblance to actual
people, living or dead, or to businesses, companies, events, institutions, or
locales is completely coincidental.

Thanks to the Flame Tree Press team, including:
Taylor Bentley, Frances Bodiam, Federica Ciaravella, Don D'Auria,
Chris Herbert, Matteo Middlemiss, Josie Mitchell, Mike Spender,
Cat Taylor, Maria Tissot, Nick Wells, Gillian Whitaker.

The cover is created by Flame Tree Studio with
thanks to Nik Keevil and Shutterstock.com.
The font families in this book are Avenir and Bembo.

Flame Tree Press is an imprint of Flame Tree Publishing Ltd
flametreepublishing.com

A copy of the CIP data for this book is available from the British Library.

HB ISBN: 978-1-78758-292-7
PB ISBN: 978-1-78758-291-0
ebook ISBN: 978-1-78758-293-4
Also available in FLAME TREE AUDIO

Printed in the UK at Clays, Suffolk

KENNETH BROMBERG

AMERICAN DREAMS

FLAME TREE PRESS
London & New York

For Jimmy. I miss you every day.
And for Carol, my beautiful angel.

PART ONE
FATHERS
CHAPTER ONE
1904

They had come to a halt on the outskirts of Tempkin, twenty kilometres north of Kiev. The burly Russian cavalryman in his long scarlet riding coat and red-crowned fleece hat took a swig from his pocket flask, then trotted his grey Lippizan to the front of the small troop. He caught up to the lead rider, who was surveying the town up ahead, its rooftops bathed gold in the light of the dying sun. The temperature had dropped, bringing the crisp chilly beginnings of evening.

"Last man to the village pays for drinks," the burly cavalryman said to his comrade, taking another swig. Then he stuffed the flask back into his coat pocket.

"I guess," the other rider replied, lifting his own flask and taking a quick drink, "that means you." And so saying, he dug his heels into his horse's flanks, hitched the reins, and galloped away.

"You bastard." His compatriot laughed, spurring his own horse into a sprint. The rest of the troops followed behind in hot pursuit.

They all slowed as they approached the village's main street, a dirt thoroughfare just wide enough for two carriages to pass without touching. Up ahead, two men in black coats and hats were crossing the manure-strewn street. When they caught sight of the approaching riders they began running, desperately, as if for their lives.

"I've got the one on the right," the burly cavalryman yelled, guiding his horse with casual expertise after his fleeing quarry.

Despite his long black coat, the villager was fast and almost made it to the steps of a small house before the burly rider caught him, his horse crashing into the man and sending him flying. The impact caused the horse to stumble but the cavalryman was an excellent horseman, and even half-drunk was able to keep the animal from going down.

The villager was less fortunate. Thrown ten feet through the air, he landed face first in the dirt, where he lay, stunned. The other cavalrymen, following behind, simply ran over him. A dozen horses' hooves broke his ribs, punctured his kidneys and lungs and shattered his neck. Looking behind him, the burly rider saw that the other villager had suffered a similar fate, crushed to death by the marauders.

His friend rode over and stopped next to him. "What do you think?"

The others were swiftly dismounting and charging into nearby houses to see what they could pillage. Most of these Jews had nothing of value, but sometimes you got lucky and found a family heirloom or even a small hoard of cash. "Let's ride ahead and see what we can find."

The two rode almost half a mile up the dirt street before the burly cavalryman turned a corner and caught sight of a woman outside her little house at the same moment she saw him. She was hanging laundry, a pale cotton frock, which she dropped in her haste as she ran inside.

"There," the burly rider said, pointing to the house with his sword as his comrade rode up behind him. "Young. And very pretty."

The young woman barely had time to close and latch the door and grab her four-year-old son, who was sitting on the floor of the front room, playing with a small painted wooden rocking horse. She picked him up and carried him to the only closet in the little house, pushed him inside and dropped clothes and a blanket over him.

"Mama, what are you doing?" the little boy said, beginning to cry.

"Listen carefully," he heard her say in the sternest voice she had ever used with him. "You must stay in here and not make a sound. No matter what you hear or what happens, you must stay here until I come back to get you. Do you understand, Max?"

"Yes, Mama."

"No matter what, not a peep. You promise me?"

The little boy choked back a whimper, and nodded, holding on to his little wooden horse and hunkering down under the blanket. His mother closed the door to the closet, leaving the boy completely in darkness.

★　　★　　★

Josif Zalensky worked his small field in a clearing of the forest that bordered the village. The penalties for operating a secret farm were harsh. Jews were not allowed to own land in Czarist Russia and as tenant farmers they were only allowed to keep a fraction of what they grew, but Josif was willing to take the risk to avoid giving eighty percent of his yield to an absentee landlord. He had started planting at dawn and had just finished turning the soil as the sun disappeared below the trees.

After carefully wrapping his tools in a canvas sheet, Josif stashed them at the base of a fruit tree at the edge of the clearing and began walking back to the village, half a mile away. As he emerged from the forest, approaching the edge of town, he sensed something was wrong. The normal hustle and bustle of working men coming home, women preparing dinner and children being summoned in for supper, was missing. Instead, there was an eerie silence.

As he entered the little hamlet, his apprehensions were confirmed. The body of Avner Levkov, the village butcher, lay in the middle of the main street, his head twisted at a horrible angle, practically torn off his neck. Another body, its face so badly crushed that it was unrecognisable, lay further down the street. Josif saw doors smashed, windows shattered, and horses tied up outside several houses. No one who lived in Tempkin was rich enough to own a horse.

Josif ran the remaining half-mile to his house. As he turned the corner off the main street he saw two horses outside his small wooden home. The front door had been kicked in and Miriam's laundry basket lay in the dirt nearby.

He raced into the house. Two men in soldiers' uniforms were passed out on the floor of the front room, one of them snoring loudly. The room stank of beer and vodka and both men were naked below the waist. In a panic, Josif rushed into the bedroom. Miriam lay sprawled on her back on top of the bed.

He took one look and fell to his knees. They had been married just over five years, and Josif thought of what a beautiful bride she had been, resplendent in a traditional wedding dress her mother had sewn. Now her pretty face was bloodied and beaten, both eyes swollen shut, lips cut, nose smashed. She had put up a fierce battle. Her peasant's skirt and undergarments had been torn away and there was blood between her legs. Her skin was cold to his touch. He could feel no breath as he put his ear by her mouth. Leaning his head against her chest, he wept. "Miriam," he whimpered through his tears, "my dearest Miriam." His body trembled with grief.

Suddenly he was seized by another thought. *Max!* Where was his son? He had been so overcome by the sight of his wife that it hadn't occurred to him. But even as he wondered this, a more primal impulse overcame him.

Josif strode purposefully back into the living room, jaw set, teeth clenched. The sword of one of the cavalrymen lay across the small dining table, still looped to the man's pants, one of the legs of which was inside out. Josif unsheathed the weapon and approached the soldier, who was still snoring loudly. He stood over this bear of a man for a long moment, grasping the sabre's handle in both hands, aiming its point straight down at the man's barrel-shaped torso. With a bloodcurdling scream, Josif plunged the blade into the soldier's chest with all the force he could muster.

Blood spurted upward, spraying everywhere. Almost instantly the room filled with a foul odour as the man's sphincter muscles involuntarily relaxed. The other cavalryman, roused from his stupor by Josif's unholy scream, began to stir, but Josif made quick work of him as well, running him through with another angry, despairing wail. Again came the expulsion of air, the foul odour, the shocking outpour of blood; life leaving the man's body as Josif watched.

He had killed the soldiers so quickly that he was hardly aware of what he had done. He found himself sitting on the floor of his living room, his knees drawn up, his face resting in his hands. His rage had been replaced by an abrupt and complete exhaustion. He suddenly felt too tired to move, resigned to just sitting in his little house and waiting until the authorities came for him.

He sat like that until a voice from behind startled him, almost making him jump.

"Daddy?" Josif turned around to see little Max, clutching his wooden horse, standing uncertainly in the doorway of the open closet where he had obviously been hiding. "Where's Mommy?"

Josif glanced away from his son, looking reflexively toward the bedroom. Before he could move to stop him, the little boy ran. "No!" Josif yelled, struggling to his feet and going after him. He caught up to Max by the side of the bed, where the boy stood motionless, staring fixedly at his dead mother. Josif awkwardly put his arms around the boy, steering him away from the frightful scene. "We must go," he said. "We have no time to lose."

Quickly, Josif gathered up some clothes, a loaf of bread and a bottle of milk. Max had run back to the bedroom, his face buried in his mother's chest, his small body heaving uncontrollably. Josif gently pulled him away, brought up the sheet to cover his beloved wife's body and led the boy out of the house. The horses stood side by side, tied to a post out front where the soldiers had left them. Josif opened the expensive hand-tooled leather saddlebag draped over one and emptied its contents, replacing them with the things he'd carried out. "We have to go," he said to his son. "They'll come looking for the soldiers."

"But Mommy," the boy said.

Josif shook his head sadly, wondering how to explain. "We must go, Max."

The boy nodded, wiping his tears with his hand. Perhaps he understood. "She fought them, Daddy. I heard her fighting but she told me to stay in the closet." He stopped for a moment, then he added, "And I'm just little."

Josif nodded. "It's good you stayed hidden. You could not have helped and they would have hurt you. Your mother would have been very sad if that had happened."

Max looked up at his father. "Did you kill them, Daddy?"

"Yes," Josif replied softly.

"I'm glad," said the boy.

What a horrible thing for a child to say. Josif shuddered inwardly. He could not imagine how such an experience would affect the boy going forward – if by some miracle they managed to survive. But there was no time to dwell on such things. They simply needed to get as far away from here as quickly as possible. Josif lifted Max onto the horse, then hoisted himself up, swinging his leg over the saddle so that Max was in front of him. With his arms encircling his boy, Josif hitched the reins and father and son rode swiftly away, leaving behind the little village where each had lived his entire life. The sky was just turning black.

At sunrise, they arrived in the town of Dansk. There, Josif sold the horse and saddlebag to a local stable owner who paid a low price but asked no questions. As little as he was paid for the horse, it was still more money than Josif had ever seen in his life. He used a portion of it to buy seats for Max and himself aboard the Eastern Express, the fastest and most luxurious train in Czarist Russia. He also spent a few kopeks to buy a meal of *butterbrots* and *kielbasa*. It felt as if they'd not eaten in a week.

Their train departed at noon. It had been eighteen hours since Josif had killed the cavalrymen, thirty since he'd last slept. Once on board, he decided it would be okay to close his eyes for just a moment. That was the last conscious thought he had until the train arrived in Minsk the next day. He and Max both slept through the entire trip.

Still half-asleep, father and son disembarked from the train onto the crowded platform. Josif had never seen so many people or so much activity. Minsk was the industrial centre of Western Russia, the Czar's gateway to Western Europe. Its large buildings, great squares and cobbled streets were like nothing Josif had ever seen. But there was no time for sightseeing. They found their way to the Jewish quarter, where Josif purchased forged papers that identified him as a Mr. Vladimir Kostoyov from Kiev. Four hours later he and the boy were back on the train, this time headed for the Polish border. It was now more than two days since he had killed the two cavalrymen. Someone had surely discovered what he had done. Josif wondered if they would be waiting to arrest him when he and Max reached the border.

★   ★   ★

In the village of Tempkin, Captain Boris Solokov of the Imperial Russian Army guided his horse through the muddy streets, the scene of the previous day's engagement. The revolutionaries had been soundly defeated. Which is to say that several old men and a few young ones had been killed, homes destroyed, young women brutally raped, some murdered. The Colonel, he knew, would be pleased, but Captain Solokov was not. He had seen too many of these so-called counter-revolutionary strikes to feel the violent revulsion he had a few years earlier. But still the brutality and mayhem did not sit right with him.

Solokov was a Cossack, born and raised in the low hills north of the Caspian Sea, where he had learned to ride a horse before he could walk. Three hundred years earlier, in return for refuge from a Polish dictator, his ancestors had pledged their allegiance to the Russian Czar. And for the centuries since that time Cossacks had done battle against Turks, Poles, Ukrainians and Serbs, shedding blood for Mother Russia as she forged westward. Tales of Cossack prowess and courage had been handed down from generation to generation. *But now*, Solokov thought bitterly, *we are reduced to murdering peasants and raping their women.* How long could this sort of thing go on before these people really did revolt?

As he made his way around the village, Solokov was distracted from his musings by the sight of a cavalry horse tied up outside a small wood-framed house. The door of the house had been smashed in and Solokov assumed he would find the horse's owner inside, probably drunk. All soldiers had been due back at regimental headquarters hours ago, and he prepared to deliver a severe tongue lashing for insubordination. Solokov dismounted his steed and bounded up the steps of the little house.

The sickening smell of human death assaulted him as he entered the front room; twenty years of bloody campaigns had not inured him to it. He covered his nose and mouth, making his way through the small house, finding first the bloated bodies of the dead soldiers, then of the woman in the bedroom. What had happened was obvious: the husband had come home and taken vengeance on his wife's attackers. Captain Solokov smiled to himself and thought, *Good for him. Any real man would do the same.*

Nevertheless, Solokov knew full well that the murderer must be caught and hanged. Order must prevail. It was obvious from the small bed in the front room, as well as the child's clothes and playthings, that a young boy lived in this house. Since the child was no longer here, the captain had to assume that the father had taken him with him. Undoubtedly, they would be heading for the Polish border. Solokov shook his head, almost sadly. He would ride back to the regiment and from there telegraph the border patrols. A lone man with a young boy would be easy to spot. The murderer would be caught and hanged, and that would be that.

Suddenly, impulsively, Captain Solokov gathered up the child's clothes, along with the toys, and threw them onto the little bed. Then he picked up the entire bed, stretching out his long arms to do so, careful not to drop the items sitting on top. After looking to make sure no one was watching, he squeezed out the front door and made his way around to the woods in back of the house. He walked thirty metres past where the forest started before dropping the bed and its contents behind a big pine tree. Now all obvious evidence of a child had been removed.

The detail that he would send back to pick up the dead bodies would almost certainly not notice anything suspicious. Only in several days, when the bureaucracy got around to sending an investigator, would they discover evidence of the boy. And if the husband made good time, if he did not panic or stop to rest, he would be safely across the Polish border by then. With that comforting thought, Solokov rode as fast as he could back to regimental headquarters to telegraph the border patrol.

★   ★   ★

Passage into Poland proved surprisingly easy. Holding Max by the hand, Josif simply joined the flow of Russian peasants and day labourers who passed through Poland on their way to Germany. At the checkpoint he presented his false papers and tipped the border agent a few rubles. There were several military policemen carefully watching the passing emigrants. Josif noticed that they occasionally pulled a man from the line and took him off to a small building next to the crossing point. These unfortunates were all about the same age as Josif, but were travelling alone. Josif and Max passed without incident.

Once across the border, they boarded yet another train, this one bound for Hamburg in northern Germany. From there, Josif used the last of his money to book passage for himself and Max in a tiny stateroom in the bowels of a Norwegian freighter called the *Rising Star*.

They were sailing to a place that Josif had heard about all his life. Although he did not know anyone who had actually been there, he did know people who had received letters and sometimes money from relatives who had emigrated. It was supposed to be a wild place, untamed, but presenting unlimited opportunity to those willing to work for it.

They were sailing to America.

CHAPTER TWO

They arrived in the new world with clothes on their backs and little else. Josif found work in the sweatshops of New York's garment district, first as a sweeper, then as a sewing machine operator and later as a cutter. He worked twelve hours a day, six days a week and, when he could get the work, laboured on the Sabbath as well. He and his son lived in a three-room rear tenement apartment on Ludlow Street, near Grand. At twelve dollars a month, it was the cheapest accommodation he could find. While he was at work, Josif left Max in the care of Mrs. Goldberg, a forty-five-year-old widow who occupied the apartment below them. She was efficient if not overly affectionate.

Mrs. Goldberg already had another charge, a girl named Sophie Feldman, who was almost exactly one year younger than Max. The girl's parents, Eli and Esther, had come to America from a small village in Poland three years before the Zalenskys came from Russia.

Esther Feldman was a beautiful and intelligent young woman who had married a man who was neither. The only remarkable thing about Eli Feldman had been his burning desire to get to America and the fact that he had the means to do so: a modest inheritance from his father. That combination was good enough for Esther, who was more than happy to trade her good looks for a one-way ticket out of Poland.

The Feldmans had sailed for America one day after their wedding, the voyage itself their honeymoon. Eli spent his inheritance on an expensive stateroom in a Swedish ocean liner so that he could make love to his beautiful new wife in luxury. The Feldmans had intercourse whenever Eli wanted, which was often, and the only way he knew, which was quickly. By the end of the voyage Esther was pregnant.

In America, with very little money, Eli and Esther rented a four-room flat in the same building the Zalenskys would later move into. Eli went to work in a meat-packing plant off 14th Street. Each night when he came home he brought the smell of the plant with him.

Esther was unable to work due to a difficult pregnancy; she vomited at least twice a day and was constantly nauseated, especially when Eli was home. The only good thing about being pregnant was that it provided her a reason to avoid sex with him.

Nine months to the day after her arrival in America, Esther gave birth to a beautiful baby girl. The baby had the same colouring and features as her mother. Eli was delighted and Esther was relieved. Eli named the baby Sophie, after his mother.

Esther's body returned to normal very quickly and her English improved rapidly. Two months after giving birth she landed a job as a file clerk with the downtown law firm of Rosen and Rosen. Three months later she started an affair with the senior Mr. Rosen, a fifty-three-year-old grandfather who proved to be a much better lover than Eli. Soon after, Mr. Rosen set her up in a Sixth Avenue penthouse with an excellent view of Central Park. The penthouse had one bedroom, two bathrooms, a kitchen, separate rooms for eating breakfast and dinner, a living room, and a room just for receiving guests. Esther had never conceived of such luxury. She left a note for her husband and money for Mrs. Goldberg and moved out. Her daughter was six months old.

Eli was furious. He walked around his little apartment for hours, shaking his fist and saying, "She's a whore. The whole time, she was just a whore." The baby girl, who had been asleep, woke up and began to cry. Eli picked her up and rocked her.

"I wish you didn't look so much like your mother. You'll probably grow up to be just like her," Eli said bitterly. The baby was asleep again and did not hear him, though she would certainly not have understood if she had.

Sophie remained in the care of Mrs. Goldberg when her father was at work, and often when he was not. Mrs. Goldberg loved the little girl and Sophie loved her in return. When Max came along three years later, the two children immediately hit it off, each providing an instant playmate for the other. They spent more waking hours with Mrs. Goldberg than with their fathers, and she thought of them like a little family. She often took them to the playground in Seward Park. A plain woman, she was delighted when strangers assumed that the two beautiful children were hers.

★   ★   ★

"I'm going to marry Max when I grow up," said Sophie.

Mrs. Goldberg laughed affectionately. "Why would you think of such things, Sophie? You're only ten years old."

"All the girls in school talk about getting married," she said very seriously. "And Elsie Schneider says she is going to marry Max. So does Rachel Cohen." Sophie wrinkled her forehead and looked at Mrs. Goldberg, who was darning a tear in the little girl's best dress. "And they don't even know him like I do."

Mrs. Goldberg shook her head, and wondered to herself if anyone really knew Max. She remembered five years earlier when she had first enrolled him in school. The teachers quickly took note of him. A genius they had said, and it was probably true. He learned to read while the other children were still struggling with the alphabet. He could do arithmetic in his head faster and more accurately than most of his teachers. His mind soaked up information like a sponge; names, dates and places devoured and stored to be instantly retrieved when needed.

But he was not like other children in ways that children should be. He was not affectionate. He did not seek approval from adults. He was, for lack of a better word, withdrawn. Mrs. Goldberg attributed this to him having no mother and rarely seeing his father. To her shame, she had not been able to compensate with the kind of affection that all children deserve. She had tried. But Max did not make it easy. He didn't enjoy being held or cuddled, and he didn't return whatever affection she tried to show him. With Sophie, so pretty and so naturally endearing, it was the opposite. She was easy to love.

Max may not have been warm or cute or cuddly from an adult perspective, but he got more than his share of attention from other children. He was easily the best athlete in the neighbourhood, and as such was automatically popular among the boys. He played both American football and European soccer and ran circles around the other children at both. Boys treated him as if he were special, possessed of remarkable qualities that might rub off if they were around him. They always wanted to be on his team and were constantly patting him on the back and looking for his approval. In school, his perpetual position at the head of the class brought him the notice of both students and teachers.

Notwithstanding all the adulation he received from other children, he had no close friends. Except for Sophie. The two of them played together every night before their fathers came home and often did their schoolwork together. She seemed to be the only person he was truly comfortable with.

"Rachel Cohen says Max is handsome," Sophie said to Mrs. Goldberg. "What does that mean?"

"It means he is nice to look at," said Mrs. Goldberg. "Rachel Cohen is correct."

Sophie wrinkled her forehead again. "Will he like me?"

Mrs. Goldberg sounded surprised. "Of course he'll like you, Sophie. He likes you more than anyone."

"I don't mean now," the little girl said. "I mean when we grow up. Rachel Cohen said that boys are different when they grow up. She said they will only like you if you are pretty." She paused for a moment. "Will boys like me, Mrs. Goldberg?"

Mrs. Goldberg could not help but smile as she looked at the girl, her sea-glass green eyes so serious in the perfect oval face. "Yes, my dear," she finally answered. "Boys will like you very much."

CHAPTER THREE
1914

The last time Jonathan Cahill saw his father was in the stockade, two weeks before Liam Cahill was to be hanged. By then, his father was something of a legend in Belfast.

Two British military policemen searched Jonathan for concealed weapons before allowing him to enter his dad's cell. They were not gentle with him, and during the frisk slapped him so hard below the belt that they brought tears to his eyes. He was thirteen years old.

Now, in the cell, standing before his father, not knowing what to say, Jonathan parroted something he'd heard one of his uncles utter. "You won't be forgotten, Dad. We'll get the bastards."

Liam Cahill smiled sadly as he looked at his only son for what he knew would be the last time. Jonathan was a handsome boy, tall for his age, with broad shoulders that he would eventually grow into, and intelligent blue eyes that held a defiant light. Liam was proud of having produced such a son.

"Someone may get the bastards," he growled in a low voice, "but I hope it won't be you." He stared intently at the boy to make sure he was listening. "You must leave Ireland, son."

"What?"

"Don't argue with me." Liam looked at Jonathan, his own intense blue eyes burning. He was a passionate man. *Committed* was the word he liked to use. He believed with all his heart that life was not worth living under tyranny, and so, not three weeks earlier, he had led a small troop of commandoes on a late-night raid of the main barracks of the British occupational regiment. They had managed to slit the throat of Major General Archibald Chapman and half a dozen others. He fervently believed that it had been worth risking his life for, but he did not want his choices to condemn his son to the same fate.

"You must leave Ireland," Liam said again. "You must go to America."

The boy was stunned. "Leave Ireland? But Ireland is everything. It's what you fought for and—"

"And what I will die for," his father finished. "Listen to me. I've kept you out of it because I didn't want you hurt or dead. That goes double now. The English have pulled most of their men from Belfast to fight the Kaiser. We've scored some small victories but we still haven't beaten them, and when the war is over they'll bring more troops here than ever. They'll be hard men, accustomed to killing and death, not the soft boys who are here now. We won't have a chance."

He gripped his son's shoulders and repeated the words. "We won't have a chance. If you stay, you'll almost certainly be drawn into the struggle. And my name will be a curse. If you're lucky, you'll live in poverty under the boot of some Englishman. More likely, you'll be shot or hanged. Like me. I don't want to die knowing that's what will happen to you. In America you can make a new start." Liam Cahill paused. "I expect you to do well there."

"What about Mother and the girls?" said the boy, still flabbergasted. "Do I just leave them?"

"They will be well taken care of," said his father. "They'll move to Dublin and live with your mother's cousin, Robert Farrell. He's a good man and he's more than happy to help. He owns a candle factory and your mother and oldest sister can both work there. It has already been arranged."

This was too much for the boy to take in. He could not stop himself from crying. His father held him just as he always had when the boy was hurt.

Two weeks later, on the day they hanged his father, thirteen-year-old Jonathan Cahill sailed for America.

CHAPTER FOUR

He had not expected it to be beautiful. In Ireland they spoke of it as dirty and crowded, grey and barren. But from the deck of the frigate steaming into New York Harbour, the cityscape glinted in the sun. The sky was a deep blue interrupted by shape-shifting, cotton white clouds. The famous Statue of Liberty loomed before the ship like a Greek Colossus. They docked at Ellis Island, a clump of dirt and rock half a mile off Manhattan that had once been a dumping ground for ships' ballast. Now it was America's major immigration centre, processing more than a million newcomers a year.

A doctor poked a flat wooden stick down Jonathan's throat, then placed a cold stethoscope against his bare chest. A man with a clipboard asked about his medical history. Then he and his fellow passengers were ferried from Ellis Island to the tip of Manhattan, a place called the Battery. On the dock he could see hundreds of people waiting for relatives or friends to disembark from the ship.

He was to meet his aunt Catherine, a woman he had never seen before. She was his mother's first cousin and had left Ireland twenty-eight years earlier with her young husband, George O'Hara. Jonathan's mother, Mary-Margaret, five years old at the time, had been flower girl in the O'Haras' wedding. Barely two weeks later, the newlyweds sailed for America. When they arrived Catherine was already pregnant with their first child, a daughter.

Over the next six years, Catherine produced three more children, all sons. George opened a grocery store on Delancey Street, and working day and night made the store a success. Now the three O'Hara boys were New York City policemen and married to good Irish girls from the neighbourhood. Aunt Catherine already had three grandchildren. The daughter, now twenty-seven, still lived at home with her parents.

Jonathan knew all this because his mother and Aunt Catherine corresponded regularly. When Mary-Margaret first learned to write at eight years old, she wrote a letter to her grown-up cousin in America. Catherine was tickled to hear from the little girl and immediately responded. Their friendship by mail had continued for twenty-five years. The arrangement was for Aunt Catherine to hold up a hand-lettered sign that said 'Jonathan'. He pushed his way through the crowd that swarmed around the gangplank without spotting any sign with his name on it. He climbed to the top of a low cinder block wall that bordered the disembarking area and surveyed the entire crowd. Still no sign. It was ten a.m. when Jonathan disembarked. By two p.m. the crowd had dispersed and still no Aunt Catherine. Something had obviously gone wrong.

He was alone and hungry, thousands of miles away from everything he had ever known. All he could think about was his father and the home he had left behind. It took effort to keep tears from his eyes. From his duffle bag he pulled the crumpled paper with Aunt Catherine's address: 174 Suffolk Street. A dockworker told him it was about three miles away, gave him general directions and told him to ask someone again when he got to Delancey.

Jonathan walked straight up Broadway, and within minutes was surrounded by the giant buildings he had seen from the ship. It was similar to a concrete canyon, with people rushing past like schools of fish in an aquarium. They walked within inches and did not seem to notice him. After forty minutes he turned on Canal Street, crossed Mulberry and was instantly transported into Little Italy. Red, white and green flags hung in storefront windows and trees lined the streets. Young housewives shopping for dinner with their children smiled at Jonathan as he walked past. The smell of fresh bread and Italian sausage made his belly growl. But the only money he carried was worthless in this country.

The dockworker had told him to turn north when he got to Orchard Street. This was past the Italian section, in a dirtier, more crowded part of town. Jonathan's senses were assaulted with hundreds of sounds and smells, and the street was so crowded that he could move forward only slowly. Vendors sold their wares from pushcarts in the middle of the street and hundreds of voices seemed to be haggling over prices, most in a harsh language Jonathan did not understand. No carriages, horseless or otherwise, even attempted to move through the sea of humanity. The street was littered with trash. Jonathan decided that he had found the New York that people in Ireland spoke of so disparagingly.

After a few blocks of this unpleasant thoroughfare he turned east onto a residential street, lined closely with apartment buildings. Three teenagers, a few years older than Jonathan, walked briskly out of one of the buildings and toward him. They were each wearing a red jersey with white lettering that read 'Manhattan Football League'. Jonathan guessed they were on their way to an American football game.

As they approached, Jonathan pulled the paper with Aunt Catherine's address out of his pocket. "Excuse me," he said to the first boy, as he approached. "Could you point me in the direction of this address?"

"Whadda ya want?" the teenager responded as if he had not understood the question. He was no taller than Jonathan, but older and heavier.

"I'm looking for 174 Suffolk Street. I would appreciate it if you could point me in the right direction."

"Get lost, mick," the young man said, shoving Jonathan out of his way. The force of the push caused Jonathan, unbalanced by his heavy duffle bag, to topple over backward. All three of the boys laughed at him as he scrambled to his feet.

Jonathan took a step toward them, his immediate thought to throw a fist into the first face he could reach. But he knew instinctively that any one of these young men would be more than a match for him, and he hesitated.

"Whatsa matter, mick, can't make up your mind?" one of them said. Again, all three laughed.

Suddenly, a rough voice came from the sidewalk behind them. "What the hell's going on here?" The laughter stopped.

"Nothing, Max," said the one who had shoved Jonathan. "Just some mick asking directions." The young man sounded nervous.

Jonathan glanced at this newest football player. He was shorter than Jonathan and appeared to be younger than the others, hardly older than Jonathan himself. But the football jersey seemed small for him, inadequate for his powerful build. He carried himself with the air of someone in charge.

"It would not hurt to help someone once in a while," he said in a harsh monotone.

"Sure, Max," said the first football player. Max looked straight at Jonathan.

"Where are you going?"

Without speaking, Jonathan handed him the paper with Aunt Catherine's address. Max told him quickly and precisely how to get there, then turned and walked toward Orchard Street, the other three hurrying after him.

Jonathan watched them depart with relief, but also with envy. They were, after all, a group; they had common interests and common experiences. And each other. Over his shoulder, as he walked away, he heard Max's amused voice calling back to him, "Welcome to America."

★   ★   ★

From the street, the house looked large and comfortable. A black, wrought-iron fence bordered a well-kept lawn and large gable windows stared down from the second floor. A very pretty young woman opened the front door in response to his knock. She looked suspiciously at Jonathan's duffle bag.

"We don't need anything today, thank you," she said, and began to close the door.

Jonathan realised that she thought he was one of the peddlers from Orchard Street. "I'm looking for Mrs. Catherine O'Hara."

The pretty woman's eyes widened a bit. "And what would you want with my mother?"

Taken aback by the unfriendly greeting, he could only say, "I came from Ireland. I'm Jonathan Cahill."

"My God, we didn't expect you until Thursday. Don't you know who I am? I'm Patricia, your second cousin." The woman came out on the porch and hugged him. Jonathan, who was dirty and unkempt from two weeks on a ship, felt embarrassed to be embraced by such a pretty woman on the front porch of such a fine house. Patricia apparently sensed his awkwardness and stepped back from him.

"Did you walk all the way from the dock?" she asked. "You must be exhausted."

"No, ma'am. But I'm hungry."

"Oh yes, of course. Let's get you something to eat right away."

Patricia opened the door and he followed her into the fine house.

CHAPTER FIVE
1917

During her fifteenth year, Sophie came to realise just how much she was liked by boys. And men. That summer had seen miraculous changes. Her hips had become fuller, her bottom rounder. And her breasts grew, springing out seemingly overnight, ungainly proofs of her femininity. At first she felt awkward and uncomfortable, but with time she grew pleased with her new shape and the attention it brought her. She had always loved attention, especially from men, and now she received more than her share.

Boys who played ball with Max fawned over her when she came to their games and used any excuse to stop and talk to her. Grown men turned their heads to watch when she walked past and smiled if they caught her eye.

But with the good, came bad. Her father, Eli, looked at her differently now. He tried to hide it but she saw him watching her the same way that men on the street often did. He also drank a lot more, and gambled. Sometimes they barely had money for rent because he had gambled it away.

She also saw less of Max now. The Zalenskys had moved out of the building after Josif Zalensky finally realised the American Dream: his own business. In ten years he had saved enough to open a small retail store for men's work clothes and suits. The store was located on Grand, a few blocks away, and Josif and Max had moved into an apartment in the back. After school and on weekends Max worked in the store. He still came by each morning to walk to school with Sophie, and on occasion she visited him in the store. But it wasn't like the old days when they had played together in the evening and on weekends.

One night several months after Sophie's fifteenth birthday, Eli came home late, after she had gone to bed. She heard the door to the apartment open and then slam, an almost sure sign that he was drunk. Five minutes later he staggered into her bedroom, walked directly to the bed and ripped off the covers.

It was a warm evening and she was wearing a thin night shirt. The light from the living room came streaming in and she could see that her father was naked. She could also see that he had a full erection. She knew about these things because Mrs. Goldberg had carefully explained to her about men and women. Eli leaned over the bed and rubbed his penis against her leg. He put his big hands on her breasts. Sophie was petrified. Finally she said, "Daddy," in a terrified voice. Eli stood up and backed away from the bed.

"I'm sorry," he said. "I'm sorry. You look so much like her now." Then he hurried out of the room.

Sophie and her father had never spoken of her mother, and they did not speak of her in the days that followed the incident. Sophie wasn't even sure that Eli remembered what had happened, he had been so drunk. Still, she was careful to never get undressed in front of him, which wasn't easy in the tiny apartment, and she slept with an extra layer of clothing. She hoped that as time passed Eli would drink less and things would be better.

But to her dismay, Eli's drinking and gambling grew worse. Several nights a week, Sophie was awakened by the slamming of the apartment door. She lay in the dark, nervous, afraid, hoping that her father was too drunk to find his way to her room.

Often, however, he did find his way. Sophie would close her eyes and pretend to be asleep, until she felt him rubbing his fleshy appendage against her leg, breathing hard and unevenly while he fondled her breasts through her nightgown. After a while he groaned, and she felt a spurt of warm, slippery liquid against her skin. Even then she pretended to be asleep, struggling to suppress her revulsion until he finally left the room. Afterward, she would lie in the dark, trembling, her stomach tied in knots, unable to sleep. During the day neither father nor daughter ever mentioned the nocturnal visits.

After work, Eli usually stopped at a local bar and drank his dinner, so Sophie either dined alone or ate with Mrs. Goldberg. Sometimes Max would join them, but usually he was busy in his father's store. It seemed that the only time she saw him anymore was when they walked to school together.

One weeknight, eating alone, Sophie thought to herself how nice it would be if he could stop by for a visit. A moment later there was a sharp knock on the door. "He's heard my thoughts," she said to herself and sprang up from the table.

But when she opened the door it was not Max who greeted her. Instead, two very large men towered in the doorway. Sophie tried quickly to shut the door but one of the men put his shoulder to the door and stepped inside.

The man was large all over; shoulders, chest, and hands. Everything except his head, which was small and bullet-shaped and set on his shoulders like a pebble on a large rock. The bullet head looked down and said, "We wanna see Eli Feldman."

"He's not here," Sophie said, trying not to sound as scared as she was.

"We'll wait," the bullet head said. As he spoke, he and the other man moved further into the living room and looked around, their large bodies seeming to fill the available space.

"He usually stops at a bar on his way home," Sophie said. "He doesn't get in until late."

The bullet head looked her directly in the eyes and held them for a moment. Somehow she knew he could tell she was telling the truth. "You're his daughter?" he said finally.

"Yes. Sophie Feldman."

The bullet head looked Sophie up and down and smiled to himself. It was not a friendly smile. "Tell your father to be here at this time tomorrow. Tell him Mr. Epstein will want to talk to him." He started to leave, then, almost as an afterthought, he turned back and said, "I'm James Becker."

Sophie did not realise how frightened she was until they had gone. Then her knees grew weak, and she had to sit down to keep from collapsing. It was obvious that her father was in real trouble. She had never met 'Mr. Epstein,' but she knew who he was. Everyone did.

There were two regular dice games in the neighbourhood. One was in the basement of a three-storey tenement on Hester Street near Bowery, the other in an abandoned warehouse near Houston Street. Both games ran seven days a week, twenty-four hours a day. Both were very lucrative. And both were owned by Arnold Epstein. Obviously, Eli had run up gambling debts he could not pay and Epstein had sent the two thugs to collect. Sophie shuddered at what would have happened if her father had been home.

CHAPTER SIX

Eli sat on the little sofa in the little living room, his knees pressed together. He had come straight home from work. His breathing was laboured and his hands shook visibly. At six o'clock there was a sharp knock on the door. Sophie opened it quickly and once again looked up at the same two men who had visited the night before.

The bullet-headed man, Becker, spoke. "Mr. Epstein is here to see Eli Feldman."

"My father is here," Sophie said.

The two big men parted to make way for a much smaller, slightly built man. He was handsome, in his mid-thirties, and was dressed in an elegant, obviously expensive suit and a black fedora. He looked Sophie directly in the eyes and seemed to be caught there, unable to pull himself away. Finally, he nodded and proceeded into the apartment.

"You wait outside," he said in the general direction of the two big men, and like obedient dogs they stayed in the hall. Sophie quickly shut the door.

As soon as Epstein entered the room, Eli began talking, almost whimpering. In spite of herself, Sophie felt pity for her father. "I'm sorry, Mr. Epstein," Eli said. "It will only take a few weeks to get the money together. Just a few weeks."

Epstein smiled and raised his hands in a gesture indicating that Eli should stop talking. "Mr. Feldman," he said in a surprisingly respectful tone. "We all make mistakes. Without mistakes there would be no people." He laughed at his own joke and Sophie realised that she should also laugh. Epstein continued talking to Eli but he was looking at her. "I'd like for you and me to be friends. Perhaps we could even help one another."

Eli was stunned. This was not at all what he had expected. He had been so nervous, so frightened, that suddenly he found himself fighting back tears of relief. But Epstein was still talking. Eli had to strain to understand, his heart was beating so hard.

"Maybe a good way for us to begin our friendship is to have dinner together. I know a nice little Italian restaurant around the corner."

What's he talking about? Eli thought. *He should be breaking my legs and he wants to take us to dinner?*

Nevertheless, fifteen minutes later Eli, Sophie and Mr. Epstein were seated in a restaurant munching on garlic bread and sipping Chianti. Epstein was given the best table in the house, one in the corner where it was possible to hold a private conversation. He ordered wine for everyone, even Sophie, who had never tasted wine before.

Eli expected Mr. Epstein to talk about the money owed him or about some great favour Eli could do to make it up to him. But Epstein never mentioned the debt. In fact, he barely spoke to Eli at all, focusing his attention almost exclusively on Sophie. What did she like best in school? Shakespeare. Epstein liked Shakespeare too. What was her favourite play? *Hamlet.* What a coincidence, it was also Epstein's favourite. There followed an animated discussion of Polonius and Ophelia, two people Eli had never heard of.

Finally, a thought crept into Eli's alcohol-addled brain as he nervously gulped down the free Chianti. Epstein had absolutely no interest in Eli. It was his daughter. Epstein wanted Sophie.

★   ★   ★

Over the next several months, Epstein took Sophie to dinner at least once a week, and there was no longer any pretense. Eli was simply not invited. Sophie, who had been to a restaurant exactly three times in her life, was thrilled by the attention. But when she mentioned it to Max, it only seemed to irritate him.

"Why is he doing this?" Max demanded. "What does a man like that want with a fifteen-year-old girl?"

They were walking to school and Sophie had described the wonderful dinner she'd eaten the night before.

"He doesn't want anything," she said, a little angry. "Not like you mean it. He's just a nice man and he likes me."

"Don't be so simple," said Max. "Your father is gambling and losing a lot, and Epstein is letting him. Epstein has never let anyone lose like that without collecting."

"How do you know about my father?" Sophie snapped back at him.

"I hear things."

"Well, it's really none of your business and I don't care to talk about it," she replied.

"That's fine with me," Max said.

And with that they fell into silence.

Max had other things to be irritated about that morning. Summer was approaching and this was Max's last year of school. He liked school. It was easy for him and the fact that he was so good at it gained him special attention. He was the star of both the football team and the soccer team and that brought him even more attention. He did not look forward to the drudgery of working full time in his father's store.

Max was also annoyed by the route they were taking to school. Instead of walking down Ludlow as they always did, he had suggested that it would be just as easy to turn on Grand and take Allen down to Canal. That way, he thought, though he didn't say this, they could avoid walking past the construction site of a new building on Ludlow and Canal where the workers always ogled Sophie and made what Max felt were suggestive sounds. Sophie had dismissed the idea. "Oh, Max," she said. "Let's just walk the way we always do." It irked him that she seemed to actually take pleasure in being whistled at. But her wishes, as usual, won out.

New York was unseasonably hot on this spring day, and Sophie was wearing a light cotton dress buttoned down the front, humidity causing the thin material to cling to her. Ruefully, Max thought about how appreciative the construction workers would be.

But as they neared the construction site, Max realised that the structure was empty. The wooden frame of the building was complete and awaited the plumbers, plasterers and other workers to do their part. For some reason, there was always several days' delay between the time one set of tradesmen finished and the next group started. Max never understood why the builders didn't time things so that one group would arrive just as the other finished, as that would obviously get the building done faster. In any case, there were no workers and Max could sense Sophie's disappointment. *She's just a shameless tease,* he thought.

The top floors of the building stood completely open, but the bottom was boarded up to form a makeshift office. Sophie never stayed angry or silent for long and as they approached the new building she was prattling on about what she would do when this school year was over.

"I might not go back to school," she said. "Mr. Epstein says he can get me a job as a fashion model for *Harper's Bazaar* or *McCall's*. He says I'm prettier than any of the girls they have now."

"Aren't you too young for those magazines?" said Max.

"They put stage makeup on your face, silly. That will make me look eighteen. And the rest of me already looks old enough." She giggled.

As they reached the construction site, Max realised he'd been wrong about no one being there. Two men stepped out of the makeshift office in front of them. They were obviously construction workers, big and brawny, wearing work shirts with the sleeves rolled up to reveal their muscles. One was blond with fair skin, the other redheaded with freckles.

They had come to work on a day when there was no work and Max knew exactly why. He glanced around. There was no one else on the street and the two men had stepped directly into their path, blocking their way.

"Excuse us," Max said in a very polite tone. "Can we get by?"

The two men didn't move. Sophie smiled slightly at them and took Max's arm, guiding him into the street around them.

But the redheaded construction worker put a huge, meaty hand around her upper arm and pulled her away from Max. He slammed her up against the building. Holding her easily with one hand he pressed himself against her while groping her chest with his other hand. He kissed her on the face and neck as she tried to turn her head away.

Max felt a sharp tightening in his chest that he had never experienced. He grabbed the big man from behind and literally threw him off of Sophie.

"Get out of here," he screamed. "Leave us alone."

Both men stared at Max, their eyes wide with surprise. They had not expected this from the boy.

"Sure, kid," said the redhead, his hands held up as if in acquiescence. "Sure. We was just having fun. Didn't mean no harm."

Max motioned to Sophie, who was still leaning against the wall, shaking, to come quickly. He saw her start toward him, then stop and begin to shout a warning. Too late, he realised the blond man had slipped behind him. A sinewy forearm clamped around his neck like a vise.

Max was lifted clear off the ground, wriggling helplessly and struggling for air. As the blond held him up, a perfect target, the redhead gave him a vicious punch to the gut. The man behind him let go and Max doubled over in pain, gasping for air. As he bent over, the redhead hit him again, a right hook to the jaw. Max fell to the ground, his world flickering in and out of focus.

He lay there, fighting to stay conscious, remotely aware of Sophie screaming, the two men dragging her inside the makeshift office, out of his sight. Willing himself to his feet, he staggered into the building after them, moving toward the sounds of the screams.

Sophie was bent backward over a small work table. The blond man had her arms pinned while the redhead tried to mount her from the front. Her dress was up around her waist. The redhead had her ripped underpants clutched in one hand. The front of her dress, where it buttoned, was torn completely open.

The red-haired man was so fixated on Sophie that he didn't notice Max enter. But the blond one did, and as Max approached he let go of Sophie and took a ferocious swing at Max's head. Max ducked the blow, in the same motion grabbing a length of stray pipe he'd noticed lying on the concrete floor. In one fluid motion he straightened up and thrust the pipe into his adversary's midsection.

The blond man folded up like a cheap tent.

Sensing movement behind him, Max whirled around, swinging the pipe like a baseball bat. He connected squarely, the pipe making a sickening thud against the red-haired man's head. His would-be attacker went down like a load of wet cement.

The blond man was still doubled over, clutching his stomach. Max kicked him in the face. Blood spurted from the man's nose and he stumbled back a few steps, landing awkwardly on the seat of his pants. Max kicked him again and this time he went all the way down. Both of the attackers were now prone and defenceless but Max kept kicking them, first one then the other, until he became aware of Sophie pulling him from behind and screaming at him to stop. "You're going to kill them!"

She was right. He would have.

Leaving their vanquished assailants, they made their way back to Sophie's apartment. As they walked, Sophie held her torn dress closed with both hands. She was sobbing quietly.

Eli had gone to work so the apartment was empty. Sophie sat slumped on the couch, her hands over her face, heaving and shaking. Max sat down next to her and put his arm around her shoulders. After several minutes she stopped crying, simply resting her head on his shoulder. Quietly, she said, "Thank you."

They sat there like that until he gently pushed her off and back against the couch. "I have to get to school."

When he was halfway to the door he heard her desperate, "Wait." He turned and she threw herself into his arms, clinging to him tightly. She turned her face up to his and the next thing he knew they were kissing. Her mouth was soft and warm and her lips parted, drawing his tongue inside. Her dress where it had been torn was completely open and he felt the warmth of her bare flesh, felt an urgent heat rise within him as her body pressed against his, pleasurable and unnerving. She took his hand in both of hers and led him back to the couch.

But as she pulled him down he said, "No," the word seeming to issue forth on its own. "I have to go." He straightened up and stepped back, a sudden timidity after his earlier display of bravery.

He was already in the hallway, the door swinging shut behind him, when she said quietly, "I love you, Max." But she doubted that he heard. His footsteps already echoed down the narrow hall.

CHAPTER SEVEN

Max did not see much of Sophie during the next several months. With school out, he worked full time in his father's clothing store. Josif believed in working hard and giving his customers value for their money. The contacts he had made during years in the garment industry allowed him to buy directly from the factory and pass the savings on to his customers. Business prospered.

Max waited on customers, stocked the shelves and kept the books. Even Josif, an intelligent man, was astounded by his son's proficiency with numbers. At any time, seemingly off the top of his head, Max could rattle off sales figures, merchandise cost, overhead and inventory for the day, month or year. He kept track of every dime that went in or out of the store without writing anything down and without apparent effort. Josif, who was accustomed to scrupulously written records, was very sceptical, at first, of his son's bookkeeping. But with time he gained complete confidence in Max's abilities and came to rely on him.

Since Max knew every penny that passed through the store, he knew about Dominic Troglia. Troglia was a large man with a swarthy complexion, hooked nose, and black hair slicked straight back from a high forehead. He appeared in the Zalensky's store every third day of every month at precisely three o'clock in the afternoon. He would chat with Josif for a few minutes, tell a joke, laugh, shake hands and then leave.

Mr. Troglia never bought anything and he never delivered any merchandise. But when he left he was always twenty dollars richer than when he came. Troglia made similar visits to every merchant on Grand Street. And everyone paid. If they refused, their store was destroyed. If they tried to stop the destruction, they suffered a more personal punishment. This cycle of extortion was commonly known as 'paying protection'.

"Why don't you stand up to him?" Max said to his father. "What if all of you refused to pay? What could he do?"

It was a conversation they had often. But Josif would just smile and shake his head. "I did all the fighting I ever want to do before I came to this country. Twenty dollars is a small tax to pay. We still make a good living."

The conversation would continue in that vein for several minutes, after which Max would silently rebuke himself for having brought the subject up. His father had achieved a lot for himself and it was not up to Max to tell him how to run his business.

★   ★   ★

Max was busy taking inventory on a Saturday morning when Sophie walked into the store. "Hello, stranger," she said, cheerful as the morning.

"Hello yourself," he replied, getting down from the ladder he had been standing on while counting dress slacks. He had not seen her for almost a month and it was a pleasure just to hear her voice. She was wearing a light silk summer dress, a pale green colour that matched her eyes. It was obviously expensive and Max knew that Epstein must have bought it for her. A spark of jealousy flickered, but he had to admit to himself that she looked even more dazzling than usual.

"You've forgotten," she said, smiling and stepping closer to him.

"Of course I haven't." In truth, he had feared that she would forget or, even worse, not care. Because it was August, and every August since they were very small they had celebrated their birthdays together. Max was almost exactly one year older, their birthdays only a few days apart. Now, within a week, she would be sixteen, he seventeen. When they were children Mrs. Goldberg had always baked them a cake with two candles on it, one for each of them. Only a year ago they had saved their money and gone out together for dinner to a small, inexpensive Italian restaurant. For dessert they had split a cannoli with two candles on it. But now, Max knew, Sophie was accustomed to much fancier fare. There was little he could offer that would compare to the elegant restaurants she frequented with Epstein.

"I'll cook," she said, as if reading his thoughts. "My father will be out late tonight and we'll be by ourselves."

"All right. What time?"

"Late afternoon, right after you close." She smiled and said, "I'll make something special for us." Then she turned and walked out of the store.

Max wanted to buy her something distinctive for her birthday, but he knew that nothing he could afford would compare to the expensive gifts Epstein casually presented her. So he settled for a dozen roses from a flower stand two doors down from his father's store.

She opened the door almost immediately, as if she had been standing right behind it waiting for him to knock. She was wearing a white cotton sun dress, sleeveless with wide straps over her shoulders. Her eyes sparkled and from her smile it was obvious how glad she was to see him.

"Ooh," she gushed, when he handed her the roses. "You're sweet." She kissed him on the cheek. "I'll go put these in water."

Max stepped inside and closed the door. Shades were drawn over the windows as protection against the August heat, so although it was still sunny outside the light was muted in the little apartment.

Sophie came back from the kitchen with the flowers in a vase. "I've got a present for you too." She giggled nervously, avoiding his eyes by looking around for a place to put the flowers. "It's something special."

"Okay. What is it?"

"First," she said slowly, "you have to tell me you want it."

Max repeated, "Tell me what it is."

She shook her head, placing the vase on a small round table. Then she looked him straight in the eyes and said very seriously, "You have to tell me you want it."

After a pause, Max said softly, "I want it."

Sophie smiled, then reached behind herself with both hands and undid something at the back of her dress. She slipped one strap, then the other off of each shoulder. The dress fell down around her ankles with a soft rustle. She had nothing on underneath. Her body glistened in the dim light, her breasts incredibly full and firm, her hips flaring out from the slim waist, her slender legs tapering down to bare feet. From across the room, Max could feel the heat emanating from her and was aware of his own heart pounding.

She came to him and carefully unbuttoned his shirt, kissed him on the mouth, then again, harder. Her lips strayed to his neck, his chest, his hard nipples. She reached for his belt, undid it, unbuttoned his pants, and pulled them down. He helped, wriggling his hips, stepping out of the crumpled heap down by his ankles. She pulled down his undershorts, and his manhood sprang free, throbbing and swollen. Circling her fingers around the tip, she stroked it lightly, and Max let out a soft moan. Then she took his hand and led him to her bedroom.

Sophie fell backward on the bed, pulling him down on top of her, pressing him against herself until she was ready. Then she wrapped her legs up high around his back, squeezing her fingers into his tight buttocks. The thrill of him entering, the fullness of him throbbing inside, brought on a sudden wave of delight. She raised her legs even higher, digging her nails into his flesh and moaning out loud as he slipped deeper into her. He rocked back and forth countless times, straining to control himself, instinctively holding back, until Sophie's brain suddenly exploded with pleasure, her body spasming uncontrollably, primitive sounds escaping her lips, her pelvis arching in and out in a rhythmic heat. Then he burst and she came again, mind and body moving out of control as if motivated by a greater force.

★   ★   ★

Later, after they had made love a second time, Max sat on the bed, putting his pants back on. Sophie sat up next to him, kissed him on the cheek and with her chin resting on his shoulder said, "I love you."

"I love you too. So, what do you say? Let's get married."

"Max, don't be silly," she said lightly, as if she knew he didn't really mean it.

"I'm serious. I love you. I've loved you my whole life. We should be married."

Sophie was taken aback. She had not expected this. She hesitated, then dropped her eyes and said, "I can't."

"I'm working with my father now. I can support us. I know our apartment isn't big, but we can make do until we can afford a place of our own." He stroked her hair.

"Oh, Max," Sophie said. "It would be wonderful. But I can't." She suddenly looked terribly sad. "I'm going to marry Arnold Epstein."

"What are you talking about?" Max thought she was making some sort of a joke.

"I'm going to marry him," she said again. "It's already been arranged."

Max felt as if he had been punched in the gut. For a moment he couldn't breathe. "But he's twenty years older than you," he said at last, as if that was what mattered.

"You don't understand. My father owes him ten thousand dollars. I don't have a choice."

It was a tremendous amount of money, more than Eli Feldman would make in the meat-packing plant in six years, but Max refused to accept the idea that she would agree to this, especially after what had just taken place between them. "You do have a choice," he said. "I can protect your father."

Sophie laughed bitterly. "You can't protect him. Not from the kind of men Arnold has working for him."

"So what? Your father made his own problems. You're not merchandise to be sold for his debts. Marry me and let him handle his own troubles."

Sophie shook her head. "It's true, it's his own fault. All of it. And there're other things he's done. But that doesn't mean he deserves to die." She paused, then said quietly but resolutely, "My mother left, he raised me by himself. I won't let him die." She was staring down at the bed, tears running down her cheeks.

Max just stared at her, stunned. "So what was this afternoon all about?" he said. "What did you...invite me over here for?"

"Because I love you," she said simply. "I wanted to make love with someone I love, just once. And I wanted to be the first for you." She looked up at him. "I was the first, wasn't I?"

"Yes, goddamn it." His voice was rising. "And now you're going off like some lamb to slaughter, selling yourself to a man you don't love. Don't do this, Sophie."

She just shook her head. "I have to," she said, bursting fully into tears. "Max, people like us, we do what we're made to do, and people like Arnold are the ones who make us."

"That may be true for you," Max said, almost shouting now, his words propelled by hurt and anger. "But not for me. I can do what I want. My father and I have our own business. I don't have to kneel to Arnold Epstein and I could protect you and your father if you let me."

"That's nonsense," she shot back at him. "You do what you're told like everyone else. I know Josif pays protection to Troglia just like all the merchants on Grand. Arnold told me he does. You're so high and mighty. You talk about protecting me. You can't even protect yourself."

He started to say something, but stopped. She was right. It was his fault. Inside, he was still that little boy in the closet, unable to protect the person he loved most. It filled him with shame. He lowered his head and turned away from her. It was the first time in her life that Sophie had seen him defeated.

"Oh, Max," she said, "I'm sorry." And she put her arms on his shoulders and kissed the back of his neck. He felt the wetness of her tears.

"It's okay," he said, his voice flat and without expression.

"I never meant to hurt you."

But she had. She had hurt him terribly. And part of him, the part that had briefly flickered back to life after all this time, was just as quickly sealed off. He would never again drop his guard or let anyone in. It was too dangerous.

Keeping his voice flat, he said, "No problem. It won't happen again." He stood up, buttoned his shirt cuffs and walked out of the little apartment without looking back. Sophie lay facedown on her bed and cried as his footsteps disappeared down the hall for the last time.

CHAPTER EIGHT

Dominic Troglia was tired. It had been a long day, what with two of his customers claiming they didn't have enough money to pay, and him having to slap them around a few times before they came through with the dough. Maybe it had been too long since he'd had to really get tough. Maybe he'd become complacent. His customers were beginning to think he was a soft touch.

He was tired as he headed for the Grand Street IRT subway station. He imagined himself at home, eating a large plate of his wife's lasagna, taking a warm bath afterward, smoking a cigar, reading the sports section. Even better, maybe paying a visit to his mistress. He smiled to himself. A little rough stuff always made him randy.

Troglia's thoughts were interrupted as a familiar figure suddenly appeared in front of him, seeming to come out of nowhere, grinning like a damn lark. That fucking Zalensky kid. Troglia was almost to the subway stairs but he had to stop short to keep from colliding with him.

"Whadda ya want?" he said, obviously in a hurry and in no mood.

Max looked up at the large man and flashed him an easy smile. "I would like to ask a small favour, Mr. Troglia."

"I'm listening. Make it snappy."

Still smiling, Max said, "Don't come into my father's store anymore."

"What the hell's that supposed to mean?"

"Just what I said, Mr. Troglia. You can keep collecting from the others. But we don't pay anymore."

"You got a lot of balls, punk. Get out of my way before I step on you." And the big man tried to shove Max aside.

As if by magic a leather sap appeared in Max's hand, at the same time he easily sidestepped Troglia's outstretched arms. With lightning speed Max thrust the sap into the big man's lower abdomen. Troglia doubled over, clutching his stomach, gasping for air. "Remember, Mr. Troglia," Max said, "we don't pay."

Troglia was bent over next to the subway stairs. Max placed his foot on the man's posterior and pushed hard. Troglia went flying down the concrete steps, his legs trying unsuccessfully to keep up with his momentum. He managed to get his arms up just in time to protect his head from real injury, but his shoulders and elbows took the brunt of it and were badly bruised. Max looked down at him and laughed. "You'd be better off not coming back," he said, and then walked quickly away. But he knew, of course, that Troglia would come back.

Three days later – four-thirty a.m. Three large figures walked out of the Grand Street station, Dominic Troglia in the middle, his dark face and thick lips set with determination. He was flanked by two swarthy Italians, each over six feet tall and two hundred pounds. With their similar builds and complexions they were almost indistinguishable in the darkness.

Two blocks before Zalensky's place, Troglia and his companions turned into a narrow alley that ran behind the shops. Even at this hour there would be peddlers on the street setting up their pushcarts for the day's sales. For what he planned to do, Troglia did not want witnesses.

Dominic Troglia enjoyed this sort of work. He prided himself on attention to detail. That was why he made collections himself, getting to know his customers and their businesses. And that was why he would take care of this matter personally. That little kike would never walk again. And his voice might rise a few octaves as well.

Actually, the timing of this business wasn't bad. You had to come down hard on somebody once in a while, just to keep the others in line. Troglia hoped the old man didn't try to interfere and get himself hurt. Zalensky was a good sort. Not his fault the kid was an asshole.

When they were forty yards from their destination Troglia could feel butterflies in his stomach and tension in his throat. Even though his two men, Vince and Joe, were several steps behind him, he thought he could sense their adrenaline rise as well.

Suddenly, with no warning, a figure rushed out of a doorway and directly into Troglia's path. At the same instant Troglia was aware of two taller figures running out of a doorway behind Vince and Joe. Even in the dim light the Italians could see that the first man held a double-barrelled shotgun aimed directly at them. The other two carried what looked like baseball bats.

Max's harsh monotone cut through the darkness. "If anyone moves a finger, I'll blow his goddamned head off."

The three Italians stood frozen, their eyes fixed on Max, straining to make out his face in the dim light. Max continued talking. "It's not often that we get to welcome visitors to our...."

Troglia realised later that this phrase must have been a signal. Upon its utterance each of Max's men whipped his baseball bat into the kneecap of the man nearest him. Almost in unison the two screamed in agony. Troglia turned and saw Joe sprawled on his side, clutching his shattered kneecap with one hand and starting to draw his gun with the other. He never had a chance. Joe's attacker swung his baseball bat in a short, downward arc that caught Joe squarely across the bridge of his nose. Joe's face seemed to dissolve into blood and broken bone as he lost consciousness. His attacker swung the bat several more times, striking the prone man in the side of the body. Troglia was aware of muffled coughs coming from Joe's blood-covered mouth as rib after rib was broken.

Vince tried gamely to stand on his one good leg. As the initial shock subsided he reached for his weapon. He was too slow. Max's other henchman had already begun to swing his bat in a wide semicircle that landed with a sickening thud on Vince's left temple. The big man dropped like a cold brick. His attacker knelt for a moment to determine if his victim still had a pulse. Then he stood up and swung the bat several more times, shattering Vince's legs while he lay unconscious.

The beatings were over in a matter of minutes. Max, still perfectly calm, pointed his shotgun directly at Troglia's right eye. He moved so close to him that Troglia was literally staring down the barrel. In his entire life, Troglia had never been more frightened. It took an act of will to keep from having a childish accident.

"Mr. Troglia," said Max, still in the flat monotone. "This part of the city is not a good place for you. It's a poor place, hardly worth the effort to get here. Do you understand?"

Troglia's throat was too dry to allow speech so he merely nodded.

"Good," said Max, and smiled. "You can go. We'll leave your trash here for the garbage man to pick up."

Troglia half walked, half ran away.

CHAPTER NINE
1918

Patricia and her mother worked in tandem to clean up after the evening meal. Her father, of course, took no part in this women's work. Jonathan wandered in as he always did, offering to help. As always, Catherine shooed him out. She felt just as strongly as her husband that the kitchen was no place for a man.

Patricia could have pointed out that Jon, at seventeen years old, was barely a man and that he ate more than she and her mother combined. So it would certainly make sense for him to help clean up after this grand meal that he received for free, just for having the good fortune to be the son of Catherine's cousin. But she knew her mother would never change her attitude on the subject, and besides, Jonathan worked a long, exhausting day in her uncle's tavern and had earned his rest.

He had been with them for almost five years now, and her mother thought of him more as a son than the offspring of a cousin she had not seen in thirty-three years. Catherine often referred to him as Patricia's brother and wanted Patricia to feel the same way. That was not likely.

When the dishes were done Patricia went to her room to read, as was her habit before going to sleep. She was grateful that her work day, one that started later than the rest of the household, allowed the luxury of reading before bed. But soon it was time for her to retire as well.

She watched herself undress in the full-length mirror. She pulled her dress over her head and let it drop unceremoniously to the floor, then did the same with her chemise. Naked, she cupped her hands beneath her breasts, just the way Tony had once done. Thoughts of him brought more thoughts, and she ran her fingers down past the slightly rounded plane of her stomach to her thighs, imagining they were his fingers. It had been nine years since she had seen or heard from Tony, but not a day passed that she did not think of him.

He was probably married now, to some dark-haired, dark-eyed Italian wife, who had already borne him four children. She, on the other hand, at age thirty-two, was a childless spinster. "It's a shame," her father had once said to her mother, unaware that she was standing just outside the door and could hear every word, "that such a beautiful girl will give no children to the world." She smiled sadly. A shame. Maybe that was why she enjoyed teaching so much. Every year the children seemed to get younger, and being around them gave her some connection to a part of life she would probably never know.

She had been twenty-one when she met Tony, already old for an unmarried Irish girl. She was bored by the fawning attention that she received from the young men she knew, and unimpressed by their lack of ambition. Then Tony Angeletti had walked into her father's grocery, introducing himself as the new distributor for Schaffer's beer. He was tall, handsome and very confident. Only twenty-five, he already owned his own truck and had landed a lucrative beer franchise. He asked her to have dinner with him that very first time they met. And although it was obviously impossible, she said yes.

They had to meet surreptitiously since her family would never allow her to date an Italian, just as his family would be horrified at the thought of an Irish girl. Marriage, of course, was unthinkable.

The first time they made love, the first time she had ever made love, was on an old mattress on the floor of a garage in Little Italy that he used as a warehouse. Despite the shoddy surroundings, despite the fact that it ran counter to everything she had ever been taught, it was wonderful. It was everything she had dreamed that it might be and everything the nuns had told her it was not. In the days that followed, she would tell her parents that she was visiting a friend or reading a book at the public library, and sneak off to the garage. Oftentimes they had lunch together but rarely dinner, since that would be too difficult to hide from her family.

For the first six months he begged her to marry him, but she knew her family would never approve and she refused to choose between them. It was an exciting time, slipping off in the afternoon for illicit, wonderful love. But after a year she was ready. She was twenty-two, and almost all of her childhood girlfriends were married. Many of the young men who had pursued her were also married, to girls three or four years younger than she. And she loved Tony. She wanted to spend the rest of her life with him, have his children and grow old with him.

But by then he was a successful businessman and able to choose from the youngest and prettiest of his own kind. He had come to think of her as a mistress rather than a potential wife. After another year, he left her. There had been other liaisons in the ensuing years, but never anyone she felt seriously about.

So she thought of him as she stood in front of the mirror, her hands wandering to her most intimate places. But it had been nine years since she had actually seen him, his face and feel no longer fresh in her memory. So as her fingers did their gentle work it was not Tony, but the image of the boy, Jonathan, that swept into her mind. As she built toward orgasm it was Jonathan's bare torso, glistening with sweat, muscles rippling as he lifted kegs of beer in her uncle's bar, that filled her vision. When she climaxed it was his face that she saw in front of her, his heaving chest and sinewy arms. And when it was over, it was him she imagined holding her trembling body and whispering sweet nothings in her ear.

CHAPTER TEN

Jonathan had almost finished setting up. The bar would not be open for another twenty minutes, so he had time to relax before the first customer showed up. The place sparkled; the wooden bar top was polished to a shine, the glasses and whiskey bottles were lined up perfectly and the brass railing around the bar top gleamed. In the six months since William had made Jonathan his bartender, business had picked up substantially, not that you would know it from the verbal abuse that William directed at him.

Still, Jonathan was happy to have the job and William was happy to have someone he could trust, someone in the family, behind the bar. Because it was too easy for your bartender to steal you blind; give drinks away to his friends for free or, even worse, pocket the money that customers paid for drinks instead of putting it in the cash box.

But to hear William tell it, he was providing work for the young man out of pure charity. He had even made a statement to that effect during a rare visit to his sister Catherine's house. Catherine had looked at him disapprovingly, which was the strongest reproach she ever gave her younger brother. She remembered when William had been desperate for some good help. "Someone," he had said, "from the old country, still willing to put in a real day's work for his wages." Catherine felt that it had worked out well for everyone. Jonathan had learned a trade and William had obtained good help cheaply. The fact that William now acted as if he were doing everyone a favour irritated her a little, but she loved her younger brother deeply and overlooked his pettiness.

The last thing Jonathan had to do before the bar opened for business was to restock the empty beer keg with a fresh one from the storeroom in the back. The keg was heavy but he knew he couldn't expect any help from William or Harry. As usual, they were in the office, drinking and talking. Or rather, William was talking and Harry was listening while they both drank.

Harry Carroll was William's only other employee. He was a big, strong brute who William employed as a bouncer. Before Jonathan was hired, Harry helped out as part-time janitor in addition to lifting the heavy kegs of beer and cases of wine. But now Jonathan took care of all that and Harry only had to act as bouncer and listen to William talk. He was very good at both and seemed to take special pleasure in beating up the occasional disorderly drunk, then pitching him into the alley behind the bar.

Two weeks earlier a drunken customer named Mulligan had raised a big fuss about the whiskey being watered down. In fact, William bought good Irish whiskey, which Jonathan poured straight from the bottle. It was never watered, and if it were, William's regular customers, many of whom drank it straight, would have known immediately. Nevertheless, Mulligan insisted in a loud, drunken voice that the whiskey was weak and that he wanted his money back. William ignored him until the noise began to disturb the other customers. Then he nodded to Harry, who had been waiting impatiently.

Harry grabbed Mulligan under the armpits and literally lifted him off of his bar stool. Then he hustled him to the back door, which both avoided an awkward scene with any customers who might be coming in the front and made certain that no one on the street would see Harry perform his dirty work. Harry came back about ten minutes later, slightly out of breath, his face and knuckles red. Jonathan saw him stuffing what looked like paper money into his pants pockets as he came through the back door.

Though he hadn't seen what actually happened, he had a pretty good idea. As drunk as Mulligan was and as badly as Harry had probably beaten him, he would not wake up until close to morning, and he would be hurting from more than just a hangover.

The next day, before the bar opened, Mulligan came back angry as a hornet. His left eye was swollen almost shut, his lower lip was twice its normal size and he was missing at least one tooth. But it was not his physical condition that had him so infuriated. He marched directly up to Harry, pointed a stubby finger in the big man's face and said very loudly, "You took my money and I'll have it back. Right now, if you don't mind." Then he took a step back and held out his hand, palm up, as if fully expecting Harry to place money in it.

Harry simply looked at the man as if he were daft. He turned away from Mulligan, shrugged and said, "I have no idea what you're talking about."

Mulligan was having none of it. He grabbed Harry by the back of the shirt collar and pulled him back. The big man was fussy about being touched and he spun around, his face reddening. Mulligan's stubby finger was back in Harry's face and he was shouting now.

"You got it all right, fifteen dollars, and you'll give it back or I'll come back here with the police." Again, Mulligan stretched out his hand as if expecting Harry to lay the fifteen dollars in his upturned palm.

Harry's face had turned the colour of a beet, his anger seething uncontrollably. Suddenly, with a motion quicker than Jonathan's eye could follow, Harry grabbed Mulligan's outstretched wrist with his left hand and pulled Mulligan straight toward him. Turning his body so that he faced toward the bar, Harry locked his right arm around the smaller man's head. Mulligan tried to struggle but he never had a chance.

Harry lunged forward, lowering Mulligan's head as he did so, so that in a terrible instant the top of Mulligan's head slammed against the newly polished brass railing that surrounded the wooden bar top. Mulligan went limp, which made it easier for Harry to pummel his head three more times into the railing. Harry let him go and he dropped to the floor, face first, unconscious and unable to break his fall with his hands. There was blood on the railing where Mulligan's head had hit it and blood on the floor where he lay. Harry kicked him once in the side so hard that Mulligan's body rose an inch off the floor. After the one kick Harry stopped the beating, partly because he was out of breath and partly because it occurred to him that Mulligan might be dead. He did not appear to be breathing and was as still as a corpse, his skin drained of its normal colour.

It had happened so quickly that neither Jonathan nor William had time to react. But William was looking very fearful and Jonathan knew he was worried. "Sweet Jesus," William said in a low voice. "I think you've killed him."

"I hope so," said Harry, his voice still filled with rage. "He was gonna go to the police. He does that, I go to jail. And you too." He levelled his eyes at William.

William glanced at Jonathan who immediately comprehended that Harry had been stealing money from all the drunks he threw out of the bar, and apparently splitting the take with William.

"He couldn't have proved anything, you stupid ass," said William. "But now we've got a murder charge to worry about. By Christ, you're so goddamned dumb, you do things without thinking about the consequences. Now I've got to figure a way out of this mess, and you might have to just—"

"Excuse me," Jonathan interrupted, "but I think he's alive." William had been so busy haranguing Harry that he had failed to notice that Mulligan was breathing again, bloody bubbles foaming from his nose as his body twitched fitfully.

"Damn," said Harry, and looked at William. "We got to kill him. When he tells the police what happened, I'll go to jail for sure."

"First off, he may never wake up. Second, if he does wake up, he probably won't even remember what happened. And if he goes to the police, so what? He's got no witnesses, and we'll all swear he was never in here tonight." William said this without bothering to look to Jonathan for affirmation, simply assuming the young man would go along with the lie.

"Take him away from here," William said to Harry. "Drive the truck around to the alley and throw him in the back. Take him over near the wharf and dump him. No one will be surprised to find a body over there." He turned to Jonathan. "You clean up all this damn blood. Make it look like nothing ever happened."

It turned out exactly as William had predicted. The police found Mulligan the next day, unconscious in an alley near the wharf, right where Harry had dumped him. They took him to the public hospital where he remained in a coma for two days. When he awoke he had no memory of what had happened. The doctor told his wife, who had been summoned by the police, that he had suffered mild brain damage. With time, the doctor assured her, he would be able to function normally, but he would probably never regain memory of whatever transpired just before he lost consciousness. Jonathan did not expect to see him in Harry's bar again.

CHAPTER ELEVEN

Jonathan was wiping down the bar when William and Harry walked out of the back office. This was the time, twenty minutes before opening, that William made his inspection. He wandered around looking for a bottle out of place, or dust on the bar top or even a fingerprint on the brass railing that he could call Jonathan to task for. This day he picked up some whiskey bottles and peered at them against the light, apparently to see if Jonathan had been secretly imbibing the merchandise. Unable to find fault, he groped for some other means to needle Jonathan. "Does my sister charge you rent for sleeping in her house, using her son's old room?"

"No," Jonathan responded. "She and Uncle George are kind enough to let me stay there for free, until I'm able to get out on my own." He was surprised at the question. It was normal within the Irish community for kinfolk in the new country to host relatives from the old. Sometimes whole families were housed with relatives in quarters much smaller than the O'Haras' house.

"How about the food you eat? I know a strong young fella like you eats like a horse. Do you pay for it?"

"No," Jonathan admitted, feeling a little defensive. It was true, he ate a lot. And since Uncle George owned a grocery store, there was always plenty in the house to eat. "I hope to make enough money to be able to pay them back someday."

"Yeah," William snorted, "I'll bet you would. I'll bet you'd like to give a little payback to your cousin Patricia, too."

"What?" Jonathan said, not understanding.

William ignored him and talked to Harry, as if Jonathan were no longer there. "You ever seen my niece, Patricia? Sweetest little piece of fluff you ever seen."

"Oh yeah," Harry responded.

"O-o-h yeah. She never got married. Too good for anyone

around here, and now she's too old. But she's still the best-looking piece around."

"She's a teacher," Jonathan interjected. "She teaches children." He was shocked at his boss's vulgarity. He had become accustomed to William's crass manner, but the man was now talking about his own niece.

"Yeah," William leered, "and I bet you'd like to be teacher's pet."

Before Jonathan could respond, the front door of the bar opened and Max, the same young man who had given Jonathan directions his first day in this new country, walked into the bar from the street. He was flanked by two hefty men, each equal in size to Harry.

It had been five years and he had grown from teenager to man, but Jonathan knew him immediately, that momentous day etched indelibly in his mind. Max, for his part, barely glanced at Jonathan, registering no recognition. After gazing around the bar, Max nodded some signal to his two men and they walked out of the bar, apparently to wait outside. He wore an expensive business suit, with closely cropped hair and a casual manner that exuded confidence.

"We're not open for business yet," William said.

"I am aware of that," Max responded. "I would like to speak to the owner."

"That's me."

Max bowed slightly and said, "I am Max Zalensky. A pleasure to meet you." He extended his hand to William, but William ignored him. After a long moment, Max let his hand drop, unfazed by the rude reception. His speech, however, was measured.

"I'm here on business," he began. "I have recently acquired the rights to distribute several brands of liquor and beer in this area. I'm quite confident that I can offer these products at rates more favourable than your current suppliers."

"You're wasting my time," William said. "I'm happy with the suppliers I've got. Maybe they ain't as cheap as you people, but they give me top product. And the service is good."

Jonathan was surprised to hear his uncle defend his suppliers, since Jonathan knew they were notoriously unreliable. William usually ordered his product to arrive a day before he actually needed it, just to make certain he received it on time. Max, seemed undaunted.

"You've had better luck than your competition," he said, looking sharply at William. "Several of them told me that they get the goods a day, or even two, after they need it. I guess that hasn't happened to you."

"No," William lied, "it hasn't."

Max nodded. "Just for your information, I will guarantee in writing that any merchandise not received on the day it is supposed to be will be charged at half price. I'll absorb the difference. Also, I'm aware of the suppliers you're currently using and the prices you're paying. I can deliver the exact same product and cut the prices by ten per—"

William cut him off. "I really don't give a shit about any of that. I ain't interested in switching." William's attitude surprised Jonathan, who would have expected a lower price and better service to be exactly what William wanted.

Apparently, William's response also surprised Max. But rather than give up, he asked, "Would a larger discount make a difference?"

"The only thing that would make a difference," William said angrily, "is you. I ain't doing business with no kike. No matter how good you sound now, you'll end up screwing me. I know how you people are. I ain't about to do business with you and I don't want you in my place. So get out."

Max shrugged and in a flat monotone said, "Obviously there is nothing I can do to change your mind," but he made no move to leave.

Max's casual disregard of his order to vacate further fed William's anger. He turned to Harry, who had been listening as raptly as Jonathan, and said, "Throw this punk out."

Harry grinned and advanced on Max. Jonathan, his panic starting to rise, could not understand why Max was not beating a retreat. The man seemed to be frozen in place.

Harry moved swiftly for a man of his size, lunging forward, his huge right hand reaching for the back of Max's neck, and Jonathan realised with horror that he was about to witness a repeat of what had happened to Mr. Mulligan. But Max seemed to have anticipated Harry's movement and, as Harry lunged, shifted his stance sideways so his body was out of Harry's line of forward motion. At the same time, Max's left forearm blocked his opponent's right hand, while he brought up his right fist so it swung into Harry's left ear as the bigger man charged past.

Harry whirled like a wounded elephant, a look of sheer fury on his reddening face, and ran straight at Max, his arms reaching for the shorter man's neck. Again, Max seemed to anticipate Harry's move, ducking his head and bringing his left fist up into Harry's liver. The liver shot was not perfectly on target, not enough to paralyse Harry, but it slowed him down, causing his knees to buckle while excruciating pain travelled his torso. Jon heard his uncle shout, "Kill him now, Harry," just before Max landed a quick uppercut to Harry's jaw. Harry's head snapped backward but the big man still managed to stay on his feet.

As Harry stood on wobbly legs, trying to regain his balance and composure, Max kicked him in the groin. Harry cried out in pain, reflexively bending over and clutching the injured area with both hands, his head lowered. With a vicious movement, Max brought his knee straight up into Harry's face and the big man toppled to the floor with a heavy thud.

William appeared to be in shock; his face was pale white and he was shaking visibly. As far as Jonathan could tell, Max was not even breathing hard. The only evidence that he had been in a fight were the flecks of Harry's blood splattered on his expensive suit. He turned to William and said, "It is unfortunate that we are unable to do business at this time. Perhaps I will persuade you to change your mind in the near future."

As he walked toward the exit, he turned toward Jonathan and with an amused smile said, "Welcome to America."

CHAPTER TWELVE
1919

Arnold Epstein slammed the ledger down on his desk, disgusted. It made a loud noise and Manny Pinkus, the little bookkeeper who had been taking Arnold through the month-end figures, looked frightened. But then, Pinkus always looked frightened. That was one reason Arnold trusted him to keep his books. Epstein was angry, but he wasn't about to kill the messenger. He knew perfectly well what the real problem was: Max Zalensky. Epstein had let the little punk get too far, too fast, and now it was costing him plenty. He hadn't taken the damn kid seriously enough. Oh well. It was a mistake easily enough corrected. Epstein smiled his tight little smile and Pinkus looked even more frightened.

"Get out of here," Epstein said to the little man, handing him the ledger. His voice was indifferent, his mind already working on the solution to the problem before him. When Pinkus left, Epstein turned to Becker, his omnipresent bodyguard, and commanded, "Get Leonetti, Schwartz, Peltz and Piluso. I want them right away." The large, bullet-headed man nodded, then left the room.

That man was a real find, Epstein thought after Becker had left. *Even if my wife is frightened of him. Oh well. That's part of his job. People are supposed to be frightened of him.* Actually, Sophie should be grateful to Becker since he was the one who had brought the two of them together. That was one reason Arnold had promoted him to personal bodyguard.

Becker had started out as just another enforcer for Arnold's bookie operation, breaking fingers or heads as appropriate. Even in that humble position, Becker's size and love of brute force made him a standout. But the big man soon demonstrated a shrewd intelligence and a subtle understanding of Epstein's needs that allowed him to rise quickly up the ladder. *When this Zalensky business is over, I'll give him a raise*, Epstein thought, smiling his tight little smile again. *He'll deserve one.*

Epstein's reverie was interrupted by a sharp knock on the office door. He yelled, "Come in!" and the four men Sophie referred to as the Brute Squad walked in, followed by Becker. They were all big men, Leonetti and Schwartz both taller than Becker although not as broad. Peltz and Piluso were slightly smaller, but still large enough to intimidate any normal person. Each man had proved time and again that he could get the job done. All of them had worked for Epstein for years, repeatedly demonstrating their worthiness. All in all, Epstein had no reason to doubt the loyalty of any man in the room.

Still, he sometimes wondered about Peltz. The man constantly worried about money. He had a demanding wife, and although Arnold paid better than the standard for this sort of work, Peltz was always looking for a raise. It sometimes got downright bothersome. When Arnold promoted Becker to be his personal bodyguard Peltz had barely been able to contain his disappointment. But at least Becker was a Jew. If Arnold put Leonetti or Piluso in charge of a project, Peltz sulked for days, whining about having to take orders from a dago. *When this is over*, Epstein thought, *it might be wise to cut him loose.* In this business a disgruntled employee was dangerous.

"We have a problem, gentlemen," Epstein began. He paused for a moment to make certain he had their full attention. "Our gambling revenues are down twenty percent this month. And I guess we all know where that money has gone."

He looked around the room again. Everybody knew. "My information is that he's going to start making book in a month or so, in addition to running tables."

All the men in the room knew what that meant. Zalensky had been running a small but well-organised gambling operation, two crap tables and a roulette wheel in the cellar of a brassiere factory on lower Washington. It had been open six months and was already taking a big bite out of Epstein's operations.

But the real money lay in bookmaking: setting odds and taking bets on the horses, the fights, the World Series or anything else where a man could back his opinion with his wallet. It only stood to reason that as Zalensky built up some capital he would want to get into the real money. But it also meant he would cut into the meat of Epstein's livelihood.

Peltz spoke up. "He gives his customers free drinks and food. Brings it right to their table so they don't stop playing. And he's got pretty girls who serve the drinks and encourage guys to bet."

Epstein stared coolly at Peltz. "That's very nice, Peltz," he said. "But we're not here to discuss the wonders of free enterprise. We're here to shut the little shit down. Permanently." He paused for a moment as the other men snickered.

"For anyone who hasn't been there, Zalensky's operation is in the cellar of the Wallich Brassiere Factory. The factory closes at six, same time Zalensky's operation opens. One of Wallich's employees stays and lets people in through the front door. But there's another entrance." Epstein emphasised this last sentence. "There's an old stairway off the back alley, goes straight down to the cellar. The door to it is always locked, but I got a man who's going to open it at eleven, tonight. That's how you guys go in."

At this point Epstein took a moment to look each man in the eye. "I want them hit so hard they can't ever open up again. And I want other people to learn the lesson too. The four of you will go in the back door with shotguns. I want the tables completely destroyed and at least two of his men shot – three would be even better. But no customers are to be hurt. We'll want them coming to our place." Epstein looked around the room. Each of the men nodded.

An hour later, Max Zalensky received a phone call on the private line in his office. He listened intently for a few minutes, then said, "You've done well. Starting immediately, we double your salary." Then he hung up.

CHAPTER THIRTEEN

Sophie knew that Arnold's men were in the house. Arnold was a man of set routine and on the first Monday of every month he liked to go through the previous month's results with his accountant. He had an office downstairs with a separate entrance from the street. This one day a month was the only time he used it. Normally, he used a desk in the back of a warehouse on Third Street from which he ran his bookmaking operation. But when he worked in his home his lieutenants loitered downstairs, in case they were needed.

Sophie loathed these men. They were big and crude and when they looked at her they practically licked their lips. So the one day a month that they were there, she did not go downstairs. The maid, Elsie, brought her breakfast and lunch in her bedroom, where she spent the day reading and sewing.

She and Arnold had been married more than a year, a life very different and yet similar to the one she had known before. She still lived on the Lower East Side, less than two miles from the apartment where she grew up. But now she lived in a large brownstone with a huge living room, dining room and guestroom. Upstairs was a master bedroom with its own bath and sitting area, and an enormous nursery for the children yet to come. Arnold had made it clear that he wanted children.

And they had tried. As Arnold was a creature of habit, they had sex every Sunday and Wednesday night. The fact that these were the slowest nights in the gambling business and therefore nights that Arnold could easily come home early did not bother the practical Sophie. Arnold was a skillful and considerate lover, always careful to bring his wife to climax before coming himself. And he never seemed to lose his awe at the sight of her unclothed body. Sophie was glad of this. Mrs. Goldberg had told her that physical lust would not last unless it was backed by a deeper feeling. Sophie was afraid of what would happen if his lust faded.

But there was no sign of that yet, just as there was no sign of children. Sophie was relieved on both counts. There had been so many changes in her life, she did not need another just yet. She still saw Mrs. Goldberg of course; life without the older woman was unimaginable. She had also had her father over several times for dinner. He knew his place and was careful not to offend.

And she made an effort to see old friends from the neighbourhood, although her life was so different now that there was less and less to talk about. Sometimes she'd meet her friends at the cinema. It was just five cents for the nickelodeon and a quarter for a movie. Moving pictures afforded Sophie an escape from the world she lived in. She went again and again, often by herself. She especially loved movies featuring strong, smart women like Marion Davies and Lillian Gish. She loved to read gossip about these stars in the fan magazines and fantasise about what their lives were like off screen; rich and glamorous and independent.

And she thought about Max. She hadn't seen him in over a year, not since that wonderful, terrible last evening. Arnold didn't know of her friendship with him and, of course, he never would. She'd heard that Max had moved out of his father's house and taken over the neighbourhood protection racket. She'd also heard that he'd assumed control of Dominic Troglia's liquor distribution business, and expanded it. She even knew where he lived. She had strolled by his house one day after she and Elsie went grocery shopping. A husky young man, a stranger to Sophie, had been standing on the stoop and watched as Sophie and Elsie walked by.

Now she had heard that Max had gotten into the gambling business. She didn't know if this would bring him into conflict with Arnold, but it seemed to her that enough people gambled to provide abundant profit for both of them. Still, in the short time that she had been married to Arnold, she'd come to realise what an ambitious man he was.

Her thoughts were interrupted by a knock on the door. Elsie stuck her head in for a moment and said, "They're gone." Elsie didn't like Arnold's men any more than Sophie did, and always made certain to tell her as soon as they left. Since it was early afternoon, this was a pleasant surprise. It meant Arnold was probably done working for the day. He had already told her he was taking her out to dinner that night, to a new little French restaurant on Broad Street. She wanted to go out and get her hair done first though, so she went downstairs to ask him for some money.

She was about to open the door to his office when she heard his voice. It was muffled, but she could sense that he was excited or angry, or both. He was speaking louder than normal and even through the door she could almost make out the words. Sophie was not in the habit of snooping into her husband's business, so she turned to go back up to her room. But just as she did she heard her husband's voice, loud and with obvious anger, say the word 'Zalensky'. She stopped dead in her tracks, not certain of anything else that Arnold had said, but sure she'd heard the name of the young man who still filled her thoughts.

Just inside the door to Arnold's office was a small waiting area, then another door that led to the office proper. Sophie knew that from inside the waiting area she would be able to hear what was being said without being seen. Very quietly, she opened the door and entered. The next voice she heard was not her husband's but Becker's. She had come to know and loathe his low, bull-like drone. She heard him say, "Okay, but how do I get in?"

Then her husband's voice, straightforward but oddly excited: "He has a bodyguard inside. I've arranged for him to leave the door unlocked. All you've got to worry about is the man on the street in front. Just get close enough to use your shiv. A gun will make too much noise. You don't want anyone on the street or in the house to hear you. Once you're inside, the coast is clear. He'll be asleep. My man inside says he's always in bed by eleven. His bedroom's the first door at the top of the stairs. Shoot the punk to make sure and if there's a broad with him, plug her too."

Sophie heard a low grunt that she recognised as Becker's way of registering compliance. Arnold continued: "Check with me about eleven-thirty, before you go over there, in case there are any changes. I'll be here. I don't want anyone at the club to see you talking to me before." Again, the low grunt of assent from Becker.

Then Sophie heard the door to the street open and close. She realised the big man had left.

Sophie backed out of the waiting room as quietly as she could, closing the door behind her. Then she rushed out of the house, her heart banging, breath coming hard, trying to absorb the fact that she was married to a man who could coldly plan a brutal murder. And not just the murder of some stranger, but of someone she had known her whole life, a man she had loved, a man whom she still loved. She felt overwhelmed, her first impulse to pretend that nothing was happening or about to happen – just as she had all those nights in her dark bedroom when her father had come home drunk.

But she knew she couldn't do that. If she did, Max Zalensky, her childhood friend and first love, would be murdered in cold blood by the man to whom she had pledged her life. There was no question in her mind what she would do. A year of marriage did not wipe out a lifetime of friendship and love. She reasoned that Max could easily enough leave the East Side and set up business somewhere else. It was not as if he were long established. How hard could it be to move? As far as she knew, he had no real friends except her, and they never saw each other anymore. But the important thing was that he get out of his house tonight.

Max lived less than a mile from the Epsteins. It took her only twenty minutes to walk there. Standing in front of the stoop to Max's brownstone was the same young man that Sophie had seen before. She walked up to him without hesitation and announced herself. "My name is Mrs. Sophie Epstein. I need to see Max Zalensky right away. Please tell him I am here."

The young man looked Sophie up and down as if to make sure she carried no concealed weapon. Then his eyes darted behind her and up and down the street, perhaps to be certain that no unseen assailant would take advantage of the attention he was giving this beautiful girl. Finally, in a polite tone of voice, he said, "I'll let him know."

The young man walked quickly up the steps and knocked on the door. It opened immediately and he went inside, closing the door behind and leaving Sophie standing on the sidewalk. In a few minutes the door opened again and the young man walked back down the stairs to the street.

"I'm sorry, Mrs. Epstein," he said flatly. "Mr. Zalensky is very busy. No visitors today."

Sophie stared at him as if she didn't believe what he had said. "Did you tell him my name?" she demanded.

"Yes, Mrs. Epstein. I did."

"Well, tell him again." Sophie was beginning to sound frantic now. "He must not have understood you."

"I'm sorry, Mrs. Epstein. I'm sure he understood."

Sophie felt desperate. She was trying to save Max's life and this blockheaded boy was not letting her. "I've got to talk to him," she said, her voice rising. "Tell him his life depends on it."

But the young man would not budge. It was as if he no longer could hear her. In desperation, Sophie charged past the young man and up the stairs. She was quick but he was even quicker and he caught her before she could get far. With one strong arm around her waist he lifted her up and carried her back down to the street.

When he set her down she turned on him, tears in her eyes, her despair obvious. "Please," she said, "I've got to see him. It's a matter of life and death. He's in great danger. You've got to make him understand."

The young man looked at Sophie for a moment, threw up his hands as if in defeat and said, "Okay, I'll ask him again."

When the young man re-entered the house, Sophie shivered with relief. She shouldn't have. He returned in less than three minutes.

"I'm sorry, Mrs. Epstein. I told him everything but he really does not want to see you." The young man hesitated, then said, "He was a little angry with me for bothering him again. I think you had better go. I'm sorry."

Sophie felt defeated and hopeless, tears welling up in her eyes. Without saying a word, she turned and walked back to her home.

CHAPTER FOURTEEN

Arnold was in high spirits. He had ordered the most expensive champagne on the menu, and told Sophie that he was thinking maybe they ought to take a vacation soon, go stay in one of the resorts in the Catskills or the Jersey Shore. Sophie barely drank her champagne. Arnold gulped his down thirstily. They were sitting knee to knee in a little half-circle booth. The restaurant was very elegant, with soft, romantic lighting, and yet Sophie's mood did not match it at all.

"What's the matter, doll? Why so down in the mouth?"

Sophie shrugged, trying to think how to talk to him.

"Drink up," Arnold said with a grin. "Things are coming together, believe me. This is a night for us to celebrate."

She looked at him coldly, hating him for his callousness. My God, he was positively giddy, knowing he had ordered someone's murder. It was sickening. Yet she sat there, helpless, racking her brain for some way to get him to call it off. In truth, she was afraid of him, afraid of what he'd do if she told him about growing up with Max, about being his friend. She nervously drummed her fingers on the plush white tablecloth.

By the time their dinner plates were cleared away, Arnold was well lubricated. He couldn't keep his hands off her. He had become so intoxicated by the combination of champagne and his power to decide another man's fate that he couldn't contain himself. He nuzzled her neck and let his hands wander down between her legs. Sophie pulled back, turning her head to the side.

"Arnold, not now!"

"What?" He was more surprised than angry. She had never denied him, and tonight he was especially anxious to have her.

"I'm sorry," she said. "I'm not feeling well. My stomach is upset." It was true, but obviously she couldn't reveal the reason for it. Instead, she said the first thing that occurred to her. "I think I might be…with child."

Arnold stared at her for a moment. "Really? No!"

She shrugged.

"You are?" he said. "Seriously? We're gonna have a kid?" A wide grin spread across his face. "Oh, Sophie! This is wonderful!" His delight was palpable. He gazed at her for another moment, and said, "And here I've only been thinking about myself."

He immediately called for the check, putting his arm around her. "What a great night this is turning out to be!" He leaned in and gave her a long kiss on the lips.

When they got home, dropped off by their driver, he helped her off with her coat. "I'll be up soon, babe. I just have a few things to do in my office." He opened the door to his office, watching her head upstairs. "Hey, Sophie…."

Sophie stopped on the stairs and looked back at him.

"This is the best day of my life. I still can't believe we're going to have a baby. You've made me the happiest man in the world, doll." He turned and entered his office.

James Becker was sitting in a chair, waiting.

"Is everything taken care of?" Epstein asked him.

"Just about everything," the bullet-headed man said in his low drone of a voice.

CHAPTER FIFTEEN

Epstein had ordered that Frank Piluso lead the way. Piluso liked being the point man for this sort of operation. He liked the excitement and the importance, and felt he was well suited to it; his reflexes were quicker than other men's, his mind able to react faster. He walked down the alley quickly, the other three close behind him.

It was not winter but all four men wore overcoats. Under Piluso's was a sawed-off shotgun. He thought the sawed-off was the best weapon for this kind of work. It wasn't accurate past about twenty feet, but up to that distance anybody who got in the way was history. And there was the psychological impact of staring down those big barrels. Schwartz carried the same weapon, while Peltz and Leonetti had long-handled fireman's axes. The latter two would destroy the tables while he and Schwartz handled the crowd, and the killings. If they got in quick it would all be easy.

It was eleven p.m. on a cloudy night and very little light from the street reached the alley. It was all very well to come in through the back entrance, Piluso thought, but he could barely see well enough to find the damn doorknob. In the back of his mind he noted that they were walking on carpet. Probably some hebe from the textile factories around them had laid down carpet in the alley, maybe excess material. Not like a Jew to waste inventory but it really didn't matter. He was approaching the third door from the street, the one that led down to the factory cellar that held Zalensky's little casino. He waited for the others to catch up to him so they could make a quick entrance. Then he reached to open the door.

It was locked. He tried again, giving it a hard twist, but there was no doubt. He was sure it was the right door. Someone had fouled up and now they would have to use the axes. Hopefully the people downstairs wouldn't hear. In this type of operation surprise was everything.

Suddenly, with a sharp clap, electric lights were turned on from above. The lights were powerful, like spotlights in the theatre, and were aimed directly at the four men. Piluso knew instantly that it was a trap. He blinked furiously, forcing his blinded eyes to focus, barely able to see the four men on the fire escape landing across the alley and hurriedly pulling the sawed-off from under his coat.

Too late. Two dozen metal pellets travelling a thousand feet per second ripped through his body, simultaneously puncturing his heart, lungs and liver, splattering blood and bone on the wall of the building behind him. The shock caused his heart to go into immediate cardiac arrest and his lungs to collapse, cutting off oxygen carrying blood to his brain, rendering him unconscious. He was dead before his body hit the ground. As were his companions.

The hit squad on the fire escape climbed down quickly, still carrying their twelve-gauge shotguns. At the same time, a horse-drawn ice wagon backed up to the entrance of the alley. The driver and a passenger jumped out quickly, ran to the back of the wagon and opened the doors. The bodies of the four dead men had collapsed on the carpet that Frank Piluso noticed just before his death. The blood that poured out of their bodies formed large puddles. The two men from the wagon picked up the carpet from opposite ends and folded it neatly over the dead men, effectively wrapping them inside. Then, assisted by the shooters, they hoisted the carpet with the four corpses into the back of the wagon, careful not to spill any blood.

The two men who had come with the wagon climbed back into the front, and three of the killers hopped into the back, along with the dead men. The driver hitched the reins, made a clicking noise in the direction of the horses and the wagon pulled slowly away.

The fourth killer, still in the alley, pulled a large towel out from under his coat. With it, he carefully wiped off most of the blood that had splattered onto the building. Then he pulled a key out of his pocket and opened the door to the brassiere factory, the same door that Frank Piluso had found locked. Once inside he flipped a switch, turning out the electric theatre lights that had been rigged in the alley that afternoon. Workmen would dismantle them in the morning. He closed the door behind him, leaving the alley in complete blackness, and hurried downstairs to the casino. He would use the telephone there to call Max with his report.

CHAPTER SIXTEEN

Sophie stopped at the top of the stairs. She knew that she had to do something before it was too late. Arnold would be angry, perhaps very angry. She was going to have to tell him that she had listened at the door, that she was friends with Max, everything. But she was certain that if Arnold would just postpone the killing for a few days, maybe even a few hours, she could convince Max to leave town, set up somewhere else. She just needed the chance to talk to her old friend.

She rushed down the stairs to his office, fearful but determined. She would use all of her wiles, including the lie of the pregnancy. At the appropriate time, she would tell Arnold that she'd miscarried, but by then he would have called off his dogs and she would have prevented this unthinkable thing from happening.

As she reached the inner door to her husband's office, she heard a sharp pop from inside. The pop wasn't loud. If she hadn't been standing right next to the door she might not have heard it, but it still seemed foreboding. She threw open the door.

Becker turned to face her and Sophie gasped. He was holding a chromed .38 automatic with a long silencer attached to the barrel. The air smelled of sulphur. Arnold was sitting in his dark leather desk chair, his head tilted back. There was a red spiderweb imposed on his forehead, a red hole in the middle of the spiderweb, a stream of blood running down the bridge of his nose and dripping off the end.

Sophie screamed.

"Shut up," Becker barked the words with such menace that she did as she was told. He pointed the gun at her, uncertain what to do. "Mr. Zalensky told me not to hurt you, but I didn't think you'd be a witness."

Sophie wanted to talk, to assure him that she was no threat to him. But she was frozen, powerless to speak. Finally, she managed to say, "I won't tell anyone."

The bullet-headed man looked directly into her eyes as if searching for the truth in them. Sophie could tell that he didn't know whether or not to believe her. "Mr. Zalensky might have me killed if I ice you," he finally growled. "But if I hear you've squealed to the cops, I'll plug you just the same. Understand?"

Sophie nodded. He gave her one last, intent look. Then he left through the door that led directly to the street, the same way he had come. Sophie knew that Becker would have killed her if not for his fear of Max. How, she wondered, could a man like Becker be so frightened of her childhood friend? She looked back at her husband, his eyes wide and unblinking, blood still running from the hole in his forehead. She could still smell the gunpowder in the air and feel the pounding of her heart.

And once again, she screamed.

CHAPTER SEVENTEEN

Avery Wachtell shuffled through a sheaf of papers on his large walnut desk. The managing partner of Wachtell, Schecter and Greene, a mid-town firm specialising in business law, he was a florid-faced man with a prominent nose and a nonexistent chin. After clearing his throat a bit uncomfortably, he peered through a thick pair of wire-rim glasses at the young woman seated across from him. Her high-collared black mourning dress and widow's veil failed to hide her remarkable beauty, but it did manage to conceal any grief she might feel at her late husband's death.

Wachtell said, "I would again like to express my deepest sympathy for your terrible loss, Mrs. Epstein." After a pause, he continued. "As I believe my associate mentioned, your husband died intestate, that is, without a will. Under New York law that means that you, as his wife, are the sole heir to his estate."

Wachtell, who had been Arnold Epstein's personal lawyer, outlined for Sophie the substance of her husband's assets at the time of his death, which included the house where she lived, a warehouse in Soho where Arnold apparently conducted business, and a second warehouse on 42nd Street. In addition, Arnold owned eleven apartment houses scattered around the Lower East Side. To her surprise, Sophie learned that one of the apartment houses he owned was the one in which she had grown up and in which her father still lived; Arnold had apparently purchased it shortly after meeting her.

Mr. Wachtell droned on, explaining that in addition to real estate, her husband owned substantial amounts of stock in some of America's finest companies. The stock, as well as the real estate, yielded a substantial return. A few times while reading the list of apartments and warehouses and rents and dividends, Mr. Wachtell glanced up at Sophie as if to decipher whether this beautiful child had the slightest comprehension of how wealthy she was.

He shook his head, deciding that she did not. "I understand, Mrs. Epstein, that this all may be a bit difficult to absorb at the moment, but I assure you that we at Wachtell, Schecter and Greene are here for you and will happily offer you any assistance you may need, and that beyond that we look forward to continuing to manage your investments."

"Thank you, Mr. Wachtell. At the moment, I'd appreciate it if you would be kind enough to call me a cab."

Slightly befuddled, Wachtell nevertheless accommodated her request.

When the taxi came, Sophie asked the driver to take her directly to Max's address.

★　　★　　★

The same young man stood on the sidewalk in front of the house. "Good afternoon, Mrs. Epstein," he said, smiling and making a slight bow.

"Good afternoon," Sophie responded. "I came to see Mr. Zalensky." She hesitated. "On the chance that he might see me now."

"Oh yes," the young man said almost immediately. "He'll see you." Sophie's look of surprise drew a laugh. "Mr. Zalensky said to show you right in if you ever came back." He smiled and led Sophie up the stoop to the front door. It was opened immediately by a neat, slender, middle-aged man dressed as a butler. "Mrs. Epstein," the young man said, "to see Mr. Zalensky."

"Ah yes. Please come in, Mrs. Epstein." He stepped aside, allowing her to enter. The young man returned to his post on the sidewalk and the butler closed the door. Max's home was spacious and elegant. The entryway was laid with white Carrera marble which led to a polished oak stairway at the far end, an expansive sitting area to the right, and large double doors, also in oak, to the left.

"Mr. Zalensky is in the library," the butler said. "If you will wait here a moment I will announce you." Then he disappeared through the double doors.

In less than a minute the double doors opened again, and Max emerged, followed by the butler. He was wearing a grey business suit and his hair was cropped short, as was the fashion on Wall Street. Other than that he looked exactly the same as when she'd last seen him, handsome and athletic. The only noticeable difference was in the way he carried himself; he seemed both more self-assured and confident than the boy Sophie had known.

"Andrew, you may want to finish up in the kitchen now," he said, his meaning clear.

"Very good, sir," the butler responded, disappearing through a small door next to the oak staircase.

"We can talk in the library," Max said. "It's my favourite room in the house." He led her through the double doors.

Sophie understood immediately why he liked this room. Max had always loved to read and now that he was wealthy he could indulge himself. The room was lined with hundreds and hundreds of books, ranging in subject from the fall of Rome to modern financial theory, from Socrates to Dreiser. There was a large, comfortable-looking leather couch, matching leather chairs and a small reading table. It was a wonderful room and for a moment, she began to relax. Then she remembered why she had come.

"You killed my husband," Sophie said, her voice edged with anger.

For a moment, Max said nothing. Then, in a calm, almost gentle voice, he said, "I'm sorry. I really had no choice."

She stared at him as if seeing him for the first time. He was so sure of himself, it made her angry and excited at the same time. "You had a choice. You could have left town, gone somewhere else, started over."

He shrugged. "If I went somewhere else there would just be another Epstein, and then I would have to leave again." He paused. "It's exactly as you once told me. There are people who do as they are made to do, and there are people who make them. I will never again be the person who does as others make him." He moved so close that she could almost feel his touch, smell the spice of his cologne. "What about you?" he said, looking directly into her eyes. "Why did you come here?"

Sophie hesitated, unnerved by his proximity, feeling her heart quicken. "I wanted to find out how the boy I grew up with became a man who could kill people. I guess I know the answer."

She was still looking into his eyes, and suddenly his arms were around her, his lips on hers, hard and passionate. Her mind told her to push him away but her body longed to open to him, her lips drawing in his tongue, her breasts and thighs yielding to his musculature. As he pressed against her, desire coursed through her like a flame. Almost without conscious thought her hands worked frantically to unbutton his shirt and remove her own black mourning dress. And she knew, as did he, that this was why she had come.

Afterward, they lay together on the leather couch, catching their breath, their bodies still warm from passion. Her fingernails traced along his upper forearm.

"Let's go upstairs," he said.

"I don't think I can move." She laughed.

"You don't have to."

He stood up, lifting her in his arms, and carried her up the oak staircase.

They spent the rest of the afternoon in his bed. Max left once to go downstairs. When he came back Sophie asked where he had gone.

"I thought you might be hungry."

"I'm starving."

Minutes later there was a knock at the bedroom door. Max went to answer it and a moment later, he carried in a silver serving tray with plates of blintzes, fresh fruits and champagne. They ate lying on the bed, facing each other with the tray between them. He fed her strawberries and they kissed with the sweet red juice still in their mouths.

★   ★   ★

In the morning, Max left Sophie asleep in the bed. He had an early morning meeting scheduled with Becker, and although he thought about letting him wait, that simply wasn't his style. So he got dressed and met the big man down in the library as scheduled.

"Went just like we planned," Becker droned in his deep voice. "He never suspected a thing."

"Good." Max nodded for Becker to continue.

"Only twist was the broad. She came in just after I put one between his eyes. Surprised the hell out of me."

"The broad?" said Max, obviously surprised himself. "You mean Mrs. Epstein?"

"Yeah, exactly. I would have taken care of her too if you hadn't told me not to." Becker paused. "And I still ain't sure it's a good idea that I didn't. She can tie us right into it."

Max nodded again. Obviously, the big man had no idea that the woman he spoke of was directly upstairs. "I don't think she'll present any problems," he said. "She knows better than to go to the police. And if she does, we'll take care of it."

Becker grunted, nodding unhappily. Then he grinned. "Gotta say, though, she's still the best-looking dame I've ever seen. Her condition ain't showing yet."

Again, Max was surprised. "What condition?"

"She's pregnant! Epstein knocked her up. He was happy as hell about it. Told her it was the best day of his life." Becker grinned again. "Too bad it was the last day."

Max listened to the words, his face blank, a knife twisting in his bowels. He finished the meeting but could barely stay focused. When Becker left, he instructed Andrew to tell Sophie that he was busy. Then he returned to his library.

She had sucker punched him. Again. And undoubtedly, when the time came, she would tell him the child was his. That was probably her plan when she came to see him. He had built this business, done everything he had done, for her. But now she'd made it impossible. Even if she told him the truth, there was no way he could stomach raising the child of his enemy. He thought he'd won. The hard work, the planning, the careful execution, it had all come together perfectly. But she had ruined it. And Becker was right. She was a material witness. She could bring him down. Of course, he could never bring himself to hurt her. That was simply not possible. But he needed to cut it off clean, end it here.

★   ★   ★

Sophie woke up alone, a shaft of light falling across the sheets, a smile on her face. Someone, she assumed it was Max, had folded her clothes neatly and placed them on a chair. She dressed quickly and hurried downstairs to find him.

The butler, Andrew, was waiting for her. He smiled in a friendly manner and said, "Mr. Zalensky was forced to leave on business. He asked me to call you a taxicab and to inform you that he would contact you very shortly."

During the ride home and all that morning, Sophie was in a state of euphoria. She knew that it was horrible to be so happy when her husband had just been murdered. But she couldn't help it. Arnold had brought it on himself. His greed and ambition and scheming had finally caught up with him. Max had been right, he really had no choice. And now, for the first time, Sophie was free to live her own life, to be with the man she loved and to live happily ever after. She couldn't help but be delighted.

She stayed at home that afternoon and evening waiting for his call. His business must have taken longer than expected because the phone never rang. Nor did it ring the next day. The following morning Sophie called him. An unfamiliar voice patiently explained that Mr. Zalensky was in an important meeting and would call back as soon as the meeting was over. Then the voice hung up.

Sophie knew, of course, that his call would never come, but she wasn't about to give up. She called him again and when that didn't work, she went back to his house. His man outside wouldn't let her in. Boss's orders.

It was his stupid pride, she thought. He had never forgiven her for marrying Arnold, and now his little revenge would destroy both their happiness. She knew that there was no remedy for it. His male arrogance would gladly accept great pain in order to inflict a small retaliation. For a moment she was angry at the entire male gender; their greed, their stupidity, their pitiful egos. But she was most angry with herself for having been dominated by one man or another her entire life. That would change, she thought. It would have to.

★   ★   ★

Six weeks later, six weeks after what should have been the beginning of a new life with Max Zalensky, she and Mrs. Goldberg boarded the 20th Century Limited on their way to California. Her furniture had been put into storage, to be sent along after she was settled. The only things she was bringing were her clothes and some personal items. She had already given a set of house keys to Mr. Wachtell, who would arrange the sale and handle her financial affairs. Although Sophie had confidence in Wachtell's ability to prudently invest her money, she had instructed him to convert her stocks into cash or government bonds. She didn't really understand the stock market and she did not want her money invested in anything she did not understand. Wachtell had actually expressed approval when she told him this, a first in their relationship.

Persuading Mrs. Goldberg to come with her had proved even less difficult. The old woman's children were grown up and gone, and to her regret, there were no grandchildren. So when Sophie told her it would mean the world to her if she would come along, Mrs. Goldberg had agreed. She was at a point where she craved some adventure in her own life. Besides, she suspected that Sophie would get homesick eventually and return east, and when that happened she would return with her.

For Sophie it was a great relief to have the only stable and loving person she had ever known travelling with her. Still, she was uneasy about moving to the opposite end of the country. That morning as they boarded the train, her stomach was so upset that she actually lost her breakfast, something that had never happened to her before.

The two women had their own compartment on the train west, a luxurious affair with its own sitting area and bathroom. This luxury turned out to be a necessity, as Sophie was sick almost every morning. She attributed it to nerves, but Mrs. Goldberg knew better. Sophie was no different than her mother had been eighteen years earlier. Esther Feldman had had a difficult pregnancy from beginning to end, and her daughter would be the same.

CHAPTER EIGHTEEN

Once again Patricia stood in front of her full-length mirror and watched herself undress, convinced that she could see wrinkles forming on her forehead, her breasts beginning to sag. It was as if the passage of time were a visible presence, announcing the loss of any chance for marriage and children. Single men her age were either not interested in women or wanted girls ten years younger. Those girls, twenty-two or twenty-three years old, were already feeling past their prime and grateful for the attention of older men. It was clear to her that any opportunity for happiness had passed her by.

As loneliness and physical need collided, Patricia's thoughts turned more and more to the young man living in her home. She found herself staring at Jonathan during breakfast, surreptitiously watching him when he helped her mother clear the table or sat in a corner reading. Her thoughts alternated between daydreams of seduction and feelings of self-recrimination. She feared that her mother would notice her obsession with the boy. Often, she thought of making her feelings known to him but worried that he wouldn't share them – or worse be repulsed and horrified. As it turned out, seducing him was easy. The difficult part was not falling in love.

It was July and New York was suffering through its worst heat wave in six years. At half-past midnight, Patricia was still not asleep. She had already been in bed for three hours and in five more would have to get up and get ready for work. The suffocating heat made it impossible to sleep. She was wearing her lightest nightgown, a fine linen that went down to her ankles, and had the bedcovers all the way back. It didn't matter; she tossed and turned, unable to think of anything but her discomfort.

The O'Haras' home had been built in the 1890s for a prosperous Dutch family. The room Patricia occupied was a former maid's quarters, separated from the rest of the house by the kitchen. She liked this arrangement as it provided a degree of privacy, but proximity to the cooking area made hers the warmest room in the house. She rose from bed and walked to the kitchen for a glass of water.

Jonathan was there. He also had wakened from the heat and come for something to drink. He was wearing pyjama bottoms only. His chest was bare, the muscles of his abdomen contracting and expanding as he gulped down the water. He reminded her of pictures she had seen of Michelangelo's statue of the young David. Her entrance startled him and he choked slightly, coughing some of the water onto the floor. Obviously embarrassed, he wiped his mouth, mumbling that he was sorry. Patricia felt as if she were in a dream, this beautiful boy not quite real.

"Don't be silly," she whispered, moving toward him. She wiped the remaining water from his chin with two fingers. She was just inches from him, concentrating on the droplets of liquid on his chin, when impulsively she reached up and drew him to her, kissing him tenderly on the lips.

He pulled back almost immediately, and started to say something. But Patricia quickly put her finger on his lips to silence him. She put both arms around his neck and kissed him again. His resistance melted. Pressing her warmth against him, she could feel his heart beating faster and his excitement growing. She took his hand and led him back to her room.

It was obviously his first time and she enjoyed guiding him, both for the physical satisfaction and the sense of dominance. That feeling of control plus his raw, youthful energy generated a carnal frenzy that left her weak with happiness. She lost track of how many times she climaxed before, exhausted, she sent him back to his own room.

But when he was gone and she was alone in her bed, anguish and guilt enveloped her. *My God, what did I do? Mama thinks of him as my little brother. What would she do if she found out?* The possible consequences horrified her and she vowed to herself that this one-time liaison would never happen again.

The next morning at breakfast she was unusually quiet, prompting her mother to ask if she was feeling well. "I'm fine, Mama, just tired. I didn't sleep well in the heat last night."

"And you, Jonathan?" Catherine turned to the young man at the other end of the table. "You're also very quiet this morning. Did you sleep well?"

"I h-had a little trouble," Jonathan stuttered, not looking at his aunt as he spoke. "But I feel fine now." Then, looking up at Patricia he said, "I slept great after I finally closed my eyes."

"Well," Catherine responded, looking directly at Jonathan, "I'm glad you're in such fine health because I think my brother's got more work for you." Jonathan glanced up quizzically, but it was Catherine's husband, George, who responded.

"From what I hear, Jonathan already does most of the work over there. Your brother and that ape Harry don't do a day's work between them. Everybody knows the place is doing a lot better since Jon's been working there, not that William gives him any credit. What else would you have the boy do for him?"

George O'Hara had trouble hiding his disdain for his wife's baby brother. He neither trusted nor liked the man, but he knew that his wife revered her only sibling, and he simply had to live with that fact.

"Dear," Catherine said, trying not to appear irritated, "there's no reason to be so disagreeable at the breakfast table. I just think Jonathan could use some extra training, learn another skill in addition to bartending. And William could teach him to do the bookkeeping at the bar. That's a skill that's always going to be in demand."

"Okay," George grunted. "You're right." And she was, of course. Keeping books would certainly be a good skill for the lad to learn. But it burned George that Jonathan would be doing even more of the work in the bar while his wife's lazy brother sat on his fat duff and drank. "But if he's got that much extra time, he could do my books. Patty could teach him, and he'll learn it a lot better than from William."

Both Jonathan and Patricia looked up from their meal. "If there's anything I could do to help out around here, I'd love to," Jonathan said. "It's the least I could do after all you've done for me."

George smiled. "It's settled then. Patricia, you can start his lessons tonight, after he gets back from work."

"He doesn't get back until late, Papa. We won't have much time before bed."

George shrugged. "Do as much as you can and you can make up for it on Sundays."

Catherine, unsettled by this change of direction, said, "Patricia, are you sure you'll have time to do this? After all, you had to give up doing William's books because you were just too busy."

Patricia looked first at her father, then her mother. "I've got the time. We can do a little every day, and more on Sundays, as Papa said. And once he gets the hang of it, he won't need help from me." Then she excused herself from the table, explaining that she did not wish to be late for work.

"As I said, it's settled," George intoned triumphantly. Catherine did not say a word. George knew his wife was upset that he had thwarted her plan to help her brother, just as she had been upset a year earlier when Patricia announced that she could no longer do William's bookkeeping. At the time, Patty had insisted that she was simply too busy to fit it into her schedule. George suspected a different reason; that it was because his wife's little brother, only nine years older than their daughter, had made some sort of improper pass at her. George had never liked the way William looked at Patricia any more than he liked anything else about the man.

★   ★   ★

That night, after her parents had gone to bed, Patricia sat with Jonathan at the kitchen table for his first lesson in bookkeeping. "I'm truly sorry about last night," she said. "What happened was completely my fault. It was the act of an old, unmarried woman just wanting something she can't have. It will never happen again."

Jonathan stared at her, obviously surprised. "You're not old," he said. "You're beautiful. And it was wonderful for me, the best thing ever."

"Thank you." She touched his hand. "You are kind and sweet. But it can never happen again and we just have to pretend that it never did."

Jonathan hesitated, then nodded, and they went on with his first accounting lesson.

CHAPTER NINETEEN

He was the best student Patty had ever had. He picked up basic bookkeeping concepts in just a few weeks, and it was a short next step for him to apply them to her father's grocery store. He was polite and thoughtful and the more time they spent together, the more attracted to him she became. It was impossible to be with him every night in the kitchen, right next to her bedroom, and not think of having him.

And so, less than five weeks after she vowed it would never happen again, she took his hand and again led him to her bed. It was more than just physical now and as she melted into him she felt emotions untapped since she had been with Tony.

*　*　*

"Can you help me out?" Catherine asked her daughter. "Jonathan left his dinner here, and I hate for him to go so late without eating anything. Can you take it to him at work?"

"Of course." It was a Saturday, Patricia wasn't working, and she was sure that he'd appreciate the bread, salted ham, and fruit that Catherine had packed for him. Saturdays were the bar's busiest nights. Jonathan got there at two p.m. to set up and would not get home until almost three a.m. the next morning. As her mother had said, it was a long time for a young man to go without eating. And, she thought happily, she wanted him at full strength when he finally came home.

The door from the street was unlocked, as she knew it would be. In the bar business, as in her father's grocery business, deliveries were received during the day. Even if the bar was not yet open for business, it was easiest to leave the door unlocked for deliverymen. Hopefully she could slip in, give Jonathan the package and slip out, without seeing William.

Jonathan was standing behind the bar polishing glasses. There was no one else in the room. He spotted the brown paper bag in her hand and realised immediately why she had come. Grinning, he said, "Thanks. I kicked myself when I realised I'd forgotten that."

"No problem. We wouldn't want you falling down on the job from hunger."

"Not likely now. Tell Aunt Catherine thanks."

She reached across the bar and touched his cheek, then said, "I'll see you tonight."

She turned around to leave, and froze. The door to William's office, closed when she arrived, was now slightly open. William was standing just inside, staring out at her. God, why had she touched Jonathan's cheek like that? She tried to hurry out without stopping but he rushed out of the office and fell in step with her.

"Patty, it's wonderful to see you. You can stop and visit if you'd like."

"Thanks," she said a little too hurriedly, "but I'm going to meet a friend. Mama just asked me to drop off Jon's dinner on my way. He left it at home."

"You seem very friendly with him."

"Yes, we like him a lot. He's become almost like a brother to me."

"Why would you see him tonight?"

"What?"

"I heard you say that you'd see him tonight. But you'll be long asleep by the time he gets home."

"Then I guess I'll see him tomorrow."

"Unless you're planning on seeing him in bed."

"What are you talking about?" Patricia said, her voice rising and her face reddening.

"Nothing. I just wouldn't want such an innocent young man to be taken advantage of. That would be an outright sin."

Patricia stared directly at him and, keeping her voice even, said, "I'm not sure what you're implying, and I don't think I want to know." She turned and walked quickly away, hearing him laughing behind her.

I hate that man, she thought, as she hurried home. Just being near him was distasteful; he was constantly fawning and leering, always trying to touch her, which was the real reason she had refused to help with his books. He was horrid to be around. Thankfully, Papa felt the same way, which was why William never came for dinner anymore. It was better for Mama to see him alone, away from the rest of the family.

When he got home that night, Jonathan visited Patricia's bedroom, just as he did every Saturday night, and just as William had suggested in his snide manner. When they were finished, and before Jonathan went back to his room, she said, "There's something I want to talk to you about tomorrow."

"We can talk now."

"No, I'm tired and this will take some time."

Hesitantly, he said, "You're not going to tell me you don't want to see me anymore?"

"No, of course not," she said and kissed his cheek. "Now go, and I'll see you in the morning."

★   ★   ★

George and Catherine had gone to church, as they did every Sunday morning, so Jon and Patricia were alone at the breakfast table. Although Jonathan sometimes accompanied his aunt and uncle to church, they generally let him sleep in after his late Saturday nights. Much to her mother's dismay, Patricia only attended on Easter and Christmas.

"So," Jonathan said. "What did you want to talk about?"

Patricia took his hand. "I want us to be partners."

Jonathan looked at her quizzically. "Partners?"

"In business. I want to open a bar. I'll put up the money, you'll run the place. And I'll help out when I can."

Jonathan looked at her, his eyebrows raised. "Is it that easy? Aren't liquor licences expensive? And we'd need inventory and furniture and a good location."

"William started with fifteen hundred dollars. I know because Mama lent it to him. Of course, he never paid her back, but that's another matter."

"Is that why your father dislikes him so much?"

"No, but it confirms Papa's view that he's a dishonourable man. I don't like you working for him."

"Is that what this is all about?"

"I just think you're wasting your time in his employ. You practically run the place now, and he still pays you like a trainee. He'll never treat you fairly.... He's a horrible man."

Jonathan nodded. He didn't know what had happened when Patricia worked for her uncle, but he could imagine. "You've got the money? And what about your mother? William won't like me quitting and he'll go to her."

"I've got plenty of money. I've been teaching for eleven years and I spend almost nothing. And Papa will help us with Mama."

"What do you get out of it?"

"I get half the profits," she said. *And you*, she thought.

★　　★　　★

Patricia arranged everything. She found a spot in the middle of an Irish neighbourhood, close to a subway stop, perfectly located so that thirsty men returning from work would pass by on their way home. Jonathan delivered his resignation to William on Sunday and started work in his own place on Monday. He called Max Zalensky and informed him of his new business. True to his word, Zalensky provided quality product at ten percent less than William's suppliers had charged, delivered right on time. The new bar was called 'Patty's', and was situated less than three blocks from William's place; customers who liked Jonathan's service easily made the trek to his new bar. That, plus the excellent location and service, quickly made Patty's a success.

In the back office of the bar were a desk and a large couch. Patricia came in to help out on Friday and Saturday nights as well as once during the week. After they cleaned up, counted the receipts and tallied the inventory, they made love on the couch. Then they went home to the same house, to their separate rooms and separate beds. Patricia knew that the relationship was becoming more emotional for her, but she was happy and didn't want to think about future consequences.

CHAPTER TWENTY

It was that bitch's fault. Always had been. He'd been his sister's favourite, more like a son than a little brother, right up until the day Patty was born. Then his spot at the centre of Catherine's universe had been usurped. She doted on Patty and expected William to do the same.

Fat chance; more likely to smother the little brat under a pillow. Many were the times young William had thought about it, but he'd never had the guts. He'd had the desire though, plenty of times. And then she grew up. Suddenly, at fifteen years old she'd turned into a woman. William remembered well; he had achieved little success with women. He was handsome enough and they were initially attracted, but he had a bitterness about him that invariably turned off the bubbly young Irish girls. He was inexplicably angry about the cards life had dealt him, although to anyone else his hand looked reasonably good.

He still remembered her graduation from St. Augustine's. Catherine and George threw a party in their backyard to celebrate the first O'Hara to graduate high school. Two of the nuns from St. Augustine's were there, sacrosanct bitches, so proud of little Patty. Proud because their little virgin was going to college to become a teacher, too good even then to just settle down and have babies like any other girl her age.

And he remembered exactly what she was wearing: a blue silk dress, sleeveless and low cut, the material so light that only in New York's sweltering summer could it be comfortable. Catherine had proudly declared that since her daughter was grown up now, she should wear a dress that showed her off as the young woman she was. It showed her off all right. Enough to make every man there grow a stick in his pants, including her Uncle William, who was only twenty-six years old at the time. William even suspected one of the nuns, Sister Ellen, the way she fawned over Patty and touched her. No wonder the Sisters were happy that she was going to college, putting off getting married.

So what happened wasn't his fault. Sure, he'd drunk too much whiskey, but it was an Irish celebration and that was normal. Patricia had excused herself from the crowd and gone into the house to use the washroom. William wandered into the house after her and waited in the hallway. When she came out he said, "Congratulations," and hugged her. She said, "Thank you," and hugged him back. She started to pull away but he held her and kissed her neck and she let him, he was sure of it.

So he put his hand down the back of her smooth dress to her round ass, which he squeezed. She pulled his hand away, but gently, like she was dealing with a harmless drunk. It wasn't until he clutched her tit that she got upset, pushing him hard, almost shoving him over. She was a strong little bitch. She screamed an obscenity at him as she rushed past, but luckily everyone else was outside making noise of their own, and no one heard. She hadn't told anyone, he was almost certain, because neither George nor Catherine acted any differently toward him afterward.

But the little bitch hated him, he was sure of it. She made that clear enough a few years ago when she was helping him out with his bookkeeping; help she only provided at her mother's insistence. William remembered how if he so much as touched her shoulder she practically jumped a foot. Finally, she'd told her mother that she couldn't come to his bar, didn't have the time anymore. William knew that was a lie, knew the truth was she couldn't stand to be around him.

And now she'd taken Jonathan away from him. Out of hatred. She was giving the kid sex, he was pretty sure of it, so that she could control him. So she could hurt William. Give the kid some sweet sack time and then lead him around by his prick. Jonathan had resigned three months earlier and William was hurting plenty. He was working hard and Harry was working hard and he had hired a new bartender, but it wasn't the same. Jonathan was a genius at having everything organised just right and doing everything in the right order, so it took less work to get things done. And the customers loved him. He remembered their kids' names and where they worked and their favourite drink. So a lot of them followed him to Patty's place. And William's profits had fallen like a meteor.

Oh sure, he'd protested. Gone to see his sister right after Jonathan resigned. He went during the day, when he thought she would be alone. Unfortunately, that asshole George came home for lunch shortly after and put his two cents in. "Why would you want him back?" George had said. "The only times we've talked, you claimed you were performing charity work by employing him. I'd think you'd be glad to be rid of him."

"Well, it was charity work in a way. He needed a job and I gave him one. Now that he's finally learned what to do, he leaves. That's hardly fair."

"Of course," said George, "you never gave him a raise, even after he was virtually running your place for you. You still paid him like a trainee. And treated him like dirt, from what I understand."

"I'll tell you what. If you get him to come back, I'll give him a raise. A big one."

George shook his head. "I think he'd rather stay with Patty. She may have put up the money, but they're equal partners. She's giving him too good a deal for him to return to your place."

William would have liked to knock George off his high horse right then and there. He would like to have said, "The good deal she's giving him is between her legs. She's humping that kid so he'll do what she wants." But he didn't know for sure if it was true, and his sister might never forgive such a serious accusation if it proved to be false. So he walked away from the O'Haras' house more angry and frustrated than when he came, and no closer to forcing Jonathan back to work for him.

CHAPTER TWENTY-ONE

It was Aunt Catherine who introduced them. "Jonathan needs to meet a girl, and I've found just the one," she said to Patricia as they were finishing up the dishes.

"J-Jonathan?" Patricia stammered. "Isn't he a little young?" Realising the hypocrisy of her words even as she spoke them.

"Don't be silly. He's eighteen years old. Your brother Danny was married by that age, and the other boys were both engaged. You know Selma Sullivan; she and her husband Robert have gone to our church for years. Their daughter Samantha is graduating next week from St. Augustine's. I think she'd be perfect for him."

And she was. Aunt Catherine insisted that Jonathan attend services with George and her the next Sunday. They sat with the Sullivans, who had brought their eldest daughter. The two young people were seated next to one another. A week later, a picnic for the two families was arranged after church. The picnic was in a nearby park and again things were arranged so that Jonathan and Samantha sat together.

After everyone had eaten, the four older folks walked off to visit with friends who happened to be picnicking nearby, leaving Samantha and Jonathan alone. They fully understood that they were being thrown together by their respective families. Jonathan was tickled, even flattered that his aunt would try to play matchmaker for him. But the slender blonde she had chosen for him was not amused. "They think that since I'm done with my education, they need to find me a man. God forbid I would go to college or work or be on my own. It's more important that they make me a match with some Irish boy as quickly as possible." She actually sounded angry.

"I'm sorry," Jonathan said defensively. "I'm only here because my aunt, who I owe the world to, asked me. I certainly don't want to cause you to be here if you don't want to be."

"Oh," she said, taken aback by his apology. "I didn't mean to be rude. You seem very nice, and I know my parents mean well. It just irritates me that they think they have to find a husband for me, as if I couldn't do so on my own."

Jonathan nodded quite seriously. "No, you would certainly have no problem."

Samantha laughed, a wonderful, unaffected laugh. "I wasn't fishing for a compliment, but thank you. That's the nicest thing anyone's said to me lately."

Jonathan smiled. "I would think people say nice things to you all the time."

"Well, I'm sure they do, but Mother and Father are very concerned that I don't have a serious beau. It's a frequent topic of conversation, and during the past few weeks they've talked a lot about you."

"Me? How would they know anything about me?"

"Your aunt has told them all about you. Father is impressed that you already own your own business; he thinks that shows great initiative. And ever since we met you last week, Mother can't stop talking about how handsome you are."

Samantha's mouth held a hint of a smile and Jonathan could not tell if she was being serious, but he was still a little flustered. "I don't own the bar by myself. I have a partner, my second cousin Patricia, Aunt Catherine's daughter. She was the one who figured out that we could do it, picked the location, and came up with the money."

"But you're a full partner?"

Jonathan nodded. "Patty put up the money, but I do almost all the work. I'm the bartender, janitor, stock boy and bookkeeper. She helps out as much as she has time for, but she works full time as a teacher."

"You don't mind having a woman as a partner?"

"What? No, of course not. As I said, it was her idea. She brought me into it." Their conversation was interrupted as the older couples returned. "I hope you two have been able to manage without us," Aunt Catherine said, smiling. Then the talk turned to church business and local politics, and soon it was time to go.

As they were cleaning up Samantha caught him out of earshot of the others. "Do I get to see you again?" she said.

"Yes," he said, obviously surprised. "I'd like that."

"When?"

"Tonight's the only night I don't work. The bar's not open on Sunday. I could pick you up later for dinner."

She nodded and pressed his hand. "That would be nice."

The Sullivans lived on Madison Street near Seward Park, twelve blocks from the O'Haras. Jonathan caught the Essex Street trolley, which dropped him a block from Samantha's house. The two of them walked uptown to a restaurant Jonathan knew across from Tomkins Square Park, chatting comfortably the whole way.

They continued talking over dinner. Jonathan felt comfortable with Samantha, able to reveal parts of himself he had never talked about with anyone. After he paid the check, they walked through the park at a leisurely pace, in no hurry to get anywhere. He found himself telling her of his father's death and how much he missed his mother and sisters, and at a certain point, she took hold of his hand. It seemed perfectly natural. He told her that he wanted to make a lot of money in America so that he could bring his mother and sisters over as soon as possible. Samantha appeared to understand completely, his concerns as important to her as they were to him. They stopped by a bent cherry tree where he put his arms gently around her and kissed her.

By the time he dropped her back home, lingering by the door, not wanting the evening to end, it was past midnight and the trolleys were no longer running. He walked the twelve blocks back to the O'Haras' and prepared for bed. He felt thirsty after the long walk, and after putting on pyjamas went to the kitchen for a glass of water. Moonlight filtered in through the kitchen window and he was able to make his way without turning on the incandescent light. He stood at the sink, looking out the window and drinking his water, when the light was suddenly turned on. Startled, he turned around to find Patricia staring at him from the doorway.

"You're back late," she said in an almost accusatory tone. "Have a nice time?"

Surprised to see her, he stammered, "Y-yes, I did."

"Mother tells me how very pretty Samantha Sullivan is. Is that true? Is she very pretty?"

Jonathan nodded. "She's not beautiful like you are, but she's pretty enough."

"Pretty enough for you. How nice."

"It's not like I could refuse to go out with her. What would I say to your mother? And you've told me many times that I should find someone my own age."

"And now you have. I should be happy for you."

"Patty, we both knew this wasn't going to last forever."

She walked close to him so that when she spoke their faces were practically touching. "Come to my room."

"I don't think we should do that."

"Please," she said.

"Patty, we don't do that in the house anymore, and it's probably not...."

But she knew precisely what he liked most, and skillfully, using both hands, she did it. In a few minutes his resistance evaporated and she led him on the familiar path to her bed.

★   ★   ★

The next Sunday Jonathan and Samantha took the new IRT extension out to Coney Island. They rode the new Ferris wheel and the roller coaster. They ate hot dogs and held hands as they walked the shore with their shoes off, the cold Atlantic Ocean lapping at their toes. It was the best day Jonathan had ever had. They went out the Sunday after that as well, this time just walking around Central Park, riding the merry-go-round, and picnicking by the ball fields. "I'd like to see you tomorrow, if I could," Jonathan said as they walked up the steps to her home. "And the day after that, as well."

Samantha smiled and said, "That will be difficult, since you work so late. And it's not as if we live together."

"Not yet," he responded quite seriously. "But maybe someday I'll get lucky."

"Maybe someday you will." Then she reached up and kissed him long and tenderly, stroking his face with her hands, ending with a reluctant sigh. She then turned and walked through the front door of her family's house, leaving him outside on the porch.

Jonathan's affair with Patty ended. He simply stopped coming to her room at home. And then at the office one night, when she tried to pull him onto the office couch, he refused to go along. She was angry and he felt badly for her, but she never again discussed it or made any attempt to seduce him.

He continued to see Samantha as often as his work schedule allowed. The fact of their limited time together seemed to intensify the urgency of their desire. One Sunday night, ten weeks after they met, standing in front of the familiar door to her house, he said, "I would love, more than anything else, to be able to see you when I wake up in the morning."

She touched his cheek, and very quietly responded, "There is a way to make that happen."

Jonathan smiled at her, nodded, and said, "Yes."

CHAPTER TWENTY-TWO

"You should have told me," Patricia said to him, her voice sharp with anger. "Instead I had to hear it from my mother." She had come by the bar after closing, something she rarely did now, since he could handle everything himself and there was no longer an ulterior motive for her visits.

"I'm sorry. I wanted to tell you," he said. "But I thought it would upset you."

"Upset me? Why? Just because you left me for little Miss Young and Pretty and now you're going to marry her? Why would I be upset?"

"Please don't be angry. Samantha is someone I can spend my entire life with, someone who can give me a family. I can't tell you how happy she makes me. I was hoping you'd be happy for me."

"Oh yes, happy. Since I'm too old and dried up for you. I'm ever so happy."

"You knew it was impossible for us to go on. You've said so many times."

"Yes, but in the meantime you managed to get this bar from me. Do you suppose she'd be marrying you without it? Do you think her parents would be so anxious to have you as a son-in-law if you were still carrying boxes for William?"

Now it was Jonathan who sounded angry. "I appreciate everything you've done for me but I didn't take this bar from you. We're owners, together. You get half the profits, and I do almost all the work. And yes, I think Samantha would love me and marry me even if I still worked for William. It wouldn't matter what her parents thought."

"Isn't that sweet? You actually think Miss Precious would still have you, even if you were poor with no prospects."

"I don't think it's any of your business," Jonathan shot back. "And since you think the bar is really yours, you can close up." With that, he turned and walked through the office door and out into the bar. Patricia heard him hurry up the stairs and out the front door, which he slammed shut.

God, she thought, bringing her hands to her face. *What is wrong with me? I've become some sort of witch.* It was as if she had no control of her own actions, as if she were watching someone else do and say those awful things.

Of course it was best that he marry someone his own age; best for both of them. She couldn't continue the wicked liaison with her young cousin. It was wrong, it had been wrong from the start, and she was certain she was bound for Hell for being so weak. If only he'd return now, she'd set things right, tell him she didn't mean any of it.

But he was gone, and there was nothing she could do. Jonathan had already cleaned the bar, counted the inventory, and put the cash in the safe. Patty had only to tally the day's receipts and record them in the ledger, which took about twenty minutes, sitting in the office with the door closed. As she finished, she heard someone moving outside.

I knew he'd come back, she thought, and rushed out of the office and into the bar to meet him. "Jona—" she began, and then froze. For it wasn't Jonathan at all, but her uncle William. He was standing in the middle of the bar, holding a large metal can, obviously as surprised to see her as she was to see him. His man Harry was standing next to him, brandishing a crowbar. The door behind them was leaning shut but not tightly closed, and Patricia realised with shock that they had used the crowbar to force the door open. Almost at the same time, she recognised the smell of kerosene coming from the can that Uncle William was holding.

"Sweet Jesus," she said, anger and fear mixed in her voice. "You've come to burn us down." She stared at them, horrified.

William stared back, stunned by her unexpected presence after seeing Jonathan leave. "You ruined my business," he finally muttered, venom in his voice. "But I'm surprised you're here. I expected you to be home in bed with your boyfriend."

"What's that supposed to mean?" her voice rising almost to a shout.

"You know what it means. You may have fooled my sister, but I always knew you were a tramp. Ain't you ashamed? Seducing that boy. You're almost old enough to be his mother."

"That's none of your business," Patty spat angrily.

"So it's true then," he said with an ugly smile, knowing he'd caught her. "I wasn't sure."

Patricia was infuriated and without thinking rushed at her uncle, her hands stretched out to wring his neck. She reached him before he realised what was happening, her hands on his throat, by pure chance her right thumb lodged just below his Adam's apple at the base of the trachea.

As Patty squeezed furiously, her left hand overlapping her right, William's oxygen was completely cut off. He had been slow to react and now, unable to breathe, he panicked. His arms flailed around for several seconds, scratching at her face before he finally got his hands on her wrists and tore them away from his neck. At that point Harry, who had been hesitant to touch Patricia, grabbed her from behind and held her, simply to keep her from doing any more damage to his boss, who was standing straight, his head bent back, desperately trying to gulp in as much precious air as he could.

It took William a moment to recover, but when he did his face contorted with rage. "You fucking bitch!" he screamed at her, his voice scratchy and painful. "You destroyed my business and now you try to kill me."

He staggered over to where Harry was still holding her and punched her in the lower abdomen. Harry let go and she doubled over, pain and nausea coursing through her. William stepped to her side and shoved her with both hands so she fell hard onto the floor. "You fucking bitch," he yelled again, and as she lay clutching her stomach he kicked her, just above her left ear. Patricia's head snapped sideways, her eyes partially closed and her face darkening. She lay still, not unconscious, but stunned. Then he kicked her again, this time in her side, under the ribcage, and Patty cried out in agony, tears filling her eyes. In a small voice she said, "Please don't hurt me anymore."

Standing above her, feeling his power and hearing her sob with pain, William grew excited, could feel himself becoming aroused. He gave her another sharp kick and when she cried out he grew more rigid. He pulled a folding knife out of his pocket, unhinged the blade and saw Patricia's eyes go wide with terror. He became fully erect.

He knelt down on top of her, knee on her chest, his weight making it difficult for her to breathe. She felt his hand reach below her long skirt to her undergarments, pull the underclothes away from her body and slice through them with the blade. She saw that he was smiling and heard him say, "I am going to hurt you more, bitch."

CHAPTER TWENTY-THREE

When Jonathan arrived the fire was out but the building had burned almost to the ground. Patricia was sitting on the sidewalk, her knees drawn up under her chin. She had a fireman's blanket wrapped tightly around her and she was rocking gently back and forth. He knelt down beside her and asked, "Are you all right?"

She didn't answer, but continued her rocking motion. He repeated the question, but still got no answer. "Were you here? When the fire happened?" he asked, hoping that a different question might elicit a response.

Finally, "Yes."

He noticed now a bruise on her face and when she turned toward him she grimaced and her hand went to her side. "Are you hurt?" Again, he had to repeat the question, but eventually she spoke.

"I hurt inside. I was bleeding but that stopped. Now it just hurts."

Jonathan, beginning to understand, said, "Aside from the fire, did someone harm you?"

Slowly, Patricia nodded. "He beat me. Then he raped me." She lowered her head between her shoulders and sobbed uncontrollably. He put his arms around her but it seemed of little help. After several minutes, Jonathan hailed a cab and took her home.

He walked her to her bed, then asked, "Do you know who did this?"

"Did what?" she responded blankly.

"Patty," he said, slowly and deliberately. "Did you recognise the man who burned our bar and...hurt you?"

"Of course. My uncle."

"What?"

"My uncle William."

Jonathan looked fixedly at her, the shock of what she had said visible in his eyes. "I'll call the police right now."

"No. Please don't."

"What? Why not?"

"He knows about us."

"Huh? So what?"

"He'll tell my mother and she'll think I'm horrible. And she'll be right." She sobbed. "I'll lose her, just like I've lost you."

"That's silly. Aunt Catherine won't blame you."

"Of course she will. It was my fault."

Jonathan stared at her, not comprehending. "What are you talking about?"

"I sinned. With you. This was my punishment."

Jonathan continued to stare. "That's absurd."

"No. It's true. I'm the one who sinned and now I've been punished."

Jonathan sighed. "You need to rest now. Get some sleep and we'll talk about it in the morning."

But in the morning it was the same. If William told her mother about them, Catherine would be dishonoured and ashamed and would disown her. She would rather die than for that to happen. She had committed sins of the flesh, she said, and had been appropriately punished. For a woman of her upbringing it was not an illogical conclusion, and there was nothing Jonathan could do to change her mind.

The afternoon of that same day, Jonathan went to see Max Zalensky. Zalensky was already aware of the fire that had destroyed Jonathan's tavern and immediately offered help. "If you need credit extended for your next liquor delivery, you have it."

"Thank you, Mr. Zalensky, but the bar was completely destroyed. We won't be reopening. Anyway, that's not why I'm here." Jonathan hesitated, as if he had difficulty finding the words. "I want to hire you."

"Oh? To do what?"

"Mr. Zalensky, you may feel this is something I should handle myself, but for family reasons I cannot." Max waited patiently while Jonathan gathered himself. "I would like you to badly hurt, or kill, Mr. William Hardy. He is the brother of my aunt, who sheltered and fed me, and as you know, I worked for him." Jonathan paused, as though suddenly realising the gravity of what he was proposing, but nevertheless continued, "I will pay anything to have this done."

"What in the world would lead you to believe that I would have the inclination, let alone the resources, to do such a thing?" Zalensky said. "And why would you make such a request?"

"It was Hardy who burned down my tavern last night. He did it because he didn't want the competition, although God knows there are plenty of other pubs. Or maybe he did it because he hates me. It doesn't matter. It's only a business. The horrible part is that my partner was there when it happened, my second cousin, Patricia O'Hara. She caught them in the act. William is her uncle, and I think he's always been jealous of her. Anyway, he beat her. And raped her."

Zalensky's eyes narrowed. "Are you sure of this?"

"Of course. I wouldn't come to you otherwise."

"Was he alone?"

"No. The brute who attacked you that day in William's bar was with him. His name is Harry Carroll, but he didn't touch her. William did that part by himself. You haven't met her, Mr. Zalensky, but she's a wonderful woman."

"I'm sure she is," Zalensky said, "but this is a serious matter. You cannot just dictate someone be beaten to death like ordering groceries from the corner store. I cannot let myself be associated with such a thing."

Jonathan did not let himself appear disappointed. He simply said, "I understand and I appreciate you hearing me out. Perhaps it is better that I take care of this myself, after all."

Max nodded. "Just do me one favour, Jonathan. Wait a few days before you take any action. Sometimes these things have a way of working themselves out."

Jonathan looked at him and shrugged. "Okay. I guess that couldn't hurt."

"Good. I'm very sorry about your cousin. Hopefully she'll pull through this. In the meantime, take care of yourself."

When they shook hands goodbye, Max said, "I'm sure we'll be seeing one another again, under better circumstances."

"I hope so."

★　　★　　★

One night later, William Hardy was awakened at four a.m. by a telephone call from Captain Johnson of the New York City fire department. A building in which Mr. Hardy was registered as sole tenant had sustained extensive fire damage during the night and they needed him to review the interior damage right away.

William jumped out of bed and threw on his clothes as quickly as he could, cursing as he did so. It was probably the kid, Jonathan, thinking he was getting some sort of revenge. He'd show him revenge, William thought grimly. He and Harry would kill the little fuck. Tomorrow wasn't soon enough. Maybe they'd do it today, he thought, as he opened the door and rushed out.

As William barreled through his front door he was struck squarely across the forehead by an eighteen-inch length of lead pipe. His body crumpled and fell like a marionette whose strings had been cut. Before he hit the floor two husky men caught his limp form and dragged him back into the apartment, shutting the door behind them. In the privacy of his living room they continued to beat him with the pipe, as well as brass knuckles, and kick him with heavy boots. When the men left, William was still alive but it was uncertain as to how long he would remain so.

Harry Carroll found William, unconscious, but still breathing, eleven hours later. Harry had gone to William's home when his boss failed to come to work and walked into the apartment after knocking on the front door and finding it unlocked. Harry first called an ambulance and then William's older sister, Catherine.

Dr. Casey of St. Francis of Assisi General Hospital patiently explained to Catherine that the broken bones her brother had suffered would probably heal with little permanent injury. However, the brain damage that he had sustained made it doubtful that he would ever be able to care for himself again. With proper training he might be able to handle his daily bodily functions as well as feed himself, but it was unlikely he would ever hold a job, cook a meal, or navigate city streets. It would be best if William were institutionalised, Dr. Casey explained. There were several Catholic Church-run institutions that provided adequate care for the incapacitated, some that were not overly expensive.

Catherine understood. Her brother had a business that still

continued to make a small profit. It could be sold and the proceeds used to pay for his support. In addition, Catherine had money of her own and could hire extra help to supplement the institutional care. She would make certain that William lived out his life in as much peace and comfort as possible.

CHAPTER TWENTY-FOUR

One week later, Max Zalensky summoned Jonathan to his home. Jon had not been surprised by the attack on William, having understood that Zalensky had not wished to acknowledge his involvement in such an enterprise, even within the walls of his own home. But Jonathan had told him he would pay anything to have the job done and he guessed that he was about to learn the price.

Max greeted him with a handshake and a smile. "How is your cousin, Miss O'Hara, doing? I hope she's recovering."

"She's doing much better, thank you." And she was, to some degree. In the time since the attack her visible wounds had all but healed, and from her terse response to his questions he gleaned that the internal bruising from the rape was also mending. Psychologically, however, Jonathan was not sure she would ever recover. She seemed to blame herself for what had happened to her uncle, as well as for what William had done to her.

"Would you like something to drink?" Max asked, his polite question interrupting Jonathan's thoughts.

"No, thank you." Jonathan waited for the other man to come to the point.

And Max did exactly that. "Are you planning to open another bar?"

Jonathan shook his head. "I don't have the capital. As you know, our entire inventory was wiped out in the fire. We were making good profits, but most of that went to reimburse Patricia for her original investment. We weren't in business long enough to generate much more than that."

Max nodded. "I thought that might be the case, so I have a proposition for you. I'd like to be your partner."

Jonathan's eyes widened as he stared in surprise. "In a bar?"

"Actually, I was thinking of many bars, maybe ten or twenty. Your joint was the most efficiently run I've seen and I'm familiar with all the businesses I sell liquor to. I'm sure that with the experience you now have you'll do even better in your next venture. But as I said, I'm talking a string of bars."

Jonathan stared directly at Max. "It wouldn't bother you to partner with an Irish?"

Max smiled amusedly. "You and I are above that bullshit. We're businessmen."

Jonathan nodded. "I still don't see how it would work. Taverns are usually family-run enterprises because the bartender can steal you blind. So you want someone you trust, which is usually yourself or someone in your family."

"I have faith in you," Max said. "You'll figure out how to keep track of what's going in and out, so if anyone's jacking us, you'll know. It couldn't be that difficult. Just set up some kind of inventory system like they do in warehouses. So you or someone who works for you can count everything up at the end of the day and calculate if anything's missing."

Jonathan nodded, his mind already starting to see possible solutions. "Yes, it might work."

"Of course it'll work. Like I said, I've got faith. So here's the split. I put up the money. You run the show. When revenue starts coming in, you take out whatever you need to live and the rest goes to pay me back. After I'm reimbursed, we split the profits down the middle. Of course, all the liquor is supplied by me at my regular prices. I make my usual profit on that."

They closed the deal with a handshake; nothing in writing. Nor was any mention ever made of what had happened to William Hardy. As Jonathan rose to leave, Max raised his glass in a sort of salute and said, "I'm sure this'll be a big success."

★   ★   ★

And it was. Jonathan envisioned, and then built, a very smooth and efficient organisation. Each tavern used an identical accounting system where receipts were counted and reported daily and matched against inventory, which was also counted daily. If cost of sales was higher than expected, the bartender was warned. If it happened twice, he was fired.

Jonathan personally chose the location of each bar. He interviewed and hired each bartender. The first tavern opened fifty-five days after his initial meeting with Max and there were already plans for two more. Of course, each bar would have its own name. New Yorkers expected any bar they frequented to be unique, not to have siblings in competing neighbourhoods. And Max was adamant that neither the authorities, nor their competition, would know how big they were, and he was confident they would be big.

Additionally, each bar was laid out according to what Max called "prohibition planning": a steel door with a peephole, a back exit, and concealed compartments in the floor where liquor could quickly be hidden.

"Seems like a waste of money," Jonathan had said when Max proposed it. "Most people don't think the amendment's going to change much of anything," referring to the Eighteenth Amendment to the United States Constitution, which had been passed earlier in the year. It would prohibit the sale of alcohol, nationwide, starting the following January.

"Most people don't know what they're talking about," Max had responded.

"I do. I've got three cousins who are policemen; Patty's brothers. They all drink and their friends on the force all drink and they're not planning to go out of their way to enforce something they don't want. At worst, we'll have to pay them to look the other way but it won't cost enough to put a dent in our profits."

Jonathan glimpsed a hard look cross Max's face, then disappear, and realised that he might be tempting the man's patience.

"I understand," Max said, "that many of New York's finest, like your cousins, may be easily bought and paid for. I conduct many such transactions in my other business. But in this case it is not the local gendarmes we need worry about. It's the federal government."

"Seriously?"

"Trust me." Max said, and Jonathan could feel the steel in his voice. "My information is that Washington is planning to form a Bureau of Prohibition. It'll be part of the Treasury Department, directly under

Internal Revenue. And more difficult to deal with than your cousins."

Jonathan ignored the slight and said, "But you still think we can make a go of this?"

"It's the reason I wanted in. Liquor is a pleasure that men have been enjoying since biblical times and only a fool would think they'd give it up. This new Bureau will eliminate much of our competition and make our business a lot more profitable."

"And you're confident you can handle them?"

Again, the hard look, and then Max said, "Already in process."

CHAPTER TWENTY-FIVE
1920

Max Zalensky had moved quickly to fill the vacuum created by Arnold Epstein's demise. His men simply walked into Epstein's two gambling establishments and took over. It was easy to do with Arnold out of the picture and his primary muscle dead, or in Becker's case having defected. The takeover was performed so smoothly that patrons of the establishments did not realise that a change in management had occurred. Of course, they noticed a distinct improvement in service; doormen remembered the names of repeat customers, pretty girls appeared at the tables with free drinks, and a friendly manager always paid the cab fare home for any patron who had won or lost a large sum of money that evening.

As soon as Max had a firm grip on his two new locations he began to plan his expansion. The Lower East Side was a poor area and as a result had only limited money-making potential; no matter how attractive he made his establishments the locals simply did not have deep enough pockets. In order to grow his business in any meaningful manner, Max would need to tap into the more lucrative midtown market. Unfortunately, there was plenty of competition, most of it already well established. Max was well aware that the players with an existing toehold would go to violent extremes to prevent any intrusion into their territory.

There was also the issue of law enforcement. As with all illegal enterprises, a casino required some amount of police cooperation. For gambling establishments already in place, this involved payoffs to the local beat cops as well as a kickback to the precinct commander. These bribes might total a few thousand dollars a year, an easily acceptable cost of doing business. But Max needed to make a much bigger investment to assure a seat at this particular table.

★   ★   ★

It had taken Michael Duffy almost thirty years to work his way to the top. He'd been a beat cop on Mulberry for twelve years, then desk sergeant, then precinct commander. Finally, eight years ago he'd made the leap to division. After surviving the politics and backstabbing, making the right friends and avoiding any powerful enemies, Duffy had been promoted to his present position of Deputy Chief of Police for the Borough of Manhattan. At fifty-one years old he was virtually on top. Sure, the big chief was still above him, but that was just a political job; glad-handing the council, public appearances with the Commissioner, assuring the public that corruption was a thing of the past. Duffy was the real top cop.

The deputy chief prided himself on being a policeman's policeman. He understood what it took to survive day-to-day police work, the give and take with thugs and hoodlums, the fact that you ultimately had to show them who was boss. Duffy could palaver with the high-society dames about how the city needed to bring understanding and education to the poor immigrants in the slums. But he also knew that a solid nightstick to the side of the head would go a lot further to make the little slimeballs into law-abiding citizens than any kind words from a bleeding-heart social worker.

Michael Duffy understood what it was like to be a cop on the beat, something that the Big Chief and the politicians had either never known or long forgotten. Duffy had been there and he remembered. He knew that for nineteen hundred dollars a year, less money than a fully apprenticed bricklayer earned, young Irish policemen risked injury and death to keep some sort of peace among the stinking hordes who poured through New York Harbour every year: Italians, Polacks, Russians, Jews and, yes, more Irishmen.

At least once or twice every year for the past decade, Duffy had attended the funeral of a young officer killed in the line of duty. It was tough seeing the teary-eyed young wives and kids, knowing that however much the widows and orphans fund helped out, it was never enough to provide proper care to the family, who had to depend upon the kindness of other relatives. Hell, Duffy knew full well that a beat cop could barely support his wife and children even when he was alive and earning his full salary.

So he understood that most regular policemen had some hand in the take. That's what they called it: the Take. The misleadingly simple word referred to the insignificant tax that authorities charged to allow ordinary men to engage in ordinary vices that were otherwise prohibited by society. Specifically, this meant drinking, gambling and prostitution. These were different than crimes such as theft, assault, rape and murder, which no policeman should ever condone. Deputy Chief Duffy knew that a street cop could pull in an extra thirty or forty dollars a month by simply failing to notice the men pouring into local pubs after work or visiting a gambling hall on Saturday night. This type of graft had helped Duffy support his own young family back when he walked a beat.

Nevertheless, he was more than a little taken aback by the offer. It was delivered to him by a man named James Becker in a meeting arranged by a councilman from the 4th district.

Duffy was not unacquainted with Becker, a kike hoodlum who had managed to stay out of police lineups the past couple of years. Word on the street was that he now worked for Max Zalensky, who was something of a mystery man. Street thugs spoke Zalensky's name with fear and respect, but he had never been arrested or even charged with a crime. Asking around, Duffy was unable to find anyone who could even describe what the man looked like.

No matter, though. What mattered was the offer. It was astounding. Ten thousand dollars. The deputy chief rolled the number over in his mind. It was more than four years' salary. In addition, Becker had assured him that an even larger amount would be available to spread among the troops, as necessary. That kind of money would buy a lot of cooperation. Duffy shook his head at the magnitude of the dollars involved. This Zalensky, if that's who was really behind it, was obviously a serious man.

CHAPTER TWENTY-SIX

There were four established gambling houses in midtown Manhattan. This was one more than in the more populous lower portion of the island, but midtown's affluent population easily supported the extra casino. Business was divided between two bosses, Enzo Capelli and Aaron Rothstein, each of whom owned two establishments. An uneasy truce existed between the two men, each apparently content with his half of the business and willing to maintain the status quo. That was about to change.

The busiest night in the business of illegal gambling was Friday, the last workday of the week for the bankers, lawyers, accountants and businessmen who comprised the most lucrative portion of the casino's clientele. Many of these men reserved Saturday night for wives or girlfriends, and Sunday for church and children. So Friday became the night to relieve some of the stress of a long work week with booze and dice. It was on such a night that Max made his move.

There had been no trouble for several years, but it was not in Aaron Rothstein's nature to be complacent. In addition to a burly doorman, his gambling den was patrolled by four guards, each large and experienced, each armed with brass knuckles and a nine-millimetre Browning semi-automatic pistol. Any trouble with drunks or irate customers was dealt with quickly and efficiently. Security was not a problem.

The five men arrived separately, arousing no suspicion. All five were perfectly groomed and dressed in dark business suits. All played quietly at one of three blackjack tables. A few minutes before nine o'clock, with the casino filled to capacity, each of the men arose from their respective seats to stretch their legs in the crowded room. At exactly nine, the short barrel of a .38 calibre revolver was thrust into the back of each security guard, along with the doorman. During the moment in which each guard hesitated, uncertain what to do, a blackjack was brought down on the back of his head, stunning him, making it easy to push him to the floor and remove his weapon.

The heavy door to the casino was unlocked by the intruder nearest the entrance, and four more men scrambled in. It all happened so quickly that Rothstein himself didn't realise anything was wrong until he saw the four men, two carrying shotguns and two with long-handled axes. He checked immediately for his guards and was met with the sinking realisation that they had been taken out of commission.

One of the intruders let off a shotgun blast straight into the ceiling. An eerie hush came over a room that just a moment before had been buzzing with activity.

"Everyone cooperates," the shooter said loudly, waving his shotgun as if for emphasis, "and everyone gets out alive."

By this time, the original five invaders had moved to the outside of the room along the wall and were pointing their pistols toward the crowd. Some of the patrons appeared nervous, even ready to panic. A few were sweating profusely.

"Relax, everybody," the man who had just spoken shouted. "Just stay calm and everything will be fine. Nobody needs to get hurt."

"You're going to be hurt when I catch up with you!" Aaron Rothstein screamed at the man, his face contorted in anger. He moved closer to the man bearing the shotgun, pointed a long finger at him and said, "You'll be easy to remember, you fucking wop, and when I find you, you'll wish you had never heard of me."

The man with the shotgun grinned. He knew exactly what Rothstein meant. He was small and slender, with a long nose, olive skin and straight, jet-black hair. He had smooth, even features and he almost glided when he walked. His name was Dominick Pastorini. He was obviously Italian and had, as Rothstein said, an easy face to remember.

Pastorini spoke again, loud enough for everyone in the place to hear. "You people should go to Capelli's instead of this dump. It's a lot safer there."

At these words Rothstein, unable to contain his rage any longer, lunged at the little man. He had been a professional boxer in his youth but he was older and slower now, and the small man moved with lightning swiftness, stepping aside, then whipping the barrel of his shotgun into the casino owner's face. Rothstein's body snapped straight backward and he toppled to the floor, blood spraying from his smashed nose.

While the original five men held the crowd at bay with their pistols, Pastorini and his crew quickly finished their work, moving table to table and emptying the contents of the under-the-table cash boxes into cloth sacks, after which they destroyed the tables and roulette wheels with the axes. Arnold Rothstein regained his senses just as the intruders rushed out the door, leaving the premises in shambles and his patrons anxious to flee the building and never return.

Rothstein slowly got back to his feet, seething with fury. As soon as he felt steady enough to walk he led his men the few blocks to Capelli's newest casino, the one that Enzo himself would be overseeing. One of Rothstein's men knocked on the door while the others stayed off to the side, out of sight. When the door opened, they rushed in, and when the doorman tried to block their way, Rothstein pulled his pistol from under his jacket and shot the man in the chest. Inside, Capelli was yelling at his men to stop the intruders.

Rothstein spotted his rival and was aiming his gun when a whistle blew and a loud voice boomed at him to drop his weapon or be shot. He looked around as two dozen uniformed policemen rushed the casino floor. A moment later three shotguns were levelled at Rothstein's head and a dozen more cops crowded into the room. Rothstein was astounded. *It's like they were waiting for us*, he thought.

And, of course, they had been. Deputy Chief Duffy made sure the local precinct commander and his men were both prepared and prepaid. They knew there would be a hit against Rothstein's main casino that night, and that the hothead Rothstein would likely retaliate. It was anticipated and planned to play out pretty much exactly as it had.

Rothstein was charged with murder of the doorman, who died at the scene. He was further charged with several counts of assault and battery with a deadly weapon. Capelli was arrested and charged with running an illegal gambling establishment, violation of anti-liquor laws, and resisting arrest. Most of their men were charged with promotion of gambling, violation of the Volstead Act, and resisting arrest. Deputy Chief Duffy felt confident that Rothstein would be in prison for the rest of his life, and Capelli for at least a decade. In addition, many of their underlings would not see the outside of a prison cell for two to three years. Duffy considered it a good day for law enforcement as well as for his own bank account.

It was also a good day for Max Zalensky, who had carefully prepared to step into the void created by Capelli and Rothstein's departure. Within a week he moved his own equipment and people into the existing casinos, making quick arrangements with the building owners, who were only too anxious to continue the lucrative leases and careful not to ask just what their properties would be used for. Max refurbished each casino, making them plusher and swankier, and he hired attractive waitresses to serve drinks at the gaming tables. Despite the recent violence, customers quickly returned, and with the upgraded facilities business was better than ever. Max Zalensky's gambling empire had more than doubled overnight.

CHAPTER TWENTY-SEVEN

Mrs. Goldberg ran down the stairs to the front door, opened it and yelled for Virgilio. The Filipino chauffeur lived over the garage, and Mrs. Goldberg prayed that he would hear her. Her sixty-year-old legs did not want to run any farther. She yelled again and saw the light go on in Virgilio's apartment. He would know to bring the Cadillac to the front door.

Mrs. Goldberg hurried back up to Sophie's room. This house was too big. Just getting out of it was work. Sophie was already stumbling out of her room. She had managed to get herself dressed, sort of. The trouble was she could barely stand up. *Just like her mother*, Mrs. Goldberg thought again. Esther had had a terrible time with Sophie. But that was in New York, a civilised city, and the doctor came to you.

Mrs. Goldberg knew she wasn't strong enough to support Sophie down the stairs by herself. She yelled again for Virgilio. Always reliable, he came bounding up the stairs. Although he was short and slender he was quite strong, and together they got Sophie down the stairs and into the car.

That was another thing about Los Angeles. In New York they had never needed an automobile, but in LA you couldn't live without one. Living up here in the hills you couldn't even buy groceries without a car. And since neither woman knew how to drive, this required a chauffeur. At least that had turned out well. As uncomfortable as she was in a car, Mrs. Goldberg had complete faith that Virgilio would get them down the hill to the hospital safely and quickly.

Thirteen hours later a nurse came out to the waiting room and asked for Mr. Epstein. Mrs. Goldberg stood up and quietly explained to the nurse that there was no Mr. Epstein. Sophie was a widow, a tragic thing, just eighteen and with a child. She, Mrs. Goldberg, was an aunt and the only living relative. The nurse seemed to take the story at face value, nodded and explained that Sophie was resting, the delivery had gone smoothly and mother and baby were both fine. If Mrs. Goldberg cared to see the baby she should come to the nursery.

The nurse handed the newborn boy to Mrs. Goldberg. "She named him Jacob," she said approvingly. "It's a good biblical name." Mrs. Goldberg nodded, still looking at the baby. Less than an hour old, he was already alert, his blue eyes staring relentlessly at Mrs. Goldberg.

"Does he look like his father?" the nurse asked in a friendly manner. Mrs. Goldberg nodded again. Nobody else would know. Even to Mrs. Goldberg, it was a surprise. No one here had seen him as a young child, but Mrs. Goldberg remembered very well. And little Jacob Epstein looked remarkably like his father, Max Zalensky.

CHAPTER TWENTY-EIGHT

While Jonathan was busy building his business, Aunt Catherine and Samantha's mother planned his wedding. It took place in June in the chapel at St. Augustine's and was, as Catherine said, a grand affair. The boisterous crowd of family and friends had a wonderful time and the bride looked beautiful. The only thing missing was Jonathan's mother and sisters, still back in Ireland. He vowed to correct that soon.

The happy couple went directly from St. Augustine's to their new home, a two-bedroom apartment overlooking Gramercy Park. The success of his business easily afforded the new flat and he needed the extra bedroom to use as an office. The wedding was on Saturday and their honeymoon would consist of spending that night and the next day in their new apartment. On Monday he would be back at work. Samantha wanted to make the most of the time they had.

He was already half-undressed, standing by the foot of the bed when she walked out of the bathroom. She was wearing a new nightgown purchased especially for this occasion, trying to appear calm but obviously nervous. It was a sheer French silk, cut low in front and lower in back, with narrow straps over her shoulders so that the thin material clung to her small, perfect breasts. The gown draped to her upper thighs, her beautiful legs visible almost to where they met. Jonathan's breath caught in his throat and his heart seemed to beat faster.

"I've never worn anything like this. Do I look silly?"

Jonathan quickly pulled off his remaining clothes and stepped toward her. In a low voice he said, "You look wonderful."

He had not known it was possible to be so happy. Most nights she greeted him when he came through the door, rushing to him in her eagerness. On one occasion they made love right there in the foyer, laughing like children. She liked to cook and during the week they usually ate at home. Weekends they dined out, often followed by a play or one of the new silent films that had become so popular.

Samantha attended college at City University of New York where she studied History and Political Science. She was one of fifty-seven females in a university of two thousand students. Neither her father nor her uncles thought it proper for an Irish Catholic girl to attend college, and they didn't hesitate to make their opinions known. She should be working to help bring in money for her new household, they said or, even better, home raising babies.

But to Jonathan it seemed natural that Samantha would continue her education. She had as quick a mind as anyone he had ever met, one of the many things he loved about her. Every night she talked to him about what she had read, or what this professor or that one had said. Her enthusiasm confirmed his opinion that this was the right thing for her to do.

Three months before their first wedding anniversary, Samantha's doctor confirmed her suspicion that she was pregnant. When Jon got home that night she was unable to contain herself, starting to speak almost before he got through the front door.

"I went to see Dr. Connell today," she said, trying to appear casual but not quite able to hide her excitement.

"Oh, what about?" He had been working hard and was visibly tired, but tried to appear attentive.

Samantha hesitated, not quite sure how to tell him. "Do you want a boy or a girl?"

Jon stopped in his tracks, his exhaustion forgotten. "Really?"

She nodded. "I'm two months along."

Jonathan grinned broadly, then picked her up, his arms locked below her bottom, and kissed her feverishly. Then he started talking, almost jabbering. "We can use the second bedroom. I'll move my office to the 2nd Street bar. Or we can buy a bigger—"

Samantha interrupted him with a long kiss. He was still holding her and she circled her legs around his waist, her hands resting on his shoulders. "Take me into the bedroom, right now," she said, laughing delightedly. She was still laughing when he lowered her onto the bed and began wrestling her clothes free. Only when his kisses left her breasts, moving slowly lower, did her mirth stop, her breath coming faster, her laughter turning to moans.

CHAPTER TWENTY-NINE
1921

Jonathan sat on a pea green couch in the battleship grey waiting room of the maternity ward of St. Mary's hospital in mid-Manhattan. Samantha had awakened him at five a.m. The contractions had started four hours earlier and were coming five minutes apart. It was time, she told him.

At the hospital, a very stern-looking nurse with a strong Irish accent stopped him at the door to the delivery rooms. "Only doctors, nurses, and mothers," she said. "Husbands wait outside."

"I would like to be with her," Jonathan responded.

"Sorry. It's not allowed."

As she talked, the nurse seated Samantha in a wheelchair and rolled her through the double doors. Samantha turned around in the chair, smiled at him and said, "I'll be fine. Don't worry."

But he did worry. Dr. Connell had plainly stated that the size of the baby, due to its lateness, could cause difficulty. And Jonathan had heard from more than one woman, including his mother, that childbearing was a painful process. It seemed obvious to him that he should be there, if for no other reason than to hold her hand. The hospital, however, felt differently and Jonathan was confined to the waiting room.

After seven hours and several cups of coffee, he was climbing the walls. He had been to the nurse's station five times in the past two hours, and they were clearly as tired of him as he was of waiting. But he could not stand not knowing and he decided to ask just one more time.

As he approached the little nurse's station, the tall, broad-shouldered woman who manned it was already wagging a finger at him. "You must—" she started to say, when the door at the back of the station opened and the Irish nurse who had wheeled Samantha into maternity came rushing out. She started to say something aloud, then stopped when she caught sight of Jonathan, instead whispering into the station nurse's ear. The big nurse listened, then looked at Jonathan, not quite meeting his eyes. She said, "I have to go. There's an emergency." Then she and the Irish nurse hurried back through the door.

Jonathan felt panic rise like a serpent in his throat. He rushed through the swinging doors that said 'Maternity' just in time to see the two nurses hurrying through another door twenty feet down the hall. Jonathan ran after them, and straight into his worst nightmare.

Samantha lay on her back on a bed in the middle of the room, her face almost as white as the pillow case it rested on. Her eyes were closed and Jonathan was not sure if she was breathing. The bottom half of the hospital bed was tilted up, so that Samantha's pelvis was higher than the rest of her body. Between her legs was a pool of blood that grew larger as Jonathan watched. There was a pile of towels lying on the floor, each one soaked red.

A doctor approached with a new towel and while the nurses propped up Samantha's legs the doctor pressed the towel between them, pushing down from his shoulders. But as the towel continued to redden he stepped back and shook his head, as if in defeat. The big nurse refused to give up. She grabbed a clean towel and continued to work until even Jonathan could see that there was no hope. The new towel was quickly turning bloody. Samantha's life was flowing out of her and there was nothing they could do to stop it. Finally, the big nurse stood up, exhausted. She picked up Samantha's wrist to feel for a pulse, failed to find one, and let the wrist fall limply down.

The doctor and the nurses were so intent on what they were doing that they hadn't noticed Jonathan enter the room. The doctor turned to walk out, his eyes cast downward, and almost walked into Jonathan, who was standing just inside the door. "Excuse me," he said distractedly. Then, sounding irritated, "Who are you?"

"I'm her husband," Jonathan replied quietly. It somehow took a great effort to get any words out.

The doctor looked directly at Jonathan and shook his head again, as Jonathan had seen him do a moment before. "I'm sorry," he said. "She started bleeding the moment the baby came out and we couldn't stop it. Sometimes that happens, particularly when the baby is so far along. I'm sorry."

Jonathan nodded slowly. The doctor squeezed his hand. "You need to sit down." Jonathan nodded again and the doctor led him to a chair in the corner. He patted the bereaved husband on the shoulder and then left the room.

Jonathan could hear the breathing of the big nurse, heavy and laboured from her futile effort to save Samantha. Other than that, the room was very quiet. He was aware that they had covered her with a sheet but no one spoke to him or looked directly at him.

He felt as if he should cry or wail, or whatever people did when the person that means everything, the person who was their entire world, had just been taken. But he was too tired. Every ounce of his energy was gone, as if someone had pulled a plug and it had all drained out. He was aware of someone asking him if he wanted to be alone with the body, but he was too tired to answer. Then the same voice asked if he wished to move to a more comfortable room, but again he couldn't muster a response. Then they wheeled Samantha out of the room and he was alone.

Sometime later, he was not sure how long, the big nurse came back into the room carrying a small bundle wrapped in a hospital blanket. She stood directly in front of him and said, "Would you like to see your son?"

Jonathan looked up at her, his eyes wide open. He had completely forgotten.

CHAPTER THIRTY
1922

Sophie was enamoured of Hollywood. Like so many others, she pictured herself on the silver screen, bigger than life, incredibly glamorous. Now, with Mrs. Goldberg taking care of Jacob, and Arnold's estate generating more income than she could possibly spend, she had the time and money to pursue her dream. So with the energy and indomitability of an innocent she set out to achieve stardom.

Sophie knew from reading fan magazines that several stars were learning a naturalistic acting technique from a former New York thespian named Leo Steinberg, who ran an acting school in Hollywood. Many silent film artists were still pantomiming cartoonish exaggerations of human expression. Audiences were becoming hungry for more realistic performances, as attested to by the popularity of stars like Lillian Gish. The recent invention of the close-up camera had only added to the audience's aversion to over-stylised acting, as the slightest nuance was magnified many times over on the big screen. Steinberg's school was less than a twenty-minute drive from Sophie's house in the hills, and with the optimism of a beautiful young woman accustomed to getting what she wanted, she called to enrol.

In addition to coaching his students on the best ways to evoke emotions like love, hate, fear and joy, without resorting to broad gestures, Leo Steinberg also taught beginners like Sophie the basics they would need for their first role in front of the camera: how to hit their marks, stay in frame and be aware of the camera's position without appearing self-conscious or awkward.

Sophie had been attending the school for six weeks when opportunity presented itself. Steinberg made the announcement to the entire class: "Metro is holding auditions for three female roles in a new comedy. They want young, untested actresses. They called, hoping I could send over a few girls to try out." After the buzz died down he continued. "I think several of you have a good shot at one of these parts." He looked around the room. "But this is not theatre. They will want you for your looks as much as for acting ability. So be a little careful. You understand?"

Sophie nodded with everyone else, but she really didn't understand. Of course film actresses had to be pretty; their faces were up on a giant screen, bigger than life. Naturally, they had to be faces that people wanted to look at. That was precisely why Sophie thought she had a chance. It was why every one of these young women thought she had a chance.

Metro Studios was located on Cahuenga Boulevard on a hundred-acre plot that had been an orange grove twenty years earlier. The studio produced as many as forty movies a year. A few of these were big budget corkers, but the majority cost less than eighty thousand dollars and were shot and edited in less than two months. The movie that Sophie auditioned for was of the latter type. Titled *The Girls Upstairs*, it was a comedy about a millionaire who courts a rich man's daughter, is pursued by her younger sister, and ends up falling for their maid. It was budgeted at seventy-five thousand dollars and scheduled to finish production in seven weeks.

The studio was ten minutes from Sophie's house and Virgilio dropped her off just inside the gate, then waited in the Cadillac in the huge dirt parking lot. The audition itself was in a large warehouse at the northwest corner of the lot. Sophie's heart sank when she entered the building and saw more than one hundred eager young women lined up for the tryout, and more coming through the door behind her.

The auditions took two days. On the first day, the director, Walter Wittsen, sat behind a large table in one corner of the warehouse. His two assistants, simply introduced as George and Edward, sat on either side of him. Each young woman took a turn parading forth and back on a ten-foot line in front of the men, then stopped, smiled, uttered her name, and performed a slow pirouette. It reminded Sophie of a dog show that she and Arnold had once attended on the Upper West Side of New York; carefully coiffed poodles being trotted in a circle in front of silent, forbidding judges.

At three minutes each, plus a break for lunch, it took almost nine hours for all one hundred forty-seven hopefuls to strut their wares for the tribunal behind the table. When it was over, the three men conferred for another thirty-five minutes before Edward, who held the title Casting Director, read the results. He was a short, stocky, balding man, and in a deep Texas twang said, "We want twenty-three of you back here tomorrow." Then he read off the names of the chosen ones. The eleventh name was Sophie Epstein.

The second day's audition was similar to a day in acting school. Again, each woman took her turn in front of the three men sitting behind the large table. But this time they were asked to display various emotions on demand: happiness, laughter, surprise, fear, love and pain. Most of the actresses tended to overdo the facial expressions and hand gestures, so to Sophie they appeared unnatural and overly dramatic. For her part, Sophie pretended it was Steinberg giving the commands and moved through the exercise easily.

Again, it was Edward who read the results. He stood in front of the assemblage and in a bored voice said, "For the role of Olivia, the rich man's daughter, we have chosen Helen Hunter, and for the role of her younger sister, Barbara Barrett. The part of the maid will be played by Sophie Epstein. Be here tomorrow morning at eight o'clock sharp."

For three or four minutes, she could not move. Other girls shuffled out, their eyes downcast and bodies slumped. She just stood in place, eyes closed, repeating to herself the words Edward had spoken: "The part of the maid will be played by Sophie Epstein." Finally, after everyone else had left, she recovered her composure enough to walk out, hardly aware of her feet touching the ground.

★   ★   ★

She arrived early, feeling excited and nervous. The entire picture would be shot in the same building that had housed the auditions. George, whose title was Assistant Director, handed each actor a shooting schedule and a ten-page story summary. Sophie's summary included notes scrawled in director Wittsen's own hand, indicating whatever characteristics he wanted her to display in each scene: innocence, coquettishness, flirtatiousness, surprise, joy, etc.

Sophie had no scenes until the third day, so she sat on a folding chair studying her story summary and watching the filming. She quickly concluded that Wittsen was a well-organised, hard-working director, if not a particularly creative one.

In the late afternoon of the second day, George asked her to go try on the maid's costume. Wardrobe was in the far corner of the building, the only section that had actual doors rather than just openings in the wall. There were racks of men's and women's clothes of all sorts and sizes, as this wardrobe served for all films produced in this and surrounding buildings. The room was roughly divided into a women's and a men's section by a wooden bench running down the middle. There were other benches in the room, as well as mirrors, to assist actors trying on costumes.

George led her to the proper section, and after sizing her up for a minute handed her one of several maid's costumes hanging nearby. He stood waiting for her to try it on. After a minute he realised that Sophie was not about to undress in front of him, and with a soft chuckle turned to walk out. "I'll let Mr. Wittsen know that you will show him the costume later."

Sophie changed clothes, laying out her own dress on one of the benches, then checked the results in the full-length mirror. The outfit was a Hollywood representation of what a young maid might wear. It had the familiar checkered apron and ruffled sleeves but was more formfitting than any actual maid's uniform. The sleeves were quite short, the bodice tight, and the skirt showed more ankle and calf than was common. She was about to change back to her own clothes when a man's loud voice said, "That looks perfect." The voice startled Sophie so much she almost jumped, not having heard anyone enter the room.

Turning and seeing who it was, she recovered her composure, curtsied like a polite servant, and said, "I'm glad you like it, Mr. Wittsen. I was thinking it might be a little tight."

"Not at all," the director said, walking up to her rapidly. "It's just right. This way it will be obvious why the millionaire prefers the maid."

Sophie nodded agreeably, wondering if she should thank him for giving her this chance. Almost as if he heard her thoughts, he said, "It was my idea to pick you. George and Edward both wanted some other girl. Now I can see that I was right."

She started to respond when Wittsen leaned over and kissed her full on the lips, taking her into his arms as he did so. Completely surprised, Sophie pulled back and put her hands against his chest to ward him off.

"Miss Epstein," Wittsen said smoothly, his arms still around her. "Have you not read the story? You kiss Mr. Peterson at the end of the fifth scene. We need to see if you are able to make it appear realistic."

Okay, Sophie thought. *If I need to kiss this lecher, I guess I can do it.* And just as she had done in acting class, she pretended that the man in front of her was Max. She closed her eyes, put her arms around his neck and kissed him passionately on the mouth. Wittsen kissed her back, slipping his hands lightly down her back and across her hips. He then bent his knees so he could reach all the way down and lift up her skirt, sliding his hands up her bare legs to her buttocks, drawing her against him.

Sophie grabbed both of his hands and forcefully pulled them away from her. He went along with this, but as soon as she loosened her grip his hands flew to her chest, pawing at her breasts. She couldn't back away from him because her thighs were up against the bench that she had used to change clothes. Instinctively she whirled around so her back was to him. Wittsen simply used this opportunity to press himself up against her. She could feel his growing hardness against her backside. Then, hand on her upper back, he shoved her forward so she was bent over the bench. He reached down and pulled up her skirt with one hand, pulling down her underpants with the other. "God," she heard him say, "you have a beautiful ass." Then his pants were undone and she could feel his erection against her.

Desperate, doubled over the bench, unable to straighten up with his weight on top of her, Sophie struck straight back with her elbow. She was bent over so the blow went straight up at Wittsen, who was leaning over to hold her in place. Sophie heard a sharp crack and Wittsen screamed with pain. He let go of her and she turned around to see him holding his nose, blood running from between his fingers. She pulled up her panties and straightened her skirt just as Edward and several of the actors charged into the room, obviously in response to the scream.

Wittsen's pants were down, his penis still hanging out in plain sight. But he seemed totally unconcerned about that. "She broke my nose!" he shrieked, pointing at Sophie. "She's like some wild animal."

"You're the animal," she yelled back at him, angrily. "You tried to rape me. I should call the police."

Calming down a little, Wittsen pulled up his pants and tucked himself back in. He looked at Sophie as if she were crazy. "I'm the director, you idiot. You have to take my direction."

"What, to have sex with you?"

"If that's what I direct you to do."

She looked around the room, expecting support from her fellow actors. She did not get any. Peterson stared at the floor, unable to look at her. Helen Hunter, who played the role of the daughter, glanced at Sophie, bit her lip, and nodded. Sophie was completely flabbergasted. How could she have been so naïve?

"I don't believe this," she said, almost to herself.

Still angry, Wittsen said, "Well, you'd better believe it, you stupid cunt. And since you can't follow direction, you're fired. Get out of here." Then he stormed out of the wardrobe room, the others shuffling quietly behind him.

Sophie changed back into her dress, carefully hung up the maid's uniform, and walked out of the building and across the lot to the waiting Cadillac. On the way home, sitting in the back seat of the big car, she finally broke down, tears pouring out, while Virgilio watched her silently in the rearview mirror.

CHAPTER THIRTY-ONE

"Why didn't you warn me?"

Leo Steinberg could hear the anger in Sophie's voice.

"I'm sorry. I thought you knew. It's one of those things that everyone knows, but no one talks about."

"Well, I didn't. And I was practically raped. How do they get away with it?"

Steinberg shrugged. "You saw how many girls were auditioning. If you aren't willing to play along, there are more than a hundred girls happy to step into your role. In fact, I'm sure one of them already has."

Seeing that this was not making her any happier, he tried another tack. "Maybe you should go to New York."

"New York? That's where I came from. Why on earth would I go back?"

"Look, Sophie, you're a real actress. A natural. You memorise lines effortlessly, you can inflect any emotion in your voice, and you do foreign accents so flawlessly a native couldn't distinguish you from the real thing. Why not put your talents to use on the stage, where they'll be appreciated?"

She looked at him as if he were daft. "I don't want to be in the theatre. I want…." Her voice trailed off.

"You want to be on the silver screen," Steinberg finished for her. "You want to be larger than life, to have millions of people looking up at you, awed by your beauty, inspired by your image." He paused. "Simply put, Sophie from the Lower East Side, you want to be a movie star."

"Yes," she said quietly, "I do."

"Sometimes," Steinberg said gently, "life requires us to make compromises. You may have to do some things you'd rather not do to get what you really want."

"No!" she said angrily. "I won't make that sort of compromise. Men have taken advantage of me too many times. I won't let it happen again."

She spoke with such vehemence that Steinberg actually backed up a step. "All right," he said, "all right. We'll try it your way. But promise me you'll let off some of that steam, have some fun. It'll make you a better actress." Then he grinned at her. "And to hell with all of them."

Sophie did exactly as Steinberg suggested: she spent more time with her son, started a rose garden in the backyard, caught up on her reading. And she made a new friend.

Deborah Gartner had ridden a bus from Saginaw, Michigan, to Los Angeles two years earlier. She was the prettiest girl in Saginaw, maybe in all of Michigan, and she knew in her heart that only time and luck stood between her plain past and her future stardom. Up until now she had only managed to land a few bit parts in shorts and two-reelers. But despite her slow progress, she had grown to love her adopted home and was more than happy to show it off to the new girl in Steinberg's class. The two ladies had discovered that in addition to their shared ambition, they both loved Mary Pickford, Coco Chanel, and French champagne. And everyone in the class had noticed that Sophie arrived each morning in a chauffeured Cadillac.

"You can have more fun here than anyplace in the world," she assured Sophie. Not that Deborah had been many places, just her family home in Michigan and now California. But this was such a perfect spot she could not imagine any place better. It was almost always warm and sunny, there were gorgeous beaches and mountains, and for a beautiful girl every door seemed to open.

They were sitting at the lunch counter at the Woolworth's on Fountain Avenue, across the street from Steinberg's acting school. Sophie gazed around the store for a moment, and then back at her new friend. "I'd like that," she said. "To have some fun."

"There's a party tonight," Deborah gushed excitedly. "There will be studio executives and producers and handsome men. It would be nice to arrive in a Cadillac. With a chauffeur."

Sophie smiled. "We can do that."

*　　*　　*

Virgilio drove her down from the hills to pick up Deborah, then back up almost the same way they had come, turning eventually onto a dark, winding street that seemed to hover above the lights of the city. Their destination was impressively large inside the gated driveway, and as a butler greeted them at the front door Sophie could hear live jazz music emanating from within. They removed their light topcoats to reveal their evening gowns, Sophie's an aqueous green to match her eyes, and Deborah's a bright red that offset her very blond hair. There were finger foods and booze and, as Deborah had promised, many handsome men.

As soon as the two women stepped from the entryway into the living room, heads turned. They were quickly approached by a striking couple; a very pretty, smiling young woman on the arm of an older, serious-looking gentleman, who seemed not to be having as good a time as the swirling party goers around him.

"So good to see you, my dear," said the woman, bussing Deborah on both cheeks. Deborah blushed, and stammered a bit. But she quickly recovered and said, "I'd like you to meet my good friend, Sophie Epstein. She's new in town and I thought she should meet you. She lives up here in the hills, practically your neighbour."

Deborah then turned to Sophie and said, "These are our hosts, Miss Marion Davies and Mr. William Randolph Hearst."

"I'm honoured to meet you," Sophie said, trying to contain her excitement at meeting the famous couple. "It's very generous of you to welcome me into your beautiful home."

"Any time." It was Hearst speaking now, seeming much more engaged than he had just a few moments earlier. "You say we're neighbours?" he asked. "How close do you live?"

"The other side of Laurel Canyon," Sophie responded. "Not far at all."

"Well, that is indeed close. Perhaps you'd like to join us in the future for—"

At that point, Hearst was cut off by his mistress. "Yes, that sounds wonderful," she said. "Oh look, darling, Louella and John just came in. They look simply parched! If you'll excuse us." And with that, she pulled the older man away, despite his obvious reluctance to leave.

Deborah could barely suppress a giggle. "He's got a wandering eye, and she's easily jealous."

Sophie shrugged, thinking that a woman who shared a house

with another woman's husband shouldn't be surprised if he was not completely faithful. After all, the mogul was more famous for his affair with the young actress than for his newspaper empire.

But she kept these thoughts to herself and said, "I take it from your reaction that we were not actually invited."

Deborah blushed once more. "No, not exactly. Usually these parties are more crowded, and Marion doesn't walk around greeting the guests. Hearst is not normally here, and Miss Davies is often entertaining a friend of her own." Once again, Deborah could not suppress a giggle, and then said, "So it's easy to slip in."

Sophie smiled. "It's part of what makes this town so fun."

"Exactly," her friend responded.

Even as she spoke, Deborah's eyes wandered the room like a predator's seeking sustenance. Sophie saw her smile, and knew that her friend had located her prey.

"Ooh," Deborah gushed. "I see William Wellman over there, and he looks positively lonely. I'll bet he'd appreciate some friendly company." Then, looking a little sheepishly at Sophie, she asked, "You don't mind if I handle this by myself, do you?"

"Of course not," Sophie responded. "You go ahead. I'll be just fine."

"Great," Deborah said, already heading off, grabbing a glass of champagne from a waiter as she made her way toward the famous director.

Left by herself, Sophie decided to make her way to the back of the house with the intention of checking out the view. Her own house nestled up against the hillside so she had no sight of the city below, and she was curious to see how things looked from this lofty perch.

The light evening dress accentuated her full breasts and long, perfect legs, but provided little protection from the cold night as she stepped out onto the patio. The chill was well worth braving. The lights of the Los Angeles basin spreading all the way to the ocean were magnificent. All the other guests were inside the house, and the only sound was that of the wind rustling though the hills as she stared out at the dazzling panorama. So the deep voice startled her, even as she realised her mistake in thinking she was alone.

"I don't know what's more breathtaking," the voice said, "the view of the city lights or you."

"Do you always get away with such cheesy lines?" Sophie responded as she turned in the direction the voice had come from.

And then she was sorry that she had said it, he looked so crestfallen. Almost simultaneously, she realised that he probably did get away with such lines. He was neither tall nor powerfully built, and he was no one she recognised. But he was tremendously good looking, almost pretty, and he obviously knew it. He had a wide mouth, straight nose, piercing blue eyes, smooth skin, and thick, wavy black hair. When he spoke again the full-bodied resonance of his voice made her want to swoon.

"You really are spectacular," he said, although his voice had a note of caution now. "You're the best-looking girl I've seen, and I've seen most of the girls in Hollywood."

"I'll bet you have," she said, and again regretted being so flippant. For in addition to being so darned good looking, he seemed sincere. To make amends she introduced herself, and asked his name.

"I'm Anthony Marston, but most folks call me Tony. I'm an actor, but I do some photography on the side to help pay the rent."

"What sort?"

"Portraits mostly. Maybe you'll let me photograph you sometime."

"Maybe." Sophie shivered slightly. "Do you mind going inside? I'm getting cold."

"I'll go inside or to the ends of the earth if you ask."

"How many girls have you said that to, Tony?"

"On my life, you're the only one."

They found a quiet corner inside, and after refilling their drinks, sat on a sofa there. Sophie was wary about revealing too much about herself, but she needn't have worried. Tony was perfectly content to talk about himself.

He was originally from Shawnee, Oklahoma, but had left there because of 'girl trouble'. Sophie assumed this meant he had gotten a young woman pregnant, and for a moment, she was astonished that he would admit to such a thing. But as he continued to speak, she realised that he was simply too self-absorbed to be embarrassed. He went on to tell her how he had worked as a photographer in

Oklahoma and continued that profession in Los Angeles. But when he'd been hired to take publicity stills for a Goldwyn film shoot, the assistant director suggested that his good looks could put him in front of the camera rather than behind it. Thus began his career as an actor. He'd landed small parts in several films, but as he had said, still did some photography to pay the bills.

Despite her doubts, Sophie was impressed with his honesty, something unusual in the men she'd encountered thus far in California. And as previously noted, he was darn good looking. Maybe it had been too long a time. Looking around, she saw the evening was winding down. They had talked much longer than she'd realised. She turned back to him and said, "If I give you my number, will you call me?"

"Of course I will. But I was thinking we could ditch this place and go out somewhere. Or even back to my place for a nightcap."

Sophie said, "I think I'd prefer it if you call me and ask me out to dinner or a movie."

"Of course," he said again. "I didn't mean anything disrespectful. I just want to see you."

Sophie smiled. "Then call me." She handed him a cocktail napkin on which she'd already written her number, then walked away to find Deborah. Her friend was almost in the same spot that Sophie had left her, listening demurely while William Wellman pontificated somewhat drunkenly about the proper place of film in the art world. She spied Sophie approaching and excused herself for a moment, then hurried over.

"I don't need a ride." The words tumbled out sloppily and Sophie realised that Deborah must have had several more drinks since she'd last seen her. "William's going to take me home." She giggled her little giggle. "He says he's got a small part for me in his new movie. It's just a week into shooting and my character hasn't been on screen yet."

Sophie nodded but didn't say anything. Deborah took her silence for disapproval and said, "It can work. A little part can be the gateway to bigger parts if I show I can act. Which I can."

"Just be careful," Sophie said.

"Of course." Deborah giggled again. "He's too old to do any real damage." Then she skipped off, back to the patiently waiting Mr. Wellman. Sophie walked out the front door of the large house to her own patiently waiting chauffeur, who opened the car door for her before driving home.

CHAPTER THIRTY-TWO

Tony Marston called a few evenings later, his voice as cool and deep as Sophie remembered. He asked her out to a movie and offered to pick her up in his Model T Ford. She was happy for the date, but told him she would meet him at the theatre.

The movie was a John Ford Western in which Tony had his biggest part yet, a handsome gambler who attracted the attention of a pretty barmaid. He was onscreen for almost five minutes and Sophie felt that he did, indeed, look very striking. But his face revealed very little of the range of expression that she felt was so important in movies of the day. Someday, she imagined, cinema would have sound, and a voice like Tony's would be in great demand. But in today's world his face needed to be his instrument of communication.

After the movie he asked if she would come to his house, "so we can have a drink and talk."

Sophie looked at him evenly, her eyebrows raised. "Is it usually that easy? The girl sees you onscreen for a few minutes and toddles right into your bedroom?"

Tony stammered, "Look, I-I didn't mean anything like that. I actually would like to talk. And I've got a photo studio in my living room. I think you'd really like it." She could see him almost sweating.

Sophie smiled coquettishly, put one hand gently to the back of his neck and drew him to her. She kissed him hard on the lips and then put her mouth to his ear, "It's okay. I'd love to toddle into your bedroom."

Tony smiled a broad, infectious smile. "Wow, you are something else. My car's parked around the corner." He took her hand to lead the way, but she pulled back.

"I have my own ride," she said, "and I'd like to have my own

way home. I'll just follow you and my chauffeur will wait for me."
She looked toward the street and Tony, following her gaze, noticed
the idling Cadillac, the driver staring stonily at the two of them.

Shaking his head, he said, "You really are something else," then
walked quickly to his car.

They became lovers, but not a couple. She came to his house twice
a week, once mid-week and once on the weekend. Sometimes they
went out to dinner, but not often. He asked her to attend parties or
go out with another couple but she explained that she had family
obligations and limited time. He took this to mean that she was
married, almost certainly to an older, wealthy man, and could not risk
her husband knowing of her infidelity.

He was a confident lover, obviously experienced. But jaded as he
was he seemed awestruck by her naked body, seemed to genuinely
believe that she was the most attractive woman he had ever seen.
Sophie loved the adulation and flattery, the undisguised lust. She loved
his uninterrupted attention when they were in bed. But when not in
bed he could become tedious.

"I can't believe they didn't call me," he said, for what seemed
to Sophie like the twentieth time. John Ford, the director of his last
movie, the Western they had seen together, was casting a new movie,
and although Tony had inquired at the studio, no one had called back.

It was late Saturday night. They had just gotten out of bed and
were standing in his kitchen while he mixed two vodka tonics. Sophie
was wearing a cream-coloured sleeveless blouse, panties, and nothing
else. Tony was in his undershorts.

"Why wouldn't they want me? Do you think I offended someone?"

"No, of course not," Sophie said. "You have a very nice manner.
They just don't have the right part. Something will come along soon,
you needn't worry so much." She touched him on the cheek as she
said this, but he did not respond, seemingly lost in his own thoughts.

Finally, he grinned and said, "You're probably right." The grin
turned mischievous. "How about we take the picture? It's all set to go.
We can do it right now."

He had converted the living room of his small bungalow into a
photo studio, complete with lights, tripod and a stool on which his
models could pose. He took great pride in the studio and, in fact, was

in some demand as a portraitist. Sophie had posed for him before and the results were excellent. He bounced light off the bungalow's nine-foot ceiling to soften the effect and used a small light behind her head so her hair seemed to shine. Sophie thought the pictures were better than the expensive headshots she had purchased to carry to auditions.

Tony had asked her several times to pose nude, "just so I'll have something to remind me how incredibly beautiful you are. I develop them myself, so no one else will see." Despite his pleas she had refused, laughing him off as if it were a joke. Now he was asking again.

"I really don't want to. You need to understand that."

For a brief moment she saw anger on his face and thought there might be a nasty scene. But it passed quickly, and his face returned to its standard cheerful look. "Of course," he intoned. "Go sit on the sofa. I'll finish the drinks and bring them over." Somewhat relieved, Sophie did as he asked.

She woke the next morning, still on the sofa. It had been dark out when she sat down to wait for her vodka tonic, but now the early morning Los Angeles sun was glaring through the living room blinds. She was still in her blouse and panties. There was a blanket over her and Tony was in the little kitchen squeezing fresh orange juice.

"Oh my God," she muttered. "I need to be home. How could you let me sleep?"

"You must have really been tired," Tony said, sounding apologetic. "You fell asleep right there and looked so peaceful, I didn't have the heart to wake you."

He sounded sincere and she nodded, but rushed into the bedroom to put back on the rest of her clothes. When she came out he was holding a glass of fresh orange juice for her. "Thanks," she said, "but I don't have time."

She kissed him quickly and rushed out the front door. Virgilio was patiently waiting in the Cadillac at the end of the driveway.

CHAPTER THIRTY-THREE

Three hours after Sophie returned home, Leo Steinberg called. It had been two months since the incident at Metro Studios and her heart leaped at the promise of his voice. Having come so close to success, and losing it, had made her want it that much more.

"I've got something for you," she heard him say, "with Clarence Rollins over at Signature."

Oh no, she thought. *He thinks for the big time, I'll put out.* Even Sophie knew that Rollins was a hot commodity who had recently directed two Wallace Reid racing films.

But Steinberg went on. "He's doing a war movie taking place in England. An American soldier falls for an English girl. They have a love affair before he goes off to war, then he's killed in the trenches, a big hero. To make it authentic, Rollins wants a real English girl. I told him I had the perfect one. You."

Sophie was floored. "Why would he care if the girl is really English? The audience never hears her speak."

"These great directors have their quirks. He's convinced that your British qualities will come through on the screen in your mannerisms, expressions, etcetera. Anyway, it's what he wants so it's what he'll get."

"And what about the little fact that I'm not English?"

"You're an actress. So act. I know you can do the accent perfectly, and you must have run into some English ladies in New York."

"Actually no, but there are a few at Roxbury Park where I take Jacob to play. They have boys the same age, so I've talked with them a few times. I think they're upper-class types from London."

"Perfect. But one last thing. You need a new name. I told him it was Susan Spencer."

"Sounds English," she said, then realised that in her excitement she had forgotten the real issue. "What about Rollins? Won't I have the same problem with him that I did with Wittsen?"

"I don't think so. He's not that type."

"What? An exalted director and a gentleman?"

Steinberg hesitated for a moment before he said, "Yeah, I guess you could look at it that way."

Signature Pictures was not the biggest studio in Hollywood but it was generally considered the most profitable, thanks to its chairman, Louis Kahn, a tight-fisted, detail-oriented dictator who personally approved every budget for every picture.

Twenty years earlier, Kahn had been one of the original Hollywood pioneers who came to California from New York to escape Thomas Edison's patent suits. Edison held the patents for early motion picture cameras and projectors, and felt that he was owed a royalty on every dollar made by a movie studio using his equipment. But laws and lawyers had difficulty reaching across state lines, let alone the Mississippi River, so Kahn and other young filmmakers moved to Los Angeles to outrun Edison's process servers.

Eventually the courts nullified all of Edison's claims, ruling that he had no more rights to a filmmaker's revenue than the man who invented the sewing machine had to a seamstress's earnings. But by that time moviemakers had become accustomed to the wide-open spaces and consistent sunshine of Southern California. The film industry had moved west for good.

Steinberg warned Sophie about Louis Kahn: "He practically invented the casting couch." She had never heard the term before, but understood it immediately. *Why*, she asked herself, *would I even want to be in this business?* But of course, she already knew the answer to that question.

From the moment she entered the Signature gate, Sophie Epstein was thoroughly and completely British. She wore a white linen sundress with gloves and bonnet to match, walked in the upright, slightly stiff manner affected by the English upper class, and generally looked as if she had just stepped away from a croquet match on the lawn of Buckingham Palace.

Clarence Rollins was enchanted. He was a slender man with blond hair and blue eyes that seemed to sparkle when the receptionist led Sophie into his office. He raised one finger to his lips as he watched her from behind his nineteenth-century mahogany desk, clinically analysing the chestnut hair that fell just past her shoulders, the high cheek bones, slim, straight nose and full lips, atop the slender, hourglass figure. But it was her eyes that caught him; widely set, green luminescent pools in which a man might easily become lost.

He jumped up from the desk and gushed, "Miss Spencer, you are absolutely lovely. Just as Mr. Steinberg promised."

"How kind of you," Sophie said in her perfect accent.

"Now, if you also act as well as Steinberg says, we're in business."

Sophie did not tell him that she was acting even as they spoke.

Rollins gave her a story summary and instructed her to "go home, read it, and show up tomorrow ready for action." Similar to the summary Wittsen had given her, the scenes Sophie would appear in were annotated with Rollins' notes of how her character should act and feel.

★   ★   ★

She arrived the next morning at seven a.m. and was on the set, in costume and makeup at nine a.m. The set was outdoors, a London street where her character, a young English heiress, would come out of a grocery store and run smack into the protagonist, a grizzled American sergeant. The heiress would drop the groceries she was carrying, the sergeant would pick them up for her, and so would begin their brief romance.

Standing behind the camera operator, Rollins said, "All right, Susan, this is your audition. If it works, you've got the part. If not, we look for someone else." He grinned. "No pressure."

It was obvious that Rollins was in some sort of bind. The movie had already been shooting for two weeks and Sophie's character was still not cast. Perhaps the original actress had quit or become ill or there had been some sort of dispute. Whatever the reason, Susan Spencer was being thrown into a real scene and would actually be in the movie, 'if it worked'.

The script called for Sophie's character to walk out the door of the phoney grocery store with bags in both arms, forcing her to back through, pushing the door open with her back side. The uniformed sergeant, rushing in to pick up some tobacco, would turn his head at the last minute to say something to his buddy standing outside and wouldn't see her coming. It was sequenced so that the audience knew a collision was imminent, although neither of the characters did.

When they collided, Sophie's character stumbled forward hard, dropping the bags and practically falling flat. The sergeant was apologetic and embarrassed, hurrying to help her to her feet and pick up her groceries. As he handed her the grocery bag they looked into each other's eyes for the first time, which, due to the odd circumstances, was also the first time the actors had seen one another. Sophie felt her knees buckle and her heart pound. *My God,* she thought. *It's Duke Hawkins.* She recovered in time to take the groceries, as the plot called for, and hurry out of the shop.

"Great," Rollins announced happily. "Susan, that was fabulous. I could see in your face how taken you were at your first sight of this man, surprised yet delighted. I could actually see it. Fantastic!" Sophie, who had barely regained her composure after coming face to face with her favourite actor, nodded her thanks.

Over the next three weeks, they completed most of the scenes Sophie was in. Although she was the lead character's love interest, her role was still a minor one. Rollins proved to be a superb director, using camera angles, scenery and lighting to set the mood and pace of the film, as well as being organised and efficient. When Sophie asked questions about camera technique and staging, he was more than happy to explain.

A few days later they shot her final scene. It was at a replica of Victoria Station, the English girl saying her final goodbye to the American sergeant as he goes off to war. "The kiss is important," Rollins said to her. "It's the only one in the movie. It must be passionate, yet sorrowful. You love him but you fear you'll never see him again." Sophie nodded. *What a great business,* she thought with wonderment. *I get paid to kiss Duke Hawkins.*

The scene was shot quickly and smoothly. Rollins was pleased and Sophie's part was over. She would put back her costume, take off the makeup, pick up her paycheck and go home. The next time she saw the set of *Over There* would be when it came to her local theatre.

But half an hour later, as she was walking toward the gate, the assistant producer of the film, Kenneth Cole, caught her. "Hold up," he said, and then stopped and caught his breath. He was a short, rotund man and he had been running to catch her. "Kahn wants to talk to you."

"Who?"

"Louis Kahn," Cole said impatiently, "the guy who runs this whole place." Of course, Sophie knew perfectly well who he was.

"What would he want with me?"

Cole heard the wariness in her voice and tried to reassure her. That was his job. "Maybe he just wants to congratulate you on making it through. You know, Clarence is damned hard to please. We had three girls doing the English part before you, and Rollins canned all of them. We would have had to hold up filming if you hadn't come along when you did."

"Can you just tell him I left before you could find me?"

Cole looked at her as if she were crazy. "He'd know I was lying. And it won't help your career to avoid him. You better go see him."

Sophie nodded, and in her best British accent said, "Where might his office be?"

★   ★   ★

Louis Kahn opened the door himself and nodded at her to come in. He was a large, fleshy man of forty-five with a once-handsome face, now red and sagging from too much booze and too little sleep. His office was spacious and light with floor-to-ceiling windows that looked down on the studio's back lot. Sophie could see the London setting of *Over There* and pick out Rollins yelling something to the cameraman. The office was richly furnished with a Pembroke mahogany desk, two leather couches and a small wet bar. Kahn nodded for her to sit on the couch by the huge window.

"Scotch or beer?" he asked. His voice was direct and rough and although he had lived in California for more than twenty years, Sophie could still hear the Lower East Side in his speech. He must have worked hard to lose his accent, but to Sophie's ear it was as obvious as the neon lights on Broadway. He'd probably grown up within a few miles of where she herself had.

"Scotch," she responded in her perfect English aristocrat accent. "Over ice, please."

"We say, on the rocks." Kahn used tongs to drop a couple of cubes into a glass. "I went by the set of *Over There* on Thursday last week. Saw you do the scene where you first meet the American." He paused, as if to build suspense, while pouring her drink. "You looked good. Real good. It was a stroke of genius for Rollins to pick a real English girl." He smiled and handed her the very full glass of scotch. "I mean, a high-class one like you."

"You are very kind."

Kahn sat down on the couch quite close to Sophie. She waited a moment, not wishing to appear nervous, and then took a sip of her drink. It was excellent Scotch.

"Thing is," he said, "that I think your part can be expanded. Audiences like romance in these war stories. Women especially. So we can give you some more scenes."

"Is that not somewhat difficult this late in the game?"

"Somewhat," Kahn responded. "But it can get done. The writer can come up with the new scenes in a day or so."

"But what about Mr. Rollins? Will he not object to you changing his movie at this late date?"

"He can object all the hell he wants to, but he'll do what I tell him." Kahn paused, then leaned over and kissed Sophie full on the lips, his hand going to the back of her neck to draw her closer.

Sophie did not respond to the kiss, but Kahn seemed not to notice. He moved his left hand from the back of her neck to the front of her blouse, which he began to unbutton. Sophie jumped up from the couch and with her voice raised, said, "What do you think you are doing, sir? This is highly improper."

Kahn looked up at her, more amused than angry. "Take it easy, lady. This is Hollywood. How it works is you want what I can give, you give what I want. No exceptions."

"Mr. Rollins did not require any such quid pro quo. Our relationship is quite professional."

"Mr. Rollins is a goddamn fagelah," Kahn said with a laugh. "Only reason anyone wouldn't wanna fuck a doll like you. All he wanted was a genuine high-class English lady for the part. I'm not sure he even realises what a hot tomato you are." As he spoke, Kahn got up off the couch and reached for Sophie. She slipped back a step, easily eluding his grasp.

As Kahn continued to come toward her, Sophie dropped the English accent completely, reverting to her native Lower East Side. "Forget about it, Louis. You and me ain't gonna happen."

Kahn was momentarily dumbstruck, his jaw dropping slightly. "Where're you from?"

"Ludlow, off Grand. How about you?"

"About a mile south of there, near East Broadway." Surprise still in his voice, he said, "You're very good. You definitely fooled me and you even fooled Rollins, which ain't easy. And your name isn't really Susan Spencer." The last was more a statement than a question.

"No, it's not."

Kahn said, "This is all very interesting and you really are good, but that don't change a thing. You're still gonna fuck me right here and right now or your part is not getting any bigger."

Ignoring the crudeness of his approach, Sophie slipped effortlessly back into the British accent. "That is perfectly fine, sir. I am quite satisfied with my role as it now stands."

"Maybe I'll cut you out completely. Maybe we'll jerk your scenes and find someone else to play the role."

Without hesitation, Sophie bluffed right back at him. "That would be expensive at this late stage of filming, and you are not known as a man who spends any more money than absolutely necessary. And it will take some time to find another perfect English lady. Particularly one who, as you say, is a hot tomato."

Kahn looked at her, shook his head, and actually grinned. "Okay, babe. You've got me beat. This time. But next time, you pay the piper."

Kahn was still grinning when Sophie walked out of his office. *I'd like to be there*, he thought, *when Rollins finds out where she's really from.* Of course, he still had one problem. He did, in fact, need to expand her part. Louis Kahn's genius was that he understood better than anyone in America what movie audiences wanted. And he knew that in this particular movie, they would want more of Susan Spencer.

CHAPTER THIRTY-FOUR

"How much power does a star have?" Sophie asked.

It was the second to last week of filming, and Clarence Rollins and Susan Spencer, director and ingénue, were lunching in the studio commissary. The extra scenes that Louis Kahn had ordered required that Sophie remain on set until the final day of shooting and she and Rollins had become quite chummy. It was Sophie who first cultivated the relationship, but Clarence had quickly become infatuated with the lovely young woman, so cultured and intelligent, utterly exquisite. He loved gossiping with her about who in Hollywood was sleeping with whom, who used drugs, who liked young girls or boys. And he enjoyed her curiosity about both the technique and politics of filmmaking.

"What exactly do you mean by power?" Clarence responded.

"I mean, can he influence the studio to make a picture he wants them to make and use actors he wants them to use?"

"No and yes," Rollins said slowly. "Someone like Louis Kahn would never make a motion picture he did not want to make. And the only pictures he wants to make are ones that make money. If one of his stars came to him with an artsy, intellectual sort of piece, he would turn them down flat. But if they proposed a picture that could draw a large audience, then I suppose he would take a serious look at it."

"And how about his ability to influence what actors are used in the picture?"

"If the star you are referring to is our friend Duke, he has a fair amount of influence. For now. The studios are trying to move to a system where they have their biggest stars under exclusive contract, in return for which the studio will pay the actor a substantial wage. Kahn is anxious to get Duke under contract with Signature, which gives Duke some bargaining power. The only problem is that Duke's star is waning. The girls don't swoon for him like they did a few years ago."

"He is still an extremely handsome man," Sophie said, almost to herself.

"I agree completely," said Rollins, in a surprisingly serious manner, and Sophie was reminded of Kahn's remarks about Clarence's sexual preference. "I'm not sure what the problem is. He just doesn't seem to radiate the same confidence that he once did. Lost his swagger, as it were."

"But for now, he does have influence?"

Clarence hesitated for a moment before responding. "Susan, I understand how desperately you want to be a movie star. Heaven knows I've seen hundreds of girls with the same ambition. And Duke may look like an extremely attractive means of getting there. But if you're thinking of…befriending him, you may be a little disappointed."

"Oh?" said Sophie, realising that she actually knew almost nothing about Duke. "Is he married?"

"My understanding is that he was, but that it's been over for many years," Clarence said.

"And does he…see anyone today?"

"No one in particular, but I'm sure he doesn't want for companionship. There seems to be a never-ending stream of female admirers clamouring for his attention."

"Yes," Sophie said flatly, "I can imagine. I'd be just another face in the crowd."

"Oh no!" said Clarence quite seriously. "There are very few faces to match yours. You'd never be lost in any crowd."

Sophie smiled. "You are very sweet to say that. But why would I be disappointed?"

Clarence smiled back, and Sophie knew that he was about to impart the sort of inside gossip that he so enjoyed.

He lowered his voice, glanced around the room as if other people might be listening and said, "Word has it that Duke's last several consorts were, shall we say, underwhelmed by his staying power. The passage of time seems to have taken its toll on our hero."

"But he can't be more than forty," Sophie offered, sounding sceptical.

"Forty-one actually, so still a young man and quite robust. But as I said, he seems to have lost his old swagger."

Sophie looked at Rollins and asked, "Do you think you could arrange a private meeting between Duke and me? Maybe to discuss publicity on the film."

"Certainly. But what I've just related doesn't...give you pause?"

Sophie smiled. "Au contraire. I think it might be a great deal of fun to help our hero get his old swagger back."

CHAPTER THIRTY-FIVE

Clarence spoke to Kahn, who set it up. Reporters snapped photos when Duke Hawkins and Susan Spencer walked into the newly popular Musso and Frank's, a few more after they sat down at the table, and then left them to enjoy their meal. It was a common ploy for the studios. Spread a rumour that the romantic leads of an upcoming film are romantically involved in real life, arrange for them to have dinner together, and tip off the Hollywood press. Kahn had responded enthusiastically when Clarence suggested it to him, thinking it would be good publicity for his newest starlet. The studio flacks would gossip that the young beauty had completely bewitched the ageing matinee idol. Duke, however, was less enthused about the idea.

"Sounds like a waste of my time," he said to Kahn. "What would I even talk to her about?"

"Tell her about your life," Louis responded. "She'll probably be fascinated."

"Right. And am I supposed to pretend I'm just as interested in her?"

Kahn grinned. "You'd be surprised, boychik. There's more to Miss England than a great set of tits." Kahn's grin turned to a leer. "Who knows, my friend? You might even get lucky."

So after the reporters left and the waiter took their order, Duke told her about his life. How he had worked, at age twelve, on a ranch in Colorado. His family had been poor and he was happy to work sunup to sundown in exchange for coffee in the morning, two meals a day, and ten dollars at the end of each week. In some ways, he actually missed that life.

Duke paused, looked down at his plate to grab a bite, and when he looked up again she was gazing directly at him. He stopped, momentarily frozen, just staring into the sea-green pools of light that were her eyes. Then, somewhat embarrassed, he said, "I'm sorry, Susan, I'm probably boring you."

"No, not in the least," Sophie protested, seemingly unaware of the effect she had. "I was just wondering how you knew how to do all of it."

"All of what?" He was back in control.

"Ride horses, work with cows. All of that."

Duke shrugged. "I grew up in eastern Colorado. Nobody had a car. You either rode a horse or a horse-drawn wagon, or you walked. We always had one milk cow. Our neighbours had cattle and I worked summers for them since I was eight. So it was just something I grew up with." He paused. "They must have horses and cows in England."

Sophie nodded. "Probably. I've never been there."

"What?"

"I said they probably have horses and cows in England. In fact, I'm quite sure that they do. But I've never been there."

Shaking his head, Duke said, "I thought you were from England. You sure sound like you are."

"No. Mr. Rollins wanted an English girl for the part and I wanted the part. So I pretended to be English and Mr. Kahn told me I should keep pretending."

"You certainly fooled me. And everyone else."

Sophie shrugged and smiled. "I'm an actress."

"So where are you really from?"

"New York City. There are some horses there, but the only experience I ever had with one was a carriage ride through Central Park." They both laughed a little. "And my name is not really Susan Spencer, though I'm becoming quite accustomed to people calling me that."

"What's your real name?"

Sophie laughed. "I'll tell you that when we know each other better. You can just keep calling me Susan."

"How do I get to know you better?"

Sophie smiled. "Tell me about yourself first. How did you get into movies?"

"By accident. I came to California eleven years ago, mainly to get away from my wife."

He tried to continue the story but Sophie interrupted him.

"Are you still married?"

He shook his head. "The divorce came through a year later. Haven't even seen her or talked to her since. For all I know she's remarried. I'm not even sure I'd recognise her anymore."

"Kids?" Sophie asked.

"No. Otherwise I never would have left." Sophie nodded and Duke continued the story. "Anyway, when I got to Los Angeles my first job was taking care of horses on a movie set."

"That's a coincidence."

"Not really. It was the only thing I knew how to do. I just answered an ad in the *Times*. The job turned out to be stable hand and blacksmith for some horses that were being used in a Western movie. This one was called *They Died with Their Boots On*. It was the first feature by a young fellow named Louis Kahn."

"You're kidding me."

"Nope," Duke said flatly, a little taken aback that she would doubt him. "We filmed the whole thing in a place called Lone Pine, an old mining town a few hundred miles from here. Most of it still looks like an old Western town, so we didn't need any special sets or anything. And they had a hotel we all stayed at, and a nice restaurant and grocery and everything. People were real nice too. Anyway, some city slicker actor who was playing one of the cowboys fell off his horse and broke his leg. He was real angry, acted like it was the horse's fault. It was a real problem for Louis since he needed the guy in two more scenes and we were out in the middle of nowhere. Wasn't like you could place an ad in the local paper and get an actor the next day."

"So Mr. Kahn asked you to fill in."

"That's right," Duke said. "It was actually kind of fun. Louis thought I did just fine and he appreciated the fact that I was willing to help out like that. So he gave me a slightly bigger part in his next feature and even bigger roles in several films after that. Then four years ago, he cast me in the lead role in *Angels with Guns*. I've been a leading man ever since. Of course, Louis doesn't make the films himself anymore, but I'm still working for him."

Sophie looked directly at him. "I saw *Angels with Guns* in the theatre on Hester Street with a girlfriend. Then I went back and sat through it three more times by myself."

"You liked it that much?"

"Not really. It was just the first time I'd seen you on film. You were the handsomest man I'd ever seen."

There was an awkward silence until Duke said, "Thank you." He actually sounded a little flustered when he said it, and yet Sophie knew there were at least a million girls who felt exactly the same way.

"I don't think Louis gave you that leading role out of the kindness of his heart. He knew very well what you brought to the screen."

Duke nodded. "I suppose you're right. But I still owe him."

After a pause, Sophie said, "Which is why you agreed to have dinner with me."

Duke's eyebrows rose. "Louis was right. There is more to you than meets the eye."

"I'm sure he put it much more crudely than that."

Duke smiled the lopsided smile that women all over North America found irresistible. "You're too hard on him."

"I don't think that's possible."

"Okay," Duke said, "I surrender. Let's switch subjects. Tell me about you."

Sophie looked down at her plate. "There's nothing much to tell. I'm a city girl who doesn't even know how to ride a horse. Anyway, it's late and we should both go home. We have to be at work early tomorrow."

Duke reached across the table and put his own hand over hers, looking again into those eyes. "We should be done shooting Saturday. Come out to my house on Sunday. I'll teach you to ride. That's something you might need to know how to do for your next movie. Or the one after that."

"You have horses?"

"Just two. Still an old stable hand."

Sophie smiled. "Sounds like fun."

CHAPTER THIRTY-SIX

Jonathan's business was going well. A little more than two years after Max had proposed a chain of speakeasies, Jon operated four neighbourhood bars spread through lower Manhattan. Each was in a working-class neighbourhood, each ran very efficiently, each was very profitable. Of course, Max was not satisfied.

"I want at least twenty locations," he complained. "At this rate, that will take you ten years."

Jonathan nodded, having anticipated Max's impatience. "Actually, it will take just three more years," he said. "Sooner, if things go well."

"You'll have to speed things up quite a bit," Max replied. "How are you planning to do that?"

"Seamus is already running day-to-day operations at all four pubs. In some ways, he's better at it than I am. So I'll be spending my time finding new locations and setting them up. I'm looking at two locations in midtown right now. Probably move on both of them before the end of the month."

Max nodded and smiled tightly. "Good to have family."

Seamus Ryan was Jonathan's brother-in-law. After Samantha's death, Aunt Catherine had become alarmed at Jon's growing depression, and had written to Jon's mother, her cousin, Mary-Margaret, imploring her to visit America. Mary-Margaret had politely declined Jonathan's earlier requests to come but now, for this emergency, she made the trip. She moved in with Jon and his newborn son, Samuel, in the apartment on Gramercy North. She took care of the baby while Jon was at work, an arrangement that worked well for both grandmother and grandson. But Mary-Margaret worried about her son's continued melancholy. After a year, she suggested he try to meet a new girl, but he claimed to be too busy with work.

Mary-Margaret could not bear the thought of being separated from her son and new grandson, so she convinced her oldest daughter,

Deidre, and her husband, Seamus, along with their two small children, to move across the Atlantic. Jonathan bought two spacious, four-bedroom homes in a new section of Brooklyn and suddenly he found himself surrounded by family. This had to be good for him, Mary-Margaret thought. But still he buried himself in his work and refused to date – or even meet – any new ladies. His mother longed for the time when she would see real happiness on her only son's face.

Seamus was immediately put to work at Jonathan's speakeasy in the Battery. Like his brother-in-law, Seamus started out carrying ice and cleaning tables. He learned the business quickly and was soon able to run the place. Within nine months the managers in each of the four pubs reported to Seamus. It was good for both business and the family.

Jonathan needed to expand northward. Just as the midtown market had yielded greater gambling revenue for Max, so would it be a lucrative liquor outlet. The two new locations Jonathan had found were perfect. Both of them were back, off the street, accessible only through an alley so that entrance and exit could be easily controlled, and they were within easy walking distance of the office buildings and hotels of mid-Manhattan. Jon was confident of success.

Of course, he knew local police as well as the feds would become aware of the new pubs in the neighbourhood. It was unavoidable. But he knew with equal certainty that law enforcement would never present a problem. Max would spread the exact combination of money, favours and threats to keep the cops off their backs.

In three months, business at both bars was booming. Businessmen and lawyers crowded in for a quick one before commuting home, and theatre patrons stopped by after a Broadway show. A group of regulars formed, men looking for good liquor and a friendly place to drink it. Jonathan could not have been more pleased.

On a Saturday night, the night it happened, Seamus Ryan was visiting one of the new bars. He lingered in the background, observing how the waitresses treated the customers, how long it took patrons to receive service, how familiar the bartenders were with the regulars. He also observed the door, a heavy steel affair with a six-inch square peep manned by a husky doorman who checked out each visitor before granting admission.

Just after three in the morning, when only a small contingent of stragglers and hardcore drinkers still remained, four newcomers came through the front door. Each man wore a long overcoat despite the mild weather outside, and each one looked carefully around the entire bar as they entered. To Seamus, they stood out from the leisure-class swells who normally showed up at that time of night.

His instincts were quickly borne out as each of the four men pulled a twelve-gauge shotgun from under his long coat. One of the four fired his weapon straight up into the ceiling, creating a deafening roar that was followed by a hollow ringing silence, all conversation and movement having come to an abrupt halt.

"This joint is officially out of business," the man yelled. He pumped the twelve gauge, swung it toward the bar, and let loose another round. He was far enough away that the pellets blasted a three-foot area, shattering the mirror and every neatly stacked bottle. A few of the pellets struck the bartender in the shoulder; he hadn't jumped out of the way quickly enough. Screaming, he grabbed for the place he'd been hit, blood spouting through his fingers.

It was over in less than ten minutes. The men were professionals who moved rapidly through the establishment, using their shotguns at close range to destroy countertops, furniture and plumbing, as well as the inventory in the small storage room. When they were done they left just as calmly as they'd entered. The remaining customers, badly shaken, waited a safe interval, then fled.

The intruder was right, Seamus thought. *This bar is officially closed.*

CHAPTER THIRTY-SEVEN

"How's the bartender doing?" Max asked. They were seated in Max's living room and Jon had recounted the events of the previous evening. Their other new speakeasy had been hit at exactly the same time as the first, also by four men with shotguns. The damage at the second bar had been equally devastating, but at least no one had been hurt.

"He won't be doing any heavy lifting for a while but he'll be okay."

Max nodded and said, "Good," then paused for a moment. "From what Seamus said, they must have paid off your doorman to let them in. Same scenario for the second hit."

"So you'll start with the doormen?"

"Yeah, but I have a pretty good idea who we're looking for."

"Really?" Jon sounded surprised. "How could you already know that?"

"You've got competition in the area. Chances are that's who hit you."

"Yes, of course. But there must be ten or twelve pubs around midtown. How could you know which one is responsible?"

"We'll start with the doormen, and see where we get," Max said without answering Jonathan's question.

The first doorman in question, the one Seamus had seen, was a middle-aged former heavyweight boxer named Francis McQuirk. In his younger days, McQuirk had fought in most of the clubs and arenas in the tristate area, always appearing on the undercard, never coming close to the big time. Still, for fifteen years he'd managed to eke out a living as a professional boxer, working just a few odd jobs to help put food on the table and pay the rent.

He'd been savvy enough to quit before getting his brains knocked out, and had managed to pick up some real money by placing bets through proxies, then taking a fall when he was the favourite to win. He'd gotten away with it, none of the money boys having realised that he'd played them for suckers. The trick was that he always went down hard, appearing to fight like a wounded tiger, looking so bloody and bruised that no one believed he was faking it.

But this latest gig was a lot easier than taking punches in the face. All he'd had to do was let some guys into the bar he was working, guys that he might have let in anyway. McQuirk had worked as a doorman or bouncer in various clubs and bars during most of the ten years following his retirement from boxing. Of course, he was accustomed to taking a few clams under the table to let someone into a club or to the front of a line. All doormen did it. But this was the first time anyone had offered him serious money to ease the way.

One thousand dollars. It was a bigger payday than he'd ever gotten boxing, almost as much as he'd make in two years as a doorman. With that kind of money involved, he knew these guys weren't coming in to read poetry, knew it could backfire, but who could resist a windfall like that? He even liked Seamus, the fella who ran the bar. But hell, it wasn't like he had any real stake in the place. There were several bars in the area and he'd picked up a similar job a few blocks away. It had worked out fine.

McQuirk's new place of employment turned out to be a little closer to his walk-up flat. He enjoyed the short walk home at four o'clock in the morning, when the streets were deserted and quiet. He was a large and strong man accustomed to dealing with rowdy customers. The early morning darkness held no demons for Francis McQuirk.

The small, wiry man slipped smoothly out of the doorway of a darkened restaurant on 43rd, just as McQuirk strolled past. Lost in his thoughts, the former boxer became aware of someone near him only a heartbeat before the hard round steel of a gun barrel was stuck into his right kidney. "Get into the car," McQuirk heard the man say in the dark. He glanced to the side and saw a black sedan parked at the curb. The utter surprise of the encounter unnerved Francis McQuirk and he moved obediently toward the sedan. The little man glided along in perfect step as McQuirk walked to the car, keeping the gun barrel pressed painfully into his back.

Climbing into the rear seat through the open car door, McQuirk found himself sitting next to a large man, larger even than himself. The man had a bullet-shaped head and was holding an imposing black revolver that McQuirk judged to be a .45. The little guy slammed the rear door shut, then walked around the car and slipped quickly behind the wheel. The engine was already running. He hit the gas and they drove off.

The car turned down Broadway until it reached Little Italy, then veered off into a maze of side streets, finally coming to a stop in front of a large warehouse. The little man hopped out and opened McQuirk's door, motioning at him with his gun to get out. McQuirk did so while the big man who had been sitting next to him got out of his own door, walking quickly around to join them. "Move inside," the bullet-headed man rasped, waving his gun toward the warehouse. McQuirk obeyed, and as he stepped through the door of the building, a searing flash of pain exploded at the back of his head.

McQuirk never completely lost consciousness. Everything around him just became very hazy and moved very slowly with no real shape or form. When his vision finally cleared and he was once again aware of his surroundings, he found himself sitting in a high-backed metal chair. He tried to stand but couldn't. His hands were strapped to the armrests and his ankles were bound in what looked like prison shackles attached to the legs of the chair. The metal shackles dug into his flesh because his shoes and socks had been removed, so his feet were bare against the cold cement floor. McQuirk knew that hours must have passed because dawn light streamed through the skylight in the roof. When they had forced him into the car it had been pitch dark.

It was the big bullet-headed one who spoke. "We need for you to tell us who paid you to let those guys into the bar the other night."

"I got no idea what you're talking about," McQuirk said.

"Would be better for you if you told us," the big man responded.

These guys got no clue who they're dealing with, McQuirk thought. *I made my living by taking pain, and they think they'll just slap me around and get me to talk.* Out loud, he said, "I'm telling you, nobody paid me nothing."

The big man shrugged, then stepped back as the little guy moved forward. In his hand was a short-handled ax. McQuirk's face blanched when he saw it, but he managed to put on a brave front. "What're you gonna do? Chop my head off? I won't be able to tell you a thing then."

The little man did not respond. He stepped close to McQuirk, in front and slightly to his side, then bent over and swung the ax in a quick arc. The blade sliced neatly through the little toe of Francis McQuirk's bare left foot.

McQuirk stared, opened mouthed, down at his foot. Amazingly, the little toe had been chopped off so skillfully that the digit next to it was not touched. "Holy Mother," he said. "Look what you did." He continued staring, as if he could not believe what he saw.

"Tell us," he heard the big man rasp.

But McQuirk was still looking down at his foot. Blood was gushing from the place where his toe had been, but it was surprisingly painless. "Fuck you," he said. "Just fuck you."

At that, the big man nodded to the little man, who once again swung the ax in its deadly arc. More blood gushed upward as a second toe, immediately adjacent to the first, was severed from the foot. This time McQuirk screamed, a loud, harsh wail, as a wounded animal might make. Then he yelled, "Stop this! You're crazy. Both of you."

The bullet-headed man spoke. "We'll do all your toes, then your fingers, then what's left of your feet, then your hands." He said it in a matter-of-fact voice, as if discussing the weather or the score of a baseball game.

Suddenly, McQuirk was feeling light-headed, the result of shock and blood loss. He blurted out, "But not if I talk. If I talk, you'll stop." His voice sounded desperate and pained.

"Yes."

"Okay. It was Bob Duncan. He's the guy who owns the bar where I work now. He paid me to let those guys in. I didn't know what they were going to do. I mean, he didn't pay me direct. A guy who works for him came to me. But if nobody had paid me anything, I might have let them in. They looked all right." He looked again at his newly deformed foot. "Get me something to stop the bleeding."

James Becker, the large man with the bullet head, nodded. "Yeah, that's what Mr. Zalensky figured."

"You gotta do something to stop this bleeding," McQuirk said again. "I told you what you want."

"Okay," Becker said. "I've got something for that right here," and he walked toward McQuirk while reaching into his pants pocket.

When he got within a few feet of the seated man, he pulled his hand free, a .22 calibre revolver snug in his vast grip. Becker shot Francis McQuirk from close range, putting a neat hole directly over his nose and between his eyes. McQuirk's head snapped back, then lolled to the side, his tongue hanging out of his mouth and his eyes wide open.

The little man, Dominick Pastorini, spoke to Becker. "What're we supposed to do with the body?"

"Nothing," Becker replied. "We leave him right where he is."

"Won't Zalensky want it cleaned up?" The small man pulled a watch from his pocket and glanced at it. "Guys'll be showing up for work soon."

Becker was already heading for the door. "This ain't Zalensky's warehouse," he said. "It belongs to Bob Duncan, the guy that McQuirk was working for."

"Holy shit! You're telling me Zalensky already knew who was behind the whole thing?"

"No," Becker replied tersely. "He didn't know. He thought. He needed us to find out for sure. He delivers liquor to this place. I paid the night guard to go away and leave me a key. Zalensky just figured it was Duncan."

Pastorini stared at Becker. "Zalensky must be pretty damn good at figuring."

Becker grunted. "Yeah. You could say that."

CHAPTER THIRTY-EIGHT

They finished filming on Saturday afternoon, exactly as Duke had predicted, so Sophie spent that evening playing with Jacob. He was the joy of her life, and now that the shoot was over she looked forward to spending more time with him. Nevertheless, on Sunday morning she told Mrs. Goldberg that she was going to visit a friend and might not be back until the next day. Along with the change of clothes that Duke had told her to bring for after riding, Sophie packed an overnight kit.

Duke lived in Santa Monica, a coastal community directly west of Los Angeles, straight out Wilshire Boulevard toward the ocean. Half a mile from the beach they turned north on Lincoln Street, an unpaved lane that led to a cluster of sprawling ranch houses.

Duke's house was set back from the street, surrounded by a tall, ivy-covered fence with a wrought-iron gate, where a guard in a dark business suit stood sentry. As Sophie's car drove up the circular drive, Duke stepped out the front door and waved. He had advised her to wear old, comfortable clothes, not too light in case it was cold at the beach, and not so loose as to whip about in the wind. She had on tight cotton slacks and an equally tight beige sweater.

Duke hugged her, then, watching the chauffeured Cadillac pull away, said, "Did Louis give you a big advance on future roles? Never known him to do that."

Sophie laughed and said, "No, that doesn't sound like Louis." Then, in a more serious tone, she said, "You said you wanted to know more about me. I'm a widow. My husband died two years ago. He was a successful businessman and left me enough money to live comfortably."

"I'm sorry," Duke said. "That must have been very hard."

Sophie nodded. "It was horrible. I guess I just wanted to run away, put it all behind me. So I came out here."

"It must be lonely, after living all your life in New York. Or do you have family in Los Angeles?"

Sophie appeared to hesitate a moment before responding. "When my husband died, I was pregnant with our son, Jacob. He's with me. And I brought the woman who worked as my babysitter when I was a child, the person who raised me. I never knew my real mother. The two of them are really all the family I have."

There was a pause before Duke said, "There really is more to you than meets the eye."

"And does the fact that I'm a widow and have a child scare you?"

"Hardly," Duke responded. "Just makes me jealous. I'd love to have a son. Never got that lucky."

"Why not? I'm sure you know how it's done, growing up around animals as you did."

Duke grinned. "I guess I just never met the right woman." And then, dourly, "After a bad marriage, I was probably a little gun shy."

Sophie nodded. "If you're nice to me, I'll introduce you to Jacob."

"I'm sure that would be quite a treat."

"Yes, it would," she said. "But first, you have to give me my riding lesson."

Duke fitted the bridle and saddle for her, then adjusted the stirrups. He lifted her up onto the pony, his big hands around her waist, as if her weight were inconsequential. Then he double-checked everything before climbing up onto his own horse, which was waiting patiently just a few paces behind.

He trotted up next to her and instructed, "Just hitch the reins and kick both heels into her, easy like, when you want her to go. Pull back when you want her to stop. We'll go nice and slow, but you can still get pretty sore the first time. Try to hold on with your knees as much as you can, let them absorb the shock."

"Okay," she said, feeling very high off the ground and sounding nervous. "Just don't leave me."

The cowboy star grinned and affected his best Western drawl. "Now don't worry your pretty head, ma'am. Ah'd never do that."

"Good. These things are a lot taller when you're on top of one."

They headed north for half a mile, then down into a canyon. Sophie felt a little anxious as they headed downhill, but Duke was right in front of her so her horse couldn't run and they maintained a slow gait just as he had promised. Suddenly the canyon swerved left and as they turned the corner, white sand and blue ocean spread out below the cliffs.

"Oh," she exclaimed, "it's gorgeous."

Duke nodded, grinning back at her.

They continued down the hill to the two-lane highway that ran the entire California coast. No cars were in sight and they crossed over to the sand, then down to the water. They rode side by side across the sand, Sophie's horse instinctively staying even with Duke's. The tide was out, the sand hard packed and almost flat by the ocean's edge.

Duke turned to face her. "You're doing good. Feel confident enough to pick up the speed a little?"

Sophie nodded. "I think so. As long as it's not too fast."

"Okay," Duke said. "Just start off like before, hitching the reins and kicking with your heels. As you want to go faster, lean a little forward and kick her a little more, or whip the reins. She'll understand you, plus she'll just naturally want to keep up with my horse."

They started off at a walk, then sped up to a trot, then a fast canter. Sophie barely had to shake the reins to get her horse to go faster, the mare eager to keep up with Duke's roan. The horse's hooves thudded into the sand just below the surface of the water, the ocean sprayed up against Sophie's boots and ankles, and the wind lifted her hair and cooled her face as they rode. It was incredibly exhilarating and exciting, and yet peaceful. After a half-mile Duke reined his horse to a halt, and Sophie pulled up beside him.

"Enjoying yourself?" he asked.

"It's wonderful!"

Duke smiled broadly. "You're a natural, but you're still going to be pretty sore if we go much longer. We ought to head back."

"Can we go back through the water? Maybe a little faster this time?

Duke laughed. "Have to go that direction anyway."

When they arrived back at the house, Duke helped Sophie down from her mount, gently lowering her to the ground. She watched while he rubbed down the horses and fired up an outdoor barbeque pit. The sun was just beginning to set as Duke finished cooking their steaks. They ate on an outside patio, looking up at the Santa Monica Mountains. Duke loaned her a huge Irish knit sweater to fend off the chill. Sophie could not think of a time she had felt more content. If Jacob were there, it would have been perfect.

After the sun set, Duke suggested they go inside.

"I've been waiting to see how the world's most famous cowboy lives," Sophie said lightly.

Duke shrugged. "Hope you're not disappointed."

The living room was furnished in early colonial, as was the large dining room, the library and both guest rooms, with hardwood floors throughout. "It's quite elegant," Sophie said.

"You sound surprised."

"I guess I expected more of a Western motif."

"Well, my bedroom is more reflective of that side of me," he said, and then, with a smile, added, "but most of my guests never get to see it."

"I bet you say that to every woman who tells you that you're the handsomest man she's ever seen."

It was a large room and was, in fact, furnished in Western motif. There was a four-poster wrought-iron bed, a small fireplace, and an old, worn, leather saddle mounted on one wall over a rolltop desk.

"There must be something special about that saddle," Sophie said.

Duke turned to face her directly. "You're the first person who's ever realised that. Everybody else just figures it's part of the theme."

"Was it a prize in a rodeo?"

"Nothing that exciting," Duke replied. "But it was the first saddle I ever owned."

"And you still have it."

"I worked an entire summer to earn the money for it. I was twelve. Before that, I just rode with a blanket under me, or bareback. I was the first in my family to actually own my own saddle. My father didn't even have one."

"How did he feel about you owning one?"

"Like I said, I'd worked all that summer, milking cows for some neighbours. The neighbours were old, in their seventies. Their children had moved to the city and they couldn't handle all the work themselves. The money I made was to help pay for household expenses. Every dime I earned, I turned over to my dad. He would use the money to help pay for food and such."

"When we'd go to the general store to buy groceries, I'd always run my hand over this saddle they had for sale. It was sitting over a barrel, right by the men's clothing section. Sometimes, when no one was looking, I'd hop up and sit on it. Of course, you weren't supposed to do that. At the end of that summer, my dad made some excuse, then went to the store without me. When he came home, he had it with him. He had put aside all the money I'd given him and used it to buy me that saddle."

"That's a wonderful story," Sophie said. "And he sounds like a wonderful man."

Duke nodded. "He was. Or at least I thought so. I never knew my mother. She left us when I was a baby. My world sort of revolved around my dad."

"Does he still live in Colorado?"

Duke shook his head. "He died when I was eighteen. Heart attack. So after that I was on my own. Guess that's one reason I got married so young."

They were silent for a moment, then Duke asked, "How about you? You said you were raised by a babysitter. What about your parents?"

Sophie turned away from him and looked toward the fireplace in the corner. "We're similar in one respect," she said. "My mother also left when I was a baby. Like you, I never knew her. But my father was not so wonderful a man as yours."

"And that's why you married so young?"

The question hung in the air, but Sophie did not answer. She continued to stare into the corner and finally asked, "Does it work?"

"The fireplace? Of course."

"Then let's make a fire." There was wood already in the fireplace and paper and matches on a shelf next to it. Without any help from Duke, Sophie arranged the sticks into a square sort of chimney configuration, placed paper in the middle and lit it.

"It will be a lot nicer if we turn off the lights," she said. Obligingly, Duke flipped off the light switch. The fire silhouetted his tall frame as she approached him.

She reached up and drew his face to hers, then kissed him long and passionately. He kissed her back, but she sensed hesitancy, almost nervousness on his part. No matter, she unbuttoned his shirt, kissing his bare chest as she did so. She slipped off her clothes and pressed herself against him, feeling his heartbeat against her chest. Concentrating on what she was doing, she used both hands to undo his large belt and unbutton his pants. Then with one hand she caressed him, felt him grow hard to her touch. When he became fully erect she took his hand and walked him to the bed.

His hand stroked her upper leg, then her hip, then moved to her breast, all the while his lips hard against hers. His large fingers traced gentle circles around her taut nipples, then moved between her legs with a surprisingly light touch. As she became aroused, she reached for him. But to her surprise he had become flaccid, his tumescence withered almost completely. With no discernable hesitation she took him in hand again, caressing him until it became clear to both of them that her best efforts would prove unsuccessful.

"I'm, sorry," he said, obviously embarrassed. "You're truly the most beautiful woman I've ever been with. I don't know what the hell is the matter with me lately."

Sophie put her finger on his lips, and then kissed him. "It's not important. I just want to be here with you." He started to speak but she stopped him with another kiss.

They lay together without speaking, Sophie's head resting on his chest. When his breathing grew shallower, and she realised he was asleep, she once again reached between his legs, stroking him with a touch so feathery it was barely perceptible. As she felt him respond she applied slightly more pressure while elongating the strokes, causing him to grow larger and harder. Soon, he was fully erect, coming awake as she kissed him. She pulled him on top of her, guiding him inside, their bodies moving together in an unhurried rhythm. She came once, right before she felt him explode, and then again as he remained inside her.

Afterward, as they lay together, he kissed her gently. "Thank you," he said quietly.

Sophie smiled in the dark. "It was my pleasure." Soon, she fell asleep, still in his arms.

CHAPTER THIRTY-NINE

Max had been fairly sure who was responsible for the attack on Jonathan's new bar. But he was a man who liked to be certain, as Francis McQuirk might have attested to if he were still alive. Max's suspicion had been based on simple fact: Bob Duncan owned seven of the eleven bars in the midtown area. Max knew this because he supplied all seven with booze, sometimes delivering directly to the speakeasies, sometimes to the warehouse that now held McQuirk's corpse. Duncan was known to be an aggressive competitor, and this was not the first time he had resorted to violence to eliminate a rival. But he had no idea that he had entered a whole new level of play.

Duncan lived in a sufficiently violent world to justify two permanent bodyguards on his payroll. They were experienced men in their thirties, both having served as infantrymen in the Great War, then as bouncers at speakeasies in Brooklyn, then enforcers for a loan shark in Queens, now as hired muscle for Duncan.

It was the best job either man had ever had. Duncan paid well and the work was rarely arduous. Some days they sat around his huge brownstone in Tribeca, drinking beer and reading magazines, and some days they shot up some competitor's bar like they had the previous week. But most of the time they followed Bob on his rounds, making sure no one gave him any trouble. That's what they were doing now, after a clerk at the warehouse had called, jabbering about a dead body. Bob was in a hurry to see what the hell was going on and his bodyguards were being extra vigilant because they knew that when he was in a hurry he could get careless. Each man kept his hand on the pistol concealed under his coat as they stepped out of the Lincoln sedan.

Duncan made his way to the door of the warehouse, sandwiched between the two bodyguards. His rap on the door was answered by a nervous voice from inside. "Who's there?"

"Who do you think? Open the goddamn door."

The door opened, revealing the warehouse foreman, Ralph Turner, who was so nervous that he was sweating, despite the cold of the warehouse. *Dead bodies must give this guy the willies*, Duncan thought as he walked through the door.

"Where is he?"

Turner, too upset to speak, just pointed into the building and to his right. Duncan and the two bodyguards headed in the direction he'd indicated. The door closed behind them, revealing the two men lying in wait, faces covered by ski masks. The men, one large, one small, stepped away from the wall, dark steel Colts held in outstretched firing position.

Bob Duncan and his two bodyguards, their attention already focused on the dead body seated in front of them, never had a chance. The shots came with a rapid *pop, pop, pop*, sending the three sprawling face first onto the concrete floor. The two killers swiftly descended, firing a second bullet into the back of each man's skull. Bits of brain and bone splattered onto the cement, followed immediately by huge pools of blood.

Ralph Turner screamed when the shooting started and now, staring down at the corpses, a gasping sound bubbled from his throat, almost as if he were finding it difficult to breathe. The bigger assassin turned to him and said, "When you stop pissing your pants, you can go untie your friends." He motioned toward the four warehousemen tied up in the back room. The masked men had been hiding in that room when Ralph and his co-workers arrived that morning, and had taken them by surprise.

The big killer was staring right at him and Ralph realised he was waiting for a response. He croaked out a weak, "Okay," nodding his head as he spoke. At that, James Becker and Dominick Pastorini walked out the front door, removed their ski masks and strolled to their car a few blocks away.

★　★　★

Four people were seated at a table that could have accommodated fifteen: the widow, Mrs. Robert Duncan, her two lawyers, and Max

Zalensky. They were in the law offices of Hannity and Cooney, who represented Mrs. Duncan. The widow was a middle-aged woman who had been pretty twenty years earlier, when she married Robert Duncan. But two decades with a violent and philandering husband had left her worn down and exhausted. Now all she wanted was to liquidate whatever cash she could from her husband's life's work and move far away, perhaps to Florida or California.

The marriage had proven childless and her only real friend, her mother, had succumbed to tuberculosis the previous winter. The death of her husband, horrible as it was, was not an unwelcome event. She was not too old to start a new life; maybe even a new romance, hopefully with a kinder and gentler, perhaps younger, man. A windfall of money could certainly pave the way to this new beginning.

"It's a very fair offer," she heard the man named Max Zalensky say. Mrs. Duncan looked at her lawyer, who nodded. Since the actual business in question was illegal, the exact nature of that business was not named in the sale. Instead, what changed hands were leasing rights, building improvements, furniture, and unnamed inventory. If her attorney felt this was a fair offer, then Mrs. Duncan was inclined to sell. The fact that this Zalensky person might be the very man responsible for her husband's murder would not stand in the way of Mrs. Duncan's best interests.

"Then it's settled," she heard Michael Hannity say. "The assets named will transfer to Mr. Zalensky for the agreed upon price, effective the first of next month."

"Actually," Max interjected, "I am only an agent for the buyer. Of course, I have full power of attorney and can consummate the transaction right now. But it will not be my name on the Deed of Trust."

"Oh," said Mr. Hannity, as this was news to him. "Who then, is the actual buyer of Mr. Duncan's estate?"

"That would be my client, Jonathan Cahill," said Max Zalensky. And with that, hands were shaken, papers drawn up, and everyone at the table was satisfied.

CHAPTER FORTY

In the morning, Virgilio came to pick Sophie up. After a long kiss, Duke said he would call her, words she knew he had probably spoken to many young Hollywood hopefuls, young women who, like her, had idolised him when they were teenagers.

But the following evening, true to his word, he did call. "I'm hoping you're up for another ride," he said. "If you drive over tomorrow before lunch, we could have a picnic on the beach."

"I'd love to." Sophie was almost gushing. "But I need to spend some time with Jacob. I was planning to take him to the park tomorrow."

"Bring him along. He'll have a great time," Duke's deep voice boomed enthusiastically.

"He's not old enough to ride a horse," Sophie said. "He's only been walking for six months. Maybe we should wait a few days, and then I'll be able to come alone."

"You promised I could meet him, if I was nice. I'm holding you to your word."

"I'd love for you to meet him," she protested. "I'm just not sure about putting him on a horse."

Sophie could feel Duke's grin across the wire. "Back in Colorado, people used to say 'old enough to walk, old enough to ride'. I've got an old saddle that'll fit him just fine. He'll be as safe as in his bed back home. If it doesn't look that way to you, we'll just have our picnic right here at my house."

"Okay," Sophie said hesitantly. "As long as we have a backup plan, I'm sure everything will be fine."

★   ★   ★

Taking along a sixteen-month-old was a bit of a production, requiring bottles, diapers and changes of clothes. But when they arrived at his house the next day, Duke appeared unperturbed. As the Cadillac pulled up to the front of his house he bounded out to the car and opened the back door. Before Sophie could object, Duke lifted Jacob out of the car and held him outstretched, straight overhead, then back down against a broad shoulder. To Sophie's surprise Jacob appeared delighted, squealing with laughter, then gurgling happily as he was held over the tall man's shoulder.

"Come on, Jake," Duke said to the toddler. "Let's show your mommy your new ride."

With Duke happily carrying Jacob, the three of them walked to the edge of the property where the two horses were tied to a hitching post. Atop Duke's roan were two saddles: Duke's Mexican, and in front of it, a small, infant-size version. The small saddle had high, padded leather sides and small leg holes at the bottom. Duke lifted Jacob into the saddle and placed a tiny set of reins into his hands. Instinctively, Jacob clutched them tightly.

"I had that saddle made special for my cousin Sarah's son," Duke explained. "He's outgrown it, but we used it a lot when he was Jacob's age and he loved it."

Sophie had been walking alongside, anxiously checking Jacob's reaction to this new experience. "You're batting a thousand so far," she said.

They took the same trail to the beach as they had a few days earlier, and again Duke led the way. He rode easily, one hand on the reins and one on the little saddle nestled in front of him. Sophie was much more at ease on a horse than she had been her first time, and Jacob seemed to instinctively feel safe with Duke. Sophie was beginning to feel that way herself.

When the trail ended they crossed the narrow highway to the beach and rode slowly across the broad expanse of sand to the water's edge. Duke halted the horses and said, "Okay, Jake, now you're in for a real treat."

The tall man swung down from the horse, removed his boots and socks, and rolled his pant legs halfway up his calf. He did the same for Jacob before lifting him down from his perch, then walked him down to where the sand became wet. Duke's large hand engulfed one of Jacob's small ones and the two of them stood together, side by side, facing the vast ocean.

"Great, isn't it?" Duke said to the toddler. "That first feel of your bare feet on wet sand. You can kind of squish it between your toes."

At that moment a wave crashed twenty feet in front of them and water raced up the sand to bury their feet. But just as it reached them, Duke scooped Jacob up and ran back up the beach, avoiding the oncoming wave. Jacob squealed with delight. As the ocean receded, Duke put him down again and they walked, hand in hand, back to the water's edge. They repeated this routine over and over, alternately chasing and running away from the waves. Several times, the rushing water overlapped their bare feet, but Duke always scooped Jacob up out of harm's way before it got any higher.

After ten minutes Duke was exhausted, but Jacob didn't want to stop and pulled with all his might, his little hand wrapped around the actor's index finger. Eventually Duke acquiesced, racing with the toddler one last time, holding him above the water before sitting down heavily on the sand, his legs splayed out flat in a V, facing the ocean.

Jacob, who had been set down a few feet away, waddled over and plopped himself down between Duke's legs, the back of his head resting against the tall man's stomach. They sat like that, silently, watching waves crash against the beach while Sophie took a blanket out of her saddlebag, spread it on the sand and laid out the fried chicken, fruit, cheese and wine that she had packed earlier, along with a fresh bottle of milk for her son.

When he finished his bottle, Sophie showed her son the sand toys that she had brought along for his first day at the beach. She demonstrated how to use the little pail and shovel, as well as the cookie-cutter implements that could make star and circle shapes in the sand. The toddler played contentedly while Sophie and Duke feasted on their picnic. "My cousin's son didn't use tools like that until he was a year or two older than Jake," Duke commented. "He's a smart little boy."

"Of course he is," his mother agreed.

On the ride back, Jacob fell asleep. His saddle held him upright while his head rested against Duke's stomach. When they arrived at the stable he was still asleep. "I need to put him down in a crib, and he'll be hungry when he wakes up. I don't have any more food for him here," Sophie said. "It's been wonderful, but I think we're going to have to head home."

Duke nodded, but disappointment showed on his face. "I was hoping you could both stay longer, but I understand. This was the best time I've had in a long time."

Sophie nodded and said, "A very long time." She tilted up her mouth to kiss him tenderly, then held him for a moment with her head resting on his chest.

★   ★   ★

He called the next afternoon. "I bought a crib today," he told her. "I've got it in the second guest room, along with some stuffed animals and toys. So the next time you and Jacob come, you can both stay overnight."

Sophie could hear nervousness in Duke's voice, as if he were a schoolboy worried about rejection.

"That's very thoughtful of you. I think Jacob would love that." She could almost feel his smile over the phone line. "And so would I."

CHAPTER FORTY-ONE

"You're leaving me?" Tony screamed the words, his face reddening. "For that cowboy? You think you can just sleep your way to the top?"

After her conversation with Duke, she'd had Virgilio drive her to Tony's house, but she already regretted her decision to tell him in person.

"It's not like that," Sophie said defensively. "He likes me for who I am."

Tony scoffed. "Maybe he likes who he thinks you are. From what I've read, they all think you're some kind of English royalty."

"He knows me better than you do," Sophie said in a steely voice. "He knows where I'm from and he knows I have a son."

Tony was taken aback and for a moment looked truly surprised. But he quickly recovered. "I figured you had a family, probably a rich old man."

"But you didn't know, and didn't care to know. All you wanted was me in your bed."

He scoffed again. "You think he wants anything more than that? You think any of us do?" His face was still red, his voice dripping with anger and sarcasm.

"He wants much more than that," she said evenly, trying to control her temper. "You don't know me and you are not capable of seeing beyond your own selfish desires. But he is."

"You're such a hypocrite," he said, some of the anger leaving him. "Are you pretending you wanted anything from me other than a good lay?"

"Of course I did," she said, "but you're incapable of giving it. Now that I've found someone who is, I don't need you."

Hostility burned on his face, and she realised too late how cruel her words were.

"You're right," she said, gently. "I wanted a physical relationship as well. It's just as much my fault that nothing more came of it." But her words did nothing to soften the rage etched on his face and she knew she needed to get away. "I've got to go," she said. "I'm sorry." With that, she turned and hurried out the door without looking back.

"This isn't the last you'll hear of me," he said, but quietly, so she did not hear.

★　　★　　★

At first they just spent weekends together, a complete little family, returning to their respective homes during the week. But the weekends soon stretched into Mondays and then Tuesdays, and eventually they were spending more time together than apart. They usually stayed at Sophie's house because it was bigger and had space for all of Jacob's things, as well as bedrooms for Mrs. Goldberg and Virgilio. And because Duke understood that she was more comfortable in her own home than moving into one owned by a man.

After five months, they decided that Duke would move most of his clothes out of his house and into Sophie's large bedroom closet. A day later he hauled his favourite reading chair, his old desk, and a stack of books into the empty guestroom down the hall from their bedroom. On the wall of the little room, he hung the old, worn, leather saddle.

Little Jacob was delighted with the new arrangement. Almost two years old now, he could walk, run, and even climb up and down the stairs with ease. He relished sitting on Duke's lap when he was reading the newspaper. Jacob would bring a favourite toy, haul it up on the chair with him, sit between the tall man's legs and play while Duke continued to read.

The World War movie *Over There*, starring Duke Hawkins and directed by Clarence Rollins, had come to movie theatres all over America, and it was a solid success. And the fact that tabloids and gossip columns were trumpeting the news that Mr. Hawkins had taken up with his beautiful co-star, Susan Spencer, wasn't hurting business.

Still, when Duke asked Sophie to marry him, she refused. She had been married before, she explained, and it had ended badly. She was happy with the arrangement they had. In fact, living in her house in the hills with Duke and Jacob and Mrs. Goldberg was probably the happiest time of her young life. She saw no reason to complicate things.

With the success of *Over There*, Duke got right to work on his next movie. Louis Kahn believed in striking while the iron was hot, and did not wish to waste his star's resurgent popularity. Duke wasn't happy that the work intruded on his new family life, but Sophie understood and was even supportive of Kahn's business motives. And despite his initial reticence, Duke seemed happy to be back on the job, trying to get back home in time to play with Jacob before bedtime, then having a late dinner with Sophie. They were indeed a happy family.

So it was a surprise, in the third week of filming, when Duke came home, obviously upset, and without so much as saying hello, stormed into his office and closed the door. This was so out of character that Sophie knew something was seriously amiss. She knocked on the office door and asked if he was okay. When he didn't respond, she knocked again, this time asking if she had done something wrong.

"No," came the muffled reply. "It's…. I just need some time to think."

Sophie, who had never seen him like this, decided the best course was to follow his wishes and made certain that Jacob did not interrupt him.

A short while later the telephone rang and Sophie rushed to grab it. There was an extension in Duke's office and, given his current mood, she did not want him bothered. But when she picked up the phone, she realised that he was an instant ahead of her and heard his angry, "This is Duke Hawkins."

A voice at the other end immediately responded with a slight laugh, and then, "So I take it you got my little package?" Sophie was shocked to recognise the resonant baritone of Tony Marston.

"Yes, I got it. Just what do you hope to gain by sending me such trash?"

"Trash?" Tony's voice exclaimed. "Those are high-quality prints, and the subject, I'm sure you'll agree, is quite beautiful."

Sophie felt a chill run through her. She kept the phone to her ear, almost without breathing.

"And most likely drugged," Duke retorted. "You worthless bag of filth!"

Without denying anything, Tony said, "A detail no one will

care about. Those photos will destroy her career and make you a laughingstock. That's all you need to be concerned with."

"How much?" Duke asked, his voice tight.

"We get right to it, don't we? Okay then. Ten grand, in cash. For a big star like you that's nothing. Tomorrow evening at your old house. I'll have the negatives as well, so you'll know you have everything."

"I'll be there. And it had better be the last time I hear from you." With that, Duke slammed down the phone. After a moment Sophie was aware of Tony putting his end down, neither man aware that she had been listening in.

★   ★   ★

Duke called the next evening, saying that he would not be home for dinner due to a late meeting. Sophie told Mrs. Goldberg that she was not sure when she would be back, and hurried out to the garage, where Virgilio was waiting. They drove straight to Duke's house in Santa Monica and up the gated driveway.

Both Tony's and Duke's cars were parked outside the house. She calmly sent Virgilio home, explaining that she would be returning with Mr. Hawkins. Then, unable to contain herself, she rushed inside the house. What she saw made her blood boil.

Duke was on the couch, Tony sitting across from him on the raised fireplace hearth. Nude photos of Sophie were spread out on the coffee table between them. Next to Tony was a brown manila envelope from which Sophie could see cash protruding.

In the photos she was lying on her back on Tony's living room sofa. Her hair was neatly combed to her shoulders, one arm extended carelessly behind her head, and it appeared that a small pillow was propped underneath her to arch her back. In the worst of the pictures her legs were spread wide, with Tony's face buried between them. In those pictures you could easily see her face, but only the back of Tony's head. In every picture her eyes were closed.

The two men had not expected her to be there and they were astonished by the extent of her anger. She walked within inches of Tony and screamed at him, "You drugged me," she said. "You took my clothes off and took your dirty pictures. Then you put my clothes back on so I wouldn't know."

"What do you mean dirty?" Tony said, his mouth in a slick smile. "These are works of art."

"That's a lie," she said, trembling with anger. "It's all about money for you, isn't it? Or do you just want to hurt me?"

Tony laughed contemptuously. "You're the one who hurt me, bitch. I had real feelings for you, and you up and left me for a bigger name. I'm just getting a little back is all."

Sophie slapped him across the face, unable to contain her anger a moment longer. One of her carefully manicured fingernails dragged across his cheek, scratching through the skin.

Tony's hand went to his cheek and felt a trickle of blood. He stood still for a moment, in shock from even this small damage to his face. Then a low, guttural sound came from his throat, and as Sophie stood glowering in front of him, he threw a roundhouse punch that landed on the side of her head. She staggered backward and collapsed onto the living room floor, arms and legs splayed outward.

Duke, who had watched the confrontation in silence, rose up with an animal instinct, stepped forward, and with the momentum of his large body struck Tony Marston with a perfect uppercut to the jaw. Tony flew straight backward, his feet leaving the floor, his eyes rolling backward in their sockets. He fell hard. The back of his head landed with a sharp crack on the polished marble of Duke's fireplace hearth.

Duke immediately turned his attention to Sophie, kneeling worriedly beside her.

"Are you all right?" he said, cradling her head in his hand.

"Yes, I think so," she responded. "I've never been punched before." And, in fact, she did seem fine, just badly shaken. A bluish bruise had formed on her cheek where Tony had struck her.

As she started to sit up, Duke watched her carefully. She suddenly bolted upright, her eyes wide with terror. "Oh my God," she said, and her hand flew to her mouth.

Duke turned, not knowing what to expect, senses on high alert. He followed her gaze to the worst sight he had ever seen: Tony lay flat on his back, an enormous pool of blood puddling the floor at the back his head.

"Oh God, no," Duke said softly. He got to his feet, forced himself to remain calm, and ripped off his white Western shirt. He knelt down and gently lifted Marston's head. He pressed the bunched-up shirt against the bloody wound at the back of Tony's skull. Almost immediately, the white cotton soaked through.

"There are towels in the bathroom," Duke said. Sophie went to get them, ignoring the unsteadiness in her legs. Duke took the towels when she returned, but each one soaked through in a matter of moments. The flow of blood would not stop. He looked up at Sophie, who shook her head, and he knew that it was hopeless.

Duke closed his eyes, opened them, and breathed out evenly. He looked at Sophie, who was crying. "I never meant for this to happen," he said. "I would never——"

"I know," Sophie said softly. "But it's done."

Duke nodded and said, "We need to call the police."

Sophie had not taken her eyes off of his, and again she shook her head.

"We need to call them," he repeated.

"It wasn't your fault. You defended me. You didn't mean to hurt anyone, just to protect me."

"I'm not ashamed of what I did," he said. "But it went wrong, and now I'll need to convince a jury."

"No, you won't. No one needs to know about this."

"Of course they do. It was an accident, but it happened. I'll take whatever punishment I've got coming."

Sophie took a breath. "If this goes to trial the pictures will come out and some people will say the whole thing was my fault. Maybe it was. And if you go to prison...." She stopped for a moment and composed herself. "I couldn't take it. I don't know what I'd do."

Duke stared at her for a moment, then nodded again. "So what are we going to do?"

"What we have to," she said.

They wrapped Tony's body in a blanket and carried it out to the stall where Duke kept his roan, where Sophie figured no one would ever look. It took hours to dig the grave. They took turns digging. Duke was much stronger but he tired easily, so Sophie made almost as much progress moving more slowly, but keeping at it longer. They tossed the body, still wrapped in the blanket, into the hole along with Duke's bloody shirt and towels. They spent several more hours cleaning up Duke's living room, scrubbed the floor and the hearth, then threw the rags and brushes into the grave atop the body and shovelled the dirt back into the hole.

When they'd finished tamping down the dirt, Sophie said, "Now we need to get rid of his car."

"Oh Jesus," Duke said. "I forgot all about it."

"I took the keys from his pocket," Sophie said, holding up the keys to the Model T. "You can drive it to Venice Beach and leave it on the street somewhere."

Duke shook his head. "I don't think I'm up to walking all the way back. And you can't drive. Are you going to call your chauffeur to pick me up?"

Sophie allowed herself a quick smile. "You're right, I can't drive a car. But I can ride a horse. You taught me."

They left just before sunrise, when the streets would be empty of anyone who might recognise the cowboy movie star, but with enough light in the sky to safely ride on the beach. Duke parked the Model T in Venice, near the beach, and left the keys in the ignition on the chance that someone would steal it. Sophie met him at the pier, riding her mare, leading Duke's roan behind her. They rode back to Duke's house without saying a word.

Inside, Duke slumped into the chair in his living room and closed his eyes. When he opened them, he said, "I was hoping it was all a bad dream, that I'd open my eyes and we'd be home in your bed."

Sophie just shook her head, so exhausted that it was difficult to keep her own eyes open.

"I don't know if we'll get away with this," Duke said. "But I sure don't want your life ruined because of something I did."

"It all happened because of me," she protested. "I was stupid enough to let him take advantage of me. You just protected me."

Duke looked at her. "People must have known you were with him. What if the police question you? You might have to tell them what happened."

Sophie shook her head. "I don't think anyone even knew about him and me. At least, I didn't tell anyone. And in any case, they can't make me testify against you."

"Of course they can," Duke responded. "Why would you think they can't?"

"Because a wife can't be made to testify against her husband."

Duke cocked his head at her, raising his eyebrows, sitting straight up in his chair.

"That is if you still want to marry me," she said.

"Of course, Susan, but that's a hell of a thing."

"Do you love me?"

"You know I do."

"Pretty soon," she said, "Jacob won't remember a time without you. He loves you and his life will be so much better with you in it."

"And you? Do you love me?"

"I do," she said. "More than you know."

Duke looked at her and sighed heavily. "I'm happy to have you any way I can. I just never thought it would be like this."

"Neither did I," she said. "But here we are."

She walked to his chair, leaned over and rubbed his cheek with her hand. Then she kissed him gently on the lips. "Right now, you need to drive us home. Jacob will be up and wondering where we are." With that, they returned to the house that would now, officially, be their home.

Later that morning, Virgilio drove her to Tony Marston's small bungalow off Doheny. She let herself in with another key that she had taken from the dead man's pocket. Duke may have been convinced that Tony was giving him a square deal but Sophie was not so trusting. The envelope Tony brought had been destroyed, but he could have made additional prints.

She found them in the first place she looked, the file cabinet in his little office off of the bedroom. There were ten copies: eight by tens, clear and sharp, really very good work. They would have provided Tony access to Duke's money for many years to come. Sophie put them in an envelope and walked out of the little house to the waiting Cadillac, hopeful that this would be the last time she ever had to deal with Mr. Tony Marston.

CHAPTER FORTY-TWO

Sy Glucksman, the twenty-nine-year-old writer of *Over There*, moved into one of the new apartment buildings on La Brea, in Hollywood, shortly after receiving his first studio paycheck. The building's primary attraction, at least for Glucksman, was a large swimming pool in a central courtyard with surrounding deck and lounge chairs. Struggling actresses, living two or three to an apartment, could routinely be observed lounging around the pool almost every afternoon and often into the evening.

Glucksman spent much of his time by the pool, usually with his Royal typewriter on a small table, pounding away at what he hoped would be his next hit screenplay. He had hoped to use the typewriter as a conversation piece, exciting the young ladies with his success in Hollywood, perhaps moving the discussion back to his apartment and into the bedroom. Unfortunately, while several of the women were curious about his work and even enjoyed discussing plot and script technique, they were uniformly unimpressed by his standing in the movie business.

It seemed that even the newest starlet wannabe, fresh off the train from Iowa, understood the lowly status of a writer in Hollywood; knew that her career could be better boosted by any casting agent or assistant director. So he was understandably excited when Susan Spencer, the gorgeous young actress who had played the romantic interest in *Over There*, called him at home. He had no idea that she knew his name, let alone that she would track down his phone number and ask him to lunch.

They met at an upscale coffee shop on Hollywood Boulevard, walking distance from the writer's apartment. Sophie guided the small talk, drawing out the shy Glucksman, listening with rapt attention to his story of growing up in Chicago, moving to Hollywood against the wishes of his father, who wanted his only son to join his law practice, and his unlikely dream of success in the movie business.

"Maybe it's not so unlikely," Sophie said. "I was impressed."

"Oh?" Glucksman responded. "By what?"

"By how quickly you wrote those extra scenes for my character. I thought they were quite good."

"Thanks. But a week to write three scenes is not particularly quick. Not by Hollywood standards."

"A week!" Sophie exclaimed. "Mr. Kahn told me about the additional scenes, or rather the possibility of additional scenes, a day before they were given to us."

Glucksman grinned. "Let me guess. He promised you a bigger part in return for…your favours?"

"You're right," she said, anger still apparent in her voice. "But he didn't get any favours."

"Good for you. He's pretty good at getting what he wants. He had me write those scenes as soon as he realised the story needed some more romance and that he had an actress who could pull it off." This last was said with a nod to Sophie.

"How much did you get?"

"What do you mean?"

"How much money were you paid for the extra work? Writing the additional material."

Glucksman shook his head. "It doesn't work like that. I get a flat fee of two thousand dollars for anything I write that the studio actually makes. For that money, I'm expected to be around for any changes that they make. It's not a bad living, but not a great one either. Of course, if you've had a hit or two in the past, your fee goes up. *Over There* will help me with that," he said with satisfaction.

Sophie nodded, listening intently as if everything the young man said was important. "I'm glad to know how it works, because I'd like to hire you."

Glucksman looked at her in surprise. "To do what?"

"To write a script for me. A drama that features a heroic man in his forties and a younger woman in her twenties. Duke Hawkins is the man. I am the young woman. Duke's character would be engaged in a struggle between his duty on one hand, and his love for my character on the other. I think a Western setting would work best for Duke. I'll give you your two thousand and then you can sell it to Kahn for whatever he'll pay you. Since you are getting paid twice it will be well worth your best effort. I think you are capable of writing something that will be remembered for many years."

"Miss Spencer," Glucksman replied, "you're the prettiest girl I've ever seen, and I'm thrilled to be having lunch with you. It's certainly possible that Louis Kahn would be receptive to the sort of story you're describing, so it may well be worth my time to write it. But two thousand dollars is more money than most folks make in a year. Are you sure this is something you want to commit to?"

Ignoring his question, Sophie said, "Then it's settled. I'll give you one thousand right now and the balance when you deliver. Duke will present the script to Mr. Kahn himself. I think that will give us more leverage."

Sophie then opened her purse and, to the young man's astonishment, pulled out what appeared to be a small stack of hundred dollar bills. The money was neatly tied with a red ribbon. She casually handed it across the table to Glucksman.

The young man stared at her, open mouthed, before taking the money and saying, "Sounds good to me."

"One last thing," Sophie said. "This arrangement is our secret."

"Of course it is," the writer replied, "since Mr. Hawkins doesn't know you're paying for this, does he?"

Sophie's eyes narrowed. "I'd like you to complete this in six weeks. Keep me updated on your progress." With that, she placed more money on the table to pay the bill, then stood up and walked out.

★   ★   ★

"Let me get this straight," Louis Kahn said to Duke Hawkins. "You're pitching me a script written by the Glucksman kid? Why the hell isn't he selling it himself? He's better at it than you are."

"Because I want the part. And I want Susan Spencer as the female lead. And you want me to sign an exclusive contract with Signature. It's all part of the same package."

"Okay," Kahn said. "I'll read it. But if the story's no good there's no deal, contract or no contract."

But the story was fantastic. That young writer must have found inspiration. It was a Western featuring an over the hill sheriff, middle aged and about to retire, who had just taken a young wife. On the eve of the sheriff's retirement, his town is threatened by a gang of desperadoes who demand a staggering ransom in exchange for not destroying the little settlement. The outlaws harass the women of the hamlet and stare lasciviously at the sheriff's pretty wife. The sheriff himself struggles between his duty to the town and a desperate desire to just take his bride and flee. Some of the townspeople turn on one another, willing to sacrifice their neighbours to save themselves. In the end, the sheriff valiantly stays and protects the town, aided by his brave wife.

Louis Kahn was thrilled when he finished reading. *We'll make millions on this*, he thought. *And Duke will be perfect for it.* He was looking like the old Duke now, walking and talking with that inner confidence Kahn had seen in the young cowboy years earlier. Obviously, schtupping the Spencer broad was doing him some good. Louis smiled to himself. Good for Duke.

CHAPTER FORTY-THREE

Los Angeles Examiner,
April 2nd, 1922, Hollywood, Ca.

Forty-two-year-old movie star Duke Hawkins married actress Susan Spencer, twenty-one, last Sunday at the Ambassador Hotel. The ceremony was attended by close friends and business associates. Mr. Hawkins will adopt Miss Spencer's child, a son from a previous marriage. The couple has asked that no photographs be taken of the child, in order to preserve his privacy. This newspaper will honour that request.

Los Angeles Police Detective Greyson Long motored his black and white Chevrolet 490 up Laurel Canyon Boulevard, past the Houdini estate, and turned onto a narrow, meandering road lined with tall hedges and gated driveways. Over the years, he'd found that a surprise visit was most effective for this sort of work, although it meant taking the chance that the subject wouldn't be home or available to talk. Still, the element of surprise was usually worth the risk.

A vehicle registered to one Anthony Marston had turned up in Venice, near the pier, key still inside and the owner nowhere to be found. After Marston failed to claim the car over a matter of weeks or answer his phone, the case had been referred to Hollywood Division, which encompassed Marston's home, and assigned to Detective Long.

The detective had contacted Marston's landlord, who reported that Marston was late on his rent and hadn't collected his mail, and he agreed to let Detective Long into the house. The place was empty, fruit rotting on the kitchen counter and milk spoiling in the Frigidaire. An expensive camera rested on a tripod in the living room, another in the bedroom, and dirty clothes were in a hamper in the bathroom. But no Anthony Marston.

A quick canvas of the neighbourhood hit pay dirt: Mrs. Carlson, a mousy-faced widow with a pinched New England accent who lived in a light blue Cape Cod across the street from the missing man, and paid rapt attention to the comings and goings of the handsome Mr. Marston.

"He's a photographer," she said. "Takes pictures of girls trying to become actresses, for them to drop with casting agents and such. They come over during the day to get their picture took. And sometimes they don't leave 'til the next day, if you know what I mean."

Detective Greyson Long nodded regretfully. He knew what she meant.

"I ain't seen him for practically two months," she said.

Greyson nodded again. That coincided with when the abandoned car had been found.

"And I ain't seen any ladies coming 'round to get their pictures took. Just the two."

"Oh?" the detective responded. "What two?"

"The one's an actress, that one who married the cowboy star. I seen her in the papers, all about her big love story with the cowboy, how's she's so sweet and beautiful and captured his heart. But I seen her coming to Mr. Marston's house in the evening and not leaving until real late, if you know what I mean."

Greyson knew.

"Last time I seen her was just after I last seen Mr. Marston. She came in that Cadillac with her chauffeur. She wasn't inside long and I never saw Mr. Marston, but he musta been home."

Greyson jotted notes in a small notebook he carried in his coat pocket. "You said there were two."

"Yeah. There was another young lady, pretty but not like the actress. Maybe two weeks later. She knocked on his door so hard I could hear it over here. She had a little baby with her. She went over to his window and looked in, but Mr. Marston wasn't home, or at least nobody answered, and she left. Then the next day, she came back."

Mrs. Carlson paused, as if in thought, and Greyson was forced to say, "She came back?"

"The next day," Mrs. Carlson said, focusing again on the detective. "She was screaming so loud, like she thought he was inside and pretending not to be there. I went over and told her to quit making all that ruckus."

Again, there was a lull in her speech and again Detective Long had to bring her back. "Did you speak to her?"

"Yeah, it was sad. I went over there mad, wanting to shut her up. But she was so upset, and with the baby, I felt sorry. She was desperate to find him, practically crying. I'd guess the baby's his, and he's nowhere to be found. She calmed down some, but asked me to have him call her if I see him again. Real sad."

"So she gave you her name?"

"Yeah, it's Mavis Hedges. She gave me her phone number, too."

Detective Long turned into Susan Spencer's driveway and pressed the button next to the gate. A few minutes later a Filipino man in a chauffeur's uniform came to the gate.

"May I help you?" the man asked.

"Detective Long to see Miss Spencer," Greyson said, showing his badge.

The Filipino man's eyes widened briefly, and he opened the gate. "You may leave your car here," he said. "I'll inform Miss Spencer that you are here."

The detective waited in a small drawing room while the chauffeur went to 'inform' Miss Spencer. It was a short wait; she must have dropped whatever she was doing when she learned a policeman was in her home. She was wearing beige slacks, a white blouse, no discernable makeup, not even lipstick, and bare feet. She was the most attractive woman Detective Greyson Long had ever seen.

"How may I help you?" she asked.

Detective Long explained why he had come.

Sophie nodded slowly. "I dated Tony for several months. It was before I met my husband. It's been a few months since I last saw him."

"Do you have any idea why he would leave town in such a hurry?"

Sophie shrugged. "I don't really know. But he left Oklahoma and came to LA because of a girl he'd gotten pregnant. I'm sure he was seeing other women when he was dating me. That can get a man into trouble. And he gambled, I think. I gave him money, more than once, to pay off some debt. I assume it was gambling. The last time I saw him he asked for more, but I wouldn't give it to him."

"That was about two months ago, at his house?" Long asked.

"Yes."

"Why did you go there?"

Sophie hesitated, then ploughed ahead, as if realising that she needed to come clean with the police. "He had something I needed. Photographs of me that would have…hurt me."

"And he wanted money for them?" the detective said.

"Yes," Sophie said, anger edging her voice. "And I paid him. Cash. He's such a jerk. I can't believe I didn't see it."

Greyson nodded with genuine sympathy for this beautiful woman. "I hope you destroyed them," he said.

"I burned them. Print and negatives." Her ire was palpable.

The detective looked down at his notes and said, "That's probably all I need for now. If you think of anything else, or if you hear from him, please call me." He handed her a card. "Thank you for your time," he said, and turned to go.

"Detective?"

He turned back. She had stepped closer, her eyes staring directly into his. He was suddenly transfixed, his voice caught in his throat, unable to respond. Finally, he stammered, "Y-yes?"

"My husband doesn't know," she said. "About Tony. I'm hoping that he won't find out, if that's possible."

"At this point, I don't anticipate the need for anyone to know about that," Greyson said.

"Thank you," she said, and smiled a smile that Detective Greyson Long thought might melt a man's heart.

Back in his car, heading down the hill, Greyson thought that this day was going much better than he'd expected. There was little upside to a case like this: a missing man who no one missed and no one wanted found. Except Mavis Hedges, who was perhaps the mother of his child.

The detective had known, before Miss Spencer told him, that Marston was from Shawnee, Oklahoma. He'd already called the local police and found out that Marston had left Oklahoma in a hurry after knocking up a teenage girl. It would be a perfectly acceptable closure to this case to presume that the same thing had happened in Los Angeles, with the same results. And, as a bonus, he'd met Miss Susan Spencer. Though it shamed him, he had to admit that he wouldn't mind seeing those photographs that she'd destroyed. No, he wouldn't mind that at all.

Fifteen minutes later, Greyson parked the Chevrolet in front of Mavis Hedges' duplex on Curson Avenue, got out, and walked to the back unit. She answered the doorbell, holding the baby. She appeared wary when Greyson showed her his badge, but invited him inside.

Mavis Hedges was, as Mrs. Carlson had said, a pretty girl. Her son appeared to be about four months old, although to Detective Long's practiced eye she showed no visible sign of recent childbirth. The apartment was spacious and light and, despite Miss Hedges' single motherhood, clean and neat. She sat on a worn couch with her son, while Greyson sat facing them in the lone living room chair.

He opened up his notebook before beginning. "You were at Anthony Marston's house approximately two months ago, looking for him."

Mavis Hedges smiled, a surprisingly sweet smile. "The old biddy across the street?" she asked.

Greyson nodded.

"I really made a racket. Probably lucky she didn't call the police right then. I was acting kind of crazy."

"I'm sure it was a difficult time," Greyson said.

"Yes," she said solemnly. "He said he'd marry me, but then he wouldn't, and after Joey was born he hardly had time for us. Then he disappeared altogether." She looked directly at Greyson. "I'm not a tramp, and I thought.... He just made me think he cared. Having a child and no husband is scary, and I panicked. But we're better off without him. I hope we never see him again."

"Do you have any idea where he is, or might be?" the detective asked.

"No, I couldn't find him. Did someone report him missing?"

Greyson shook his head. "We found his car, but not him. He's not at his house and no one has seen him so we think he's missing, but no one's reported it."

Mavis nodded. "I'm not surprised. I don't think he had any friends. He's just a self-absorbed pretty boy." Then she smiled. "Maybe he left because of me. I told him my brothers were going to hurt him, bad. I don't any have brothers. I just wanted to scare him."

"Did it work?"

"Yes. Or at least he looked scared. He's a coward. But he probably left because of the gambling."

"Oh?"

"He played poker," Mavis said. "And wasn't very good at it. He asked me for money to help out, but I didn't have any." She paused. "If I had, I'd have probably given it to him. I'm such a fool."

Suddenly, the pretty young girl looked sad, and Greyson had an urge to put an arm around her and comfort her. But instead, he stood up. "That's probably all I need," he said. "I thank you for your time. If you hear from him, or think of anything else, please call me." He handed her a card.

That was that, Greyson Long thought as he got back into the Chevrolet. *No one cared if Anthony Marston was ever found alive, not even the mother of his child.* Hollywood Division could keep whatever proceeds they received from selling the Model T, and Greyson would keep whatever he got for Marston's expensive photo equipment. He might search Marston's house when he swung by to pick up the cameras, just in case the slime ball had made a few extra prints. Greyson certainly would have.

He'd file a report stating that the subject had probably left town of his own volition, either to avoid a pregnant girlfriend or to flee from a gambling debt, or both. There was no reason to suspect foul play at this time, and given that there had been no complaint, further investigation appeared unwarranted. Case closed.

★   ★   ★

One week later, Sophie met Mavis Hedges in the dining room of the Hollywood Roosevelt Hotel. Mavis had her son with her, so they were seated near the back where the infant was unlikely to disturb other diners.

This was their third meeting, here at the Roosevelt. The first had been two months ago, before the incident with Tony Marston, and had been at Mavis's request. They had originally met in Steinberg's acting class and like all the girls in the class, Mavis knew Sophie had money.

"I need two hundred dollars," she'd said, her tone desperate. "It's for my son, Joey. He's got a cough, a croup, that won't go away. And the doctor is expensive. But if he has just a few more treatments, they say he'll be fine. I'll pay you back as soon as I can."

"Don't worry about the paying me back," Sophie had said. "Just make sure that Joey's taken care of." And she'd proceeded to take two hundred dollars out of her purse. Mavis had just stared at Sophie, her face glowing with awe and gratitude. "You don't know what this means," she had said. "It's a life saver." Then she'd got up and left. Sophie had watched her, thoughtfully.

Five weeks later, one week after the death of Tony Marston, the two ladies met again, this time at Sophie's request. "I'll get directly to it," she said. "I need your help, and I'm willing to pay for it: one thousand dollars up front, and one thousand more if the police ever come around."

At the mention of police, Mavis became nervous. "I don't want anything to do with the police."

Sophie shook her head. "Don't worry, that probably won't happen." She explained that her friend, Tony Marston, had gotten into some trouble with gamblers and needed to leave town in a hurry. Sophie had promised to cover up for him, make sure that any investigation into his disappearance would result in a dead end.

But now Mavis shook her head. "This Tony, is that the guy you used to date? Did something happen between him and Duke?"

When Sophie remained silent, Mavis continued. "I can't be involved with anything like that."

Sophie stared at her coolly, and in a voice so cold that Mavis was stunned to hear it coming from the sweet Sophie, she said, "Yes, Mr. Rossi might not be happy if he were to find out about it."

Every drop of colour seemed to drain from Mavis's pretty face. Her mouth opened, then closed, then opened again to gulp in air, as if she were having trouble breathing.

Sophie continued very calmly. "I don't know of any doctor who charges two hundred dollars to treat the croup, and I like to know how my money's being used. So I had an investigator look into it." Sophie paused. "I don't think Mr. Rossi would approve of the abortion. Was it his child?"

Mavis at first just nodded, then finally got words out. "He'd kill me if he knew. And he'd take Joey."

Sophie felt sympathy for Mavis, for what her investigator had found out. She'd come to Los Angeles like the rest of them, hoping to find fame and fortune in the movies. But instead, she'd found Joe Rossi, who ran the largest loan-sharking business in the city. Rossi was a short, handsome, sometimes violent man, who was happily married. But that didn't stop him from supporting three mistresses in three different duplexes he owned across the city.

"He's Joey's father," Mavis continued, having recovered her voice along with her composure. "He loves Joey, and he's good to us. But then I got pregnant again, just three months after Joey was born. She looked directly at Sophie. "I had a real hard time with Joey, and the doctor said I shouldn't have any more children. I didn't know it could happen so soon after."

She dropped her eyes, then looked back up at Sophie, her voice pleading. "You're a really good person. I know you are. If he finds out what I did...." Her voice trailed off.

Sophie looked back at her, and spoke softly, reassuringly. "It'll all be okay. But you need to understand that I do need you to do this." She paused. "And that I will do anything to protect the one I love."

Mavis hesitated, but then nodded. They went through the scenario. Mavis went to Tony's house, raised a ruckus, and she and Joey went home. Two months later, Detective Greyson Long showed up.

So now, the two young women sat one last time in the dining room of the Hollywood Roosevelt Hotel. Sophie took an envelope out of her purse, the envelope containing one thousand dollars, and handed it to Mavis. "Thank you," Sophie said. "I was confident you could do it."

Mavis moved her head up and down, but said nothing. She started to stand up, but Sophie halted her, saying, "I think we might have something for you."

"Oh," Mavis said, obvious dread in her voice.

"A role," Sophie said. "In Duke's new movie. They need a pretty girl to play a barmaid. Nothing big, just a few scenes. But it's a paycheck. And a start. If it goes well, we can help out more in the future."

Mavis nodded again and said, "That sounds great." Then she did get up to go, looking back at Sophie. She really was thankful for the role, as well as the money, but could not help but be apprehensive about becoming even more beholden to Sophie.

CHAPTER FORTY-FOUR
1928

Louis Kahn tossed the typewritten sheaf of papers on the table in front of him. "Damn good," he said. "And I suppose you want to direct it?" This last statement was to Clarence Rollins, one of two men seated across the table from him. Next to Clarence was Sy Glucksman, the writer of the script in question.

"I agree with you, Louis," Rollins said. "It's very good. In fact, I think it will be perfect for your first talking picture. And yes, I'd like to direct it."

Louis nodded, almost imperceptibly. The queer was right, as he usually was about these things. It was high time for Signature Studio to come out with a talkie. Technology had advanced impressively in the year since *The Jazz Singer* had introduced sound to moving pictures. In truth, that film had contained little more than a few songs poorly synchronised with popular singer Al Jolson's celluloid lip movement. But now the technological wizards of the film industry had made spoken dialogue a true reality, comparable to watching someone speak on stage. It would mean huge changes to the industry. Louis knew that once movie audiences were accustomed to sound, they would no longer settle for any movie without it. Signature had some catching up to do, and this script would be a great first step.

"Okay," he said. "I'm willing to entertain the idea of producing this." Then, turning to Glucksman, he said, "It's your script. You can pitch it on your own, and you've never shown much interest in who directs. So why is he here?" As he spoke, Kahn nodded toward Rollins.

"Because he shares my vision of this film," Glucksman said slowly.

"Vision," Kahn almost snorted the word. "And what, exactly, is your vision?"

"In regard to casting," Rollins spoke up, and Kahn realised why the writer had brought him along. Glucksman was still afraid to challenge the studio head, but he knew the queer had no such weakness.

"What about the casting?" Kahn said.

"We see Susan Spencer in the lead role." Rollins was still doing the talking.

Louis grimaced. "*Over There* was the first really big hit for both of you, and I can understand that you'd want the same actress to launch your talkie careers. But I can't do it. You know that. I've offered her a contract on at least ten different occasions. She's not interested."

"You could still use her for this part." To Kahn's surprise, it was Glucksman who spoke up. "You've cast her in other films, even though she's not under contract. You probably won't even have to pay her as much as one of your contract players."

"You're a smart boy," the studio head said. "But I'm sure you understand that a picture like this, Signature's first talkie, will give the female lead a huge step into the new era. Hell, if it works out, this film alone could make her a star. That means I want her to be someone I've got under contract."

"Look, Mr. Kahn, she'd be perfect." Now it was Rollins taking up the argument. "And she's already a star. Having her as the lead will draw in a million men. We all know she can do the accents flawlessly. She can act the part of the sweet country girl or the high-society bitch, and make them both believable. And the audience will completely believe it when the older, happily married husband falls for her. Hell, every man in the audience will fall for her." Rollins paused a moment. "It's important that Signature's first talkie be a hit, hopefully a big hit. With Susan in the lead, it will be."

Louis Kahn would not say so, but Susan Spencer had immediately come to mind when he read Glucksman's script. It was the story of an engaging and innocent country girl who travels to Hollywood hoping to become a star in silent pictures. Of course, her movie land plans prove elusive. She finds it difficult to make ends meet, directors and producers take advantage of her, and she is forced to sacrifice both innocence and virtue to obtain even a small part.

So she reinvents herself as a girl from high-society Boston, complete with Brahmin accent and elegant manners. She is befriended by an older, successful actress who is married to a thriving producer. She lands a major movie role by seducing her friend's husband, ruining her friend emotionally as well as professionally. In the end, she achieves all of her dreams but is unrecognisable as the sweet young woman the audience knew earlier in the film. *Susan could act the part perfectly,* Louis thought, *and even the fagelah understands her raw sexual appeal.*

"There may be some truth in what you say, Clarence," Kahn intoned. "But I simply can't invest the time and money it would take to produce and promote this film and then have the star go off and make a movie for someone else. A big part of the buildup for the picture would involve publicity for the star herself. She could just take all the celebrity I create for her to another studio. That's why I'd rather use someone I've got under contract."

"I'll tell you what," Clarence said. "I'll talk to her and convince her to commit to doing her next two or three films for Signature. I'm pretty sure that if she doesn't have to sign a lifetime contract, she'll be fine with doing a few films. It'll work out great for her, move her into talkies, and you'll still get the benefit of her popularity for several more films."

Kahn paused before answering, as if he had to ponder this scenario, as if it were not something he had already thought of. "Okay," he said. "Make it four films, and I think we can make it work."

Clarence nodded. *Of course it'll work,* he thought. *It'll make her an even bigger star, and a proposal from Clarence, her friend, would be much better received than one coming from the studio head whom she loathed.* Clarence smiled at the thought of working with her again.

CHAPTER FORTY-FIVE
1930/1931

"We've saturated the market in the New York area. If we open any more pubs we'll be cannibalising our own businesses," Max said.

"What are you suggesting?" Jonathan responded. "No new bars?" They were sitting in Jonathan's office, which occupied a large room above one of the midtown pubs on 36th Street near 7th.

"What I'm suggesting is we move to new territory."

Jonathan looked at him quizzically, thinking to himself what a nuisance it would be to drive to New Jersey on a regular basis. "Okay," he finally said, "where?"

"Hollywood, California."

Jonathan laughed. "That would be a long commute."

"I was thinking you could move there."

Jonathan stared at him for a moment. "You're serious?"

"Look, Jonathan, you've done a great job, an incredible job. You've surpassed my highest expectations for this business. But like I said, we've saturated this territory, and since the stock market crashed, business is down. We both know that. But California's still wide open. They've got a lot of people with a lot of money and not enough places to spend it. And I'm told the bars out there are second rate. You would blow away the competition."

"What about the business here?"

"Like I said, you've done a great job. You've set up such smooth operations, they practically run themselves. Seamus can handle it. And you can talk to him every day on the phone if you want, or take the train back every few months. Or both. And Prohibition's not going to last forever."

"No?"

"It was a stupid idea in the first place. Even Congress is starting to figure that out. I don't give it more than another three years. And when it goes, so do a lot of our profits."

"Really?"

"Hell yes. When it's legal, any schmuck can be in the business. So there'll be lots of competition and our profit margin will be cut in half. Or worse. And the guys in Canada who I buy from will figure they can deliver it in the States themselves, so I'll have to compete with them as well as buy from them."

"I'm sure you'll figure out a way to…discourage competition."

"Sure," Max said with a wave of his hand. "But that'll still cost me, and it's always better to avoid any rough stuff, cheaper and safer. So we need more territory to maintain our overall profit when the margins drop, and to give me more clout on the distribution side." Max grew even more serious. "Look, Jon, a move to California could be good for you. You need to meet some new people, get your social life moving. And Sam could grow up in the sunshine, become a tennis player or surfer, or whatever they do out there."

"We've got family here."

Again, Max spoke while gesticulating with his hand. "You and Sam and your mother can move to California. Seamus and family stay in Brooklyn and he runs the business here. Every couple months, your mom takes the train out to visit. Sam and you can come with her and you'll catch up on the business with Seamus."

"Okay," Jonathan said. "I'll give it some thought."

"Thanks. I appreciate that."

★   ★   ★

A year later it was obvious that Max had been right. Hollywood proved to be fertile ground for a growing liquor business. There were, as Mr. Zalensky had said, lots of folks with lots of money, looking for places to spend it. And since the onset of the Depression, people in California were comparatively better off than their brethren back east. With movies, oil, and airplane manufacturing, life in the Golden State was good, even while people went hungry in Oklahoma.

Mr. Zalensky made the trip out west to attend to the 'political end' of things, ensuring that local police agencies would present no obstacles to the illegal sale of alcohol. The Los Angeles Police Department was notoriously corrupt, and gaining their favour proved an easy task. As had been the case in New York, the LAPD had never experienced anyone willing to expend the large amounts of cash that Max casually threw their way. Jonathan had to modify his standard formula. The movie land bars required extra booths to afford privacy to patrons and fewer stools at the bar. In one tavern off Sunset Boulevard, he put curtains around some of the booths and thin walls and a door around several of the tables, thus creating small private rooms for elite customers. This particular bar also served food, so patrons could come for lunch or dinner in addition to drinks.

Although no sign could be hung outside a speakeasy, the Sunset Grill, as it became known, proved a popular spot for Hollywood producers to bring up-and-coming actresses. More than one starlet owed her first on-screen role to a lunchtime performance in one of the private dining rooms at the Sunset Grill.

The California operation grew so quickly that before long it was bringing in more profits than New York. At thirty years old, Jonathan earned an annual income of two hundred thousand dollars, a majestic sum in 1931. Of course, Mr. Zalensky would earn a share equal to Jonathan's, plus profit from the wholesale side, all without devoting the long hours that Jonathan did to day-to-day operations.

Sam loved Southern California. Max had been right about that too. They lived in a four-bedroom Spanish-style bungalow in Santa Monica, and ten-year-old Sam and his friends could walk to the beach or to the amusement park on the pier, or to the local public park with its baseball diamond and tennis courts. And he never seemed to be alone. There were lots of boys around, sons of men who worked at the Douglas airplane factory a few miles away. If Jonathan made it home by late afternoon, the house was usually filled with ten-year-olds who might have just returned from the beach or were playing ball in the large backyard, or enjoying one of the snacks that Grandma always had prepared.

After a lifetime in cold climates, Jonathan's mother, Mary-Margaret, had moved west with them, and she seemed to enjoy the California sunshine as much as her grandson. The two went to the beach together and it tickled Jonathan to see his fifty-one-year-old mother dipping her toes into the surf.

Jonathan, too, was happier in the new environs, and had managed to come out of his shell a little. He had begun dating one young woman who handled the bookkeeping for several of his new bars, and another, an aspiring actress and a teacher at Sam's elementary school. Neither woman was Samantha and he didn't see a long future with either one, but it was a step in the right direction. California, it seemed, was good for everyone.

CHAPTER FORTY-SIX
1931

"I have a proposal," Jonathan said, aware that Max could hear the nervousness in his voice. He was in Manhattan for a few days and the two men had just finished trudging through the quarterly results, which had been quite favourable.

"I'm listening."

"I'd like to get into the movie theatre business. Timing's right, money's good, and we have a high probability of success." Jonathan looked at Max expectantly.

"Keep talking."

"In 1929 there were twenty-one thousand theatres in America. There is still the same number today, but more people are going to the movies. The existing movie houses can barely handle the traffic. But here's the topper. Only fifteen thousand of the existing theatres have sound equipment; the other six thousand can't handle talking pictures. Next year, three quarters of the movies made will be talkies and in a few years they all will. So there will be a real shortage of theatres."

"Why haven't the established players built enough to keep up?"

Jonathan talked more intensely, his nervousness disappearing as he warmed to his subject. "Their funding dried up after the market crashed. Also, they got nervous about whether people would go to the movies during hard times. But it turns out, people go more than ever. To be honest, I don't think anyone realised that talkies would become so popular so quickly."

Max looked at him thoughtfully. "For you to find locations and build new theatres will take a few years. By that time the majors will equip their other six thousand theatres for sound, and probably build some new ones. So by the time you've got your cinemas up and running, there may not be any demand."

Jonathan actually smiled. "Exactly. Which is why I'm not going to build new. I've got a contract to buy the Balaban and Katz chain of vaudeville houses. They've got five houses in Los Angeles, eight in San Francisco, fifteen in the Philadelphia area, and twelve here in New York, which is where they're based. With talkies coming in strong, vaudeville's dead. So these guys need to sell and we get a good price. Most of these old vaudeville houses are bigger and plusher than your normal movie house, and they're in good locations. The normal conversion costs for live stage to theatre, plus projector and sound equipment, will cost us about three thousand five hundred dollars each, and take maybe two months."

"You know how to do this?"

Jonathan nodded. "I've already got the technicians lined up. The cash flow on this thing will be great. Almost half the revenue from a successful movie goes to the theatre owners. And that's just the successful movies. The flops either never get to the theatres or don't stay there for long, so the studios absorb the losses."

"This contract you have with the owners of the vaudeville houses: You had to give them money to tie up the deal?"

"Of course. I put down five percent. Had to."

"That's a lot of cash for you, which you will have difficulty recovering if the deal doesn't go through. You had a lot of confidence that someone would come up with the rest of the money."

"It's an excellent opportunity."

Max paused, then nodded. "What sort of split do you propose?"

They shook on it, as always, nothing in writing. The new theatres opened just in time to carry the new Susan Spencer talkie, *Country Girl*. They were sold out for five weeks.

CHAPTER FORTY-SEVEN

Los Angeles police vice squad Lieutenant Walter Parker was hunting for high-profile homo, just the thing to boost his already fast-track career. The citizens of Los Angeles, an otherwise conservative community of blue-collar workers and citrus growers, had carved out a special tolerance for the excesses of Hollywood glitterati. There was no advantage to busting a Lionel Atwill orgy or a Wallace Beery coke party; the studios would have their lawyers down to the station faster than the police could process their precious movie stars into a jail cell. Besides, the top brass and politicians loved to glad-hand the motion picture moguls, maybe get to rub shoulders with a headliner now and then. Rather than helping his career, pulling in a matinee idol on a vice rap would just make Lieutenant Parker a nuisance to the big bosses.

But busting a homosexual was a different matter. Most of the police bigwigs were truly repulsed by the image of two men getting it on sexually. Or at least they had to pretend they were in order to not come under suspicion themselves. And the studios, who five years earlier had not hesitated to cover up for Ramon Navarro and Rudolph Valentino, now tried to distance themselves from 'fagelahs' as the Jew moguls called them. America had been tempered by the stock market crash, and certain excesses were no longer tolerated as they had been during the roaring twenties.

So a high-profile homo bust was just what the doctor ordered to boost Walt Parker's career temperature. Not too high profile, of course. Not a real star. Someone just big enough to get Parker's name in the newspaper without causing any real suffering at the studios.

To that end, Lieutenant Parker employed Arthur Lindquist. Arthur was a seventeen-year-old pretty boy from Minneapolis, Minnesota, who had come to Los Angeles to be a movie star. He'd been arrested a month earlier in a raid on a male brothel in East Hollywood. At the time of the raid, Lindquist was engaged in what vice cops called a dog and pony with an Episcopalian minister from Pasadena. Parker, who was impressed by the boy's striking good looks, pulled him aside for questioning when they got to the station.

"Ever do any Hollywood people?"

"Sure, all the time."

Parker smirked. "Right. Anybody I've heard of?"

"Probably not. But I got invited to a party. Supposed to be some producers and directors there."

Parker nodded, suddenly more interested. "Okay, let me lay it out for you, Arthur." He looked straight at the kid and spoke in a very serious and, he hoped, threatening manner. "I could process you right now, but we're a little crowded here in Vice, so I'd have to stick you over in Central, downtown."

Lindquist's face turned almost white.

"Now we both know what'll happen to someone like you in a place like that, don't we?" Parker said.

The boy nodded.

"And of course, neither of us wants that to happen. Right?"

The boy nodded again.

"So here's what I'm thinking. You help me out, I kick you out of here, keep your papers in my pocket and everything's jake. You don't, I arrest you, and boot your pretty ass over to Central. Then, when I lose your papers, it's at least a week before you're out of there. Capisce?"

"So what is it you want me to do?"

Parker smiled and told him.

★   ★   ★

Clarence Rollins patted back his hair in the mirror and smiled excitedly, thinking about Artie, the boy he'd met last week at Stevenson's party. Seemed like a nice kid. Didn't want any money or anything, just help with his career. That shouldn't be too hard, considering how good looking the boy was. After all, Clarence was at the top of his profession. He'd been one of the most respected directors in silent films, and now that *Country Girl* was a runaway hit, he could write his own ticket in the talkies.

They went to dinner at Café Monmartre, then drinks at Del Monte, then to Rollins's place. He had a small house in the hills, overlooking the lights of the city. Artie asked if he could use the phone to call his parents to let them know he'd be late. Clarence, a little embarrassed, excused himself while Artie used the phone. After Lieutenant Parker received the call, he placed his own call to a friend at the *LA Examiner* before leaving the station.

★   ★   ★

Sophie burst into Louis Kahn's office, anger reddening her face.

"How could you do it?" she shouted. "Don't you think you owe him a little more than this?"

Kahn, who was sitting at his desk looking through a script, looked up at her, his eyebrows raised. He knew exactly what she was referring to. "We didn't have a lot of choice. The fagelah hadda go." Then he returned to reading his script.

Kahn's response made Sophie so angry that she pulled the script he was reading out of his hands and threw it on the floor. "How can you say that so easily?" she screamed at him. "You were almost his friend. Now, just like that, he's fired? He won't be able to get any work in this town. What is he supposed to do?"

Kahn looked down at the script on the floor, then back up at her again and shrugged. "Yeah, I like him, but you understand as well as anyone that I gotta do what I gotta do. The cops walked in while Clarence was getting a blow job. From a boy. And I mean that legally. The kid was underage. And there was a reporter there. The damn thing would have been all over the newspapers by now."

"And there's nothing you can do to help him?"

"Are you listening? I've been working on this full time for three days. The kid was underage. It cost me five G's to keep it out of the papers, then another five plus three goddamn lawyers and a lot of promises to keep Clarence out of jail. One of those promises was to fire him and never bring him back."

Sophie was taken aback. Louis was notoriously tight with a dollar. She never would have expected him to expend this sort of money for an employee's welfare. At least, not for one who would be worthless to him in the future. "I'm sorry," she said. "I had no idea of all you'd done." She paused a moment. "You did good."

Kahn shrugged again. "I'll be honest with you, Susan. The public's fed up with this sort of thing. They'll put up with male stars making it with lots of different women, figure it's part of the manly thing. But even that has its limits if it involves underage girls or drugs. But banging another man!" Kahn shook his head. "Not even a man, a boy. That looks really bad. We've gotta come down hard, at least publicly, show how we stand against this sort of thing."

"Gotta do what you've gotta do," she said sarcastically.

"Yes," he snapped back. "And you and everyone else needs to understand that. Clarence was arrogant and careless. The kid actually called the police from his house. And the door was left open so the cops waltzed right in without even having to knock. With the goddamn reporter. Clarence didn't even bother to check that the door was locked. Thought he was such a big shot that nobody could touch him. That's never true. For anybody."

Sophie was surprised that Louis had gotten so excited, even angry. "You think there's a possibility of this happening to more people?"

"I don't know, but I worry about it. I just think people need to be discreet. Not act like they're untouchable."

"I'll remember that," she said, "and thank you for giving him the help that you did." With that, she turned and left his office.

CHAPTER FORTY-EIGHT

In 1931, Alphonse Capone, the most infamous mob boss in the United States of America, was sentenced to eleven years in the newly established federal prison at Alcatraz, not for bootlegging or murder, but for failing to pay his taxes. The government no longer had to prove that you made your money through illegal means, only that you had not paid taxes on it.

Organised crime ran lucrative businesses: gambling, booze, extortion, prostitution. These businesses required accurate, comprehensive records kept by trained accountants. Suddenly those records as well as the men who kept them represented a grave danger.

It was part of his genius that where other men saw obstacles, Max Zalensky saw opportunity. He reasoned that men who worked very hard and at great personal risk for their money would not want to just give it away to the government. It was an opportunity that could bring him more money and power than any other aspect of his business.

It took him almost a year to set it up. He worked through several subordinates who, in turn, worked through subordinates of their own. Large sums of cash were delivered to Max's organisation from all over the country. That cash was bundled up and transported to a friendly bank in a friendly foreign country, then placed in the account of a newly formed foreign corporation. The foreign corporation then sent the money back into the United States for investment in legitimate businesses such as hotels, apartment houses, or oil wells, or simply to pay expenses for their American representatives.

Foreign investment was welcome in America and the US government did not care how the foreigner had earned his money. That was the concern of the country it came from. Of course, the real owners of the corporation were Max's clients, who now had access to their money, tax free. The operation merely required friendly foreign governments and greedy bankers. Max found that key politicians of the Caribbean island nation of Dutch Antilles could be friendly for a reasonable fee. And bankers, of course, were bankers.

For reinvestment in the United States, Max favoured real estate and oil wells. The income from these ventures was protected from taxation by legal loopholes such as depreciation and depletion allowances that were available to all legitimate businesses in America. In addition, foreign investors enjoyed special investment tax credits that Congress had established to encourage foreign investment in America, advantages not available to homegrown businessmen.

So underworld figures could run legitimate businesses, report their income honestly to the government, and pay no taxes. Of course, they had to pay a slight fee to Max for his services. And if he arranged for the purchase of an oil well or a hotel, he charged a fair commission, as would any legitimate broker.

The potential payoff was enormous: a four percent fee for a 'global reroute' and three percent for investment commissions. Max could receive seven percent of all illegitimate revenue earned by organised crime in America. And best of all, this scheme would make him indispensable to the very men he competed against, men who up until now had been his enemies. The possibilities were staggering.

CHAPTER FORTY-NINE
1932

Senator Alton Standish climbed naked from his hotel room bed and headed for the shower. It was his habit to rise early and get to the office before his staff arrived. The young woman still asleep in the bed would not cause any change to his routine. He thought of her and the night they had spent together as he stood under the high-pressure shower, feeling the full force of the water against his skin. She was a petite thing, small and slender in every way, except for her breasts, which were full and remarkably firm. Her skin and musculature were as smooth and taut as fine silk, and she had inspired the senator's fifty-four-year-old body to perform at a level he had no longer thought possible.

His thoughts were interrupted by a quick rush of cold air as the shower door opened and she stepped in behind him. The suddenness of it, as well as the soft crush of her breasts against his back, both startled and excited him.

"Let me bathe you," she said softly, as she took both soap and washcloth from him. She started at his shoulders, her hands surprisingly strong, and then worked her way down. She washed his back, moved quickly past his buttocks, kneeling down to carefully wash his thighs, calves and feet. Rising up, she used both hands, still slippery with soap, to massage his private parts. He felt himself harden against her touch, a throbbing ache accompanying the stiffness as she skillfully caressed him. She kept at it until he was on the brink of orgasm, then stopped abruptly.

"Oh my God," he said desperately. "Don't stop now."

She smiled, and as if in penance knelt on the floor of the shower before him, and with the water spraying her back began to work him with her mouth. Her tongue flicked in and out, teasing him mercilessly until, with a moan of ecstasy, he thrust himself into her. She sucked gently at first, then harder. As he was about to come she reached a hand between his legs and inserted a slippery finger from behind, as her lips drew every ounce of him. It was more pleasure than he remembered ever experiencing. He gasped out loud, then collapsed against the shower wall, his energy spent.

★　　★　　★

In the back of the taxi on the way to the Senate Office Building, he kept thinking about her, reliving their night and morning together. Her name was Kathleen Collins and they had met the previous afternoon following a speech he had given at Georgetown University. She was working on her doctorate in Political Science and along with other students had stayed after the speech to ask questions and speak in person to the great man.

Kathleen was obviously interested in contact of a more intimate nature, a fact she communicated with unmistakable body language. But a man in his position had to be careful, and it had taken him some time to decide. He had been attracted, of course, by the pretty face almost hidden behind the owlish glasses, and the slender body in pleated skirt and sweater. But the deciding factor had been the knowledgeable questions she had asked about his banking bill, of which he was particularly proud.

So he had his driver discreetly ask if she cared to join the senator for dinner, which they had at an elegant café just outside the District of Columbia overlooking the Potomac. Afterward, they went straight to his hotel. Senator Standish liked the ladies, a fact not unknown to his colleagues, his wife, or his constituents. But he had never been with anyone so fully and completely devoted to bringing him physical pleasure. Or so well suited to it. Just the thought of Kathleen Collins' flawless body excited him. He was already thinking about when he would see her again.

CHAPTER FIFTY

For Spencer Buckley, the trouble began when a friend from work took him to an underground gambling den near their Wall Street office. Spencer had gambled a bit when he was at Princeton, but at the age of thirty-five, with a pretty young wife, two children, and a top job at one of the country's leading investment banks, those days were behind him. He was a responsible man now, with a responsible career, and lived with his family in a spacious brownstone on Manhattan's Upper East Side.

But as he walked down a back alley off Water Street, his heart was pounding with excitement. A window-slot on the steel door slid open, his friend gave the password, and they were in. It was dark and noisy inside, craps tables, roulette wheels, one-armed bandits, and everywhere men in suits and white boaters whooping and hollering, smoking cigars and drinking whiskey. Spencer was in heaven.

The first couple of times he played at the Water Street casino, he won big. It was as if the dice were an extension of his fingers and his brain could command their movement just as it commanded his own limbs. But the dice moved to their own random destiny, and in the weeks that followed he started to lose, sometimes heavily.

At first he was down only a few hundred dollars, then a thousand, then five thousand, and finally a massive ten thousand dollars. He'd become friendly with the pit bosses and managers of the casino, and they were surprisingly generous in extending him credit. But as his losses mounted he became wary of showing his face.

It was perverse, if logical to Spencer, that he found relief from the high pressure of work by engaging in an activity that ran so counter to the discipline he exercised at the office. As a senior vice president and one of the top private money managers at the bank, he stood out amongst his colleagues by being a conservative investor. Even when the market crashed in '29, Spencer's clients fared better than most, thanks to the careful research that he used to place clients into companies with real value to back up their paper promises. But as protective as he was with his clients' money, he was a gun-slinging cowboy with his own. Throwing dice, lending his fate to sheer chance, gave Spencer the same high other people got from alcohol or drugs. The more he played, the more addicted he became.

Unable to pay his losses and afraid to go back to his usual haunt, he found a new place off Washington Square, where he could start fresh. At first, Spencer's luck seemed to change in the new surroundings, but within a month everything went downhill. He had an unbelievable streak of bad luck at the craps table, a streak that he just knew had to end at any moment. So he kept pouring in more money, the new casino even more accommodating than the old one about extending credit. But the streak did not end. It got worse. Before he knew it, he was down almost twelve thousand dollars in the new place. The croupiers and doormen addressed him by name. They smiled and brought him drinks. They never seemed to question his ability to pay. And he continued to believe that his luck would turn, that he would win his way out of debt.

But, of course, he never did. And one night as he entered the casino the pit boss asked to speak privately to him for just a moment. It was very smoothly done. He was led by the elbow to a side room just off the entrance, and asked to sit on an elegant Louis XVI divan. Then the door shut and the pit boss left, leaving Spencer alone in the small room. It did not occur to him to be frightened. He had already skipped out on his debts at one casino with no adverse consequences. At worst, he would promise to pay, walk away as he'd done before and never come back.

The door opened and a well-dressed man about Spencer's age walked in. Spencer started to stand, but the man indicated that he remain seated. "I am Max Zalensky," he said, "and I believe you owe me twenty-one thousand, seven hundred eighty dollars."

"What?" Spencer protested immediately. "No! I owe a little less than twelve grand."

Zalensky paused a moment. "I am including the total you owe

me, both from your losses at this casino and the one I own near Wall Street. I'm sure you understand that switching your play over here does not cancel your debt at any of my other establishments."

Spencer sat stunned, his mouth slightly open. The quiet monotone with which this Mr. Zalensky spoke was unnerving, even a little frightening. How could they have let him gamble like this if he already owed them money? And how many 'establishments' did this guy own? "I can p-pay it all back," he sputtered. "Soon. Just let me sell a few positions, get the cash."

Zalensky nodded. "Can you bring me the money in, say, a week?"

"Yes, of course," Spencer responded, seeming to regain his equilibrium. "That should be easy."

Zalensky nodded again. "That will be fine. I'll see you in a week then. I would suggest you go home tonight, and not do any more gambling." Zalensky then walked out the door, leaving Spencer by himself in the small room.

As soon as Zalensky left, Spencer hurried out of the room and out of the unmarked casino. At Washington Square he caught a cab for home. He had the cabbie circle all the way around Central Park, to make certain he was not being followed.

The truth was there was no way he could pay back the money. Not even close. He had about seven thousand in his savings account, just a fraction of what he owed. His 'positions' as he called them consisted of two hundred shares of American Telephone and Telegraph. It was a very solid company, but at two dollars a share only worth a total of four hundred dollars. How on earth, he wondered, had they let him keep gambling? Of course, it wasn't real money to them, just credit extended to another sucker at the table. No real skin off Zalensky's back. If he gets any money at all, he comes out ahead.

As Spencer jogged up the stairs to his brownstone, a plan formed in his mind. Again, before opening his front door he looked around to make sure he had not been followed. He decided that the best course of action would be to never return to that particular casino. Probably not to any casino in Manhattan for that matter, no telling how many this Zalensky character actually owned. From now on Spencer would do his gambling across the river in New Jersey, or Brooklyn.

After all, Zalensky had no way of knowing where he lived or what he did for a living. For that matter, he didn't even know Spencer's full name. Buckley had simply signed his credit slips 'Spencer', and the croupiers had addressed him as 'Mr. Spencer'. They probably thought Spencer was his last name. Illegal casinos were not the kind of places that asked to see proper identification. No, it was unlikely they would ever catch him, as long as he never went back.

The big mystery to him was why they had extended him so much credit in the first place. Back in college, he had been down only a few hundred dollars when the goons came calling. Maybe Zalensky figured it was better to have bodies at the table, and if he collected even a fraction of what people like Spencer owed, he would make a very good living. Which, if they found him, he would pay. Give them a couple thousand, call it even, everybody wins. But only if they found him – which was unlikely.

Despite these rationalisations, Spencer was so unnerved by the experience that he did not indulge his addiction for a week. Even then, when he finally succumbed, he had the common sense to put a river between himself and Mr. Zalensky's establishments. Another friend at work had spoken repeatedly about a gambling house just across the Brooklyn Bridge. "You'll love this place," his friend told him. "It's better than any of the spots in Manhattan."

And it was. It was in a huge warehouse on the edge of Brooklyn Heights. There were more craps tables, roulette wheels and poker games in the vast space than in any three Manhattan establishments combined. And if you stood for long at any one table a pretty girl in a low-cut blouse brought you a good stiff drink, served with a smile. Spencer loved it. Not only that, by the end of the night he was ahead by seven hundred dollars.

He arrived home after midnight. His wife was accustomed to this and had gone to bed two hours earlier. The master bedroom and the children's rooms were upstairs, so he could let himself in without disturbing them.

His usual custom was to pour himself a brandy, then relax with it in the library before retiring. Tonight was no exception, and with snifter in hand he headed for his favourite wing chair. The library was just to the right of the stairs, and light from it reached the upper floor, some even seeping under the bedroom doors. For that reason he walked all the way into the pitch-black room and closed the door behind him before reaching for the familiar wall switch.

He turned on the light, then shrieked in horror, dropping the brandy snifter, which shattered on the hardwood floor, scattering glass and brandy across the room.

"Please try to be quiet, Mr. Buckley. You'll wake the missus and kiddies." The gruff voice came from a large, dark-suited man sitting in Spencer's favourite chair, the one he relaxed in every night. The man was holding a pistol in his right hand, waving it around as he spoke. Spencer's lips trembled, and his knees grew weak.

"Sorry to just drop in like this, Mr. Buckley, but Mr. Zalensky wants to see you. Now."

CHAPTER FIFTY-ONE

A car waited in the street. Spencer sat in front, next to the driver, and the large man sat directly behind him. As they drove, Spencer's shock wore off, replaced by sheer terror. It was his worst nightmare come true. They not only knew his full name, they knew where he lived. And they could waltz right into his home on a well-lit street in a fine neighbourhood despite the best locks money could buy. They were even able to anticipate that he would relax in the library before going up to sleep. With a sinking feeling, he realised they must have been watching him for some time, probably spying through the library window, the only one not draped at night. He'd have to negotiate, convince them to accept what little he could pay. It had seemed like a fine plan when he'd believed he would never need to sell it, but now that they had found him he knew it would be very difficult.

The large man led him into the same small room that he had been in the last time and asked him to sit on the same sofa. The man stayed in the room even after Mr. Zalensky arrived a few moments later. Zalensky looked briefly at Spencer, then nodded. Too late, Spencer realised that Zalensky was not nodding at him, but at the large man who was now standing directly behind him.

A huge forearm circled Spencer Buckley's neck and began tightening. He was helpless. His lungs gasped for air, his heart quickened, his brain went wild with panic. Spencer tried to rise from the chair but the big man's other hand on his shoulder held him down, seemingly without effort. He pulled desperately at the offending forearm, his strength fueled by adrenaline, but to no avail. The big man continued to squeeze air and the life it afforded out of Spencer Buckley. The image of Mr. Zalensky standing in front of him slowly faded, turning into black and white spots. Then the spots disappeared, replaced by blackness. Spencer's last thought was that he was dying and there was nothing he could do about it.

Then suddenly it was over. He was on the floor, gasping air into his lungs, gulping in all that he could as quickly as he could. It took him several minutes to recover, and when he did he heard Zalensky's voice. "Please get off the floor and sit back in the chair, Mr. Buckley."

Still in shock from his ordeal, Spencer did as he was told, staring fearfully at the man who had ordered this.

"Are you all right now?" Zalensky asked.

Spencer nodded, not sure if his voice box was capable of forming actual words.

"It is not my intent to kill you. I just want you to know I'm serious. Understand?"

Again, Spencer nodded.

"I would like for you to pay me what you owe me. Can you do that?"

"I can pay some of it now. It'll take me some time to get the rest."

"Unfortunately," Max responded, "that's bullshit. You've got seven thousand dollars in your savings account and you hold less than a thousand dollars' worth of stock. Even if you sell your home, it won't fetch much more than ten grand. That, plus the seven hundred you won tonight at my Brooklyn Heights casino, still leaves you three thousand short. Your annual salary is just over fifteen thousand dollars, which is a very nice income, but at the rate you save it'll take you two years to come up with what you owe me."

Spencer Buckley sat stunned, his mouth wide open. He wasn't sure if he was more horrified that Zalensky knew every detail of his personal finances or that he owned the casino he had just visited in Brooklyn. It was common knowledge that gambling was controlled by local mob elements, emphasis on 'local'. But Zalensky's reach apparently crossed the East River and who knew where else. Beyond that, he had access to Spencer's bank and employment records.

Spencer's throat hurt as he croaked, "If you know so much, if you knew I couldn't pay you, why did you allow me to keep gambling? What is it you want?"

For the first time, Spencer Buckley saw Max Zalensky smile. "I'm pleased that you're so astute. I think we'll work well together."

Buckley's eyes widened, uncomprehendingly. "Work well together at what?"

Again, Zalensky smiled, so coldly that it sent a chill through Spencer. Then he nodded at the big man who was still standing behind Spencer, and for a moment he feared the worst. But the big man just walked out of the room, closing the door behind him, leaving Spencer alone with Max Zalensky.

Max began speaking. "I'm going to tell you things that only I know about. Other people know parts of the story, but those people do not know each other and would have no reason to converse. So you will be the only person, other than me, who knows the whole picture. If I ever suspect that you have told anyone, I will kill you. But before I do so, I will kill your lovely wife, Ellen, and your adorable children, Thomas and Amanda. Do you believe me?"

Spencer knew perfectly well that no one could gain dominance in the New York gambling business, as Zalensky apparently had, without absolute ruthlessness. Quite honestly, fear apparent in his scratchy voice, Spencer said, "Yes, I believe you."

"And do you believe that I will be able to find you and your family, regardless of where you might run?"

"Yes."

"Good. I believe we have the basis for a long and profitable relationship. Basically, I wish to open a bank, perhaps several, and I need a successful Wall Street banker to help me. Someone like you, Mr. Buckley. If you agree, I can promise you will make many times the fifteen thousand dollars a year you make now. In addition, all your outstanding debt to me will be erased. On the other hand, if you decide not to take the job...." Max's voice trailed off, but his meaning was clear.

Spencer Buckley, although surprised, recovered his composure. "How would you find customers for this bank of yours? And why would you want to get into a business that you're unfamiliar with? Making money in banking is never easy and the profit margin is not nearly as attractive as in gambling."

"True," Max said. "But banking has the distinct advantage that your competition doesn't usually try to kill you."

Spencer did not say anything, and Zalensky continued speaking.

"Actually, I'm already in the banking business. I just don't have my own bank." He paused. "Are you familiar with Al Capone, and how he ended up in prison?"

Buckley shrugged. "Same as anyone else, just what I read in the paper. The government couldn't prove that Capone was doing anything illegal, so they grabbed his accounting records along with his accountant and prosecuted him for not paying his taxes."

"That's essentially correct. And as you might imagine, men who make their living though unconventional means were quite distressed by the circumstances of Capone's incarceration. A man might work very hard, endure great expense and risk, and then face imprisonment simply for protecting his hard-earned fortune from the government vultures."

"Uh huh," Buckley said, "or he could just pay his taxes like everyone else."

"Yes," Max responded, "but then he would have to explain all that income from gambling, prostitution, narcotics and loan-sharking. That might prove a little awkward."

"And that's where your bank comes in?"

Max smiled and nodded. "That's where my bank comes in."

Max explained his system to ship cash off shore, set up a foreign corporation, then send the money back to an American bank in an account set up for the foreign corporation. The American bank account was under the control of an American agent appointed by the foreign corporation. That American agent was actually Max's client and owner of the offshore company.

"So you take dirty money and make it clean," Buckley said. "You're sort of like a laundry for illegally gotten gains."

"I hadn't thought of it that way, but I guess the metaphor is appropriate."

"But it must be expensive to bundle up that much cash and physically move it across the ocean. If you owned your own bank, your client could simply deposit it into that bank. Then you could move it overseas through legitimate banking channels: wires and letters of credit. You wouldn't necessarily send it directly to its final destination. You might move it through several different countries so that it would be very difficult, maybe impossible, to trace back to its origin."

Max smiled broadly. "You catch on quickly. Your job will be to set up and run my bank. Or banks. We're already quite profitable from my laundering business, to use your metaphor. And as you've pointed out, using normal banking channels to ship money overseas will substantially reduce costs. I'd like a branch in every big city, so my clients can just walk in and deposit their cash. I won't have to worry about collection and transportation within the United States, which is also a big cost for me. Of course, you'll need to build a fairly large legitimate business to support this infrastructure."

"Legitimate business?"

"Hell yes," Max said, warming to his subject. "I've checked around. Most of your clients really appreciate what you do for them, good solid investments with decent returns. You should have no problem bringing those folks over to your new venture. The investment arm of our bank will offer them exactly the same safe investments that you're providing them now. But in addition, we'll also be able to provide significantly better returns for those who are willing to take higher risks."

"Exactly how will we do that?" Spencer Buckley asked, not certain he wanted to hear the answer.

"The men I deal with require occasional capital for new ventures, like any businessman. But the usual lending options are not open to them. So they are generally forced to pay many points higher than standard rates to obtain funding. We could charge them significantly lower rates than they pay to their current sources, and still make an extremely attractive profit by normal banking standards. Our legitimate clients who invest in these loans will make an excellent return, and we slice off a nice cut. Everybody wins."

"Except that these loans are risky. Somebody uses the money to open up a bordello or to buy drugs, and they get caught, the money is down the drain. I don't want to put my people in anything where they might lose their entire investment," Spencer said.

"The risks in these businesses are different than in more conventional businesses," Max said, "but I don't think they're any greater. And just as with any investment that you put your clients' money into, you will carefully analyse the risk. And you will not put anyone's money into just one loan. You'll spread it around to minimise the risk. I believe that is a key part of portfolio management, as they teach it over at Columbia University. Given the high rates that we will be able to charge on these loans, I think you'll find that the risk/return is very favourable."

Spencer immediately understood, and realised the logic of what Max was saying. All businesses were risky, and all business loans had to take that risk into account. Due to the limited sources of funds available to illegal businesses, they would be more than willing to pay extraordinarily high interest rates, at least by standard business practices. The high margins would easily cover the extra risk. As Max said, everybody wins.

That is, Spencer thought, *unless they get caught.*

Of course he didn't give voice to that possibility. Instead, he said, "The problem is that as a legitimate bank we're regulated by the federal government. If the feds got suspicious and some congressmen wanted to make trouble for us, we could have real problems. They could put us though some nasty audits, investigate our clients, ask for information about our offshore depositors, etcetera. Even if they don't find anything, I would worry about our reputation being sullied, which would scare away many of my legitimate clients."

"You're right," Max said. "The government would not appreciate what we are doing, and if they start nosing around it can only hurt us. Fortunately, I pride myself on being able to anticipate such problems and head them off. It's really just a matter of being willing to make the investment."

Spencer Buckley was not sure what that meant, and was not sure that he wanted to know. So he nodded, as if to agree.

Zalensky asked, "Are you in?"

"Yes, definitely."

The fact that the alternative was a bullet to the back of his head made the decision an easy one. In addition, he held no illusions that he or his family could flee Zalensky's wrath in the event that he later became unhappy with the arrangement. Given the inevitability of the situation, he might as well make the best of it. Hell, he'd always wanted to run his own bank, and under other circumstances he'd be thrilled. If he played his cards right he'd probably get rich.

★   ★   ★

Spencer Buckley worked hard to make the bank as successful as possible. They opened up the first branch of Manhattan First Savings Bank six weeks after that fateful meeting. Mr. Zalensky did not like his money to sit idle, and the bank grew quickly. As Zalensky predicted, Spencer was able to bring in some of his old clients as large depositors in the new venture, more in fact than he had dared hope. It was both flattering and surprising to Spencer, but Zalensky acted as if he had expected it. Perhaps he had.

But the real growth was from people right off the street. At Zalensky's instruction, Manhattan First Savings advertised savings interest rates one-quarter percent higher than the going rate in Manhattan. Customers flocked into the clean new quarters on Broad Street to receive that little bit extra on their hard-earned money. Spencer hired his chief operating officer from a rival New York bank, a man considered to be the best operations guy in the city. Zalensky told him to simply offer the man twenty percent more than his current salary.

"But we don't need anyone this good yet," Spencer had responded. "We're not that big."

"Don't worry, we will be. Pay a little bit more, hire people who are smarter and work harder. You'll run a lot more efficiently, and your overall costs will be lower. Then you can pass the savings on to your customers."

"And that's how you run your own operations?"

Zalensky nodded. "Something I learned from my father."

"Oh, you're close to him?"

Zalensky looked at him sideways. "We don't speak."

★　★　★

Ten months after the opening of the first branch, they opened a second one off Washington Square. It also got off to a rousing start, and Zalensky was already planning an expansion to Chicago. The branch there would be called Chicago First Savings Bank, as Zalensky believed in local pride. Spencer was now making thirty-two thousand dollars per year, more than twice what he had been making on Wall Street. He loved his job, with one small caveat: Max Zalensky made his blood run cold.

CHAPTER FIFTY-TWO

Senator Standish was not looking forward to his ten o'clock appointment. It was not that the thought of meeting a gangster intimidated him; he had met more than his share of rough characters during his climb to the Senate. It was just distasteful to have a person of such low character intrude upon the elegance of his office.

He had never met Zalensky but he knew the type: Lower East Side thug, always ready for a fight, never quite able to leave the smell of the street behind him. And a Jew to boot. Truth be told, such men were usually intimidated by Standish. Or at least the senator felt that they were. His high intelligence and obviously superior breeding, as well as the rich surroundings of his office would naturally be discomforting to such scoundrels.

Not that Zalensky was known as a criminal. Standish had checked, and Max had never been convicted or even arrested. The local police were barely aware of his existence even though they had to deal with his subordinates on a regular basis. But Standish made it a point to know what was going on in his old district and he had been aware of Max Zalensky for years. His informant network told him that Zalensky controlled illegal gambling and the inevitable loan-sharking that accompanied it throughout the five boroughs of New York and half of New Jersey. It was suspected, although no one could confirm, that he also controlled several legitimate banks.

Standish could not imagine what a man like Zalensky would want with a real bank. Maybe, the senator thought, he just needs a place to park his money. To Standish's knowledge, no one man had ever controlled a gambling empire of such proportions. It would take superb organisation backed up by complete ruthlessness. The cash flow must be enormous, which is how he had gotten an appointment with the senator. Two of Standish's most generous supporters had arranged the meeting. Standish had resisted but the two contributors had made it clear that without the meeting, there would be no more money. It was obvious that Zalensky had the two men in his pocket.

★   ★   ★

He was not at all what the senator had expected. He arrived precisely at ten o'clock, a handsome man in his mid-thirties. He looked to Standish like a Wall Street lawyer: perfectly tailored pinstriped suit, neatly cropped hair and carrying a dark leather briefcase. He shook the senator's hand quickly and firmly, and when he spoke there was hardly a trace of the Lower East Side.

"Thank you for taking the time to see me, Senator," Zalensky said graciously. "I will come directly to the point so as to take as little of your time as possible."

The senator nodded, and Zalensky continued. "I realise that what I am about to ask may seem an imposition on your personal sphere of influence. However, I assure you that if you help me, I in turn can provide substantial financial assistance for your next senatorial campaign. My people tell me that these campaigns are very expensive."

Standish had expected something of this sort when the meeting had been arranged. Like many of his colleagues, he was not above trading favours. And if the favour Zalensky wanted was not too big, and the reward significant, this meeting could be well worthwhile. Without any hint of commitment in his voice, Standish said, "Go on."

"Senator Standish, you are well aware that Congressional Seat 102, your old seat, has been vacated by the retirement of Congressman Horne. You have endorsed Councilman Fenton for that position, which makes his election almost a sure thing." Max hesitated a moment. "I would like you to withdraw your support for Fenton and issue a very enthusiastic endorsement of Arthur Simmons. You will then follow up with several campaign speeches for Mr. Simmons. With your support, I feel confident that Mr. Simmons will be elected."

Max noted the look of surprise on the senator's face but continued undeterred. "As I mentioned, your help would not go unrewarded."

The expression on the senator's face changed to one of contempt. "In your world," he said coldly, "people may be bought and sold very cheaply. I, however, am not part of your world. Congressman Paul

Fenton is a personal friend of mine, a protégé of sorts. He is my choice to fill my old position. I will not betray a friendship, a trust, for any amount of money." The senator reached into a file cabinet for some papers, placed them on his desk and began reading. Without looking up he said, "You may go."

Max, however, did not go. Instead, he smiled slightly and spoke. "I am sorry, Senator, but there is another issue I must address with you."

Standish glanced up at him and said, "Yes?" in an impatient manner.

"Senator," said Max, "there are some unscrupulous men, enemies of yours, who would like to do you harm."

"What are you talking about?"

Max took a legal-size manila envelope out of his briefcase. He passed the envelope across the table to Standish. The senator fingered it for a moment, then opened it and pulled out five eight by ten photographs. The photos were of excellent quality, obviously taken by a professional.

The subject of all five pictures was Senator Alton Standish and Miss Kathleen Collins in bed together. The covers of the bed had been thrown off, something Kathleen loved to do, so that their naked bodies were completely exposed to the camera lens. The face of each subject was easily distinguishable, and it was quite clear that they were engaged in sexual intercourse. Standish could even make out the insignia of the Williamsburg Inn on the lamp next to the bed.

He looked up at Max, his face red with anger. "You cheap hood. You think this bullshit scares me? You think I'm going to kiss your ass for crap like this? You stupid kike, this won't cost me one vote. My people know I play around, my wife knows it, everybody knows it. Hell, it's part of my manly image." Then he said, "Now get the fuck out of my office or I'll have you thrown out."

But again, Max made no movement to leave. Instead, he spoke in a very placid, almost gentle voice. "Please, Senator, you misunderstand. The unscrupulous men who commissioned these pictures do not care about your political career. They are actually aiming to deprive you of your very freedom."

"What the fuck are you talking about?"

Still in the gentle voice, Max said, "Senator, it is plain from the photographs that this particular incident occurred at the Williamsburg

Inn, in Virginia. In that state, as in most of the South, sexual intercourse between an adult and a minor under the age of eighteen is statutory rape, punishable by up to five years in prison. In addition, this girl resides here in Washington, DC. Under the Mann Act of 1924, transportation of a minor across state lines for the purpose of sexual intercourse is a federal offence, also punishable by up to five years."

Standish's eyes narrowed as he looked at the pictures spread across his desk. It occurred to him that the female body in the black-and-white glossies was so taut and firm that it could easily be mistaken for that of a teenager. That was precisely what made her so wonderful. He looked up at Zalensky and said, "Those laws are irrelevant to my situation. The young woman in question, Kathleen Collins, is a twenty-six-year-old graduate student at Georgetown University. Some of my constituents would consider the difference in our ages to be scandalous, but it is hardly illegal." Standish allowed himself a small bit of vanity. "Some of my constituents would actually consider it evidence of my virility."

Max nodded respectfully, but his voice no longer held the endearing quality that it had the moment before. In a cold monotone he said, "You have been misinformed, Senator. The name of the young woman in question is Dorothy Mislowski, not Kathleen Collins. She is sixteen years old, seventeen next month, and a student at John Madison High School here in Washington, DC. In legal terms she is a child, not a young woman."

"Bullshit."

Without speaking, Max took three objects out of his briefcase and slid them across the desk to Standish. The first was a Photostat of a Washington, DC driver's licence. The person pictured on the licence was definitely Kathleen. She was wearing neither makeup nor glasses. She looked like a teenager. But the name on the licence was not Kathleen's; it was Dorothy Mislowski. It had been issued ten months earlier, one month after Dorothy turned sixteen according to the birthdate given.

The second object was a 1932 yearbook for John Madison High School. It had been published a month earlier, when the school year ended in June. Max opened it to the junior class. There, under the Ms. was a Dorothy Mislowski. She was wearing makeup, which made her look older than on the driver's licence, but it was definitely the same girl. Kathleen.

The third object was a copy of Dorothy's high school transcript, dated June 2. At the bottom it stated that this student would begin her senior year in September. The senator noted that the girl had received good, but not outstanding, grades.

Max then took three papers which had been clipped together out of his briefcase and placed them on the desk. "This is a copy of a deposition given by Dorothy Mislowski, signed by her and sworn to, in the presence of a court reporter and a notary public. It states that she met you on April 12th of this year when her high school government class toured the Senate office building. According to her, you asked her to stay after her class left. She was thrilled to be singled out for special attention by a famous senator."

"You took her out for an early dinner and then to a hotel, where you seduced her. You have been meeting on a regular basis ever since. In fact, her high school class did visit the Senate Office Building on April 12th and if you check your calendar, you will find that your office was on the tour and that you were in your office that day. In addition, the school records show that Dorothy did not return to school with the rest of her class."

The senator sat down in his chair and buried his face in his hands. When he looked up again and spoke, his voice was shaking. Max could not tell if it shook from fear or anger, or both.

"How could this have happened? I did meet her at Georgetown. She came on to me. Presented herself as a graduate student."

Max responded in his monotone. "The unscrupulous men that I spoke of set you up, Senator. Dorothy lives with her mother, who is a working prostitute. Although Dorothy is a legitimate high school student, she could have been hooking on the side, maybe filling in for her mother on occasion. A girl like that is often sophisticated beyond her years, possibly very intelligent. Perhaps these enemies of yours spent some time teaching her about politics, particularly in the areas of interest to you, such as banking. That would give her credibility as a graduate student. Everyone knows your proclivities. A meeting is arranged, the rest is easy."

Standish spoke again, his voice still shaking. "I suppose you can guarantee, for the proper quid pro quo, that none of this becomes public."

Max nodded. "Exactly." Then he gathered the documents, placed them back in the envelope, and stood to leave. On his way out the door he turned and said, "I'll expect you to pull your support from Fenton and issue an endorsement of Simmons by Friday. You can call Simmons' office to arrange the details of where and when you will perform campaign speeches. I think ten personal appearances on his behalf would be about right."

"What do you expect to get out of this, Zalensky? Total control of a young congressman?"

"No," Max responded coldly. "I do, of course, expect to gain some influence over the young Mr. Simmons. But I expect total control of a middle-aged, senior senator." Then he walked out of the senator's office, shutting the door behind him.

CHAPTER FIFTY-THREE
1933

"Your new business has done very well," Max said. It had been two years since Jonathan had proposed converting vaudeville houses into movie theatres. Max had come out west for his regular visit, and they were discussing business over breakfast at the Sunset Grill.

"Thank you. It's your business too."

"I appreciate that. And I'm thankful for it. However, since you have brought up my interest, I do have one concern that I'd like to share with you."

"Oh?" Jonathan looked up from his French toast.

"It seems to me that our one competitive weakness is that we don't control the product."

"Meaning we don't make movies?"

"Exactly."

"That hasn't caused us any problems so far."

"No, not so far, because there are lots of movies, and not enough theatres to show them in. You did a great job of getting us into the business right when there was a shortage. But as the majors build more theatres, that'll change. MGM owns the Loews chain, right? If things get to the point where there're too many movie houses and not enough movies, MGM is gonna take care of its own."

"But we're not close to that point. Loews has fifteen hundred theatres, but there're still a lot more movies than places to show them."

"My understanding is that Loews wants to open another five hundred houses in the next two years."

"What?" Jonathan looked up so fast he almost spilled his coffee. "Where did you get that information?"

"I can't tell you where I got it. But trust me."

Jonathan looked at him glumly. "So you're saying the solution is for us to get into the movie-making business. Only little problem is, I don't know how to make a movie."

Max shrugged. "You'll learn. Louis Mayer was a junk dealer, right? Goldwyn was a glove maker, and Zukor a furrier. You're as smart as any of them, you already know a lot about the business, and you know lots of people in it. You'll do great."

"Producing a movie is expensive. Anywhere between two hundred fifty grand and a million for a feature with big-name players, and sometimes more than that. Even the bargain-basement pictures cost almost a hundred grand."

Again, Max shrugged. "I imagine we can find the money somewhere. Look, Jon, it isn't just a matter of producing product to put in our own theatres. If we have even a few hit movies, MGM will want to show them in their two thousand theatres, so they won't want to piss us off. That means they'll have to let us show their movies in our forty theatres. They'll have a lot more to lose than we do, so we've got leverage."

"So," Jonathan said sarcastically, "all I have to do is turn out a few hit movies a year."

Max brightened. "Exactly."

On August 26, 1933, Jonathan and his silent partner bought Film Studios of America Inc., a small production company based in Hollywood. Film Studios of America, or FSA, did not actually own any studios. It rented space on the Paramount lot where it churned out bargain-basement Westerns at the rate of one every eight weeks. FSA's two biggest assets were Bob Benson, its cowboy star, and his horse, Silver Savage, who received equal billing on movie marquees. FSA movies were popular in small towns but had never broken into the much bigger urban markets. When Jonathan talked to the manager of his San Francisco theatres about showing an FSA feature, the man responded, "I don't think so, Jon. This month our biggest hit is *Dangerous Curves* with Susan Spencer. Our audiences want female flesh, not horseflesh."

For FSA's next picture, called *Sunset over the Rockies*, Jonathan ordered the writer to add a hint of romance for Bob Benson and a few less scenes for the horse. The romance consisted of a rancher's daughter, played by a pretty young girl with no acting experience, who developed a crush on Benson when he saved the family ranch from cattle rustlers and the girl herself from the rustlers' evil lust. Benson returned the girl's advances by walking her around the ranch after supper, gazing into her eyes, and granting her a quick brush on the lips before galloping off into the sunset. Jonathan forced his San Francisco theatres to show the film, over his manager's protests. The feature proved to be a hit and was picked up by urban movie houses all over the country, effectively tripling FSA's normal revenue. From that point on, FSA films featured less horse and more female.

CHAPTER FIFTY-FOUR
1934

"Thank you for seeing me."

"The honour is mine, Mr. Cahill. It's been a long time since I've had an audience with the head of an American studio," Clarence Rollins said.

"Yes, that's unfortunate," Jonathan said. "I know you've been doing good work in Europe and I'm glad to catch you while you're here in Los Angeles. But I'd have flown to Berlin to meet with you if I needed to."

"Okay, I'm very flattered. What's this about?"

"I'd like you to direct movies for Film Studios of America. Are you interested?"

Rollins gazed at him coolly. "Yes, of course I'm interested. But I don't do horse pictures. Don't get me wrong. Working in Europe isn't the same as working here, no matter what anybody tells you. The equipment's not as good, the sets aren't as good, the actors aren't as good and the money's not as good. Also, I'm sick and tired of the goddamn Huns clicking their heels and barking away in German. But I get to make movies that I'm proud of and I get to be in charge. Besides, FSA isn't exactly a major studio, no offence. You probably won't pay me any more than what I get over there, and your overall budget is probably smaller. Now give me some good news and tell me I'm wrong."

Jonathan spoke slowly. "I have some good news, and some bad. If you agree to work for us, we will pay you the same rate that is paid to any top director at a major studio. That's because I consider you the equal of any of them. You will be allowed to make any sort of film you want, as long as it's not a horse picture. Furthermore, you will be responsible for every aspect of the film. That includes hiring actors, cinematographers, sound men, grips, etcetera, and when or if you allow bathroom breaks. We already have all those people working for FSA, but whether you use our in-house folks or hire your own is up to you. Of course, you are known as a man who brings a picture in on time and under budget. You will be expected to do that here."

"And what's the bad news? You expect me to do all this for seventy thousand dollars. That's your usual budget, right?"

"Your first film will have a budget of five hundred thousand dollars. I'm sure you can do the job for that figure."

Rollins stared at him. "So what's the bad news?"

"At Film Studios of America, it is not our purpose to be artful or intellectual or on the cutting edge. Our purpose is to make good pictures that make good money. To that end, I will have veto power over the script, the actors, and anything else that I feel it necessary to stick my nose into. Speaking honestly, I know very little about making movies, but I do feel that I understand our audiences. So I will only interfere if I feel something or someone is not commercially viable. That is, if it will not play in Peoria. Or New York."

Looking Jonathan up and down, as if sizing him up, Rollins said, "I can live with that."

"And your name will not appear anywhere on the screen."

Rollins looked as if he hadn't understood what Jonathan had said. "Excuse me?"

"I'm sorry, but we can't give you on-screen credit. That would put the film in real danger of being banned, in which case our five hundred thousand-dollar investment would be lost." Jonathan winced slightly. "My partner would not appreciate that."

"I guess people here have long memories."

Jonathan shook his head. "Actually, I've found memories in this town to be remarkably short and four years is a long time by Hollywood standards. Unfortunately, your case is special. It didn't really hit the papers. Someone did a good job with that. But the Vice Squad seems to have a special beef with you. They promised to shut down any studio that employs you - made a special trip out to see me when I purchased FSA, just to let me know. If your name appears on the screen, we would have some trouble.

"If it's that serious, aren't you running a risk to employ me at all?"

Again, Jonathan shook his head. "I don't think it'll present any problems. We're in a unique position with the LAPD and there's not much chance they'd actually shut us down. But that doesn't mean I want to spit in their face. If anything does come up, we'll say you were employed as an errand boy, no real responsibility. The proof of that is that you're not listed in the credits. Eventually, I do hope to get your name back on the screen, which would be beneficial for both of us. But that'll take some time. Please understand that I'm a great fan of yours and I am truly amazed that people care so much about so-called crimes that have no victims. That said, I need to run a profitable business. So I'd love to have you, if you can live with the conditions."

Rollins hesitated a few moments before saying, "I guess I'll have to." He stuck out his hand. "I look forward to working for you."

Jonathan smiled. "As I look forward to working with you."

CHAPTER FIFTY-FIVE
1935

"Be reasonable, my dear," Louis Kahn said, edging a little closer to her. "This offer is comparable to what we pay our top stars. I really can't go any higher."

Duke was on the lot, filming a Western, and Sophie would soon be starting work on a new romantic comedy. More than ever, Kahn wanted her under contract. She was a big star now, a certain box-office draw, and it killed Louis to have to compete for her every time he wanted her for a particular part.

"And I'm not asking you to," Sophie responded. "To be honest, I only took this meeting because Duke asked me to." And then she said, as if in response to Kahn moving closer, "And he assured me that you would act like a gentleman."

"I'm always a gentleman," Louis protested. Then he grinned, reminding Sophie of a leering satyr in a Botticelli painting. "Of course, there are some young ladies, such as the one I was with last night, who don't like it so gentle, if you know what I mean."

"How about your wife?" Sophie couldn't stop herself from saying. "Does she know what you mean?"

Kahn shrugged, a gesture that extended through his entire upper body. "She's wife number three. She knows the way it works. How the hell do you think I met her? But enough about me, we're here to talk about you. You're not gonna make this much money anywhere else, or staying independent. So how 'bout it?"

"Why would you want me, or any actor for that matter, to sign a contract?"

Kahn nodded to himself, as if her question confirmed something he already suspected. "You're the first actor to ask me that," he said. "My Board of Directors, yes, but never an actor. Actors just ask how much."

"What do you tell your Board of Directors?"

"That I want my movies to be made by the best people: actors, directors and writers. Since I want the best people, I've gotta have them available when I want them. That means I need those people under contract and I'm willing to pay damn good money for that."

"I'm flattered that you consider me one of the people you want. But I want to have a little more control—"

Sophie was interrupted by Kahn's secretary rushing into the room through a door that was suddenly thrown open. Kahn looked up, more irritated than surprised. The secretary started to speak, then seeing Sophie, stopped. Instead, she walked over to Louis and whispered quickly in his ear. Louis blanched, stood up from the couch, and started to walk toward the door. "There's an emergency on one of the sets," he said, without looking back at Sophie. "I'll be back as soon as I can." Before he closed the door behind him, he said emphatically, "Don't leave."

Sophie wasn't sure if she should be irritated or not by Kahn's abrupt departure. Whatever had happened was apparently important and required his presence, but he had begged for this meeting and she at least had expected him to finish it. *Oh well*, she thought, *for all practical purposes it was over anyway*. She simply was not interested in what he had to offer. Sophie got to her feet, but before leaving decided to take a look out Kahn's oversized picture window, the one overlooking the studio lot. Perhaps she'd be able to spot the big emergency.

At first, she saw nothing unusual. But then Kahn came rushing out of the building below her, and headed toward the west side of the lot. Sophie stepped up close to the window so that she could follow his path. Her eyes automatically moved ahead of him to where a small crowd of people huddled in a circle. They were in front of an Old West set, complete with saloon and sheriff's office. Sophie's brain immediately flashed to Kahn's secretary, the way she had become silent upon seeing Sophie, and how she had looked at her. "Oh my God," she whispered, and then turned from the window and sprinted for the door.

The wait for the elevator seemed interminably long, and Sophie was about to take the stairs when the bell rang and the door slid open. She hurried in and practically yelled at the operator, a small, grey-haired man, to go straight to the lobby. He did as he was told, ignoring the flashing buttons on intervening floors.

A man at the edge of the cluster of people saw her approaching and moved out of the way. He tapped the sleeve of the next man, who also stepped aside wordlessly, as did the next, so that a path was cleared for her.

As soon as she broke through the crowd Sophie saw Duke lying on his back, in the middle of the make-believe Old West street. Dr. Ornstein, the studio physician who Kahn employed for the benefit of his contract players, stepped forward as Sophie approached, forcing her to stop. He was a short, stocky man, and had a reputation as a top-notch internist. "I'm sorry," he said. "He appears to have had a heart attack. It was very quick. He didn't suffer."

Sophie stared at him as if he were speaking some language she did not understand, then brushed past him. Louis Kahn was down on his hands and knees, bent over Duke's prone body. He appeared to be talking to him, in spite of the obvious fact that the cowboy star could no longer hear him. Sophie dropped to her knees beside him and Louis moved aside, as if he knew who it was without having to look. Instinctively, Sophie bent over and kissed the dead man, then caressed his face with her hand.

To her surprise, his cheek was slippery with moisture. She looked quickly over at Kahn, and saw that the studio chief was crying profusely. His back was to the onlookers, and he was leaning over so that nobody but Sophie could see. Few people in Hollywood would have thought Louis Kahn capable of feeling actual grief. But Sophie was not surprised. *He has lost the only man he could truly call a friend*, she thought, and wondered if she should say something to comfort the old lecher.

But then she flashed to Jacob, her son, and an overwhelming grief crept over her like a dark cloud blotting out a sunny day. Poor Jake would be crushed. Absolutely crushed.

And as Kahn had done, Sophie found herself speaking to Duke, softly, as if they were lying next to one another in bed and he could hear her. "He thinks of you as his father," she said. "I don't think he can remember a time without you. It will be terribly hard on him."

With one hand on Duke's face and the other grasping his cold fingers, she continued to speak to him: about that first time he had taken her horseback riding, about the family vacations in Cabo San Lucas, about Jacob and how smart he was. Duke had seen that first, and she wanted him to be there when Jake became a great doctor, which was her secret hope. Sophie wondered who she would turn to now if she needed career advice, or if Jake needed counsel. It wasn't easy getting him to listen to her anymore, but if Duke backed her up the boy would always see the wisdom of her words. And it would just be so lonely.

Sophie realised suddenly that Louis Kahn was pulling her by the hand away from Duke. She had forgotten that he was there, but he was saying something in a gentle tone that was very unlike him. "They have to take him now," he whispered. "The people are here with the ambulance, and they need to take him."

She nodded, acknowledging that she understood. And then she began to sob, uncontrollably and in great waves, her shoulders and chest heaving heavily, and Louis Kahn, whom she so disdained, held her gently as her sobs turned to slow, gurgling wails of despair.

CHAPTER FIFTY-SIX

Sophie returned to work two weeks after the funeral. Louis Kahn had uncharacteristically told her to take as much time as she needed. But Jake was back in school now and sitting around the house that she and Duke had shared only deepened her depression. Perhaps going back to work would take her mind off him, help her to move on with her life.

She had been back on the set of the new movie for almost a week when she got the call from Mrs. Goldberg. There was some trouble at Jake's school. The principal, Mrs. Stanley, had called the house. Sophie needed to go over there right away.

Virgilio drove the five miles from Signature Studios to Hollywood High in slightly under twelve minutes. Sophie jumped out of the car before the chauffeur could come around to open her door, then walked rapidly to the school office. Behind the reception desk sat a neatly dressed, meticulously coiffed woman poring over a schedule of classes. Sophie announced to the woman that her name was Susan Spencer and that Principal Stanley had asked her to come in.

The woman stared at Sophie for a moment, then rose from her desk and strode purposely over to where Sophie stood. She stuck out her hand and said, "I am Mrs. Stanley." She waved a hand toward the reception desk. "Our receptionist, Annie, called in sick and we were unable to get a replacement. I brought some of my work out here so I could do double duty. Please, come into my office."

It was only then, as she followed Principal Stanley, that Sophie noticed Jake. He was sitting in a chair off to the side of the entrance area. He had obviously seen his mother's entry, but hadn't said a word. There were scratches on his face, a cut on his right cheek, and some swelling over his right eye. But what made her pause, caused her heart to catch in her chest, was the cold, almost uncaring manner in which Jake looked at her. It was a look that reminded her of another young man she had once loved, a man whom she no longer wished to think about.

She heard Mrs. Stanley say, "He's fine, the nurse looked at him and it's just some minor bruises. But we do need to talk."

Sophie took one last long look at her son, then kept walking behind Mrs. Stanley down the short hallway into her office. The principal settled herself behind the desk and Sophie sat in one of the visitor's chairs, facing her. The furniture was utilitarian rather than stylish, but the office was arrayed with pictures and personal touches.

Mrs. Stanley began, "Jacob got into a fistfight today. That's why I called you in. He's not in trouble with the school, it was clearly self-defence, but...." Mrs. Stanley's voice trailed off. She looked away from Sophie for a moment and said, "It was troubling."

"I'm not sure I understand."

The principal nodded. "The boy that Jacob had his run-in with is named Martin Holten. Martin is a senior, two years older than your son and quite a bit bigger, although not nearly as athletic. He's a known bully, both violent and mean, and he's been quite a problem for us. According to every witness, Martin started the fight, calling Jacob names, shoving him, then hitting him. Most of the students at the school and, I suspect, some of the teachers, were thrilled to see one of Martin's victims stand up to him."

"So, what is so troubling?" Sophie's voice had a slight shake; she was afraid that she knew the answer.

"Apparently," Mrs. Stanley responded, "Jacob had no problem gaining control of the situation despite the fact that Martin struck first. He was able to dodge and duck and connect several blows, while Martin was only able to land a few punches. Martin was knocked to the ground and Jacob continued to kick him, even after he was down. Martin suffered several broken ribs and a slight concussion. The reports I've received are that Jacob showed no signs of letting up, and if several male teachers had not arrived in time to pull him off...." Mrs. Stanley's voice trailed away.

Sophie shut her eyes, picturing another young man who looked so much like Jake that he could be his brother. She could see him in his single-mindedness, focused only on the enemy in front of him and his need to destroy that enemy.

Sophie said, "His father died recently. They were very close and it's been difficult. Jake seemed to be doing okay, but I think he's actually quite angry."

Mrs. Stanley nodded. "Of course. And I'm so sorry for your loss." She hesitated a moment. "I'm not much of a moviegoer, myself, Mrs. Hawkins, but everything I've read makes it clear that your husband was a wonderful man."

"Yes," Sophie said, "he was."

Sophie and Jacob drove home without speaking and walked into the house, still not saying a word until Sophie broke the silence. "I know how you feel. Exactly how you feel," she said, "but you can't do this."

"Do what?" Jake snapped. "Defend myself?"

"It's fine to defend yourself. Your father would have said it's the only thing to do. But you can't just hurt someone. Once that bully is no longer a threat to you, once you've beaten him, you need to stop and walk away."

"Maybe he deserved more than that. Maybe he deserved for someone to really kick the hell out of him."

"And maybe if no one had been there to stop you, you would have hurt him very badly. Or killed him. And then what?" Sophie asked, desperation in her voice.

"Then maybe he still deserved it," Jake said. "He picks on everyone and maybe now he won't."

Sophie spoke very softly. "What about your father? Would he want you doing this sort of thing? Hurting people?"

Jake looked at her for a moment, then lowered his eyes. "No, I guess he wouldn't."

Sophie walked over to her son and put her arms around him. He buried his face in her shoulder and cried, the tears soon turning to deep sobs. Sophie held him tightly, stroking the back of his head and whispering that everything would be okay. Because now she knew that it would be.

CHAPTER FIFTY-SEVEN
1937

Jack Warner set up the meeting. Jonathan did not normally meet with union representatives himself, but since the chairman of Warner Brothers had made the request, he felt he should oblige.

The man wore an expensive suit, smoked an expensive cigar and smelled of cologne. He reminded Jonathan more of a gambler from his old New York neighbourhood than of a working man. He could not picture this fellow running a movie projector.

He got straight to business. "I'm Willie Bioff," he said, "and I represent the International Association of Projectionists. But I guess you already know that."

"Yes, I do. But Jack was not clear about the nature of this meeting."

"The nature. Yeah. Well, like I said, I represent the projectionists and that's the nature of this. To put it to ya straight, we're thinking of putting in a strike at all your theatres. I know your movie houses ain't a part of Film Studios of America, they're yours personally. But then, we also could strike all the theatres across the country that are showing FSA movies. Turn your movies off, so to speak."

Jonathan stared at Bioff. "Let me make certain I understand you. You are telling me that the Projectionists Union is thinking of striking all the movie theatres I own, as well as theatres I do not own that are showing an FSA movie."

"You got it exactly right."

"I don't understand. I pay my projectionists more than the prevailing wage. And I have certainly not heard about any discontent among my employees."

"Yeah, well you're hearing about it now. And that's the point, see. You actually got it in your power to fix the problem right here and now and prevent any strikes. Everybody'll be happy, just like before."

"How would I do that?"

"Write a check for two hundred thousand dollars."

"Excuse me?"

"You heard me. That's a hundred grand for your movie houses, and a hundred grand for your studio. And your business goes on like usual."

"And if I don't write you a check?"

"We shut you down. We're not asking for much, considering what we can do to you. It's not like this will even make a dent in your budget. I think the other studios call it public relations expense or something."

Jonathan felt his blood begin to boil, but outwardly remained completely calm. "And to whom should I make out this check?"

"To me is to whom. That's B-I-O-F-F."

"Mr. Bioff, until five minutes ago I had never met you. And before Jack Warner called a few days ago, I had never even heard of you. I'm sure you understand that I cannot pay what amounts to extortion without checking things out."

Bioff shrugged. "Yeah, of course. But remember it was Jack Warner who called you. Call him back. Call the other studio heads too. Just don't take too long at it. I'll be back in a week for my check."

★   ★   ★

"The majors all pay this guy," Jonathan said into the phone. "I talked to Jack Warner at Warner Brothers, to Ernst Lubitsch at Paramount, and to Bill Fox at 20th Century. They all think it's worth it. Apparently, Sam Goldwyn told Bioff to go to hell. A week later three hundred and twenty theatres showing Goldwyn features were shut down for five days. It cost Sam a small fortune, so now he's paying too."

"Bioff's taking a big risk," Max Zalensky said. "If one or two of these Hollywood big shots calls the FBI and testifies against him, Bioff goes to jail for a long time."

"That may be, but the studio heads are worried about their personal safety. No one wants to be shot on the way to the courthouse."

Jonathan could hear Max scoff at the other end of the phone. "This punk isn't about to hurt a big-time movie mogul. J. Edgar Hoover would be all over that like white on rice. Think of the headlines the FBI would get, which is mostly what Hoover cares about anyway."

"Be that as it may, I don't think anyone's about to call the feds. If Bioff's asking us for two hundred grand, he's probably asking the big guys for five or six hundred G's each. That's a drop in the bucket for them, and if they call it public relations or consulting or something like that, it's tax deductible."

"Yeah, maybe. Look, put this guy off. I need some time to see who's behind him."

"I'll try, but he said he'd be back in a week."

"A week should be enough."

CHAPTER FIFTY-EIGHT

Four days later, Special Agent David Normand sat in his small office in the Washington, DC headquarters of the FBI and stared at the special delivery he had received an hour earlier. He had asked the postal service to trace the package back to the sender, but he already knew that the effort would be futile.

The package was extraordinary, not only for its contents, but for what it said about its sender. Whoever mailed this package had a remarkable ability to reach into and extract information from the American banking system. The FBI itself, with all its resources, would have had difficulty finding these documents. No less unsettling was the fact that the package was special delivered directly to Normand, meaning the sender had access to confidential case assignments, because there had been no announcement, either publicly or within the Bureau, that David was working on this particular case.

Normand had been assigned the case two months earlier, when headquarters began to suspect that the new president of the International Association of Projectionists had ties to the Chicago crime syndicate. Disgruntled delegates to the union's convention phoned in that they had been intimidated into voting for Willie Bioff. The calls were anonymous and no one was willing to come forward, but Bioff was a known pimp who had been arrested twice and had served time. More importantly, he was a known associate of Chicago mob boss Frank Nitti, and like any pimp in that city had to operate under the mob boss's protection.

FBI Director J. Edgar Hoover would give his right nut to put Nitti away, so this close a connection between a national union and the mob had to be investigated. But given Hoover's paranoia about information leaks, plus his fear of Hollywood's political clout, the investigation had been kept close to the vest. Normand reported directly to Clyde Tolson, J. Edgar's right-hand man, and other

Bureau personnel knew only what was necessary to get the job done.

But the investigation had gone nowhere. Until today, and the delivery of this package. Normand again looked at the contents spread out across his desk. There was a typed letter explaining that the heads of each of the major studios were paying extortion money to Willie Bioff to prevent the Projectionists Union from shutting down their theatres, either by sanctioning union strikes or creating individual mishaps such as projector breakdowns, sound cut-offs, film being destroyed, etc. The anonymous letter writer went on to say that Bioff was backed by Frank Nitti but that, faced with federal prison time, he would likely rat him out. None of this was surprising. In fact, Normand already suspected all of it.

But then the coup de grace: spread out in front of Normand were cancelled checks from each of the five major studios, signed by each of the five studio bosses, and made out to Willie Bioff. The signatures on the checks were a who's who of Hollywood moguls: Jack Warner, William Fox, Neil Schenk, Ernst Lubitsch and Sam Goldwyn. The checks were for six hundred thousand dollars each. Someone had known about the payoffs and who was making them, and had been able to reach right into private bank accounts and pull out the cancelled checks. Normand knew that the Treasury Department had been talking, for a while, about requiring banks to send such checks back to the depositors, but as of now each bank still held them. And someone had somehow gotten them. Under other circumstances David Normand would be investigating this intrusion into the US banking system. But right now he was grateful for it.

The phone on his desk rang loudly, startling him. He picked it up, assuming it was Clyde Tolson asking for an update.

"Normand here."

"Did you get the package?"

Surprised, Normand asked, "Who is this?"

"Let's not play games, Normand." It was a male voice, a bone-dry monotone. "Tomorrow morning you'll receive a call from a studio executive named Jonathan Cahill. Don't hand out any indictments or confront any of the people who wrote the checks until then. Okay?"

"Why not?"

"Because you just received a package that contained evidence of payments made by industry executives to Willie Bioff and because the person who sent that package is trying to help you build a stronger case."

"Wait a minute. I need more than that. Tell me what—"

The caller hung up.

★   ★   ★

The next morning, David Normand got a call from Jonathan Cahill. Normand had done his homework and knew that Cahill was president and chief executive officer of Film Studios of America, as well as a string of forty big-city theatres. FSA was not in the same league as the majors, but in the past four years it had turned out twenty-two full-length movies, each of which had yielded respectable profits.

"I'm told you'll know what I'm calling about."

"I do if it concerns Willie Bioff."

"It does. He's paying me a visit day after tomorrow and I'm supposed to hand him a check for two hundred thousand dollars."

"I can be there. You go ahead and give him the money, and I'll arrest him on the spot. That check will never be cashed...assuming you're willing to testify."

"I am. Unfortunately, I don't think there's any way around it. I just need to know that this guy's not going to come after me."

"Don't worry. Once I nab him I'll stick him in prison so deep he'll never get out."

"Let's hope so," Jonathan said.

CHAPTER FIFTY-NINE

"Good morning, Mr. Cahill," Bioff said jovially. "How ya doing today?"

"Fine, thank you."

"Ya got something for me?"

Yes, I do, Jonathan thought. *I've got three G-men next door, recording every word we say on studio-grade recorders.* But to his visitor, he said, "Yes, in fact I do. And just to make sure we're both totally clear on our deal, tell me again what I'm getting for my two hundred thousand dollars."

"You're getting that we don't shut down every one of your theatres and every other theatre that shows one of your movies. Just ask Sam Goldwyn if we can't do it. But you probably already heard about that." Bioff snickered.

"Yes, I did. So here is your check, which I trust will spare me from the same problems that befell Mr. Goldwyn."

"You trust right." Bioff snickered again, taking the check from Jonathan, holding it up to make sure it was legit.

His smirk faded when the door burst open and the three FBI agents rushed into the room, guns drawn. "Federal Bureau of Investigation," David Normand said to Bioff, holding out his badge. "You're under arrest for extortion and racketeering."

Bioff turned white. Jonathan could not tell if this was from fear, anger or just surprise, but by the time the government men had the cuffs on him he was sputtering with rage. He screamed at Jonathan, "I'll get you, you fuckin' mick. I can get you any time." They turned him around but he twisted his head to face Jonathan one last time. "I promise you, if I see you on any witness stand, I'll get you. I'd better not see you again." His eyes looked ready to burst from his face.

The other two agents hustled Bioff away while Normand stayed behind with Jonathan, who was obviously shaken up.

"Look," Normand said, "don't worry about Bioff's threats. They all do that, it's just part of the repertoire. But this guy's not going to be in a position to do you any harm, trust me."

Jonathan looked at the FBI man. "Easy for you to say."

★　　★　　★

Ten weeks later, with Bioff's trial set to start, Normand said that he would have plenty of testimony from much bigger players than Mr. Cahill, and would only need Jon to walk the jury through the tape recording. It was a devastating piece of evidence, Bioff incriminating himself on tape.

The prosecutor, a young man named Steven Leary, recently out of Stanford Law School, had subpoenaed the head of every major studio in Hollywood. His first witness was Joseph Schenck, chairman of Loew's corporation. Loew's owned the largest theatre chain in the United States in addition to being a major stockholder in MGM, the country's biggest motion picture producer.

"Mr. Schenck," Leary started, "do you know the defendant, Mr. William Bioff?"

"Of course. Willie's the president of the International Association of Projectionists. Basically, that means he's their top negotiator, the fellow who deals with the large theatre chains like ours."

"So you dealt with him in regard to projectionists' wages and benefits, and other work-related issues?"

"Exactly."

"Did you ever make a large payment to Mr. Bioff's personal account?"

Schenck shook his head. "No. We pay wages to our projectionists, not to Mr. Bioff."

"So Mr. Bioff never extorted money from you under threat of shutting down your movie theatres? And you never paid him for that purpose?"

"No, of course not."

Leary then picked up a cancelled check from the table where he had been sitting and placed it in front of Joseph Schenck. "Do you recognise this, Mr. Schenck?"

Schenk stared at the check as if in shock. He did not respond to Leary's question.

Leary raised his voice. "I would like to remind you, Mr. Schenck, that this is a trial in federal court and that you are under oath. Lying to this courtroom is perjury and may result in your incarceration in federal prison. With that in mind, would you care to change your last answer?"

Schenck, still stunned, did not respond until the judge interceded. "Mr. Schenck, please respond to the question."

"Yes," Schenck finally said, "I'd like to change my answer."

"Go ahead," Leary said.

"I made a payment of six hundred thousand dollars to Willie Bioff to prevent him from shutting down my company's theatres as well as any other theatre that showed an MGM movie. Mr. Bioff demonstrated on several occasions that he had the ability to do this."

Schenck's testimony continued, with Leary drawing out all the details of Bioff's threats and the subsequent payoffs. After Schenck testified, Leary called the other studio heads who all told essentially the same story. Jonathan's testimony and the playing of his tape was last. It took the jury less than a day to convict Willie Bioff of extortion, racketeering and accepting bribes.

After the verdict was read, and Bioff was led away by the bailiff, Agent Normand stopped to speak to Jonathan. "Nice job, Mr. Cahill. Your testimony put it all together nicely, made it easy for the jury."

"Yes, it worked out well for the prosecution. Now, I guess, we find out if Mr. Bioff makes good on his threat. He was pretty clear about what would happen if I testified."

Normand shook his head. "He's not in any position to order a glass of water, let alone revenge. He'll be held on Terminal Island for a few days, then shipped to Alcatraz. He won't be seeing any visitors for a while. I wouldn't worry. You're not important to him anymore."

Jonathan stared at him for a long moment before replying. "I suspect it's the prosecution to whom I'm no longer important. Bioff, however, will still want his revenge."

"Look," the FBI man responded. "I think you're worried about nothing. These guys make ten threats every day that they never carry out. But if it makes you feel better, I'll have a couple of our guys keep an eye on you for a while, until things die down. They won't be obtrusive or anything. You can give them a little office at your studio, and they'll watch your house from a car. We're well trained at this, and I guarantee you nothing will happen while they're around."

"Thanks," Jonathan said. "I appreciate it."

★   ★   ★

That evening, Jonathan received a call from Max Zalensky, who wanted a blow-by-blow account of the day in court: testimony, the verdict, and everything else that Jonathan remembered about the trial. Jonathan mentioned his trepidation at Bioff's possible retaliation, and once again Zalensky expressed his lack of concern.

"I told you, Hoover would never allow anything to happen to a Hollywood mogul. It'd be bad publicity, which is all that pervert cares about."

But Jonathan Cahill was hardly a household name, and his death would never promote the same headlines as a big-name studio head. It struck him how fearless his partner could be from three thousand miles away.

Jonathan also knew that Zalensky had his own sources of information about the trial and wondered what the man was really calling about. It didn't take long to get to it.

"I'm hoping that you can do me a favour," Max said. "I've got a fellow who works for me, name's Becker, who's been doing some good work. I want to reward him with a trip out west, show him a really good time. Can you help me out with that?"

"Sure," Jonathan said, annoyed that he'd have to play host to one of Zalensky's thugs at a time like this. But he just said, "Send him out. We'll show him a real good time."

CHAPTER SIXTY

The moment James Becker walked into his office, Jonathan felt an icy chill run along the back of his neck. It wasn't just Becker's size, although certainly that was a factor. It wasn't even his bald, bullet-shaped head, though that too was a factor. It was that the man seemed to have an unflinching sense of purpose. Becker had come because Max had told him to, and he was determined to relax and have a good time because Max had told him that as well. Jonathan hoped he was never on the wrong side of whatever else it was that Max told Becker to do.

"Good to meet you, Mr. Becker," Jonathan said, rising to shake his hand.

"Same here," Becker spoke fast and shook hands briskly, as if getting distasteful social functions out of the way as quickly as possible.

After small talk about his trip out to LA, Jonathan asked, "Do you enjoy the movies?"

The big man shrugged. "Like anybody else."

"Have you seen our new film, *The Love Parade?*"

Becker shook his head.

"Well, I'd like to show you a few scenes." He led his visitor into a screening room down the hall from his office. *The Love Parade* was a sexual farce about the love affairs of the royal family of a fictional duchy in modern-day Europe. The movie was a mild hit and featured a small part by a young actress named Jean Harper. Harper was a tall, slender, platinum blonde, pretty not beautiful, with a sensuousness that some men found irresistible. In the movie she wore a slinky evening dress that accentuated her best assets. Jonathan had arranged to show only those scenes in the movie that included the young actress.

When they returned to Jonathan's office, Jean Harper was waiting for them. She wore a white cashmere sweater and a slim A-line skirt. When she stood up and walked over to greet them, the sexual heat was palpable.

"James," Jonathan said, "I'd like you to meet Jean Harper, the young lady we just saw on screen. Jean will be your guide around town for the next few days."

Jean moved close to the big man and looked up at him slowly, taking in every part of him. "Hello there," she said in a surprisingly deep voice, and stuck out her hand to shake. Becker, struck dumb, took her hand without saying a word.

"Strong, silent type," she purred. "I like that. I can talk enough for the both of us." Turning to Jonathan, she winked and said, "Don't worry, I'll take good care of him." Then, holding a small bag she had brought with her in one hand and Becker's large paw in the other, she led him to the door.

They left the studio lot, and Jean drove them to the Sunset Grill for drinks. The maître d' led them to one of the large booths with curtains around it. Jean sat next to Becker. When the waiter brought their drinks, she slid close to him and clinked glasses. He spoke little. She spoke a lot, telling him about her childhood in Kansas City and her decision to come to Hollywood to seek stardom. Her face was close to his when she talked and the hand that wasn't holding her drink came to rest on his thigh, moving slightly when she emphasised a point in the conversation.

After drinks they drove directly to the Beverly Hills Hotel and checked into one of the bungalows. Becker carried in Jean's small bag as well as his own suitcase. "They've got a great pool here," she said. "We should go swimming before dinner."

"Okay. You got a suit?"

"In my bag. I'll put it on." And then, standing directly in front of him, her eyes locked on his, she took off her clothes. They made love on top of the bungalow's king-size bed before visiting the pool, and again afterward.

She took him to the canals in Venice, a section of Los Angeles where a man named Abbott Kinney had built a replica of Venice, Italy, and they went for a ride in a gondola that was almost like a real gondola in the real Venice. They went for a roller-coaster ride on Lick Pier that was almost like the one on Coney Island, and they spent one afternoon watching a movie being made so Becker could see how a street in Paris, France, was really on the back lot of Paramount

Studios, California. But most of the week was spent at the hotel, often in a private cabana at the pool. They made love many times in the cabana as well as in their room, and once, very late at night, in the pool. Becker discovered the back massage and the steam room, sensual pleasures he had never known in New York. Jean wanted to have sex in the steam room but Becker laughingly begged off, explaining that he didn't want to be responsible for giving a heart attack to any of the nice old men who used the steam.

At the end of the week she drove him to the train station. "Thanks, doll," Becker said. "You sure know how to take care of a guy."

"So I take it you enjoyed yourself, Jimmy?"

He grinned. "You know I did."

"Me too," she said, and kissed him goodbye.

Jean drove directly from the station to Jonathan's office. "He's gone," she said. "I watched him get on the train."

"Did you show him a good time?"

In a matter-of-fact tone, as if reading a weather report, she said, "I showed him the best time a man could possibly have. He'll never forget it."

Jonathan nodded approvingly. "Thank you."

"And that part we talked about?"

"Don't worry. It's yours."

★   ★   ★

Two days later, Jonathan put both the trial and Becker out of his thoughts, and concentrated on work. Sam would be sleeping at Grandma Mary-Margaret's for a few days while Jon caught up at the office. Clarence Rollins was making his third picture for Film Studios of America and it looked like this one would be even more successful than the first two.

Rollins brought in Sy Glucksman, whom he knew from his days at Signature studios, to write the script. It was a solid drama about a farm boy who follows his dreams to Chicago and becomes a meat-packing baron and multimillionaire in the early nineteen hundreds. In the process of building his empire the farm boy cuts corners, compromises his ethics and sees his family life crumble before his eyes. It was a neat, watchable story. Best of all, Rollins had landed Susan Spencer to play the spoiled, self-centred wife who cheats on her husband with a rival meat-packing mogul. Jonathan was surprised to learn that Spencer was not under contract with Signature, where she had made her most recent pictures. She was anxious to work with Clarence and had agreed to do the film for a reasonable price.

Jonathan was in the office until late in the evening, reviewing the script, so it was midnight when he pulled into his driveway. He took no notice of the white Chevrolet sedan parked half a block down the street. He stopped in the driveway, too tired to open the garage, got out and ambled up to his front door.

As he pulled out his key, the cold metal barrel of a .22 calibre Smith & Wesson revolver was stuck into the right side of his neck. Jonathan was so startled he dropped his key. "Pick it up and open the door, quick," said a high-pitched male voice.

Shaking and afraid to look at his assailant, Jonathan picked up the key. "If you're going to shoot me, I'd prefer you do it out here, not in the house." His voice quivered audibly when he spoke.

A heavy fist clubbed him in the left kidney. Sharp pain shot through his back and for a moment he thought he might vomit. A different, low, raspy voice said, "We prefer privacy. So shut up and do like you're told." Christ, he hadn't even realised there was a second man. Jonathan put the key in the lock and opened the door.

They all walked inside and one of the gunmen closed the door. It was dark in the house and as they stood in the foyer, Jonathan could feel two large shadows just in back of him. He heard the high-pitched voice say, "Let's give it to him here," and Jonathan knew with certainty that he was about to die.

Suddenly he heard two thumps coming from either side of him, and two bodies pitched straight forward onto the entryway tile. Something metallic, probably a gun, skidded across the tile floor. Someone flipped the light switch by the door and he could clearly see the two killers laid out cold on the floor. They were both dressed in black pants and shirts, had dark hair and olive complexions, and one was about half a foot shorter than the other. A black .22 calibre revolver was resting on the floor four feet from the outstretched hand of the shorter man. Jonathan noticed all this as he whirled to see who had turned on the light.

And there was Becker. So large that he seemed to fill the foyer, holding a billy club in each hand. He had simultaneously whacked each killer on the top of the head. It occurred to Jonathan, even in his state of shock, that with his brute strength James Becker was easily capable of crushing a man's skull with one swing.

"You got a rug or something?" Becker asked. "Don't want them bleeding all over the floor." Jonathan's face was white and his heart was beating hard. Becker had to ask the question again before Jonathan responded by pointing to a throw rug in the living room.

The big man carefully laid it out next to the bodies. It was a hand-knit wool that Jon's mother had brought as a present from Ireland. Becker tossed each body onto it as easily as Jonathan would toss a stick of firewood. Then he took a towel out of his jacket pocket and wiped up the blood that had already spilled onto the tile.

Both men were at least out cold; Jonathan wondered if they were dead. As if reading his thoughts, Becker said, "I'll plug them once or twice before I get rid of them, just to make sure."

Badly shaken and not wanting to continue this line of conversation, Jonathan said, "I thought you were gone, back to New York."

"That's how it was supposed to look," the big man responded. "I hopped off in San Bernardino and rented a car to get back here. These two have been following you for a few days. There were a couple feds on you too, but they pulled out this morning. These guys weren't gonna waste time after that. I saw 'em hanging around outside your house and knew they'd bring you inside. Neighbourhood like this, folks don't know enough to keep their mouths shut. So I came in through the back and waited."

"Will Bioff send more men, now that these two have…failed?" Jonathan asked.

The big man shook his head and said, "These ain't Bioff's men. They belong to the guy Bioff worked for."

"Great."

Becker shook his head again. "You don't need to worry. Mr. Zalensky doesn't think it's going to be a problem."

"What if Mr. Zalensky's wrong?"

Becker pondered this as if someone had asked him the origins of the universe. "Never known that to happen."

He then rolled up both bodies inside the rug and used cord that he found in the kitchen to tie up each end. With little discernable effort he slung the whole bundle over his shoulder and turned to walk out. As he opened the door he looked back toward Jonathan and said, "Thanks again for having Jean show me around. It was a great time."

Jonathan nodded, his face still ashen. "No problem. Come back anytime and I'll set something up."

The big man smiled, then turned with his bundle and walked out Jonathan's front door, closing it gently behind him.

CHAPTER SIXTY-ONE

Frank Nitti picked up the phone, his personal line, known only to a few people. A voice he did not recognise said, "Is this Mr. Nitti?"

"Yeah, it is. Who the fuck is this?"

"Hold for Mr. Zalensky, please," the voice said.

A few seconds later, an irritated Nitti heard the recognisable monotone: "Hello, Frank."

"Whatsa matter, Max? You gotta have somebody make your calls for you now?"

"My apologies," the monotone said without any real feeling behind it. "I was on another line and sometimes it takes a while to get you."

"Yeah, sure," Nitti responded. Zalensky was a great banker. The best. But he could be a little too impressed with his own importance. "So what's up? No problems with my money, I hope."

"No, of course not. This is something else. Call it a personal favour."

"Okay," Nitti said, growing impatient. "I'm already thankful. Now what the hell is it?'"

"Willie Bioff has agreed to testify against you in regard to the Hollywood racket. The indictment should come down tomorrow or the day after."

"What? How the fuck would you know that?"

"I've got sources. Don't worry about it. I just want you to know that my information's good. I'll call you back." Then Zalensky hung up.

★   ★   ★

Nitti's indictment came down two days later. "That shit-eating little prick!" he roared when he got the news, throwing a chair across the room and into the wall, leaving a dent in the plaster. "That little traitor. I'll kill him with my own hands."

Johnny Pescatelli grew more and more concerned as he watched his boss's violent tirade. When Frank got this angry, nobody was safe. Johnny had seen Nitti smash a subordinate's head into the wall just for making a sarcastic comment when he was in this kind of mood. Best thing to do right now was just keep quiet.

But Pescatelli also knew that these indictments represented real danger, for himself as well as his boss. After Al Capone went away, Frank Nitti, Capone's second in command, had taken over without much trouble. There'd been some guys thinking they could use the opportunity to grab a bigger piece of the action, but Nitti had savagely cut them down without mercy. After that, everyone had kept nicely in line. But if Frank went to jail there would be chaos, everyone trying to take over everyone else's territory. A lot of people would get dead. Problem was, the feds were holding that rat Bioff in solitary at Alcatraz. Nearly impossible to get anyone in to kill him. It was a bad situation no matter how you sliced it.

Nitti's personal phone rang. And rang. Nitti was too angry to pick it up and Pescatelli didn't dare. What if it was news of another indictment? Nitti had been known to kill the messenger. Literally. Finally, Nitti said, "Pick it up." Johnny did as he was told.

Johnny Pescatelli listened for a few seconds, then handed the phone to his boss. "It's Max Zalensky."

Nitti took the phone. "What? You calling to say I told you so?"

"I'm calling to offer my services."

"Services? To do what?"

"To take your friend Bioff out of the picture."

"What? You're telling me you can get to him?"

"That's what I'm telling you."

"How the fuck can you do that when I can't do that?"

In a tone that sounded almost bored, Zalensky said, "Are you interested or not?"

"Does a drowning man say no to a life preserver? Of course I'm interested."

"It'll cost."

"Naturally. How much you got in mind?" ·

"Two hundred and fifty thousand."

Nitti guffawed. "Be serious. I could get a thousand guys dead for that. More than a thousand."

Again the bored tone. "You may take it or leave it."

After a moment, Nitti said, "You know I can't say no. You'll get the money when the job's done."

"Up front. In cash."

"For Christ's sakes, Max. Why don't you just ask for my whole operation? How do I know you can even deliver?"

Max's response was quick and Nitti sensed that the always calm Zalensky was growing impatient. "I've got to pay people to get my man in and out again. Then I've got to pay to keep them all quiet afterward. And then to make sure the whole thing is not investigated too closely. Then, I'll need to do follow-up to make sure no one's tempted to renege on the deal. It's not going to be cheap and I'll have to oversee it personally. But like I said, it's up to you, take it or leave it."

When Nitti still hesitated, Zalensky said, "Look, Frank, we do a lot of business. Your money's always been safe with me. I've never promised anything I couldn't deliver."

Nitti knew this was true. In fact, he had been one of the first to bank with Zalensky. He hadn't wanted to end up like his old boss, jailed for tax evasion. So every month he deposited all his receipts, mostly cash but sometimes checks, into Zalensky's bank, which was called First Chicago. It was a legitimate bank and had legitimate customers. Probably made a legitimate profit. *Max is certainly high and mighty now,* Nitti thought. *Maybe he's had been away from the street for a little too long.* "I'll get you the money," he said. "But you gotta come yourself. I wanna look in your eyes when I give it to you."

★   ★   ★

Two hundred and fifty thousand in one hundred-dollar bills fit nicely inside a medium-size briefcase. Twenty-five stacks of one hundred bills, each stack two thirds of an inch high and worth ten thousand dollars.

Max and Becker took the train to Chicago to collect the money. They had their own private car, the very last one on the train.

Frank Nitti and Johnny Pescatelli drove their automobile right into the Chicago railyard, and pulled up alongside Zalensky's train. Pescatelli got out of the car carrying the briefcase in his left hand and a .45 calibre Colt revolver in his right. Nitti carried his favourite weapon, a

Thompson sub-machine gun. In Nitti's hands that same gun had once killed six men in less than two seconds.

Of course, he did not think there was any danger here. No one but himself, Johnny and Zalensky knew about the money. Max wouldn't try to jack him, not because the man was so trustworthy, but because he would want to continue doing business with him. And there would be plenty more business. As soon as Bioff was taken care of he would find a new guy to handle the Hollywood enterprise, someone a lot smarter than that little pimp. Frank felt pretty sure that if he killed just one of those California creampuffs the rest would fall in line.

They climbed the steps into the railroad car and Johnny handed the briefcase to Zalensky. "Close the door and let me take a quick look," Zalensky ordered.

Christ, the damn banker's going to count it, Frank thought. "It's all there," he growled, obviously irritated.

"I'm sure it is," Max responded. "But I'll just make a quick check while you're here, and then there won't be any questions later."

Annoyed, Frank grunted, "Uh huh." Max placed the briefcase on a small table in the private cabin, opened it, and began to riffle through the bundles of cash. Frank kept his eyes on Becker. He noticed that Johnny was doing the same. The big man stood quietly, arms crossed over his chest. The only weapons visible in the room were Frank and Johnny's heavy armament. Still, this was James Becker and Frank was taking no chances.

Max counted the cash in the open briefcase, the top of the case raised between him and his guests, hiding his hands and waist. Perhaps because his attention was on Becker, perhaps because it was so unexpected, Nitti noticed too late Max swinging his right arm straight up from behind the briefcase. The arm was fully extended, moving smoothly and rapidly. At the end of it was a .38 calibre Beretta automatic pistol.

The automatic exploded and a red hole appeared in the middle of Johnny's forehead. Cursing, Nitti brought up the Thompson. But before it cleared his waist, Max had moved his pistol two feet to the right and pulled the trigger a second time. The bullet caught Frank in the right cheekbone, spinning his head and flinging his body a foot backward. Max stepped closer to him and standing over the fallen man, put a second bullet into his chest. The shots were extremely loud, leaving a ringing in Max's ears, but in the noisy railroad yard it was very unlikely anyone would notice.

They left the two dead bodies in the railway car, blood spouting over the rich red carpet and walnut veneer. They walked through the doorway at the end of the car that led to a linkage to the next, and the next, all the way through the length of the train. The cars were mostly empty, as this was the end of the run and people were either departing for Chicago or changing to a connecting train.

A few passengers were still on board, slow to depart, but Max and Becker moved quickly and did not look anyone in the face. All anyone would remember were two men dressed in business suits, one quite large, the other carrying a briefcase. Their compartment had been paid for in cash, under a phoney name, by someone who did not look like either Becker or Max. They departed the train, crossed the tracks and walked into the station. Once inside they bought two first-class tickets on the next train headed back to New York.

PART TWO
SONS
CHAPTER SIXTY-TWO
1942

The Second World War came at an opportune time for Jacob Epstein. He had graduated from UCLA the year before, earning Summa Cum Laude and Phi Beta Kappa honours as a biology major. But now, with school over and no job, he was just hanging around the house. It was Artie who called him, saying that he and Buddy were thinking of signing up.

Artie Molene and Buddy Thompson were Jake's two best friends, had been since pee-wee football. At Hollywood High, Jake had quarterbacked the team to a city championship, throwing passes to star receiver Artie and handing off to all-city halfback Buddy. Off the field the three were inseparable, hanging out after school and on weekends, spending summers at the beach, and chasing girls.

Of the three, only Jake had gone to college. Buddy was working in his father's Chevron station on Highland Boulevard, and Artie was selling insurance for one of the big companies downtown. Now, with the big conflict looming on the world horizon, Artie and Buddy wanted to do their duty, and they wanted Jake to join them.

Jake's rich and famous mother hoped desperately that he would apply to medical school. Of course, she never pushed it, never made a big deal of it. But Jake knew that the thought of her son, the doctor, was like a beam of sunshine that radiated warmth within her soul.

He told her what he was planning to do over dinner.

She was horrified. "You have no idea what war is like. It's not glamorous or exciting like they show in the movies. People just die."

"I have no choice," he protested. "They've announced a Selective Service, starting in a few months. Every able-bodied man will be drafted. If I go now I should get my choice of assignments, and proper training. Guys who wait will be rushed out in a hurry, without preparation."

"Who told you that? A recruiting officer?" From the sheepish look on his face, she knew she was right. "They'll tell you anything. It's their job."

"Well, sooner or later I'll have to go. Everybody will. I'd rather that it be sooner."

"No!" she said, shaking her head for emphasis. "You don't have to go. I'm sure our lawyers can find some way to exempt you. My doctor will write a note. I'll pay the people on the draft board." She sounded nearly hysterical.

"Mom...." He took her hand in his and spoke very calmly. "I want to go. It's the right thing to do. In the long run, it's what I must do."

"Don't you understand?" she pleaded. "Men are always fighting and killing each other. It's what men do. If you miss this war there will be another one later and another after that. Let someone else go fight. It won't make any damn difference."

Jake waited until this outburst was over, letting the silence hang in the air for a few minutes. Finally he said, "Hitler is a madman. England won't be able to hold out much longer. When she falls, Hitler will control the Middle East oil fields, the African diamond and mineral markets, and all the wealth in Western Europe. And the Japanese will own the rubber plantations of Southeast Asia." It was obvious that he had thought this through.

"At that point," he continued, "it'll be almost impossible to stop him." He looked directly at his mother. "And we're Jewish. There are rumours, stories, that he's doing horrible things to Jews in Germany and Poland. Rounding them up and putting them in work camps, making them slaves, even murdering them. Even more than the rest of the world, it's our responsibility to stop him."

Sophie hung her head, feeling defeated. Her son was right, of course, and she should be proud of him. But her fear of losing him was excruciating. She could feel the tears welling up. She knew her son perhaps better than he knew himself. She couldn't, didn't dare, tell him of the ways in which he reminded her of the father he had never known. She suspected that he secretly looked forward to the excitement of soldiering, of fighting, even of killing. The fact was, she thought with a shudder, he would probably be very good at it.

★　　★　　★

And he was. Drill Sergeant Richard Mathews, who had been training recruits for almost twenty years, had never seen anyone quite like the young man from California. It wasn't so much his physical abilities, although those were impressive. Epstein had set a new camp record in the obstacle course and earned top scores as a marksman. But what made him truly stand out during training exercises was his ability to see and understand the field. He was able to quickly judge the strength of the opposing squad, where and if they were hiding, and what their objective was. Thanks largely to his leadership, his unit had won all the training skirmishes they had engaged in.

Of course, the drill sergeant also knew that a training exercise was a far cry from a real battle. They'd see how Epstein performed when real bullets were flying and real bodies were being blown to bits.

In addition to regular duty, Jake volunteered to be a medic, an infantryman who received special training in first aid, dressing wounds and binding broken limbs. In theory, medics served as any other soldier, but they carried a first-aid kit into battle and were expected to assist wounded soldiers when the fighting subsided. Due to his college degree in biology, Jake was completely familiar with the skeletal system, the human heart, and the arterial and vascular systems, an advantage other medics did not have. He felt confident that he could make a real contribution in this field, but like all untested men he was uncertain how well he would behave in the heat of battle. It wouldn't be long before he found out.

CHAPTER SIXTY-THREE

For Samuel Cahill, the war was an inconvenience. He still had another year to go at Stanford Law School and was anxious to finish and get on with his career. But he also understood the impending disaster if the Nazis were not stopped. Several of his Stanford classmates had already volunteered, as had several old friends from Santa Monica High. Sam had no intention of appearing a shirker when his best friends were stepping up to the plate. But it was inconvenient.

His movie-mogul father was desperately opposed to sending his only child to a war that would only help 'those bastards who killed your grandfather'. Sam, born and raised in America, viewed the situation differently.

"Japan attacked us, Dad. They dropped bombs on American soldiers and ships. And Hitler declared war on us."

"Roosevelt manipulated the whole thing," Jonathan argued, his voice rising. "We've been shipping provisions and providing help to their enemies. The Japanese didn't think they had any choice but to attack us. And the Russians couldn't make any kind of fight without all the supplies we give them."

Sam tried to contain his emotions. "If Roosevelt thought that England and Russia could stop the Nazis by themselves, he'd have let them, Dad. In fact, he'd probably love to see them all beat the hell out of each other. But at this point, it looks like the Germans could win. That would be a disaster for us and for the whole world. So we've got to step in."

Jonathan hung his head and sighed. "Maybe you're right. You're probably right. But that doesn't make me like it any better." He looked up, staring Sam directly in the eyes. "I just want you to come back to me in one piece."

"I'll do my best."

In May 1942, one week after finishing final exams, Sam Cahill stepped onto the train that would take him from Union Station, Los Angeles, to Fort Benning, Georgia. His father stood by the tracks as he watched the train disappear, tears sliding down his cheeks. Then, feeling much older than his forty-one years, he walked back to his car and drove to his office.

CHAPTER SIXTY-FOUR
1943

Sergeant Cordell Campbell lay on his back in a makeshift hospital in the little Sicilian town of Bagheria on the Mediterranean coast. He stared at his leg, elevated and wrapped in bandages. Hell of a way to spend his birthday, not that anyone over here would care. He was just thankful to have lived twenty-nine years.

The hospital unit had been set up only two days before in a stone building that eighteen hundred years ago had been a Roman armoury. The doctors and nurses were Americans who had shipped in via Egypt and appeared nervous to be this close to actual combat. You had to hand it to General Patton; he tried to do right by the fighting men. Campbell supposed he was lucky, if you could call it that. The medic had been stingy with the morphine and the wound in his leg throbbed like the scorpion sting he'd gotten as a teenager back in Mesa, Arizona. He was looking forward to some painkillers.

The doctor, whose nametag identified him as Henry LaBrot M.D., didn't really speak to the sergeant, just gave a short, tired grunt of acknowledgement, then went right to the leg. Campbell understood. He knew the docs and nurses had been up for more than twenty-four hours taking care of the flood of wounded from Palermo.

After a few minutes LaBrot spoke, this time in actual English. "I guess the medic must have gotten to you right away, treated the wound just after you got it."

"How'd ya know that?" Campbell asked, gritting his teeth against the pain, which the doctor's exam was exacerbating.

"Because if he hadn't you'd be dead. Bullet went clean through the femoral artery. Blood must have been spouting like water out of a hydrant. Ten minutes of that and you'd have bled out. If the medic hadn't been right there to clamp it off, you'd be dead by now."

"Uh huh. Guess I'm fortunate."

LaBrot snipped though the stitching to examine the wound more closely. "I'll be," he exclaimed out loud as he looked more closely at the wound. "The medic didn't use a clamp. He tied it off."

"Is that bad?"

"No, it's what I would do now, but it's already done. Did a good job, from what I can see. Normally in the field they use a clamp because you need good conditions to tie off an artery. The patient needs to be elevated properly, plenty of light and air, and a decent nurse to hand you equipment as you need it. Normally, that sort of situation only occurs in a hospital, but I guess you had good conditions where you were."

"I guess," Sergeant Campbell responded. "Me lying flat on my back in the dirt, the medic stretched out on his stomach next to me, reaching up with both hands and doing everything by touch 'cause he couldn't raise his head to look at what he was doing. If you call them good conditions, we had 'em."

LaBrot stared at his patient in disbelief. "You're kidding me."

"I'm not."

"Why could he not raise his head to watch what he was doing?"

"'Cause some Nazi son of a bitch would have shot it off. We were in the middle of a fire fight in a fox hole about twelve inches deep, bullets buzzin' over us like flies on a dead horse."

There was a short silence before LaBrot spoke again. "Well, we're going to have to take the leg below the knee. I'm sorry. But you're very fortunate to be alive."

"Lucky me."

LaBrot turned to go and finish his rounds, but looked back for a moment to ask, "What was this medic's name?"

"Staff Sergeant Jacob Epstein."

CHAPTER SIXTY-FIVE

After six months in Basic, Jacob's unit had shipped out to England. They were greeted like heroes and quartered in large tents at the northern end of London. They marched and drilled and chased after English girls for ten weeks before clambering back onto troop ships to be ferried to Tunisia, recently liberated by British General Bernard Montgomery.

The ten weeks in London's damp, cold weather were followed by four months in the dry, dusty, intense heat of North Africa. The young men from California were not sure which environment they liked least. But, as Artie pointed out, at least there were girls in England.

Jacob had been promoted to squad leader, so he was a non-commissioned officer now, as well as being one of four hundred medics in a brigade of twenty thousand men. There was little to do but wait, and Jacob found himself wishing that their part in the war would come soon, just to relieve the boredom.

And then it did. With exactly sixteen hours of warning the men of units 1 through 6, 2nd Brigade, 1st Infantry Division, 7th Army, under Lieutenant General George Smith Patton were loaded onto barges and floated across the Mediterranean Sea. They were offloaded onto landing craft manned by Marines, who would deliver the soldiers to the shores of Sicily.

Units 2 and 3 of the 2nd Brigade landed July 10, 1943 on Scoglitti Beach on the southeastern coast of Sicily. To Jake's amazement, there were no enemy troops to meet them. The Americans took the beach without opposition and proceeded inland. They didn't encounter enemy fire until two days and thirty miles later, outside a small hamlet called Villarosa. The forward observers had assured the lieutenant that the Germans were gathering at Palermo, that there would be no resistance until they approached the Sicilian capital. Jake's squad was second in line. He and Buddy and Artie marched in front, the other six men stretched behind.

Jacob heard the sharp thunk from his left, like a baseball striking a watermelon, and felt the splatter of Artie's blood before he heard the rifle report. "Get down!" he yelled as he dropped to the ground. But Buddy was still standing, staring with open mouth at what remained of Artie Molene. Jacob tackled him, careening them both into a ditch at the side of the road just as more bullets pounded the earth where Buddy had been standing seconds before.

When he was finally able to form words, Buddy said, "Did you see? His face is —"

Jacob cut him off, his voice cold. "Stay right here. Don't move. You'll be fine." Then he handed Buddy his medical kit and said, "Hold on to this."

Jacob felt amazingly calm, as if this was all happening outside of himself and he was just an observer. He could tell the direction from which the bullets had come by the way Artie's body had landed. After the sound of the second set of shots he thought he had a good idea where the sniper must be hidden: up behind a row of rocks at the top of a hill that stood three hundred yards away. It was a spot that he might have chosen if he were the sniper.

He was able to scramble out of the ditch and cross the uneven countryside to a small clump of olive trees that he knew would hide him from the shooter. He followed the trees to the hill where he could use the natural topography for shelter. As Jake climbed the little hill he could hear more shots coming from the unseen attacker, as well as returning volleys from the Americans pinned below. He judged himself to be about fifty yards south of the shooter and kept climbing until he was well past the point where the enemy was stationed. He ran fifty yards north and then circled back.

His eyes scoured the slope below, and when he caught sight of movement, he realised there were actually two of them, crouched behind a line of rocks, their helmets removed, only their rifles sticking out. They were completely focused on the scene in front of them and it was easy for Jake to sneak up behind them without being detected. He crawled the whole way, not because they would otherwise see him, but because he did not want any shots from his companions below to accidentally strike him.

When he got within forty yards of the two snipers, he stopped, stretched out on the ground, forearms resting on the earth, his Browning Automatic Rifle nestled into his shoulder. It was a perfect shooter's position and he never even thought of asking them to surrender.

He shot one, then the other, easy kill shots to the back of the head. Then, as they slumped forward over the rocks, he shot each one again, just to make sure. It was the first time Jacob had ever killed a man, the first time he had killed anything other than a fish or an insect. It occurred to him that he should feel something, regret or grief or queasiness. But he felt nothing. He'd simply done what was necessary, what needed to be done. He was satisfied with a job properly completed.

*   *   *

Jacob and Buddy buried their friend, Artie Molene, in the shadow of an olive tree near the road where he had died. Standard procedure was to leave the body where it fell until a clean-up crew hauled it back to base camp and performed the burial. This allowed the fighting men to move straight to their objective without losing any time. And in fact, the six other victims of the snipers had all been left where they fell. But it was uncertain as to when the cleanup might occur, and Buddy and Jake had heard too many stories about dead soldiers being eaten by animals or rotting in place.

When the lieutenant saw what they were doing he hurried over and ordered them to leave the corpse behind and rejoin the march. Both men ignored him, remaining intent on their task. The lieutenant barked the order again, a threat buried deep in his voice, a tone that brooked no insubordination.

Jacob looked up from his shovel. "He was our good friend from back home. We'll just be a few minutes." His voice was emotionless, totally unconcerned about the lieutenant's position of authority.

The lieutenant noticed other soldiers stopping to watch the confrontation, their faces grim. They all knew what Jacob had done for them that morning, and the lieutenant knew that they knew. Jake and Buddy had already begun to shovel the dirt back into the grave. It truly would be just a few more minutes.

"All right," the lieutenant relented. "Finish the job, then catch up with your platoon." He added, "Good work," as if they were only doing as he had asked them. Jake smiled to himself, impressed with the lieutenant's quick understanding.

They encountered no more resistance until Palermo. The enemy occupied the low hills outside the city with mortars and machine gun nests implanted in the earth. It was their first encounter with mortar fire, the terrifying low whine that indicated an incoming round. It soon became second nature for Jake and Buddy to leap into the nearest foxhole, lie flat, helmet pulled low, and wait for the explosive to scatter its lethal charge before popping back up to fire a retaliatory few rounds at the enemy.

It was at Palermo that Jake's legend began to grow. He was never reckless or overconfident, was in fact quite deliberate, seeming to plan every move. But he was always in the right place at the right time, as if he had some extra instinct for where the enemy was and how many there were. Men around him developed great confidence in his leadership, certain that their best chance of remaining alive was to follow his directions.

It was at Palermo that Jake administered medical care to Sergeant Cordell Campbell in the midst of a nasty fire fight. For those who saw it, and those who heard about it, Staff Sergeant Epstein became not only the soldier other men wanted to follow but the medic every wounded man hoped would come to his aid.

★ ★ ★

After capturing Sicily, the Americans wasted little time before pursuing the enemy to the mainland and up the boot toward Rome. The capital of Italy was of symbolic if not strategic importance, and the Germans did not wish to give it up easily. Progress was slow and bitter, with enemy defences making every foot forward costly in lives and munitions.

They were attacked outside the small village of Fondillo from behind a stone wall that ran the length of a wide olive grove. It was a poor choice by the Germans, as the wall provided little actual cover. The lieutenant immediately commanded his troops to return fire, then set up mortars and blasted the attackers. The mortar fire ripped right through the stone wall, destroying it. At the end of a five-minute-long barrage, the return fire ceased, and it became obvious that most of the enemy had been killed or wounded.

The lieutenant and his troops advanced cautiously across the open field, each man with rifle at the ready, alert for any movement. When they finally reached the shattered wall and climbed over the rubble, they saw a tangle of bodies, dead and nearly dead. The mortar fire had sown horrific devastation, terrible to witness. No matter that just moments before these same men had been trying to kill them, many of Jacob's comrades felt sympathy for their victims.

On the other side of the wall, the Americans could see an old barn about two hundred yards away, down a slight decline. The dilapidated structure must have been built by the farmer who owned this land, and used to store goats and chickens during happier days. Like everyone in this unfortunate region, the farmer and his family had fled at the approach of the Germans, taking with them whatever animals they could.

Now, however, none of that mattered. It was clear to the lieutenant and his troops that if an enemy soldier had survived he was surely in that barn. Without any order being given, every man turned toward the weathered building and moved deliberately forward.

They had barely taken a step when two riders mounted on horseback burst from the big open barn door and raced full speed toward the road. The two German officers had unhitched the horses from whatever load they were hauling, saddled them up, and were riding away like the wind. Perhaps because they were surprised, perhaps because it was so beautiful to watch, the Americans made no move to stop the two men galloping away.

Jacob had done enough riding with his father to recognise excellent horsemanship when he saw it, and he watched for a moment, admiring the fluid beauty of the horses and their riders. Then he raised the Browning to his shoulder, aimed, and shot one fleeing soldier in the back, then the other. They fell almost in slow motion, thumping to the ground while the horses continued running for another thirty yards before meandering to a stop.

Several of the men stared sharply at him, and Buddy said, "Jesus, Jake, did you have to kill them? They were just trying to get away."

"You know they'd regroup at some point, try to ambush us,"

Jacob responded. "Better them now than us later."

Buddy shook his head. "They just looked so pretty."

The other men continued to stare at Jake, who did not bother looking back at them, just slung his rifle over his shoulder and turned toward the road. The rest of the patrol followed him.

CHAPTER SIXTY-SIX

Samuel Cahill started his army career exactly as Jacob Epstein had, with boot camp at Fort Benning. But Sam did not take to the soldiering business as naturally as Jake. He could keep up on the forced marches and the obstacle courses. He was a decent shot. He became proficient at disassembling and assembling his rifle and did well on the mortar range. In rational disciplines like map reading and orienteering, he was the equal of any man. But he realised that despite the brave logic with which he had supported the war to his father, it was simply not in his nature to kill people.

Other men in his unit spoke easily, or even enthusiastically, about shooting Krauts and Japs. But Sam could not imagine purposely killing a man, even his sworn enemy. He lay awake some nights, wondering what would happen if the time came and he couldn't pull the trigger. Would his weakness result in his own death or the death of a comrade?

Despite this self-doubt, Sam graduated with the rest of the boots. There was a short but formal ceremony, complete with a speech from the fort commander, and then it was on to the bloody business for which they had been trained. Within a few days the new soldiers were herded onto troop carriers and caravanned east to the coastal city of Savannah. From the back of the truck it looked like a beautiful town, but they weren't there to explore. The carriers drove directly to the port and the newly minted soldiers were off-loaded to a waiting transport ship and sent to war.

★　　★　　★

Two weeks after completing basic training, Sam Cahill and two thousand other recent graduates of Fort Benning arrived in Tunisia. Upon arrival, almost all of them were parcelled to various combat or support units. Sam, alone, was ordered to report to a Major Kinney at camp headquarters.

Sam walked through the front door of the recently erected Quonset hut, his duffle in one hand and his orders in the other. The building was so new that the corrugated metal shell was still shiny in the dusty North African clime. Major Kinney's office was one of four in a row along the right wall of the long, narrow structure. The door was open, but Sam knocked anyway. A small, middle-aged man sitting at the steel desk looked up from the papers he was perusing. "May I help you?"

"Private Cahill, sir, reporting as ordered."

Kinney looked at Sam with a disinterested expression and yelled, "Markley."

A young man sitting at the desk just outside the major's office rose slowly and squeezed past Sam through the door. The man, whose sleeve bore the two stripes of a corporal, stood ramrod straight and said, "Yes, Major."

Kinney looked back down at the papers on his desk, waved his hand in Sam's direction and said, "Show Cahill to his quarters and give him the lay of the land."

"Yes, sir," said Markley, and started to leave, signalling for Sam to follow.

"And one more thing," the major's words reached them as they neared the door. "Try to make him presentable."

"Yes, sir," Markley responded.

Once outside, Markley grinned and held out a hand to Samuel. "Phil Markley," he said. "Glad to meet you."

"Sam Cahill. Same here."

Markley was tall, probably six-foot-four, with broad, square shoulders, neatly cut sandy hair, and a smooth, handsome face that flashed perfect white teeth through his big grin. Sam had to look up to speak to him.

"Major Kinney has been looking forward to your arrival," Markley said. "He thinks you'll be a lot of help."

Sam was genuinely surprised. "Why would he be looking forward to me? What would I be of help with?"

Markley grinned again. "We are at the critical centre of the entire war effort. Of course, we don't actually shoot anyone, or make strategy, or lead men into battle. We do logistics." He made an expansive gesture with his hands. "We figure out how much food and water the company will need, how many blankets and canteens and tents and trucks and cots and tyres and k-rations. And, of course, how many guns and how much ammo. Basically, we're in charge of keeping this Company fully supplied with all necessities at all times."

Sam looked at Markley. "In other words, in the biggest armed conflict in the history of the world, we're the desk clerks."

"Exactly," Markley exclaimed. "But it's important. Battles can be lost because one side runs out of ammunition. Or gasoline. Or the other side wins because they got their people in position first, which can depend on tyres or replacement parts for tank tread. So what we do and how well we do it matters."

Again, Sam nodded. "Okay. I'm convinced. But you were looking forward to me coming because…."

As Sam expected, Corporal Markley grinned. "We know you studied law at a top school, and that you got good grades. We figure you're smart and organised. We have more work than we can handle and we need someone who can pick up the ball and run."

"Sounds like you need an accountant, not a lawyer. This is just a numbers game."

"Yeah, but accountants get picked off fast. Everybody wants them. So we decided to settle for you."

"Well," Sam said in a less-than-enthusiastic tone, "I'll try to live up to those high expectations." Then he looked up at Markley and returned his grin.

★   ★   ★

With troops marching on Rome, Sam decided to concentrate on ammunition. There were standard estimates for how much each man on the front line should use, how much more would be used during an assault, and how much less when simply marching forward. Sam did the arithmetic and came up with estimated ammo use, then upped the estimate to accommodate what he supposed would be fairly heavy enemy resistance. Finally, he looked at transporting the ammunition to the men who needed it. As it turned out, there were neither enough trucks nor enough gasoline on the Italian peninsula, so Sam had to figure out where the necessary trucks and fuel were, and how to get them where they were needed.

All of this had to be coordinated with the food and clothing and medical supplies that Markley and Kinney were busy calculating. After a week and a half of fourteen-hour days staring at maps, shipping logs and troop deployments, and endless paper and pencil calculations, they had the answers they needed. Now would come more hours of checking and rechecking their calculations before actual execution.

Over dinner, at the long metal tables they used as desks, Major Kinney asked Sam, "Are you glad I chose you for this work?"

Between bites, Sam responded, "It's boring and it's tedious, but somebody's got to do it."

Kinney nodded. "Exactly." Then he smiled, thinking he had chosen well.

CHAPTER SIXTY-SEVEN

Sophie needed a place away from home to hold meetings, read through scripts, and perform the numerous business tasks of a successful actress. The majority of her roles were still with Signature but she wanted it to be clear that she was not a part of Louis Kahn's fiefdom. So her friend, Clarence Rollins, arranged for a small office on the back lot of Film Studios of America.

Even so, Kahn still thought of her as one of his own and did not hesitate to call her anytime he wanted something.

"Whad'ya think of the script?" Kahn's voice blared through the receiver so loudly she had to hold the phone away from her ear.

She was certain he reverted to a Lower East Side accent just to annoy her, but she chose to ignore it. "It's not bad," she said calmly. "I assume you'll be getting a subsidy."

"Sure," he said. "But it still has to sell and I think the public will like this one."

"Of course," Sophie agreed. The War Department gave financial backing to films that supported the Allied effort, but Kahn still required that his films tell a good story and appeal to the public. This story took place in an English hospital that treated wounded soldiers. The two main female characters were nurses; one a sexy spy for the Germans who uses her allure to extract information about troop deployments, the other an experienced nurse who suspects and then exposes the young spy. It was a decent suspense tale involving murder, attempted murder, and a climactic fight between the two nurses. It would certainly sell.

"I assume that I'll play the older nurse."

"We could put you in either role," Kahn said, and Sophie was surprised at how seriously he said this. "But I agree. You're a better fit as the heroine."

She refrained from adding that she was also a better fit as the older woman, and simply said, "Sounds fine."

"I'll send over a contract and you can look it over," Kahn said. "There's also something else. I know you'll do whatever you can to help our soldiers?"

"Yes, of course."

"Good. We're putting together some posters for the troops. Kinda like the Betty Grable legs photo, but from the front with lots of cleavage."

She could feel the studio chief's leer over the phone line, but refused to take the bait. "You know I have a son in the war," she said calmly, "and I'm sure you have a more appropriate use for me than a display of cleavage."

"Well, yeah," he said. "I guess Jake might get upset if his buddie's got the hots for his mom. So I was thinking of the Red Cross blood drive. They'd love to have a star for their poster. You'd pose in a nurse's uniform, then maybe show up for some of their fundraisers."

"Sounds perfect," she said. "I'd be very happy to do that."

"Okay. And one other piece of charity?"

"Yes?"

"Someday you could pretend to let me get the better of you."

"I'll think about it, Louis," she said, and hung up.

CHAPTER SIXTY-EIGHT
1944

With the Allies controlling the southern half of Italy, the invasion of France became a certainty. It was merely a matter of exactly when and exactly where. General Patton had been recalled to England and the assumption was that he would lead the invasion. Jacob Epstein's company and Sam Cahill's logistics team were both transferred to England to become part of the 3rd Army under Patton's command.

Patton was not quiet about the fact that the invasion would take place in Calais, and that it would happen in mid-June. Most of the men under his command felt a certain pride, knowing they would be part of the force that would bring this war to an end. Jacob and Sam, though unaware of each other's existence, nevertheless shared similar emotions. They had a job to do and would do it. But both men knew that the price would be high, paid for with the lives of many compatriots, and perhaps even with their own.

★   ★   ★

When the invasion came it was a shock to most of Patton's army. It happened on June 6th, weeks before the great general had promised, and it took place on the beaches of Normandy, more than a hundred miles south of Calais. One hundred fifty thousand British, Canadian and American troops took part in the invasion, but Patton's army did not. They were simply a diversion, a head fake to draw German troops north to Calais, the closest point to the English cliffs of Dover and the obvious attack point.

It worked. The invasion, although bloody, was a success, and within a few days the Allies had firmly established a beachhead. If the Germans had not diverted a considerable portion of their defences to

Calais, the outcome might have been very different. By the end of June allied troops controlled Saint Lo, the area of Normandy where the invasion took place. It was gently sloping farm country, subdivided into a crazy quilt of small farms which were separated by hedgerows.

Hedgerows had originated in Roman times, built to fence in cattle and mark boundaries. They were long hillocks about eight feet deep and six feet high, consisting of dirt and shrubs and trees built over low stone pilings. Roots had permeated the dirt and rock and water ditches had been cut alongside the rows, forming a maze that was easy to defend and difficult to penetrate.

The Germans took full advantage, burrowing machine gun nests into the shrubbery and even drilling tunnels in the hedgerows where they could crawl through undetected and surprise the Allied soldiers. The American Sherman tanks were unable to plough through the hedgerows and trying to drive over them proved disastrous. It was slow and noisy, and by the time a tank reached the top of a hedgerow, the Germans were well alerted. Also, the unarmoured underside of the Sherman would be exposed for several minutes as the back treads dug in before the vehicle crested and toppled down the other side. In those moments, the Germans' heavy machine guns could rip right through the bottom of the American tanks, killing every man inside. When the Americans sent platoons over the hedgerows to clear the way, enemy fire picked them off like clay pigeons on a shelf.

At this point Patton's 3rd Army was finally brought into the fray. Jacob and Samuel were both part of the 1st Division consisting of ten thousand men under Major General Norman Cota. The General surveyed the situation and ordered three dozen bulldozers brought in to pulverise the hedgerows. It became Sam's job to find the dozers and arrange transportation to Normandy. He was on the shortwave radio for twenty straight hours rounding up all the necessary machines, arranging overland transfer to Dover and shipping to Normandy. It would be another ten days before they would all arrive, but the bulldozers were on their way and soon the Krauts would have nothing to hide behind.

Until that equipment arrived, however, the enemy could wander through the hedgerows at will. The Nazis knew it was only a matter of time before the Americans blasted through the barriers, and General

Cota was wary that they might attempt a quick assault before that happened. He ordered all combat personnel to be grouped into twelve-man platoons with orders to patrol the area, pick off Germans as they could, and scout and report enemy activity. All noncombatants, including Sam, were ordered to carry a sidearm. Sam was reasonably certain that he would have no need to fire the weapon, but even the slight possibility made him nervous.

On the morning of the ninth day after ordering the bulldozers, Sam was working on a new project to obtain proper rain gear for the upcoming wet season. Phil Markley was engaged in an equally mundane assignment, estimating boot and sock requirements for the next six months. Major Kinney was at General Officer's quarters on the other side of the camp, delivering his weekly supply forecast.

Markley muttered something about heading out to the latrine. Sam was vaguely aware of him stepping outside, but he barely registered it or looked up from his work. A few seconds later, however, he heard a startled Markley yelling, "Fuck!" followed by the loud sound of automatic gunfire and voices shouting in German.

Instinctively, Sam realised what was happening, knew that in the next few seconds enemy soldiers would rush into the Quonset hut and kill him. Almost without thinking he pulled his Colt .45 single action from its holster and dropped behind his metal desk, the pistol propped firmly in front of him, his right index finger on the trigger.

The two Germans burst through the door, sweeping their rifles as they came. Sam, to their left, fired the instant they breached the opening, hitting the first soldier cleanly, then swivelling his elbows and firing again. The second German was able to fire a wild shot just as he was hit, splintering the end of the desk, spinning it around and knocking Sam off his knees, onto his side.

He recovered almost immediately, adrenaline pumping, leapt up and rushed at the Germans. He had aimed low and his first bullet had struck his enemy in the groin. The man was in a foetal position on the floor, gasping and groaning almost silently, both hands to his crotch as if to staunch the stream of blood pulsing out. The second German had been hit at the top of his right thigh and had fallen to the floor, his rifle dropped and forgotten. The .45 calibre bullet, shot at such close range, had shattered the bone and the man's leg was protruding at an unnatural angle. Sam quickly finished off each of them with a shot to the head.

Seeking a more effective weapon, he grabbed the Sturmgewehr .44 assault rifle the first German had dropped, then dove back behind his desk. Outside, there was more shouting in German, running footsteps, and, further away, more gunshots and shouting. Then suddenly silence.

In his mind, Sam pictured the German platoon leader stopping by Markley's body outside the hut. He pictured him seeing the bodies of his dead comrades through the open door, and silently holding up his hand as a sign for his fellows to halt. In a moment, they'd come in with guns blazing and this time Sam wouldn't have a chance.

So he decided not to wait. He aimed the Sturmgewehr to the right of the door and pulled the trigger, sweeping it in a wide arc. It was a heavy, powerful weapon, and Sam correctly guessed that its bullets would easily penetrate the thin shell of the Quonset hut. Even over the deafening roar of his automatic rifle, the screams from outside were audible. He waited, uncertain what to do next, afraid to venture out from behind his overturned desk. He knew he should be horrified at what he'd just done. But it had been necessary.

It was only a minute or two before there were more voices, this time American. "Is it clear out there?" he shouted, still not moving.

"Yeah," came the response. "How 'bout in there?"

"Just me," Sam replied.

A young lieutenant, followed by three privates, entered the Quonset hut, rifles at the ready. The lieutenant looked at the two dead Germans, then at Sam and at the bullet holes in the wall of the Quonset hut. "You got three dead Krauts outside. Did you know that?"

"I figured two or three," Sam responded. "I wasn't sure."

"How'd you know they were Germans?"

"I could hear them talking," Sam said.

The lieutenant nodded before he said, "You'll need to come back with us to General Officer's quarters and file a report."

Sam followed the young lieutenant past the dead Germans and then past Phil Markley, sprawled awkwardly on his back, his lifeless eyes staring upward. Sam had an urge to stop for a moment, touch his friend, but he dutifully walked on.

At the General Officer's quarters Sam was personally interviewed by General Cota. When he had finished giving his account, Sam asked, "How did this happen, sir?"

"It was basically fubared," Cota replied. "I had too many men out hunting Krauts, not enough guarding our hindquarters. Somehow a German patrol got through our lines — not that there are really lines with these goddamned hedgerows — and in broad goddamn daylight walked right in and started shooting. Killed twelve of our people and wounded ten others before Lieutenant Mazzacoli and his men stopped them. Actually, Mazzacoli and his guys got three of them. You killed the other five."

The general paused and looked directly at Sam, who felt compelled to say, "Yes, sir."

"What do you do?" the general said.

Taken aback, Sam said, "I'm not sure what you mean, sir."

"I mean, I know that you are assigned to headquarters, but what's your exact job?"

"I'm in Logistics, sir. It's important."

The general nodded. "I know. As a matter of fact, I just had Major Kinney in here running me through the supply requisitions. But I'm thinking you might be more valuable in a combat unit. You seem pretty good at it, Cahill. Any problem with that?"

"No, sir." Despite Sam's heartfelt fears about how he would respond in a combat situation, he'd had absolutely no hesitation shooting the enemy, or any sense of regret for having done so.

"Good," the general said. "Mazzacoli lost a squad leader in this mess. I'm sure he could use another one."

Turning to the lieutenant who'd brought Sam to him, the general said, "Isn't that right, Mazzacoli?"

"Yes, sir," Mazzacoli said immediately.

"Sir, just so you're clear," Sam said, "I've never been in combat, let alone led a squad. I'm not sure how the men would respond to me."

Both Mazzacoli and the general looked at him, but it was the young lieutenant who responded. "Don't worry about it," he said. "You'll do fine."

And with that, Sam was a staff sergeant.

CHAPTER SIXTY-NINE

The war had been profitable for Max Zalensky. He'd had the foresight, when he saw conflict coming, to buy two small arms manufacturers in Connecticut as well as machine shops in New York and New Jersey. When demand for guns and ammunition boomed he was in perfect position to make large, legitimate profits. His friends in Congress assured that a fair share of military contracts were sent his way, and of course those friends were generously rewarded for their helpfulness.

But the biggest profits were derived from the black market. Wartime shortages made normal household goods like sugar, coffee and gasoline scarce, and many citizens were willing to pay a premium to attain a modicum of luxury. Max, who'd always had a sweet tooth, decided to concentrate on sugar.

Sugar importers were closely watched and regulated by government bureaucrats, making extralegal activity on their part difficult and expensive. But Max's banking contacts in the Caribbean connected him to sugar farmers in that region who were happy to sell to the highest bidder, and who had no interest in what was or wasn't legal in America.

The difficult part was transportation into the US, since the coasts were carefully protected. Again, Max's connections in government paid dividends. Senator Standish was able to assure the proper paperwork to pass Coast Guard inspections; cargoes were well documented as United States Department of Agriculture imports headed for government-controlled distribution centres. But in fact, those cargoes were headed for a Max Zalensky-controlled pier in northern New Jersey and distribution on the black market.

"This is more than we agreed upon," Senator Standish said, surprised but obviously pleased, as he opened an attaché case full of cash. They were in the senator's office, and Max, who liked to keep this powerful man close, was making the payoff in person.

"Your help has proved invaluable," Max responded. "We've been able to get our shipments through without problem, and the margins are even higher than I had hoped. You deserve the bonus."

Standish smiled broadly. "I appreciate your fairness. I guess not all you people are as cheap as everybody thinks."

"No," Max responded, as he turned to leave. "Apparently not." And once again, he was amazed that such a fool could become a US senator. Because only a fool would not realise that this transaction simply tightened the noose that Max Zalensky already held around the neck of the influential Senator Standish.

CHAPTER SEVENTY

General Patton's 3rd Army crossed the Seine, bypassed Paris, and continued full speed toward Berlin. Patton pushed his troops at breakneck pace until they reached the town of Metz near the junction of France, Germany and Luxembourg. Metz had been a German city prior to the Fatherland's defeat in the Great War, and it was not a prize they wished to lose a second time. The assault began in early November. The battle was brutal and the weather bone-chilling, but American forces broke through the enemy lines and into the city on Thanksgiving Day.

The main German force fled when the Americans breached their defences, pursued by the bulk of the 3rd Army. But small squads of the Wehrmacht remained in the city and Jacob's company was assigned to clean them out. His squad was put on point.

Jake's protocol was to send two men at a time running forward, covered by the other seven. The city's streets were narrow and cobbled, dating back to before Julius Caesar, and they were challenging to say the least. The squad progressed, slowly but surely, for a mile without incident, until they reached a large open square, surrounded by narrow apartment houses. There was no choice but to cross it.

"Spread out," Jake commanded. "Buddy, Haggarty, Schmidt and Kirby on the left, everyone else, right. I'll take the middle."

They were halfway across when three shots rang out in quick succession. As had happened before, Jake wasn't sure which he heard first: the shot itself or the horrible thunk of bullet hitting flesh just a few yards away. He dove to the ground, rifle extended in front of him.

As his knees and elbows hit the ground, he saw the three enemy soldiers at the far end of the square. They had jumped out from behind the near corner of a low apartment building, taken one shot each, and were now scurrying back for cover. By the time Jake got off his shot, two of them were already behind the building, and the third, a tall blond, was halfway there. Jacob was almost certain that his shot had grazed him.

Kirby was down, and Jake yelled at Haggerty to stay with him. As he got to his feet and started running, the others followed his lead. He let loose a round of automatic fire as he followed their attackers around the corner, but the narrow passageway behind it was empty. At the alley's end was a small square bordered by trim, neat houses. Jake was so sure his bullet had hit the tall blond that he actually looked for blood on the cobblestones.

He could barely believe his eyes when he saw it. Red droplets, wet and glistening, leading to the wooden door of an incongruously modern house. Jacob was certain the three Germans were in there, unaware of the trail they had left.

Buddy was ten yards to his right, Schmidt the same distance to his left, the others covering the perimeter of the small square. When they were fifty feet from the house Jacob snatched a grenade from his belt, pulled the pin and hurled it through a small window near the front door. The ensuing explosion blew out every window in the front of the house and blasted the door off its hinges and out onto the street. Jake pulled a second grenade and tossed it through the open door frame. He dropped on all fours to avoid the blast, then sprang up as soon as it passed. Yelling for Buddy and Schmidt to follow, he raced into the house.

The place was filled with dust and smoke, but he could see enough. The big blond must have been standing behind where the door had been and had apparently taken the brunt of the second grenade. He was lying in a pile of rubble, the midsection of his body half blown away, stomach and intestines and blood spilling out onto the floor. The other two Germans were in better shape, but not much. One was slumped against the back wall in a daze, blood spouting from an open gash in his right leg. Jacob put three bullets in him before he was even aware of the American's presence. The other German was lying face down on the floor, semi-conscious. At the sound of Jacob's fire he started to rise but Buddy, running in behind Jake, swept his machine gun around and dropped him permanently.

At the far end of the front room was a hallway that led, probably, to bedrooms. Jake was almost certain that only the three German soldiers were in the house but he had to be sure. Crouching low, he moved down the hall and into the first room.

He saw movement as soon as he was through the door. He raised his gun and swung around, his shadowy assailant making the same move. In the split second before he fired, Jacob could make out the man's face. It was almost black from dirt and sweat, and his eyes were blood red. Jake felt he was looking at the devil himself. In the next moment, there was a twin flash as they both fired, and then the sound of glass shattering and Jacob's antagonist disappearing in a clattering crash. He realised that he'd just shot out a full-length mirror.

He backed out of the room just as Schmidt and Buddy emerged from the other bedroom. "Everything okay?" Schmidt asked breathlessly.

"Yeah," was Jake's terse reply. He didn't want to explain that he'd just killed his own reflection. "How 'bout you?"

Schmidt nodded. Then all three walked out of the house to see if Kirby was still alive, and resume the patrol.

CHAPTER SEVENTY-ONE

Things worked out exactly as Jonathan had thought they would. The uncertainty of war initially hurt film sales, but as the conflict settled into its second and third years, people needed relief from their day-to-day grind, and movies provided that relief. Even better, the war effort created huge numbers of jobs, so nearly everyone had extra change in their pocket. The year 1944 was looking like the best on record for Film Studios of America, and Jonathan was confident that 1945 would be even better. FSA's latest release, *Bombs Over Tokyo*, about the Doolittle raid, was the number one hit in the country.

Max, of course, acted as if he expected no less. He breezed quickly through FSA's quarterly results and then segued to a new order of business. "I happen to have access to large quantities of sugar," he said. "I'm sure your Hollywood friends would love to partake. You interested in being my distributor?"

Jonathan stared at him a moment before replying, "No, thanks. Not something I want to do."

"Seriously?" Max responded, unable to keep the surprise out of his voice. "Everybody needs half a cup or so for every cake they make, every batch of cookies, every pie. My understanding is that the war hasn't slowed down the parties in this town. I would think there'd be a big demand."

"I'm sure you're right. But Sam's fighting in Europe. I'm not about to do anything that might have a negative effect on the war effort."

"And you really think that's what sugar rationing is about? Helping the war effort?"

Jonathan shrugged. "That's what they say. Who am I to doubt the government?"

Max nodded. "Okay, understood. It's not a big deal. I've already got a great business on the East Coast. I just thought you might like to play Santa Claus to some of these Hollywood big shots."

"I appreciate it," Jonathan said, "but I'm sure you see that I can't be involved with this."

Max nodded again. "Absolutely."

They quickly moved on to other subjects, and sugar was never again mentioned. But Jonathan had known Max Zalensky for many years and he could almost hear the wheels turning. He knew that Max was registering new information, to be retrieved and utilised at the appropriate time, and probably not for anything good.

CHAPTER SEVENTY-TWO

Four days after the battle for Metz, word came from Allied Headquarters: the Germans were making an unexpected attack to the north, an area called Ardennes in Belgium. It was Hitler's last great attempt to save his empire, so getting as many Allied troops to the area as quickly as possible was crucial. The 4th, 26th and 80th divisions of Patton's 3rd army travelled the two hundred twenty miles to Ardennes in three days, a feat considered the most efficient troop deployment in military history.

Company C, 4th Division, positioned itself along a four-mile parallel in the Ardennes Forest, ten miles north of the city of Bastogne. Sam's platoon settled near a temporary headquarters area where a small field hospital had been set up. Two men were added to the existing guard at the headquarters, the rest handed basic maps of the area and instructed to march east, the direction from which the Germans were advancing. Jacob and his platoon arrived at the same spot thirty minutes later and were similarly deployed, a few men staying at headquarters and the rest heading east.

Sam and his men trudged through the forest, snow up to their knees, gloved hands gripping their rifles. It was heavy work but the officers worried they would be sitting ducks if they took the icy road that ran parallel to their route, simple targets for anyone hiding in the woods. So they laboured through the forest until they heard the rapid bursts of automatic rifles and knew they were close to battle. Then, suddenly, the dark woods opened onto a large, beautiful meadow that was thick with noise, bullets and black smoke.

Sam dropped to the ground and signalled his men to do the same. Enemy soldiers came out of the woods at the far end of the meadow, picking off the hundred or so Americans caught in the open. A single German Tiger tank wheeled slowly down the middle of the meadow. One soldier stood in the open hatch and manned the machine gun. A phalanx of German infantry, perhaps twenty men, moved behind the tank, and used it for protection as it crawled forward. Sam estimated that a few hundred more enemy soldiers were scattered along the far end of the field, advancing cautiously, letting the tank and the men behind it clear the way. Fog swirled off the snow at the Americans' end of the meadow. It chilled Sam to his bones, but he realised that the fog prevented them from being seen clearly, the only thing that inhibited the Germans from charging at full speed.

Then, just a few minutes after Sam and his patrol arrived, an American tank destroyer rolled out into the meadow eighty yards to Sam's right. It had come up the same road that Sam and his men had avoided and was now trying to race up the far edge of the meadow. Sam knew the game well. The German tank carried inch-thick hardened steel plating over its front armour, and an extra half-inch along the front side portion running halfway to the rear. The weight of all this extra protection slowed the tank down but made it practically invulnerable to a direct frontal attack.

Sam had heard stories of one Tiger going toe to toe with as many as four Sherman tanks and demolishing them all. With time, the Americans learned that in the open field they could use their superior speed to run around the side of the German tanks from which point they could take them out. The destroyer was trying to get within killing distance of the Tiger, but slightly to the side and behind it, before the slower tank could swing its turret in the Americans' direction. Sam held his breath, watching this contest.

The tank destroyer rolled up the road at a good clip but suddenly, a hundred yards up, it stopped short, wavering like a wobbly infant as it struggled in vain to go forward. The fog hid the bottom half of the destroyer, but even without seeing it, Sam could guess the situation. A tank destroyer was really just a basic army-issue truck with tyres in front and treads in back, with a three-inch anti-tank weapon and a .50 calibre machine gun mounted on top. The front tyres were probably stuck in some hole in this godforsaken ground and the treads in back couldn't find enough traction on the frozen earth to force the truck free. The driver of the tank destroyer shifted gears from forward to reverse and back again, trying to free himself from the hole, knowing death was closing in with every second that he remained immobile.

The soldier manning the three-inch gun, Private Ben Luckley from Amarillo, Texas, was not about to sit like a wooden duck and wait for the German tank to use him for target practice. So although the plan was to shoot only after they had passed the rear end of the tank, Private Luckley improvised. Bending his long legs so he could look directly through the sights, he calmly but quickly trained his weapon on the Tiger.

He estimated that it was just less than a hundred yards away and he set the distance adjustment accordingly. Luckley had received the highest marks in his artillery class back at Camp Lejeune, North Carolina, and his aim was nearly perfect. But just as his finger began to tighten against the curve of the big gun's trigger, the half-track's back tread finally found traction. The truck jumped backward out of the hole it had been stuck in and lurched a full fifteen feet in reverse before the driver regained control.

Luckley was taken completely by surprise and went careening sideways, his feet leaving the truck bed. The only thing that prevented him from falling flat was his tight grip on the gun, which was bolted down. He recovered quickly and scrambled back into position, swinging the three-inch barrel back toward the target. He had the tank focused almost exactly between the parallel lines of the site when a shell fragment ripped off the top of his head.

The commander of the Tiger had seen the tank destroyer racing up his left flank and slammed his control lever to the left, knowing it was time to kill or be killed. The movement of the long cannon was maddeningly slow, and the German realised he wouldn't catch the destroyer in time. Then, abruptly, the half-track was stuck in place, and he knew he had a chance. He was close when the truck suddenly lurched backward, directly into his site. He let go of the lever and bellowed at the top of his lungs, "Fire!"

The fifty-centimetre shell landed ten feet short of the half-track and detonated on impact. The explosion created a one-foot-deep, three-foot-wide crater in the frozen ground. But most of the shell burst upward and out, killing both men in the tank destroyer. A half-inch shard of metal flew through the door of the cab, entering the left side of the driver's body and exiting his right, tearing through two ribs, his left lung and the bottom-left ventricle of his heart.

A second piece of shrapnel, almost two inches long and an eighth of an inch thick, flew higher and caught Private Luckley above the bridge of his nose. Its upward arc cut through him like a scythe through wheat, cleaving his skull and separating the top two thirds of his brain from the bottom. Ben Luckley's lifeless body fell away from the anti-tank gun, flailing for several seconds before coming to rest.

★　　★　　★

Sam's heart sank when he saw the explosion near the tank destroyer, the gunner blown away. He knew, as did every soldier in that field, that with nothing to stop it, the Tiger would roll right through the meadow with hundreds of German soldiers following behind it. Then it would speed up the same road that the tank destroyer had come down, right to headquarters and the makeshift hospital. American soldiers in the meadow were already retreating. Soon, it would be a rout.

"Maybe we should get the hell out of here." It was Wolinsky speaking, expressing the thoughts of all as they saw the impending disaster.

Sam swung around to address all of the men. "Stay right here. Dig in and do your job."

"There're too many of them," Wolinsky responded. "At least, with the Tiger tank. That thing'll blow us to kingdom come, even if we could dig in this frozen dirt."

Sam looked straight at him. "Private Wolinsky, you're in charge. Dig in as best you can and shoot Germans if you get the chance. If it looks totally helpless, then get everyone the hell out. But not until then."

"What? Where're you gonna—"

But Sam was already off and running. He left the Browning so as not to slow himself down, carrying only his .45. He ran with his bottom low and his body bent almost in half at the waist. The fog was covering most of the meadow now and it would be difficult for the enemy to see him. He moved along the edge of the meadow to the road, then over the road to the woods beyond. Once in the woods, hidden by the trees, he straightened up and moved as quickly as he could in the direction of the tank destroyer. The snow was deeper in the woods than in the meadow and it was slow going, but he eventually caught sight of the tank destroyer between trees.

Like everyone else, Sam had seen the explosion and the top of the gunner's head blown off. And from the gaping hole in the cab, he assumed the driver was also dead. But he thought there was a good chance that the gun itself had not been touched, that it might still be usable if he could get to it without getting killed first.

The German tank and the enemy soldiers using it for cover were almost parallel with the tank destroyer, but their focus was straight ahead. Sam took a deep breath, let it out, and then dashed out of the woods and across the road. He clambered up the short ladder to the elevated truck bed and crawled toward the three-inch gun. He was so focused on his goal that he did not notice the lifeless body of Private Luckley until his right hand slipped on something slick and wet, sending him face first onto the deck. He found himself only inches from what was left of Ben Luckley's head. His hand had slipped on the unlucky man's blood and brains. Long past feeling revulsion, Sam pushed himself back up and continued his crawl to the gun.

Once there, he sprang to his feet. Luckley had been blown straight back so the big gun had hardly moved. With very little manoeuvering Sam was able to sight directly on the tank. He had trained for one day with heavy artillery back at Fort Benning, and had not been particularly skillful. Sam remembered that it was critical to properly adjust the distance setting, but had no idea how to calculate it. He figured that the tank was no more than twenty yards past where it had been when Luckley adjusted the setting. He cranked the handle one eighth of a turn, slightly raising the three-inch barrel. Then he pulled the trigger on the right-hand grip. There was a two-second delay that would normally give the gunner time to cover his ears, but Sam had forgotten about this and was temporarily deafened by the tremendous noise.

The deadly projectile hit the rear left side of the German tank, easily piercing the unreinforced section of armour, ripping it apart and instantly killing the five-man crew. Dozens of shards of metal flew through the rear and sides of the tank, killing or disabling eight of the soldiers walking behind it. The other Germans, stunned by the unexpected explosion, were slow to react. By the time they did, Sam had skipped across the truck bed to the mounted machine gun. He had practiced extensively with a .50 calibre back in Basic and even manned one in combat at Verdun, so he was on familiar ground.

He aimed at the troop of soldiers behind the tank and in seconds had decimated them, the large bullets pulverising anything they came in contact with. A man hit squarely in the arm or lower leg by a .50 calibre volley would find that limb almost torn off and his life ebbing away from loss of blood if help did not arrive quickly. For the enemy soldiers in this meadow this day, help would never arrive.

★   ★   ★

Private Jacob Epstein and his patrol had followed the same route as Sam's squad, albeit half an hour behind. On their way in, panicked men had run past them back toward headquarters. As they neared the meadow, soldiers were easing back into the trees while bullets shattered branches with thunderous cracks. Jacob got down on his hands and knees and signalled his men to do the same. They crawled out of the woods just a moment before the tank was hit.

The situation soon became as hopeless for the Germans as, moments before, it had seemed for the Americans. The soldier behind the .50 calibre was shooting any Kraut he could see, and he looked to Jacob to be damn good at it. The Germans were trying to return fire but the American's bigger weapon and elevated position gave him the advantage. Scores of German bodies littered the meadow now, either dead or dying. The Americans had stopped their retreat and were moving forward, although not as quickly as their enemies were running away. Even as they ran, many Germans fell victim to the quick death spitting from the crippled tank destroyer.

Sixty yards away, Jacob noticed a German uniform dive forward into the snow and disappear. He assumed the soldier had found a blast hole or ditch that afforded him temporary respite from the rain of .50 calibre bullets. He'd be better off running like hell as most of his comrades were doing, Jacob thought. In a few more minutes the Americans would be sweeping the entire meadow and the Kraut would be caught in his hole and shot like a rat in a barrel. Nobody was in the mood to take prisoners.

"Take Schmidt and Haggerty," Jacob shouted to Buddy. "Go up the road and make sure it's secure. I don't want any Krauts coming back down it." Then he pointed to where he wanted the men to go. And as he did so, following the sweep of his own arm, he saw the brown uniform pop up out of the snow not more than thirty yards from where that machine gunner was still firing at the struggling Germans. Knowing where the man had come from, Jake was able to spy the ridgeline of a slight mound that ran across the meadow from the spot where the German had first disappeared, all the way to the road. By diving into the snow bank built up on the lee side of the mound, the German had been able to slither across the field undetected.

But now he was standing upright, his rifle extended. The battle was too noisy and the soldier too far away for Jacob to hear the shot, but he saw the heroic gunner on top of the tank destroyer, the man who had saved the day and maybe all of their lives. He saw him spin around, blood spurting from his shoulder, falling backward onto the raised bed of the truck. Jake looked back at the German but the man was nowhere to be seen. Of course, Jake knew where he was. He was down on the ground crawling toward the road, where he would race to the other side of the destroyer, out of sight from the men fighting in the meadow. He would climb up a few steps onto the truck, kill the helpless gunner, and then use the .50 calibre on the Americans.

Jacob was up and running. He couldn't see the enemy but he knew approximately where he must be. As he ran he pulled a grenade from his shoulder strap and drew out the pin. He'd been able to toss a football farther than anyone else back at Hollywood High, farther than any high school boy in Los Angeles. Still, he wasn't sure if he could do this.

He was still almost sixty yards away. He threw the grenade hard and high on a full run. To his delight, it landed almost exactly where he had aimed it, just on the other side of the mound and twenty yards from the tank destroyer. Jacob saw the German fly two or three feet into the air, landing in a jumbled heap. Jacob knew he wasn't getting up again.

After sprinting the rest of the way to the destroyer, Jacob

clambered up the small ladder and dove onto the platform. The gunner was spread-eagled on the floor, his head and left arm hanging precariously over the side. There was a dark red wound where his left shoulder met his chest, blood covering his upper torso and spilling onto the platform beneath him. Like so many wounded men Jacob had seen, the gunner was semi-conscious; not really out, but not aware of anyone or anything around him.

Jake pulled the man all the way back onto the platform, then ripped back his shirt so he could see the wound. The bullet seemed to have gone all the way through, taking several square inches of the gunner's flesh and muscle with it. Stopping the bleeding as quickly as possible would be critical to whether this soldier lived or died. Jacob cursed himself for not having brought his medic kit. He looked back to where he'd left it and saw Buddy jogging toward him. God bless him, he was carrying the kit.

"Toss it," he yelled as his friend got close, but Buddy didn't have to be told. He threw the kit up onto the truck bed even before he had stopped running. Jacob tore it open, had the gauze and tape out in an instant, and bandaged up the wounded man. Then he wrapped the excess cloth that he had added to the standard medic's kit around the soldier's arm and chest, securing the arm against the man's side.

Jacob slung the gunner, whose dog tag identified him as Samuel Cahill, over his shoulder and carried him down the short ladder to solid ground. Buddy found a stretcher inside the truck. They lowered Cahill onto it, fastened him with the strap, and set off at a fast trot. The field hospital was a little more than three miles away. They made it in less than thirty minutes.

CHAPTER SEVENTY-THREE

Sam was in the little hospital in Bastogne for ten weeks before the doctors felt he was ready to travel. Then he rode overland by jeep to Marseilles, and by merchant marine to New York. Eighteen months earlier such a trip would have carried the risk of attack from German submarines and battleships, but today the Allied navies owned the Atlantic Ocean. In New York he boarded the train to Washington, DC. The entire trip took three weeks.

A Lieutenant Basker met him at the railroad station in DC. Sam had to put down his bag to salute, since he could not hold anything with his free hand. Noting the problem without seeming to, Basker said, "Let me carry your bag, Sergeant." Sam was amazed that such an offer would come from a man who outranked him, but tired as he was he didn't argue. The lieutenant had a car waiting that took them to the Hay-Adams Hotel. Basker checked him in, then told him, "Ceremony's tomorrow. I'll pick you up at eight hundred sharp. Be in dress uniform." As if Sam would not know that.

Samuel assumed the ceremony would take place at the War Department, but to his amazement the car turned up Pennsylvania Avenue and into the long driveway at 1600. They stopped at the guardhouse, but when the MP saw Basker, he opened the gate and waved them through. They rolled around to a beautiful rose garden on the north side of the White House, where tables and chairs were set up, along with food and drinks. Red, white and blue banners were strung through the air, and a pianist played 'God Bless America'.

There were eight other soldiers in uniform, representing all branches of the armed forces. Two of the soldiers were in wheelchairs; one appeared to be missing both legs. Another man, in an air force uniform, had obviously been severely burned, the right side of his face and neck disfigured by angry white blotches, a black patch covering his right eye. Two of the soldiers walked with the help of a cane, and one appeared to have sustained a shoulder wound similar to Sam's. Only two men appeared unscathed.

After about five minutes, the music suddenly stopped, almost in mid stanza. A few men stood straight and saluted. Sam turned in the direction they were facing and saluted along with them. President Franklin Roosevelt was rolling toward them, his wheelchair pushed by a dark-suited man, a United States Marine flanking him on either side.

"At ease, fellows," he said with that familiar Brahmin accent. Sam dropped his arm. The president then rolled around the garden, shaking hands with each man, and saying, "Thank you, son," or "Great job, soldier."

After the initial greetings, the eight soldiers lined up and, one after the other, the President of the United States presented each of them with the Congressional Medal of Honour. The medal itself was a bronze star suspended from a bar bearing the word 'Valour'. On top of the bar perched an eagle with outspread wings, and on the back of the medal given to Sam were the words, 'The Congress to Samuel J. Cahill'. Sam bent over so the president could hang the blue ribbon from which the medal was suspended around his neck. Roosevelt seemed to have a difficult time lifting his arms to perform the simple task, his face becoming red from exertion.

The president excused himself immediately after the ceremony, explaining that although he "would rather stay and chat with you fellows", he had work that he must attend to. "But please stay," he pleaded, "and enjoy the food and company." To Sam, Roosevelt appeared to be exhausted and he wondered if the president was really going back to his office to work, or whether he was sicker than was generally known.

In the car, on the way back to the hotel, Lieutenant Basker informed him that he would be returning to Germany. "Patton's most of the way to Berlin," he said. "I honestly don't think the war's got much longer to run, at least not in Europe. Maybe six months. The Japs are a different story. They don't seem to want to give up."

"I'm not sure I understand," Sam said. "I'm not in any condition to fight anymore. I don't know if I could even hold a rifle. What am I going to do in Germany?"

"General Patton has requested that you join his staff."

Sam looked at the lieutenant in surprise. "How would Patton even know who I am?"

"Are you kidding? Of course he knows. He had to approve your medal. And he likes having heroes around him."

Sam shrugged. "Okay. When do I ship out? I'd hoped to call my father, see if he could pay me a visit."

"Sorry, you leave first thing tomorrow morning. And calling home is not a good idea. Technically, you being here is a war secret."

Sam grimaced and Basker continued. "Don't worry. Like I said, I don't think this war is going to last much longer."

Basker's prediction proved correct. By the time Samuel caught up with General Patton at his headquarters in Magdeburg, the Russians had entered Berlin. A week later, the war in Europe was over. Sam was going home.

CHAPTER SEVENTY-FOUR

Jonathan stretched to his full height and stood on his toes to see over the crowd gathered at Los Angeles' Union Station. Sam's train was coming in and Jonathan was so anxious to see him he could hardly contain himself. It had been nearly four years and seemed like a lifetime. Sam's unit had docked safe and sound in New Jersey, each man formally discharged and handed a train ticket home. And today was the day. Judging by the crowd of parents and sweethearts, there were many soldiers on this train.

With a wheeze and exhale of steam, the train came to a stop. Suddenly, young men in uniforms were hopping off, jubilant, looking for familiar faces in the crowd. Sam was one of the first off. He looked a little awkward, one arm hanging limply at his side, the other holding his duffle, so he had to step down carefully without aid of the handrail. Jonathan was confused for just a moment, but then he remembered. Of course, he'd been wounded. He hadn't realised it was something permanent. No matter. Jonathan was running now, and shouting, and then he had him, hugging and laughing and hugging him again. Sam finally pulled himself loose. There were tears in Jonathan's eyes.

Jonathan took hold of the young man's good shoulder and said, "Come on, let's get out of here. I'll bet you're starving." Both of them grinned as they turned and made their way through the crowd. Up ahead, Sam caught sight of a stunning woman, waving in the direction of the train. "Say, isn't that..." he said.

Jonathan nodded. "Susan Spencer," he said, finishing Sam's thought. "She must be meeting someone."

As they looked on, a young soldier hopped off the train and strode toward her. Susan rushed to meet him, and the soldier, who was half a foot taller, reached down and picked her up in a bear hug. Susan smothered his cheeks with kisses and then put her arms around his neck as if she had no intention of letting go. It looked to

Jonathan like she was both laughing and crying. He knew exactly how she felt.

"Holy shit," Sam said. "That's Epstein. I didn't realise he was on this train."

"Your language has not improved in the army," Jonathan said, looking sideways at his son. "Do you know him?"

"Not exactly. But he did save my life."

"What?"

"He saved my life, Dad."

"Seriously? Then I need to thank him."

"Me too, actually," Sam said. "I never had the chance. But I'm not sure this is the time."

Sam was right. Susan's feet were back on the ground but she was still hugging the young man and sobbing profusely.

"I guess young Epstein must be Susan's son," Jonathan said.

"Her son?" Sam's tone was incredulous. "I figured maybe her boyfriend or something. How could she have a son my age?"

"Easily. She's about the same age as me."

"You're kidding. She looks so much...." Sam's voice trailed off.

"So much younger? Susan started in the business before I did. She was a star in silent films twenty years ago."

Sam laughed. "No offence, Dad. You look good. I just don't think of her as that old. Maybe because of the roles she plays. I guess she probably makes them put her in young parts."

Jonathan shrugged. "Actually, she's been asking for middle-aged roles. We're the ones who make her play younger."

"You mean you know her?"

Jonathan nodded. "She's done several films for my studio. She even keeps an office on the FSA lot. So I know her through business, but we don't see each other socially if that's what you're wondering."

Sam looked at his father and then back at Susan. "Maybe you ought to work on that."

Jonathan looked back at his son, smiled, and said, "Let's go home. Your grandmother is anxious to see you."

★　　★　　★

They had met, of course, since she had starred in several of his studio's films. But they had never exchanged more than brief pleasantries, so she was surprised when Jonathan Cahill knocked on the open door of her office. It was located in a bungalow on the outskirts of the back lot, not a place a studio chief would wander by accidentally.

Sophie put down the script she was reading and stood up. "Hello, Mr. Cahill. To what do I owe this honour?"

Jonathan grinned. "I assure you the honour is mine. Actually, I came to invite you and your son.... This is horrible, but I'm not sure of his name. Is it Jason? I'm hoping that the two of you will join me and my son, Sam, for dinner at our home."

Clearly surprised, Sophie said, "His name is Jacob. And it's very generous of you." Then, after a slight hesitation she said, "But why? I mean, it sounds nice, but it's so out of the blue. And with my son?"

A little flummoxed that she didn't know, Jonathan said, "To celebrate the boys' return from the war. And, of course, to thank Jacob for saving Sam's life."

Sophie was taken aback. "What? I mean, I read about what a hero your boy Sam was, and how he was wounded. But Jacob never even mentioned that he knew him."

Jonathan nodded. "Technically, they never met. Sam was unconscious when your son rescued him. He only learned of it later, and never got the chance to thank him. We'd both like to do that."

Sophie shook her head as if in wonderment. "He never said a thing." Then looking directly at Jonathan, she said, "We'd love to come, of course."

CHAPTER SEVENTY-FIVE

Jonathan wanted it to be perfect, and it came close. To make Susan more comfortable he also invited Jack and Deborah Wallis. Jack was an independent producer who was currently working for Film Studios of America on a World War Two film involving two brothers, farm boys from Iowa. Jack's wife, the former Deborah Gartner, had been a successful actress before retiring to raise their children and maintain their Beverly Hills home. She was taking a brief break from real motherhood to play the movie mother of the two protagonists in the film. Jonathan and Jack had worked together several times over the years, and Jon knew that Deborah and Susan were good friends, often meeting for lunch or shopping. He knew this because he'd asked Selma Williams, his executive secretary, to find out whatever she could about Susan's personal life.

The food was catered by Chasen's, a West Hollywood restaurant famous for its Texas-style chilli and chocolate desserts. Dinner was excellent and from Jonathan's dining room his guests looked out over the moonlit, glittery Pacific Ocean. Below them were occasional headlights from cars on the Pacific Coast Highway, and in the distance, lights from the Santa Monica Pier.

"What are your plans now?" Jack Wallis directed his question at Sam as he speared a forkful of Caesar salad. "Now that you've won the war?"

Sam swallowed a mouthful before answering. "I'd finished two years at Stanford Law before I joined the army. I'll be going back to finish up next month."

Wallis grimaced in an exaggerated manner. "A lawyer in the family. How do you feel about that, Jon?"

"I can live with it," Jonathan deadpanned, trying to underplay his obvious pride in his son. "He's already had calls from several of the top firms, inquiring if he'd be interested in working for them when he graduates."

There were words of congratulations from around the table. Sam nodded politely and said, "What about you, Jake? Are you planning to go to medical school?"

The room went silent, waiting for Jacob's answer. Sophie stopped eating, obviously interested, and said, "Why would you ask that?"

Sam shrugged. "He was a medic in the army. I guess you knew that. He was great, sort of a legend in our company. Word was that he could stitch up a wound or splint a broken leg in the middle of a battle, better than the doctors in one of those little field hospitals. I'd heard stories about him even before he rescued me."

Sophie beamed, obviously delighted at this news. It confirmed what she had always hoped for her son. She looked at him expectantly.

"It's a real possibility," Jacob finally said. "But I haven't decided yet."

"Better not wait too long," Jack Wallis intoned. "You may not have decided, but it looks like your mother has." At that, Sophie reddened a bit and everyone around the table laughed, including Jacob.

Of course, Sam didn't mention the other stories he'd heard about Jacob Epstein; stories about the young soldier's naked aggression and cold brutality. It was part of his legend in the battalion, the contrast between great medic and cold-blooded killer. From what Sam had heard, Jacob was one of those who volunteered to go behind enemy lines when the troops were punching into new territory, risking his life to kill a few more Germans. And, if the stories were true, he didn't take prisoners, even if the Krauts had dropped their weapons and were waving their hands in the air. He simply killed them.

This was not as unusual as people back home believed, and had its practical advantages. When you were on the front lines, as Jake often was, taking prisoners meant you had to backtrack with them to field headquarters, often in very difficult conditions. So you were removed from the action for at least half a day, sometimes longer. By the time you returned to the front the battle might be over.

So while the generals didn't condone shooting enemy soldiers who were in the process of surrendering, they didn't discourage it either. And the great medic, Jacob Epstein, had been absolutely ruthless. Knowing what he knew, Sam could fully understand Epstein's mixed feelings about becoming a doctor. Still, Sam would be willing to put his life in Jacob's hands anytime. It seemed to him that medical school made a lot of sense.

"So, Susan," Jack Wallis asked over dessert, "what are you working on these days?"

"Actually, nothing," Sophie replied. "I've been given some scripts to read, but nothing interesting. They're all parts for someone half my age."

"That's because you look half your age," Deborah chimed in.

"That's nice of you to say, even if it's not true." Sophie smiled at her friend.

Without looking up from his chocolate soufflé, which was excellent, Jonathan said, "I've got something that will interest you." The completely casual yet certain manner in which he said it caught the attention of everyone at the table.

But when he just continued to eat his soufflé, Sophie finally said, "What?"

Jonathan smiled. "Come around this week, and I'll show it to you. You can make an appointment with my assistant."

"I'll do that," Sophie said, her curiosity obviously piqued.

As the evening wound down, Sophie said to Jonathan, "This was a wonderful idea, getting together with our boys. Next time you and Sam will come to our house."

"If that's an invitation, we accept," Jon responded. "But don't forget to come look at that script I mentioned."

"Oh, did you mention a script?" Sophie asked, completely straight-faced.

CHAPTER SEVENTY-SIX

Three days later, Sophie called Jonathan's office as promised. When she arrived for their meeting he got to his feet and kissed her on the cheek. "You look sensational," he said. It was the standard line of all studio heads to all female stars, but in this case he meant it sincerely.

"Thank you. I really had a wonderful time the other night, and I know Jake enjoyed it too."

"I'm so glad." He paused a moment. "We're lucky, you know. They're great boys. And the fact that we got them back in one piece."

"I know." Sophie nodded. "Thank God. But now you're going to tell me a story."

"I am. It's about a woman in her early forties, a former small-town beauty queen who marries the handsome son of the town's leading family and has two children with him, a girl and a boy. Her husband takes over the family business, a paper mill that employs more than half the local workforce. He's an excellent businessman and the town prospers, earning him the gratitude of the entire populace.

"Unfortunately, he's not so excellent a husband. In fact, he's been unfaithful since the birth of their first child, and he's now engaged in a serious affair with a much younger woman. The heroine's two children, now both grown and in college, have become tired of small-town life, their father's philandering, and their mother's meek acceptance of it. Son and daughter both make it clear that they plan to move to 'the big city' after graduation, effectively destroying any remaining joy in their mother's life.

"Desperate and angry, she dives into a reckless affair with a younger man, the golf pro at her country club. The affair turns disastrous when friends and family find out. What is socially acceptable for her husband is simply not for her, and eventually leads to divorce, ostracism and ruin."

"Is she redeemed in any way?" Sophie asked.

"Not redeemed so much as her soul is bared, and she comes to grips with who she is and what she wants. It's a little heavier than our usual story, but I think it will work," Jonathan said. "But only with you playing the role."

"You really think so?"

"I won't make it without you."

"Well, I've been dying for a chance to do some real acting." She looked into his eyes in a meaningful way.

Jonathan smiled. "Let's do it, then." He glanced at his watch, and Sophie, taking the cue, stood up to leave.

"No, I didn't mean for you to go," Jonathan protested. "I was just noticing that it's almost lunch time. Perhaps you could join me."

"Perhaps I could."

They ate at one of the power corner tables in the small outdoor patio of the studio commissary, where the other stars and executives lunched. After their lunch plates were cleared they kept talking for nearly an hour, in between chatting with the actors and producers who stopped by to say hello and pay their respects. Finally, Jonathan signed the check and looked at his watch. "I wish I didn't have this meeting in ten minutes. I feel like we're just beginning."

Sophie nodded. "Me too." She cocked her head the same way that she did on screen sometimes. Her eyes sparkled. "Thank you, Jonathan."

"I was thinking.... I'm attending a charity ball for the Veterans' Association next Saturday. Would you like to join me? As my guest? If you're not busy?"

Sophie smiled, amused by his slight awkwardness, and said, "That would be very nice."

★   ★   ★

The day after the event, a society columnist for the *Los Angeles Times* would refer to Susan Spencer and Jonathan Cahill as 'an exceptionally attractive couple'. And that night they did seem a perfect pair. In any other circumstance, the highlight of the evening for Jonathan might have been the special award he received honouring his contributions of time and money to the rehabilitation of wounded veterans. But in this case, it was getting to spend time with Sophie.

She was charming and witty and beautiful as the two of them spent the evening drinking and dancing. Jonathan could feel the envious stares of every man in the room as they watched this glamorous movie star cling to him and whisper in his ear. Outside of time spent with his son, it was the best time he could remember since the death of his wife.

Afterward, on the way back to Sophie's home, slightly tipsy from champagne, the movie star and the studio head reclined in the back of his limousine. Jonathan, his tongue looser than usual, spoke of the hopes he had for his son and of the loneliness he had felt for twenty-six years since losing Sam's mother. Sophie took his hand, which led them to a long, exploratory kiss. When the driver finally guided the large car up the long driveway and stopped in front of her door, Sophie said, in a tone so tender and so vulnerable that it surprised him, "Maybe you could come inside for a little while."

In an equally serious tone, Jonathan said, "I'd like that." And after only one date, the middle-aged couple spent their first night together.

★   ★   ★

For the next several months, Jonathan and Susan Spencer had dinner several times a week and were often seen in one another's company at a play or party. On the occasional weekend when Sam drove down from Stanford, Sophie and Jonathan and their two sons spent time together, usually dining at one another's home. The two boys had become friends and seemed pleased by their parents' involvement.

The time he spent with her filled the void that he had carried for so many years. But Sophie turned him down when he asked her to move in with him, and marriage was out of the question. He asked, and she said no.

"We have a good thing going. Let's not ruin it." She loved his company and conversation, the sex was good, and Sophie was flattered by his obvious infatuation. But for now, at least, that was all she wanted. Jonathan understood this and was careful to allow her adequate space, always with the hope that she might grow to love him the way he loved her, allowing himself to believe that it might happen.

CHAPTER SEVENTY-SEVEN
1946

For Jimmy O'Brien, the time seemed right to expand his little empire, which was why he was sitting in the first-class car of the Southern Pacific Starlight Express, headed for Los Angeles. O'Brien's official title was Northeast District Coordinator for the Democratic Party. In practice, that meant he was a cigar-chomping, deal making, back-room political boss.

Jimmy had started out twenty years earlier in the Irish wards of South Boston. He had garnered votes in exchange for money, favours, and civil service jobs. People in the neighbourhoods came to him if they needed help getting a relative from the old country into America. Or if their son wanted a job with the police force or fire department, or their other son was in trouble with the law and needed a friend in court. Or any one of the myriad interactions that average citizens had with their local government.

Of course, in exchange for his help, people voted for Jimmy's candidates. They were more than happy to do so, since it served everyone to have elected officials who were responsive to the voters. *Democracy at its best*, Jimmy thought.

From South Boston he moved up to District Coordinator for the city, then for the state of Massachusetts, then the entire Northeast United States. Now he had local coordinators working for him who were Italian, Polish, Jewish, even Negro. In local politics Jimmy was one of the most powerful men in America. And if the national big shots wanted to get out the vote in one of Jimmy's precincts, they had to show their respect. His office walls were lined with pictures of himself standing arm-in-arm alongside all the great Democratic politicians: Roosevelt, Truman, Smith, Stevenson and the rest.

But when it came down to it, Jimmy was still no more than a local fixer. The highest-level pol that he had personally picked was just a councilman or mayor. In the worst way, he wanted to go national; influence the really big decisions, the really big money. Which was why he was heading to California.

The war had established airplane and automobile factories in Southern California to complement the banks and insurance companies in San Francisco. People were moving west in droves, looking for good jobs, affordable houses, sunshine and open spaces. O'Brien foresaw a day when California's huge population and economic strength would make it a political power, and he wanted to own as much of that power as possible.

The war had done one more thing. It had created heroes, and the people loved heroes. Jimmy felt that the perfect candidate for national office would be a good-looking young warrior, flush from victory, brimming with confidence. Jimmy would just plop him down in front of a grateful and patriotic public and let them sweep him into office. It would be like stealing apples from a blind man.

★   ★   ★

Tom Stern, the city councilman for his district, had set the meeting up and Jonathan assumed it was just another fundraising expedition. Max had taught him the value of supporting local politicians and he was happy to contribute, so long as this O'Brien character didn't take up too much of his time. Unfortunately, this seemed to be exactly what he was doing. "Maybe we can get directly to your business," Jonathan said, looking at his watch as O'Brien strolled around his office, checking out the personal photographs that lined the walls.

"Of course, Mr. Cahill." But O'Brien made no move to get on with it. Instead, he continued to peruse the walls, then said, "From what I see here, you seem to know all the big wheels in Hollywood – movie stars, producers, directors. Everyone."

"I've been around a few years now. So, naturally I've gotten to know most of the main players." Jonathan thought, *This guy not only wants my money, he wants me to introduce him to other people who can give him money. Probably a smart thing for him to do.*

But just as Jonathan thought he understood where O'Brien was heading, the man zigged once again. "Your words have just a slight twinge of the old country," O'Brien said. "Quite lovely really. You must have been young when you came here."

"I'm impressed. I was thirteen and I worked hard to lose the accent. Not many people would be able to pick up on it."

O'Brien nodded. "And your son was born here, in Los Angeles?"

At last Jonathan's patience ran out. "It occurs to me, Mr. O'Brien, that I don't really know why you're here. I assumed you were looking for money, which I'm willing to give you, within reason. But I'm not sure why you would care where Sam was born or when I came to America."

O'Brien stopped his pacing and looked directly at Jonathan. "I read about your boy in *Time* magazine, a piece they had on returning heroes. I'm sure you know the article. It had a very nice picture of Sam. Actually it was Mary, my wife, who first saw it. She commented on what a handsome young man he is. You'd be amazed how important that is nowadays, what with women making up half the voters."

Jonathan stared at him, surprise showing openly on his face. "Samuel was born in New York. He was seven when we moved out here." He paused. "What exactly are we talking about?"

"We're talking about the United States Congress. I am proposing that your son, Sam, be the next Democratic candidate from this district. He's young, he's good looking, and most importantly he's a hero. Having moved here when he was seven qualifies him as a local boy. In fact, the LA papers have already played him up as a hometown hero." O'Brien smiled. "I don't think it'll be too hard."

Still staring, disbelief showing on his face, Jonathan said, "How do the local Party people feel about this?"

"The short answer is that they'll feel however I tell them to. The long one is that they want a winner, and he can win. And starting this young, there's no limit to how far he can go. After three or four terms, if things go well, we'll run him for Senate."

"You might be getting a little ahead of yourself," Jonathan said. "First he has to agree to run."

"I was assuming, I should say hoping, that you could help us out with that. You could speak to him for us."

After a moment Jonathan nodded, then said, "Yes, I'd be willing to do that. But he loved law school. He's looking forward to being an attorney."

O'Brien snorted. "So he can join Cromwell and Fiske? And write contracts for corporations? Or help them form offshore affiliates to get around their tax obligations?"

Jonathan was a little shocked that O'Brien was so well informed about which law firm Sam was thinking of joining.

Reading his look, O'Brien said, "Don't get me wrong, nothing against the corporate lifestyle. I just mean that he could help his country, be a leader. He's already accustomed to being a hero."

"I'll talk to him," Jonathan said.

★　　★　　★

Sam warmed to the idea much more readily than Jonathan had expected.

"Do you think it would work?" Sam asked when his father broached the subject. "That I actually could win?"

"This O'Brien fellow thinks so. I've asked around and he's quite a power in the Democratic Party. If he says they'll back you, they will. And from what I hear he's got a history of picking winners." Jonathan paused. "You sound interested."

"Hell yes, I'm interested. I've always thought about politics. I just thought I'd have to have a career first." He noticed his father's raised eyebrows. "Well, I've thought about it since I mustered out. There are a lot of things that the government needs to do."

"Like what?"

"Like rebuild Europe, so the fascists don't come back. And make it easier for young people to afford college. And their first house. Maybe build a national highway system."

"Oh." His father sounded sceptical. "Who's going to pay for all of this?"

Sam shrugged. "With the war over, we won't need to spend so much on defence. There should be plenty of money for building up the infrastructure here at home, and in Europe."

"I have no idea what 'infrastructure' means," Jonathan said, "but somehow I'm sure that I'll be the one paying for it."

Sam grinned. "The fat cats won't be happy with my ideas, but the people will love them."

"You might bear in mind that you'll need at least one fat cat to finance your campaign."

Sam's grin widened. "I appreciate that, Dad, and I want you to know how much I'll enjoy spending your money."

Jonathan shook his head, then patted his son on the shoulder. "You'll make a fine politician," he said.

★　　★　　★

The first speaking engagement O'Brien arranged was at the Douglas Aircraft plant in Santa Monica. Sam talked to the workers about how they had achieved victory together, he in the field of battle, and they in America's prodigious war factory. Together they had won the war and together they would forge a great peace. The audience loved it, and by the end of the day O'Brien knew that Sam had captured the hearts and the votes of these blue-collar labourers and of their bosses as well. He gave essentially the same speech at the Hughes plant in Westchester, with the same results.

After that, O'Brien arranged Sam's introduction to the Jewish voters along Fairfax Avenue. Sam spoke of how the American army had saved the world from the Nazi scourge, and how proud he was to have played a small part. He spoke about how important it was to rebuild Europe the right way, so that the greatest evil in human memory could never return. Here was a handsome, articulate young man who had been willing to risk his life to defend both the Jewish and world community against persecution and oppression, who talked the talk and had obviously walked the walk.

Jimmy O'Brien could not suppress a smile as he watched Sam work the crowd. He had looked for a hero, confident he could teach him to be a politician. He had not dared to dream of such a natural.

Sam campaigned tirelessly, from PTA meetings to bridge clubs to downtown business groups. He spoke of Europe as a great potential market for American goods, and of how the government needed to assure free and open trade. Some of the businessmen appeared sceptical of the young man, but many had been soldiers themselves and liked the look and sound of this fellow. Their wives, for the most part, loved him.

It was, as Jimmy O'Brien had predicted, like taking candy from a baby. Samuel Cahill won election to the 53rd congressional seat with almost seventy percent of the vote. That landslide margin, plus his war-hero status, assured that he would be taken seriously by the congressional leadership. That and the fact that he could provide access to Hollywood money, which the Democratic Party was just beginning to appreciate.

CHAPTER SEVENTY-EIGHT

He took it as a personal affront. Fifteen years ago Walter Parker had driven the faggot out of Hollywood, but now he was back. Worse, he'd been back for quite some time. Detective Parker had done some investigating and found that Jonathan Cahill, over at Film Studios of America, had been employing Clarence Rollins for more than ten years, keeping it low profile, letting him use an on-screen pseudonym. But now, with the passage of time and war, Rollins's name was back in the credits.

This Jonathan Cahill had taken it upon himself to negate Parker's work. So he decided to investigate Cahill. Everyone had something to hide. It took Parker a while, but he found Cahill's secret. The man was tied to Max Zalensky. The tip-off was a thug named James Becker.

It had been an unlikely catch. A detective in the NYPD had alerted a Detective Nash in Los Angeles, who happened to be his cousin, that a known thug named James Becker was travelling to LA on a regular basis. The Los Angeles detective followed up only because the request had come from his cousin. When he found that Becker's business was at the Film Studios of America lot, the investigation was dropped. FSA and their chief, Jonathan Cahill, were off limits. Everyone in the LAPD knew that.

By coincidence, Parker heard someone talking about it in the lunchroom, and followed up with Detective Nash.

"Yeah," Nash said. "My cousin really hates Becker. The guy's been a suspect on a dozen assaults and a few murders over the past twenty years. But no one's ever been able to put together enough to charge him. He's smart, or at least the guy he works for is."

"Who's that?" Parker asked.

"Max Zalensky. You heard of him? Becker's his primary muscle."

Parker arched his dark eyebrows. Hell yeah, he'd heard of him. What cop hadn't? The man was reputed to control gambling up and down the East Coast and be the biggest money launderer in the country. And yet somehow he'd never even been arrested, was seemingly untouchable. Nash continued. "Becker comes out here about every three months. Every time he comes, he checks in with Cahill at FSA. They usually have lunch or dinner or something. Seem friendly. And Becker always spends some time with a real cute piece of trim named Jean Harper. She's an actress, early thirties now, never a headliner but she gets steady work. The leading lady's best friend or the sexy cocktail waitress at the road stop, you know the type. Anyway, I reported it all to my lieutenant and was ordered to drop the whole thing." Nash shrugged. "Fine with me. It wasn't going anywhere anyway."

Parker nodded and thanked the other detective. The skinny from Nash had triggered an old memory in the former vice cop. It took seven hours, breathing dust, leafing through papers that hadn't been touched in sixteen years, but he found what he wanted. Jean Harper. Seventeen years earlier she'd been busted for solicitation, and had served three months in the Camarillo juvie facility. Six months after that, she'd landed her first role at Film Studios of America. Now he remembered the whole thing.

He called her, then drove out to Venice where she lived in a cosy two-bedroom bungalow three blocks from the beach. She opened the door before he knocked. "It's been a long time," he said.

"What do you want?"

"You've done well for yourself. I wouldn't want that to change."

"What do you want?" she repeated. She remembered him. She had been just seventeen, off the bus from Kansas City. A man who was supposed to be a Hollywood agent had taken her and some other girls to a party and told them that the men there were movie producers who would put them into the moving pictures, if they were nice. And so she was nice. But the party was busted by a Hollywood vice unit and Jean and the other girls were booked for solicitation.

It turned out that one of the men at the party really was a big producer and had enough pull to get himself and his friends out of jail that same night. But the sergeant in charge of the vice unit insisted on getting something for his efforts, and the young ladies were charged and convicted. That sergeant was Walter Parker. Now, he was back.

"It worked out real well for you," Parker said. "I heard that producer felt guilty, introduced you over at FSA, got you your first part, and everything's been gravy ever since."

"What do you want?"

Parker shook his head and laughed. "You're not one for small talk, are ya?" Then, very seriously, he said, "I want to know everything you know about James Becker. And if you don't cooperate, your past is going to destroy your future."

It took a while, but Parker cajoled and frightened her and eventually wore her down. She told him everything she knew.

CHAPTER SEVENTY-NINE

"Captain Robertson called me today," Max said.

It took Becker a moment to place the name, then he said, "Head of robbery-homicide for LAPD. What'd he want?"

"He wanted to tell me that your friend, Miss Harper, has been singing like a canary."

They were in the living room of Max's house on Long Island and Becker had been lounging back in a Louis XV armchair. Now he sat straight up. "W-what?" he stammered. "She doesn't know enough to sing about."

"Fortunately for us both, that's true," Max said. "Robertson says he's got a detective, a Walter Parker, who's been showing special interest in you."

"Because he knows I'm connected to you?"

"That, and for some reason, Parker's got it in for Jonathan. They've known for a long time that you and Jonathan meet on a regular basis."

Becker shrugged. This didn't seem like anything to worry about.

"And they have some random source that saw you meeting with the councilman but they have no idea what about. They don't know about our connection with Dragna."

Becker nodded. Jack Dragna ran all of the illegal gambling throughout Los Angeles. Max used his connections on the city council and the police force to alleviate pressure on Dragna's operation. Becker acted as bag man.

"This Detective Parker dug up a prostitution fall that Jean took seventeen years ago," Max said. "Sounds like bullshit, but Parker's convinced her that he'll make it public and ruin her career. Such as it is. So she's willing to tell him anything."

Becker shook his head and said, "Still. She doesn't know anything."

"She knows when you come and go. She knows you know

Jonathan and have for a long time. And she promised Parker that she'd try to find out more about what you do when you're out there."

There was a pause before Becker said, "Yeah, it's true she's been asking about that. But obviously, I didn't tell her anything."

Max nodded, and Becker realised that his boss already knew this much.

"She's gotta go," Max said.

"No," Becker said. Max remained silent. "There's no need," Becker said. "Nothing'll come of this."

"You know," Max said softly, "that we can't have this hanging over us. It's just business." Then Max rose and walked out of the room, leaving the big man by himself. Becker did not move for several minutes, just staring straight ahead.

★　★　★

The homicide detective had been instructed to conclude that it was a burglary gone bad, and there was certainly enough evidence to support that conclusion. The house was in disarray, closets and drawers had been rifled, and the actress had been shot just as she entered her bedroom. The police photographer took pictures, the coroner collected the body, and a report was filed.

The neighbours were shocked; there was no history of burglary in this neighbourhood, let alone murder. But the evidence was clean and there was no reason to suspect anything else. The papers reported it just as the police had stated. A small funeral was held at First Lutheran of Venice. The one reporter who covered the event noted that Jonathan Cahill, head of Film Studios of America, was in attendance.

The day after Jean's funeral, Captain Robertson instructed Detective Parker, in no uncertain terms, to end his investigation of Jonathan Cahill and James Becker. The investigation seemed to be going nowhere anyway, and now Parker's one and only lead was gone. The Los Angeles Police Department's Detective Bureau had better things to do with its time.

CHAPTER EIGHTY
1947

In January, when Congressman Sam Cahill headed to Washington, DC for his first inauguration, Jacob Epstein was four months into his first year at Johns Hopkins University School of Medicine. He had taken the entrance exams primarily at his mother's urging, and after scoring in the top one percentile, had enrolled in med school for much the same reason.

Because of this, he was thoroughly surprised at how much he enjoyed it. He was fascinated by the biological makeup of the human body, and hungered to learn as much as he could about its workings. Back in the war he had felt an individual victory with every life he saved as a medic, but in med school he realised that he could live an entire life of such triumphs. The thrill he'd gotten every time he killed an enemy had receded to the level of a curious quirk of character; besides, it was hardly a practice out of which one could make a career. But the medical profession certainly was. So he proceeded happily down the road his mother had so desperately wanted for him.

CHAPTER EIGHTY-ONE

In April, Max came out for his annual visit to go through the numbers. The previous year had been good for the movie industry in general, and especially good for Film Studios of America. Zalensky, however, had more on his mind than the movie business.

"I need to ask you a favour."

"Sure," Jonathan replied, a little surprised. In all the years they had known one another Max had never asked for anything, other than a good return on his investment. "I'd be glad to be of any service."

They were in Jonathan's office, and as Max spoke he rose from his chair and walked around the room. "Really, the favour would be from Sam," Max said, picking up one of the many photographs adorning the shelves in the office. "But I'd like you to be my intermediary."

Jonathan just nodded, although the sight of Max Zalensky fingering a family picture, and asking a favour from Congressman Cahill, caused a discernable tightening in his stomach.

Max asked about the people in the photograph he was holding, one of whom was Susan Spencer. Jonathan answered, amused that even Max Zalensky was distracted by movie stars. Not for long though. He returned the photo to its original position and continued with his plea.

"Samuel is a member of the House and Senate Joint Banking Committee. The one headed by Senator Standish."

Jonathan nodded. "Yes, he was quite pleased to be selected. He applied because banking is an area that interests him, but it's very unusual for a junior congressman to be appointed to such an important committee."

"I'm aware of that," Max responded. "In fact, I used my influence to ease his way."

"Really." Jonathan was truly surprised to hear this. He had no idea that his partner's influence ranged all the way to Washington, nor could he imagine why Max would be interested in the banking committee. He was certain, however, that any help Zalensky gave Sam would involve a quid pro quo. The uneasy feeling in his stomach ratcheted up.

"My reason," Max continued, "for putting your son on that committee was to have him support Senator Standish, not oppose him. There are voices calling for bank regulators to look more closely at certain transactions involving overseas banking. Standish is opposed to greater regulation in this area, and has enough support to carry any vote on the issue. But Sam is one of those speaking up in favour of more controls."

Jonathan nodded. He knew exactly what Max was referring to because Sam had told him about it. As Sam had related to his father, there were rumours that organised crime was moving large quantities of money out of the country into overseas banks, then bringing the money back to America in the name of foreign corporations that were actually owned by the crime bosses.

At this point there was no evidence of any wrongdoing, just an accusation by a second-tier Chicago crime boss convicted in a police bribery scandal and hoping for a softer deal. Even if the rumours were true, it might be impossible to trace the transactions and prove wrongdoing. Nevertheless, Sam thought it would be a good idea for the regulators to investigate, if only to verify the integrity of the American banking system. But Jonathan now knew what his son did not: the rumours were indeed true and Max Zalensky played a key role.

"So you would like Sam to drop his calls for more investigation of these particular banking activities and move closer to Senator Standish's position."

"Exactly."

"But you said that Standish has the votes with or without Sam, so what does it matter?"

"In the world of congressional committees," Max said, "a snake that you think you've killed may come to life again. So when you kill that snake you have to make certain its head is cut off and properly buried. I would like this proposal buried so deep that it will never again see the light of day. Therefore, I'd like the vote to be unanimous, or as near unanimous as I can make it. Standish tells me that although Sam is just a freshman congressman, he is influential. If he changes his mind, so will others."

Jonathan shook his head. "I don't know, Max. Sam will not be easy to convince. He makes up his own mind on everything and it will take more than a word from his father to change it."

"You must make sure that he changes it," Max said. "You must make sure that he understands that he has no choice." Max did not raise his voice when he spoke, nor did his tone convey anger or emotion. But his manner was so matter of fact, so certain, that Jonathan felt a chill go down his spine.

"I'm not sure I understand," Jonathan said.

"I think you do," Max said, "but let me clarify. You, my friend, have dark secrets in your closet. If those secrets should come to light they will destroy this life you have so carefully built for yourself and end your son's very promising political career."

"C'mon," Jonathan responded, his voice rising. "I owned a few speakeasies. Back then everyone drank illegal liquor, including almost every big businessman and politician. Do you really think the public will get upset about it? Prohibition's been over for fifteen years and most folks realise it was a mistake."

Max nodded, almost absently. "I understand," he said, "that Samuel's grandfather was hanged for murder. He was a hitman for the IRA."

"How did you know..." Jonathan began, then stopped himself. "It doesn't matter," he said, his voice confident but his gut beginning to twist. "That was a long time ago, in another country, before Sam was born. The only people who would care are people who dislike the Irish, and they would never vote for Sam in the first place."

"I agree," Max said. "In general, at least. But that background makes it all the more credible that Sam's father would be a criminal and a murderer."

Jonathan practically sputtered his next words, he was so outraged. "What on earth are you talking about? I've never murdered anyone."

Max paused to gaze at the photo that he had been examining just a few moments before. Then he turned back toward Jonathan. He said two words: "Bob Duncan."

"What?" Jonathan stammered.

"You remember Bob Duncan." Max's monotone had become amazingly cold. "He owned seven speakeasies in midtown. He was mysteriously murdered, and then his establishments bought up at a very good price by one of his competitors: You. Your operation doubled overnight."

Jonathan was sitting down now, in one of the office chairs. "But I didn't murder him. It was you who arranged the purchase."

Max shrugged. "It's your name on the lease. In fact, I happen to have a photostat of it, with your signature. I don't believe there is any record of my involvement."

Jon could feel nausea rising in his throat. "It's absurd. I didn't murder anyone, and there's certainly no way I can be tied to it."

"Actually," Max said, "there's a fellow named Dominick Pastorini. He was a hitman in New York back in the thirties and worked for a number of bad people. Anyway, seems he was involved in the Duncan murder and knows a lot of details that only someone who was there would know. He claims to be one of the shooters. Says it was you who hired him, which makes perfect sense, given how soon after Duncan's death you bought out his widow."

"That's nuts," Jonathan protested. "First off, I have never even met this Dominick Pastorini, and second, he would be confessing to murder."

Max again shrugged. "The man has been diagnosed with cancer. They tell him he has less than a year to live. He got married late in life, has a wife and young son. Now he's worried about how they'll support themselves when he's gone."

"And you've assured him that his family will be taken care of."

"Something like that," Zalensky said.

Jonathan sat in the chair and put his head in his hands. His life, he realised, had turned a corner. Nothing had really changed but he now fully understood the deal that he had made with the devil so long ago. It was crystal clear. And that devil was standing right in front of him.

He lifted his head and said, "Okay, I'll talk to Sam."

CHAPTER EIGHTY-TWO

It had been so many years that she did not recognise him. She noticed only a handsome, dark-haired man about her own age sitting at a table across the room from her at the Polo Lounge. Louis had asked her to lunch to discuss a sequel to a movie she had made almost twenty years earlier. They were discussing script and supporting cast when she noticed the dark-haired man looking at her, a not uncommon occurrence for a successful actress. But this man smiled and nodded as if he knew her, then got up from his table to approach her. He had the same powerful build, the same easy walk, and in a flash she realised it was him.

"Hello, Sophie," he said in a low voice. "It's been a very long time."

She put a hand to her chest. "It certainly has, Max. A very long time. But you look well."

"As do you. But I knew that, of course. I've seen every one of your movies."

"I never would have thought of you as the movie-going type."

"I'm not," he said, smiling.

Sophie became aware of Louis nudging her with his foot, under the table. She had temporarily forgotten about him, so focused was she on the man in front of her. "I'm sorry," she said. "Max, this is Louis Kahn, the head of Signature Studios. Louis, I'd like you to meet my oldest friend, Max Zalensky."

Kahn, famous for never appearing nonplussed, was visibly shaken. He looked at Max, then back at Sophie. "Susan," he said, "you never cease to amaze me."

"That makes two of us," Max said, and both men laughed. "Forgive me for interrupting, but I'm only in town for a few days and I'd love to get together. If you give me your number, I'll call." He listened as she did so, writing nothing down, and walked back to his table.

★   ★   ★

She had just arrived home when his call came. He was staying at the Beverly Wilshire. Was she free for dinner?

They met at a restaurant on Rodeo, just up the street from his hotel. "You're more beautiful than ever," he said, looking into her eyes. They were sitting across from one another in a corner booth.

"Untrue." She laughed. "But appreciated."

Max nodded, as if in agreement, but he had meant what he said. There were small lines now, at the corners of her smile and her eyes, as well as slight furrows in her forehead. But it was still an extraordinary face. "Seriously," he said, "you look wonderful. And what you've accomplished is remarkable. I was a little nervous about calling you."

"Oh? I don't recall you ever being nervous."

He shrugged. "We didn't part under the best of circumstances."

"It was a long time ago. We're different people now."

"I have a confession to make. Our meeting today was not accidental."

"Oh," she said, not entirely surprised. It had seemed like quite a coincidence. "Why, after all this time?"

"I saw a picture of our son. And I knew."

Sophie was stunned. She'd always been careful to keep Jake's picture out of the papers, and for Max to turn up under these circumstances, after all these years, triggered her deepest fears.

"When I left you," he said, "after that last time together, when I never called you, it was for a reason. I thought you were pregnant, with Epstein's child. I thought—"

Sophie interrupted him. She spoke slowly, deliberately. "You thought that was why I came to you so soon after Arnold's death, why we ended up in bed. You thought I'd pretend that the child was yours and use that to trap you." She spoke evenly, but the great actress could not conceal her anger. This was a man whom she had loved, who had loved her, and yet his covetous nature, his instinctive mistrust, had doomed any chance of happiness. She thought immediately of Duke, who so generously had welcomed another man's child into his life.

"Yes," Max said. "Yes. But it was a mistake. I was young and stupid and full of myself. I thought everything revolved around me. But I loved you. I've always loved you. I still do. It was just a stupid mistake."

Sophie shook her head, trying to process this. She couldn't deny his sincerity, nor his obvious pain. But there was still the cold fact of what he had done. And who he was. "Tell me about yourself," she finally said. "Tell me about your life since we last saw each other."

So he did. He was a man who had planned out his work, and worked his plan. He had done some things that he was not proud of, but they had been necessary. And worth it. He now controlled a vast empire, including thousands of people and hundreds of millions of dollars. The government, the politicians, law enforcement, all were aware of him. But no one realised just how powerful he really was. Or how rich. He had not told anyone else what he was telling her.

He lived on Long Island, in an estate overlooking the water. He derived most of his income from legitimate businesses, like banking. "Or, at least," he smiled, "semi-legitimate."

He asked about her life, and she told him. He seemed enraptured by her rise in Hollywood, the famous people she casually mentioned, the fact that she lived in a world that he only read about in newspapers. And when he listened, it was as if she were the only woman in the world. But she never mentioned their son and he did not push her on the subject.

The remarkable thing was that even after all these years, there was still a connection between them. Max had an energy, a charisma that drew her in and made her feel as if the past twenty-seven years were but a moment and he was still a part of her life. As he talked, his right hand was resting on top of the table. She reached over and took it, almost expecting to see a spark jump between them.

After dinner, they walked back to his hotel, still holding hands. The attraction was irresistible, and Sophie knew she would spend the night with him. Despite what he had done, despite what he was, despite the fact that she would be betraying Jonathan.

When they reached his room, he took her in his arms and kissed her. She held his face with her hands as she kissed him back, then unbuttoned his collar and moved her lips down to the base of his neck. He lifted her chin back up and kissed her hard on the mouth, pressing himself against her. Sophie was overcome with desire.

They undressed in a frenzy, hands flying, lips locked. She pulled him back onto the bed, frantic to have him. She reached for him and he was there, hard and pulsating. Then he was inside her, filling her, and it was both exquisite and familiar. She felt her body shudder and explode repeatedly, but it was not only physical pleasure. It was also the wonderful feeling of coming home to a place she had always belonged.

Afterward, as they lay in bed, Sophie was quiet, her body spent and satisfied. It was Max who spoke. "Maybe it was meant to be."

"What was?'

"The mistake I made. The years I made us miss. It was terrible, but it made me the person I am, gave me the drive to build my organisation. And it made you what you are. If I hadn't made that horrible mistake you never would have come out here, never would have become a star."

And, she thought, *I never would have met the finest man I've ever known, and Jacob wouldn't have had the best father a boy could have.* The thought of Duke made her smile. Max saw her expression and, misinterpreting, continued.

"Now I have everything I've ever wanted."

"Oh?"

"I have the woman I've always loved," he said. "And a son. Maybe he could continue my legacy."

It took an act of will for Sophie to restrain herself from screaming at him. But as calmly and quietly as she could, she said, "Jacob already has a career path. I don't think he'll be interested in your…business."

"Yes, I know. He's in medical school, at the top of his class. And he doesn't even know about me yet. But there's still plenty of time."

Sophie nodded, using all her craft to conceal her horror. She said, "It would probably be best if I tell him about you, about us, before you meet him."

Max looked directly at her. "I understand," he said. "This is a big step. You need to get more comfortable with us before bringing me into our son's life. Like I said, there's plenty of time."

Sophie smiled, and it was still a dazzling smile. "Thank you," she said, "for understanding." Then she kissed him gently on the lips, laid her head in the crook between his shoulder and chest, and pretended to fall into a satisfied sleep.

In the morning they had breakfast together in his room. "I'm flying back to New York this afternoon," Max said, "but I'll be back in Los

Angeles next week, negotiating the purchase of a small bank here. The deal is almost done but there are still some details to iron out. I can arrange to extend the next trip for a few days. If that would be all right?" There was hopefulness in his voice.

"That would be wonderful," she said, hoping that perhaps it would be.

★   ★   ★

True to his word, he called the next week. He was at the same hotel, but this time he had rented a large suite so she could spend more time there. His meetings would take a full day, but after that, if she wanted, they could spend a few days together. She did, and made an excuse to Jonathan as to why she would be unavailable.

It was, in many ways, a wonderful two days. Max energised her, made her feel as if she were truly the most beautiful, intelligent, special woman on earth. He seemed totally enamoured of her, and she used that to her advantage. "Jacob is happy with his studies," she said proudly. "He looks forward to using his skills to help people." She paused, then said, "I want him to stay happy." They were at dinner in a small Italian restaurant on Roxbury, and as she spoke she placed her hand on his. She looked him directly in the eyes, and she was fully aware of the effect that still had on him.

"Of course," Max said. "He can decide for himself what he wants to do. The important thing is for us to be a family." It was exactly what she wanted to hear.

Taking him to the airport, she sat with him in the backseat while Virgilio drove. When it came time to say goodbye they shared a long, sweet kiss and Max said, "I love you, Sophie. I always have." Then he was out of the car and gone. Sophie breathed in the smell of him, still in the air, and smiled.

CHAPTER EIGHTY-THREE

"Is he ready?" Sophie asked Selma Williams. Selma sat behind a desk that held two telephones and a typewriter in the large waiting room outside Jonathan's office. She was known throughout the studio as someone who could talk on the telephone while typing seventy words a minute. Her primary responsibility, however, was to keep unscheduled or unwanted visitors from troubling her boss. Sophie was a few minutes early for their appointment. "He has someone in there, Miss Spencer," Selma informed her, "but they should be done in a few minutes."

"Thanks," Sophie said and sat down. This was not a conversation she was looking forward to, and she had purposely chosen a location where Jonathan would be most comfortable. She would have to tell him that there was someone else in her life, someone from long ago, and that she and Jonathan could be no more than friends. She loved him as a friend and she did not wish to cause him pain. Unfortunately, there was no avoiding it.

Selma's desk was next to the door to Jonathan's office, and the chair Sophie chose was on the opposite side of the large desk from the door. Most people walking out of the office would not glance back and notice her sitting there. This was convenient since many of Jonathan's visitors were bankers or lawyers from outside the studio and, even in Hollywood, many were starstruck. Sophie was in no mood to have some young lawyer ask for an autograph, or even worse, try to engage her in conversation. So she sat where she was unlikely to be noticed, a magazine in front of her face.

A few minutes later, the door to the office swung open and Jonathan walked his visitor out. The visitor said something and the studio chief laughed, patting the other man on his large shoulder. Neither man turned around or noticed her, and Jonathan walked his visitor to the end of the reception room and out the door to the hallway.

Sophie felt as if she'd experienced an electric shock. It had been many years and she could only see him from the back, but she still recognised the giant body with the bullet head, and that low, bull-like drone of a voice.

Suddenly, the pieces fell into place.

When Jonathan turned back into the waiting room and saw her, his face lit up. "Susan," he said happily. "I didn't see you there."

But she gazed at him coldly and said, "What was he doing here?"

Jonathan looked at her without comprehension. "Who?"

"Becker," she said, her voice flat. "James Becker."

Jonathan stared for a moment, as if seeing her for the first time, then hurried her into his office. "Let's talk in here," he said, closing the door behind them. As soon as they were alone he said, "How do you know Becker?"

"From a long time ago, back in New York, before I came here. Why is he here?"

"He works for my partner. You know I've got a silent partner from the East Coast; the fellow who put up the money for all this." Jonathan waved his hand around at the office. "Becker comes here sometimes, for vacation. I arrange for someone to escort him around, make sure that he has a good time, that sort of thing. Actually, I like the guy."

Sophie raised her eyebrows at this last piece of information, but continued smoothly to her next question. "How long has Max Zalensky been your partner?"

Now it was Jonathan's turn to be shocked. "How did you know that?" When she didn't answer, he continued, "Since before I came here. In fact, it was his idea that I move here and sell liquor. And it was his idea that I go into the movie business. But before that he put up the money for the chain of bars I owned in New York." He looked harder at her. "How do you know him?"

"We were children together. We grew up together." She lowered her eyes. "Once upon a time we loved each other."

Sophie then asked more questions that were not questions at all, since she already knew the answers. "Since he's your partner, he comes here and checks things out every so often?"

"Yes, he comes once a year."

"The last time he came was about two weeks ago?"

"Yes, on April 13th," Jonathan said, eyebrows raised, wondering how she could possibly have known this.

"He was in this office?"

"Yes."

"There's a photograph on your credenza of you and me and our boys, the one we took at Jacob's birthday dinner. It shows the birthday cake. Max saw that photograph and picked it up and asked who the young men were and whose birthday it was. You told him."

"Yes." Jonathan was fascinated now, his mind racing.

"Then he asked when the birthday took place, and how old Jacob was, and you told him that too."

"Yes, but how could...?" Jonathan's voice trailed off as his thoughts sped forward. Finally he whispered, as if it could not be said out loud, "He's Jacob's father."

Sophie nodded.

"And he didn't know. Until now."

Again, she nodded.

Jonathan said, "I never would have thought of it, but now that I know you knew him, loved him even, the resemblance is obvious. Especially since I knew Max when we were young. Jacob's likeness to how he looked then is remarkable."

"Yes," Sophie said dryly. "Isn't it."

"And he's contacted you since he saw the photo?"

"The very next day." She hesitated, but decided she owed him the truth. "It's complicated, but he left me, thinking I was pregnant with another man's child. Then, when he saw the picture, he realised the truth."

Jonathan looked at her, his face flushed. "And after he abandoned you, after all this time, you're going to take him back. That's why you wanted to meet with me today."

"I'm sorry," she said. "I really am. But he wants Jake too. He wants a legacy. He's got a huge empire and no one to run it when he's gone. No one to pick up the work as he gets older. That's what he wants for Jake." She hadn't been looking at Jonathan as she spoke, her eyes downcast. But now she looked at him directly. "I can't let that happen."

Jonathan shook his head. "How do you think you're going to stop it?"

She spoke rapidly, as if in a hurry to get the words out. "He loves me. He's said it and I believe him. If I'm with him, if I stay with him, I can make him understand that Jacob should choose his own course, that it'll be better for all of us. I've already got him mostly convinced."

Jonathan spoke slowly, choosing his words. "It's been a long time since you knew Max. He's a very different person now."

"I realise that. I even had him investigated. And you're right, the findings were...eye-opening."

"Oh?"

She gathered herself as Jonathan waited, reminding herself that she owed him the truth. "I used a top investigator and he used two of the top forensic accountants in the country. He also has a contact on the Senate Banking Committee, an aide to one of the senators." Again, she hesitated, then said, "Max is one of the richest men in the country. The accountant's best guess is that he is worth over one billion dollars. And," she paused, as if for dramatic effect, "they didn't even find this place." She swept an arm around Jonathan's office.

"There's almost no way that they could," Jonathan said. "He has no part in running this business. He just shows up once a year and I take him through the results. I deposit his share of the profits in a New York bank account that's in the name of a South American holding company."

"Of course," she said. "His primary business is banking. He owns several, probably including the one you deposit his money into. And they are legitimate, well run, and profitable. Too profitable. The word in Washington is that his banks are money-laundering centres. He takes dirty cash from top mobsters and converts it into clean American dollars."

Jonathan nodded, listening intently, as Sophie continued. "He controls senators and congressmen on the banking committees to keep them from making laws that would stop him, or allow the bank examiners to look too closely into what he does. The word is he buys them off, and if that doesn't work he blackmails them. The Senate aide told my investigator that Max has so much control

over the most powerful lawmakers that he is virtually untouchable."
She looked at Jonathan and said, "You don't seem surprised by any
of this."

"No, I learned something about it recently. The hard way."

"What do you mean?"

"Sam recently was appointed to a spot on the House Banking
Committee."

"Oh God," she said. "He wouldn't do that."

"There's apparently very little he wouldn't do." He told her how
Max was using Jonathan's own background to blackmail his son.

"But a lot of people's fathers were bootleggers. Why would that
affect Sam?"

"I funded his campaign. So, essentially, he ran on dirty money.
And there are much worse things in my background. Or that he can
make appear to be in my background."

"I won't ask. I just can't believe he would do this to Sam."

Jonathan shrugged. "As Max would say, it's just business."

"Have you talked to Sam yet?"

"No, I've been putting it off. But I'm not going to be able to wait
much longer."

Sophie looked again at the birthday photograph, then back at
Jonathan. "I am truly sorry. But it makes my decision even clearer. I
need to do whatever it takes to make sure he doesn't force anything
on Jacob."

"I understand." There was a weary resignation in Jonathan's voice,
a final realisation that Max Zalensky was taking both his son and the
woman he loved. He looked at Susan, all humour drained from his
voice. "I think I'll just have to figure out how to make the best of it."

Sophie gave him a kiss on the cheek, hugged him, then turned
and left.

CHAPTER EIGHTY-FOUR

Stepping out of Jonathan's office, Sophie took a little-used hallway that led to a side exit, closer to her own office. As she walked down the lonely hall, a large figure stepped out of an alcove and towered in front of her. "Hello, Sophie," came the low, drone-like voice. "It's good to see you." He looked her up and down, the same way he had that first time he had seen her, thirty years earlier. "Really good."

"I can't say the same," she said, and hurried past him.

He made no move to stop her, instead saying, "I understand congratulations are in order. In regards to your son."

She whirled on him. "What are you talking about?"

James Becker shrugged. "I understand he'll be my boss in a few years."

"That will never happen," she said in a controlled voice. "Why would you think that?"

"Max wants it. He wants the kid, and he wants you. Max gets what he wants." After a pause, he said, "I imagine that's what you were in there telling Jonathan."

She flinched at this, but said, "Jacob has his own life to live. He'll make his own decisions. Max understands that. And it's not like he can make Jake do anything he doesn't want to."

A small smile flitted over Becker's face, in obvious scorn of her naiveté. It infuriated Sophie, but she contained her anger.

"Max can be very persuasive," he said. "I'm sure you understand that. And there're other buttons he can push if he needs to."

"What buttons?"

"The kid has to pass medical exams to become a doctor. Max can make that not happen. And there are licensing boards in every state. Those boards are made up of men – with jobs and wives and children." Becker looked directly at her. "Max gets what he wants."

The horror of it struck her, stopped her in her tracks for a moment.

"That won't happen," she said, then continued past him, through the exit door and back to her own office.

She didn't sit down right away, just leaned over, her stomach in a knot, hands resting on the desk, her breath coming hard. Becker was a dreadful man. She had hated him twenty-seven years ago and she still hated him today. But his words were difficult to ignore.

She could wield influence of her own. Max loved her as much as he was capable of such a thing. She would use every ounce of her energy, every feminine charm, to convince him that it would be best to let their son follow his own path. She would be in New York in a few weeks, in connection with a new movie. It was a part that Jonathan had arranged for her months ago, a meaty, dramatic role that had Academy Award potential. She would arrange to see Max and continue her seduction of him, make him see things as she saw them. Love had certainly achieved greater miracles.

At the same time, she knew that her son had a dark side, inherited from his biological father and buried deep in his psyche. She had heard stories about the war. With just the right stimulus, that side of him might be brought out. As Becker had said, Max could be very persuasive. Perhaps that was what she was truly afraid of.

CHAPTER EIGHTY-FIVE

Max stepped out of a cab in front of the Waldorf Astoria. Sophie had called to say she was in town, something about checking out a New York location for a new movie. She had been almost giddy, telling him how, if things worked out, she would be in New York for the next several months. Their son was in Baltimore, not far away, and he'd be visiting her if he had time. This might be an opportune time for them to meet, and she wanted to talk about that first introduction. Max smiled to himself. Everything was falling into place.

He was in the habit of never dining at the same restaurant two nights in a row, never following a set routine. Call it paranoia, but he did not want his whereabouts to be predictable. It was a habit that he had developed early and that had served him well. He took a side entrance into the Waldorf, wandered around a bit in the underground hallways to make certain no one was following him, and then found his way to the elevator bank without having to pass through the lobby.

Sophie's room was on the twenty-first floor. When he knocked, the door swung open almost immediately, and he realised that she had been waiting for him eagerly. She was wearing a light pink negligee and the sight of her took his breath away. The sheer material was cut low over her breasts, which were still extraordinary. It showed off her flat stomach and slim waist and ended high up her slender, still perfect legs. Her full lips were smiling, her beautiful face glowing.

She pulled him through the door, kissing him hard on the lips, pressing her body against his. He instantly felt himself becoming aroused. She pulled back from him, smiling coquettishly, and said, "Let's get into the bedroom," then pranced happily across the living room area of the suite toward the king-size bed, visible through the open bedroom door. "C'mon," she called.

He couldn't take his eyes off her, hurrying after her while she leaned back at the foot of the bed, waiting. He stepped into the bedroom, simultaneously pulling off his shirt and.... Something was terribly wrong. There was a figure to his left. It had stepped out from behind the half-open door.

Max whirled and saw Becker, huge and menacing, his gun out and pointed. Most men would have never had a chance. Focused on the gorgeous woman in front of them, they'd not have noticed him in their peripheral vision. Even if they had realised the deadly threat, they would have been too surprised to react with sufficient speed.

But this was Max Zalensky. His mind immediately processed the situation and acted appropriately. With no apparent hesitation he pulled the Beretta automatic out of the holster at the back of his waist, his motion a blur of purpose and speed.

But James Becker knew Max well, knew what he was capable of. His .38 calibre Colt automatic with a silencer attached to its barrel was already out, held at arm's length and shoulder height. As soon as the door closed and Max came into view, Becker aimed and pulled the trigger.

The hollow-point bullet pierced Max's right eye socket and continued through the right frontal lobe of his brain and out the back of his skull. It expanded upon impact, creating a much larger hole where it left Max's skull than where it had entered. Brain and blood spewed out of the back of his head as his lifeless body fell backward to the floor. He lay there, twitching for a few moments before his body stopped moving.

Sophie fell to her knees, her hands covering her face, shaking uncontrollably. She had known this would happen, had carefully planned for this to happen, yet was still shocked to actually see it. Her body began to shake, desperate sobs escaping her lips.

Becker ignored her as he went about his work. There was a large laundry cart in the corner of the room, the kind the hotel staff used to pick up dirty towels and sheets. He moved the cart next to Max's dead body, casually hefted him into the cart, then stuffed towels over and around him. He used other towels, along with cleanser from the cart, to clean up the mess. When Sophie vacated the room he did not want the hotel staff to have any clue as to what had happened here.

The bullet that had snuffed out Max's life had not had enough energy left to penetrate the opposite wall. It lay flattened and spent on the floor. Becker picked it up and dropped it into his pocket, then retrieved the ejected shell. He walked to the closet where a large jumpsuit identical to those worn by the Waldorf's maintenance people was hanging. He put it on over his clothes and wheeled the cart with Max Zalensky's corpse out of the room. Sophie was still on her knees on the floor, her hands over her eyes, still sobbing. Becker was not sure if she was aware of him leaving.

The big man took the cart down the service elevator and out to an alley behind the hotel. He dumped the body, swathed in towels, into a dumpster. He took off the jumpsuit, threw that on top, and walked away. The city workers would probably discover the dead man when they collected the garbage.

It had been Mr. Cahill who approached him. Becker was in his late fifties and ready to get out of the game, a fact that Jonathan could easily discern. And he intuited that Becker resented Max, maybe even hated him. Cahill didn't know why, but he was insightful enough to see it.

They had offered him two million dollars. Two fucking million. It was enough to live like a king for the rest of his life. An incredible amount, impossible to turn down. Half was paid by Jonathan and half by Sophie.

The cops would look at Max's known associates, of whom Becker was numero uno. He had always wanted to see the south of France, find out if the booze and broads were as good as everyone said. Now would be a perfect time to go. Come back in three or four years, when everyone had forgotten Max Zalensky.

He walked the few blocks to the IRT stop at 51st and Lex, taking no chances that some nervous cabby would give the police his description. He took the 6 train to an apartment he kept in Brooklyn Heights, where his passport, luggage and plane tickets were waiting. There was a picture of Jean Harper on his nightstand, a head shot she'd given him on one of his trips to LA. He took one last look at it. Then he called a cab to take him to LaGuardia airport.

James Becker stepped out of the taxi at the TWA terminal and smiled. Perhaps Max would have understood. It was just business. But not entirely.

EPILOGUE

Aaron Wachtell, junior partner at the firm of Wachtell, Schecter, Greene and Wachtell, was given the assignment of contacting Jacob Epstein, a first-year medical student at Johns Hopkins University. Epstein lived just off campus in housing reserved for attendees of Hopkins' revered medical school. Wachtell had called ahead to arrange a private meeting in Jacob's room.

The lawyer shook hands, then handed Jacob a business card. He appeared to be only a few years older than the medical student, and judging by the slight limp, a fellow war veteran. Jake immediately liked him but could not imagine what could constitute the 'important and secret' matter that Wachtell had mentioned on the phone.

As if reading his thoughts, Wachtell said, "I'm sure you're wondering why I'm here, what could be so urgent."

Jake nodded, and Wachtell continued. "For many years, my firm has represented Mr. Max Zalensky. Are you familiar with that name?"

Jake shook his head, glancing over at his desk. The lawyer caught the glance and, realising that young Epstein was anxious to get back to his studies, rushed ahead with the rest of his rehearsed speech.

"We're not familiar with the exact nature of Mr. Zalensky's business, but he engaged us to manage certain assets of his and those are very substantial. He also engaged us to draw up his will and to execute his estate in the event of his death." Jacob looked at the attorney with some curiosity.

"Mr. Zalensky passed away less than one month ago. He has willed all of his assets to you," Wachtell said, then he paused a moment, as if gathering himself. "We estimate those assets to be worth at least one billion dollars, and they are yours, contingent on just one condition – that you fulfil Mr. Zalensky's highest hope and agree to take over and carry on his business."

Jacob Epstein looked stunned. "This is either a joke or some sort of mistake," he said. "I don't know this man. I've never even heard of him. There must be some other Jacob Epstein and that's your guy. You need to find him and I need to get back to my books."

Aaron Wachtell shook his head. "There are, in fact, several other Jacob Epsteins. However, Mr. Zalensky specified the Jacob Epstein born February 17th, 1920, son of Arnold and Sophie Epstein, the latter who became an actress, assuming the name Susan Spencer. Mr. Zalensky's Jacob Epstein fought in Europe during the war and is now a medical student at Johns Hopkins Medical School. You are, without doubt, that Jacob Epstein."

Jake shook his head, his scepticism obvious. "Let me get this straight. You walk in here and tell me that some billionaire I've never heard of has left me his entire fortune. And all I have to do is take over his business, which conveniently, you have no knowledge of. Is that about right?"

Instead of giving a direct answer, the lawyer opened the leather briefcase he carried and withdrew a large brown envelope, the kind used to hold written contracts. Wachtell placed the package carefully on Jacob's desk and said, "This envelope contains documents provided by Mr. Zalensky, which my firm was instructed to deliver to you upon his death. We have not seen what is inside but were assured that the contents would answer any questions you have regarding your relationship to Mr. Zalensky and the nature of his business. I ask that you read these documents and then call me with your answer. My number is on my card."

With that, Wachtell stood up, closed his briefcase, shook hands once more and walked out of the room. Jacob, eyebrows raised, watched him leave and then stared for a minute at the brown envelope sitting by itself in the middle of his desk. He finally gave a small shrug and opened it.

It did, as promised, explain everything. There was a short narrative revealing that Mr. Zalensky and Jacob's mother had been childhood sweethearts, but due to poverty and an abusive father, Sophie had been forced to marry a wealthy, older man named Arnold Epstein. Still in love, Zalensky and Sophie had a brief affair, the result of which was Jacob.

After Arnold Epstein's untimely death, Sophie moved west in

search of a new life. Due to Mr. Zalensky's unorthodox career and lifestyle, she chose to separate herself from him and never informed him of Jacob's existence, which he found out about only recently. Jacob was Mr. Zalensky's only living relative.

There was also a photograph of Mr. Zalensky as a young man. He was a well-built youth wearing a 1920s business suit with wide lapels, tab-collared white shirt, and cuffed, striped pants. At first glance the young man could have been mistaken for Jacob himself, but on closer examination was clearly a different person, albeit one who looked very much like him. Jacob stared at the picture for several minutes.

And then there was the explanation of his businesses. It included a long list of assets: real estate, stocks, restaurants, illegal gambling casinos and banks. The man owned banks. It was a veritable empire, and Jake realised that Wachtell's estimate of a billion dollars was probably low.

But most shocking was Zalensky's half ownership in Film Studios of America and its related movie theatres. Jacob shook his head. How could this be? Was it just coincidence that his biological father had half interest in the studio where his mother had made several movies, run by a man whom she recently dated? Jacob's instinct told him that such a coincidence was unlikely.

Zalensky's narrative then gave a complete description of what Mr. Zalensky called his 'laundering' business, and the role his banks played. This sort of thing was not unknown territory to Jacob; his friend Sam, the young congressman, had explained to him how the Congressional Banking Committee, of which he was a member, was looking into exactly this sort of thing. It was quite interesting and Sam had enthusiastically explained how the whole illegal process worked.

But then came the real stunner: a list of congressmen and senators whom Mr. Zalensky controlled and paid, precisely so that they would not look too closely at his business. Sam's name was on that list.

But Sam was not yet under control. There was a note that Sam's father could be blackmailed to force Sam to go along with whatever Zalensky wanted. There were more notes about business between Zalensky and Jonathan going back almost thirty years. Zalensky's ownership interest in Jonathan Cahill's studio was indeed no coincidence.

My God, Jacob thought, shaking his head at the monstrosity of the whole thing. Still, he knew something Zalensky did not. His friend, the young congressman, had explained it to him. "All these guys would have to do," Sam said, "is establish a bank in a foreign country, and then open a branch in the States. They'd have to comply with our normal regulations, but we can't dig too deeply into a foreign bank's records so they could probably do everything they do, and we couldn't catch it."

It was something to consider.

Finally, the narrative reiterated what the lawyer had said: that Max Zalensky considered his business to be his legacy and his fondest desire was that his son, Jacob, take over the business and continue to expand it, probably reaching heights that Zalensky could only dream of. He knew that Jake was an intelligent and courageous young man, and that he could be ruthless. He knew this because he'd made inquiries about the young man's war record. Mr. Zalensky could not imagine anyone better suited to take over his business.

And, to his horror, it did appeal to Jake. The sheer size of it, the power it conferred. Jake could easily enough switch the laundering business to a foreign bank, as Sam had told him, and that problem would go away. Or he could get rid of that part of the business altogether, and just run legitimate banks. He could liquidate the illegal casinos and start up in the growing town of Las Vegas, where gambling was legal. The resources he would inherit from Zalensky were almost limitless, and Jake could use them for great good as easily as great evil.

The money was not the attraction. His mother, a multi-millionaire, was only too happy to bestow upon him any gift he might desire. In addition to her own money, Susan Spencer had inherited her husband's millions and she had already made it clear that Jake could have any or all of Duke's money, if he wanted it.

Power, however, was a different matter. In addition to Mr. Zalensky's vast fortune there were all those senators and congressmen he controlled. It was indeed seductive to think about the things you might accomplish.

Jacob could feel the Zalensky blood flowing through his veins. He had always known there was something in him not inherited from his mother, and not learned from Duke Hawkins. A desire for control, a desire to bend the lives of other men to his will. Now he knew where it had come from. This inheritance would allow him to fulfil every long-hidden desire, to be the man he was destined to be.

But the thought of Duke Hawkins changed his mind. What would his father, his real father, think of any of this? Duke would be appalled by the whole concept of illegal profits and blackmailed congressmen, let alone strong-arm tactics. The whole business ran contrary to the entire way he had lived his life and to everything he had taught his only son. Jacob had been amazingly lucky to have had Duke in his life. He was not about to betray him.

So he slipped the papers back into the brown envelope and picked up his textbook. He wanted, above anything else, to be the man his father would have wanted him to be, and there was no doubt what sort of man that was. He would call the lawyer tomorrow and tell him that he wasn't interested.

But for some reason he couldn't bring himself to throw away the brown envelope. Instead, he stuck it into the bottom drawer of his desk and slowly slid the drawer closed.

After all, you never knew.